www.Bolajieyo.com

Good Girls
DON'T PUT OUT

BOLAJI EYO

Copyright © 2017 Bolaji Eyo

All rights reserved, including the right to reproduce this book, or portions thereof in any form. No part of this text may be reproduced, transmitted, downloaded, decompiled, reverse engineered, or stored, in any form or introduced into any information storage and retrieval system, in any form or by any means, whether electronic or mechanical without the express written permission of the author.

This is a work of fiction. Names and characters are the product of the author's imagination and any resemblance to actual persons, living or dead, is entirely coincidental.

The views expressed in this work are solely those of the author and do not necessarily reflect the views of the publisher, and the publisher hereby disclaims any responsibility for them.

ISBN: 978-1-326-84139-3

PublishNation
www.publishnation.co.uk

This book is dedicated to every young girl who knows what it feels like to hold on to her integrity in the face of adversity and ridicule.

CHAPTER 1

1998

"Mr Sunday, please, can you drive faster?" I leant forward to tap the back of the driver's seat. The head in front of me nodded, and as the car shot forward, I gripped the front seat to steady myself. Ignoring the jolts as the car hit bumps and potholes, I stared out the window as a woman with a large round tray balanced on her head jumped out of the way of a motorbike.

I imagined how my conversation with Josh would go.

"Hi, Josh."

"Hi, Jade," he would respond, staring dreamily into my eyes.

"Would you like to go on a date with me?" Wait... where would we go? If we went to a restaurant, would he pay or would I have to pay since I was the one who'd asked him? That doesn't matter now; I admonished myself; we'll cross that bridge when we get there. But first I need to focus. Where was I?

"Yes," he would say, taking my hands in his and rubbing his thumbs over my knuckles. "I thought you'd never ask."

Okay, I'm not sure what my chances are, but unless I've read the signs wrong, I'm feeling confident. The thing is, I don't understand why he hasn't asked me out yet; heaven knows I've given him enough opportunity.

I'd decided to take action today after the principal had called me to the front of the school during assembly and announced that I was the new Head Girl. Standing next to her on the podium, listening as she listed my accomplishments and the awards I had won for the school, I realised something about myself. I was a go-getter. And while the way I felt about Josh wasn't a secret, I wondered if perhaps my hints might have been too subtle for him. Well, from today onwards, no more hints or playing games. My mind drifted back to the first time we met.

1992

I was nine, and Josh's family had just moved into the house opposite ours. There had been only three houses on my street when my family had moved there. On both sides of the house were many empty plots of land, most of which were fenced up to deter fraudsters from selling them to unsuspecting victims. The road was untarred, with numerous potholes of varying widths and depths.

Our house was a two-storey one. From the outside, it looked as if it was divided into three sections: the outer ones were painted cream, and the middle one was built with grey bricks. The tops of the fences had sharp metal spikes to keep out any unwanted visitors. There was a big black gate in front of the house, and a couple of metres to the left of it stood a gatehouse where the security guard was stationed. My brothers and I used to sit on the stoop in front of the gatehouse after school, playing card games. We were excited that we'd be getting new neighbours, and we made guesses as to what sort of people they would be. I hoped that they'd have a little girl of my age whom I could play with. I had three brothers and one sister. I got along with my brothers but had nothing in common with my sister: it was like we were from different planets, rather than the same family. She was five years older than I was, and I could never understand a word she said as she always felt the need to yell every time she spoke to me. It was as if my existence was a constant source of annoyance to her, so I tried to stay out of her way as much as I could. Unfortunately, that wasn't an easy feat, since we shared a room. I wished that if a little girl my age moved in next door, she would have her own room so that we could play without being yelled at to be quiet. She would be beautiful and smart, not like the girls in my class who taunted me because I always put my hands up in class whenever Miss Ochuko, my class teacher, asked a question.

One day, I was lying on my bed reading a Nancy Drew book when my sister, Tayo, breezed into the room.

"How was your day at school?" she asked, plonking herself at the foot of my bed.

I lowered my book and eyed her. I wondered what it could be. My sister didn't talk to me unless she wanted something. She wasn't yelling so that meant I wasn't in trouble. I told myself to relax.

"What do you want?"

Tayo shrugged. "What are you reading?" She tugged the book from my grasp. "Hmm, yeah, I've read this one." She snapped the book shut so my place in the book was lost and tossed it on the bed. I groaned inwardly but taking a deep breath, forced myself to smile; the last thing I wanted was a fight.

"Can I help you?"

She made a non-committal noise. "Just wondered if you'd like some biscuits and Baba dudu… I know you love Baba dudu." She held out a ten naira note. I'd been fine before, but now that she mentioned Baba dudu, I could taste the juicy stickiness of the dark coconut candy. I swiped the note before she could change her mind.

"Really?" I asked, the money safely squeezed in my palm. "Why?"

"Nothing. Just while you're there, can you get me sanitary towels?"

"Yuck, why don't you get them yourself?"

"Pleeaase."

"Fine, but I'm keeping the change."

"Thanks, lil' sis. So, I need you to get the heavy-flow pads. Get 'Always' pads, not 'Simple', okay? And I need them now, so hurry up." She punctuated her last words by smacking her palm on the bed twice; then she got up. I stuck my tongue out as she walked out of the room.

I was on my way back from the aboki's stall a few houses down the road when I heard a dog growling: a low guttural growl that sent chills down my spine. My eyes locked on a big Alsatian standing between me and the gate to my house, and I froze. A boy stepped out of the new house opposite mine.

"Whatever you do, don't run," he said in a calm, steady voice, his eyes fixed on the dog. He held out one hand to it, beckoning it, and he held out his other hand in my direction, ordering me to stay where I was.

I took a deep breath and nodded, trying to appear nonchalant. I would stay put until the boy took his dog inside, no biggie; it wasn't like I had anything to do. That is until I heard the growl turn into a full-blown bark, and the massive animal bounded towards me. I shrieked and flung the black carrier bag at it; then I turned and ran. I hadn't got far when the dog threw itself at me. I stumbled under its weight and fell, screaming and fearful for my life. I shielded my face with my arms as I anticipated the inevitable pain, but all I felt was the dog's wet tongue. I kept on screaming after the weight was pulled off me.

"Okay, you can stop crying now. He only wanted to play with you."

I eased my arms down off my face and got off the ground.

"You need to put a leash on that thing!" I sobbed, looking down at myself and grimacing. I was covered in dust and dog slobber.

"He has a leash," said the boy in a patronising tone, holding it up for me to see.

"You only just put that on him. Do you think I'm stupid?" I tried to dust my clothes off, but a large light-orange smear remained. Sighing with resignation, I looked up, and that was when my eyes met his. He was the most beautiful boy I had ever seen. He was taller than I was and he had a beautiful olive complexion. His mouth was heart-shaped, his eyes were a lovely shade of hazel, and his jet-black hair was short and curly. I felt my heart beat faster as I looked into his eyes. I couldn't understand what I was feeling or why I couldn't tear my eyes away from his. I willed my lips to move, but it felt as if they were glued together and my tongue felt heavy. I tried to look away, to make a move: any movement was better than just standing there, staring. I succeeded in shutting my eyes, and when I opened them, everything came into focus suddenly, like air rushing into a vacuum.

"You dropped this," he said, handing me the dusty black nylon bag.

I felt my face grow hot. I snatched the bag from the boy and without another word I dragged myself, on shaky legs, back into the house and upstairs to the room I shared with my sister. Leaving the door ajar, I shuffled to Tayo's bed where she sat eyeing me from behind a Mills and Boon novel and dumped the plastic bag by her feet, then I turned to my bed, threw myself on it and buried my head into my pillow.

"Oi, is your hand broken? Go and shut the door!"

I stuffed my head into my pillow over and over again, groaning each time.

I was furious with myself for acting in such a silly way. But every time I thought about him, there was a small ache in my chest, and I found myself sighing.

I met him properly two weeks after the dog incident. My brothers and I were sitting on the stoop in front of the house after school one afternoon, just whiling away time. There was never anything on TV before 4 p.m., and we were bored. We watched the cars going and coming on the dusty road, struggling through or manoeuvring around the larger potholes.

A car stopped in front of us. A man alighted and walked towards us; he was slim and handsome, though his hair was thinning and speckled with grey. He smiled at us in a diplomatic manner: the smile of someone who didn't quite know what to do with kids and addressed them, in the same way, as he would to adults.

"Hello there," he said, waving us over. My brothers and I looked at each other: none of us moved.

"Come along now; I won't bite." The man waved us over again as if becoming impatient. His wife got out of the car and came to stand by his side. She was almost as tall as the man, with really blonde, long hair that flowed around her like little caresses. I tried to imagine how we looked to the couple as we sat there, still in our school uniforms. I was light-skinned, a scrawny child with an oval face and hair woven into cornrows in a style called 'calabash' because the hair plaited from the ends of the head to meet in the middle. My brothers were darker than I was and they were all tall and gangly. Timi, the oldest, was only twelve, and he was as tall as an Iroko tree. (I'd never seen an Iroko tree, but I'd heard my mum use the expression when she referred to Timi; all I knew was that it must be a very tall tree.)

The lady smiled and held out her hands to us; we got up, looking at one another for the reassurance that we were doing the right thing. When we got to where they stood, I curtsied, and my brothers bowed their heads in greeting. I took one of the woman's outstretched hands; it was soft, and her skin felt cold and smooth, even in the October heat. She squeezed my hand before releasing it.

"Bawo ni?" she asked. *How are you?*

I blinked in disbelief that a white lady spoke Yoruba, my language. The man asked our names and we told him. He shook our hands as we introduced ourselves.

"I'm Colonel Bankole, and this is Sue," he said, holding his wife proudly by the waist.

"You should meet our boys." Sue clapped her hands and walked around the car to open the back door. I heard protests from the car's interior.

"You will get out this instant," Sue spoke sternly without raising her voice, and I marvelled; to me, words didn't carry enough authority unless yelled or spoken in an aggressive tone.

"Yes, Mommy." Two boys emerged from the car.

"Well then, Ben and Joshua, these are our new neighbours: Timi, Gbenga, Femi and Jadesola." Impressively, she had remembered all four of our names, though they rolled off her tongue with misplaced accents. When she uttered my name, I looked up and found myself staring straight into the face of the boy I'd already met: the boy with the dog. I looked away quickly.

"Hello," Ben and Joshua said.

"Hi," said Timi.

"Hello," said Femi.

"S'up?" said Gbenga.

"Hi," I said, waving shyly. I felt like my head too big for my shoulders, and my arms felt too long. I couldn't quite get myself to stand right. I shuffled to support my weight on one leg, placing my other foot behind it, and I folded my hands behind my back. I really wanted to look at Josh again; I could look at him forever. I willed myself to be strong, to avoid looking at him. Did I affect him the same way he affected me? My curiosity got the better of me, and I snuck a peek at him under my lashes: he was staring at me. When he caught my eye, he winked, and I looked away quickly. My face grew hot, and I drew lines in the dirt with my foot. Sue was speaking, and I struggled to tune into what she was saying.

"...and you're welcome to come over anytime," she ended, with a smile. I smiled back at her: anything to keep me from glancing back at Josh.

I felt scared and excited at the same time; something was happening to me. I couldn't explain it, but the world felt different: brighter, cleaner and more beautiful than it had ever seemed. As I stood there on that sunny afternoon, employing every ounce of self-restraint I had not to look at him again, I knew that my world would never be the same again.

CHAPTER 2

1 9 9 5

Three years went by but my feelings for Josh in no way diminished; if anything, my infatuation with him had grown stronger. I scribbled his name and mine all over my notebooks, drawing large hearts around them with Cupid's arrows. I dreamed up my versions of fairy tales in my head. One day I would be Sleeping Beauty and he would show up on his trusty stallion and kiss me, rousing me up from my thick, dark and murky sleep; the next day I would be Rapunzel, throwing down my long hair from the window of my high tower. All my dreams ended the same way: we always lived happily ever after.

I tried various ways of getting Josh to pay more attention to me; it seemed as if he would only speak to me if it were unavoidable. One day I found him alone in my house, walking from the bathroom back to the living room where Ben was playing video games with Timi, Gbenga and Femi. I snuck up behind him and shoved him; he tripped and fell forward, catching himself with his elbow on the terrazzo floor. Clocking the angry look on his face, I laughed and ran to my room. I shut the door and leant against it, my heart beating in trepidation, the expression on his face haunting me. I waited in vain for the pounding on the door and the voice raised in anger. After what felt like forever, I went back out to investigate what was taking him so long, and he was back in the living room as if nothing had happened. My heart sank. He was supposed to make an effort at retaliation or at least show some form of indignation; the last thing I expected was that he would ignore me. Why? Did he not like me? Did he think I was ugly?

The more I thought about it, the more it infuriated me that he didn't think I was worth reacting to. It made me want to make more of an effort, so, whenever I knew Ben and Josh were coming round to ours, I would put on my best outfit, not caring that it was evident that I wasn't going anywhere. I walked in and out of whatever room I knew they were in so I could catch a glimpse of him. Some days I would plant myself in the living room, say hello nonchalantly when he arrived and then steal glances at him while pretending to be engrossed in Lara Croft shimmying across a wall or Ryu pounding Zangief to a pulp on the TV screen. I would drink in the sight of him, memorising his little quirks like the way his brows furrowed in concentration and he stuck his tongue between his teeth when he played.

One day I walked into my brothers' room when I knew Ben and Josh were there. Gbenga, Femi, Ben and Josh were huddled around Femi's bed looking at a magazine. They were laughing and joking about whatever it was they were looking at, but as soon as I walked in the room fell silent. Gbenga snapped the magazine shut, shoved it under his bum and sat on it.

"What do you want this time?" Femi said, rolling his eyes.

"Erm... I was wondering if I could borrow a pen." I risked a glance at Josh, but he wasn't looking in my direction. He picked up a comic book and flipped through its pages; a strand of curly hair fell across his face, and I held my breath as he lifted his hand to brush it back in a smooth and fluid motion, almost as if he knew he was being watched. I was hoping he would look up and say hello, or at least smile at me, but he didn't. Femi sighed and got up to find me a pen, which he thrust it into my hand.

"Thank you," I said, grasping the courage to glance at Josh one last time. Finally, our eyes met. He looked at me funny, like the way my mum looked at the maid when she burnt Mum's favourite lace blouse with the iron. I stepped out of the room, and the talking and laughter resumed as if I had never interrupted it. My heart sank. Did Josh hate me? What could I do to make him like me? He probably thought of me as his friend's younger sister; maybe that was why he wouldn't let himself like me. Well, I would show him that I wasn't a baby, that I could be grown-up and sophisticated.

I would give myself a makeover. By the time I was done, Josh would look at me in a different light.

I had watched my mum put on makeup a few times, and I figured I could do it on my own, so I snuck into my parents' room. My parents always locked their room whenever they left the house but unknown to them we had a spare key. Usually, my destination would be the little store room where they kept treats and other bits and bobs, but I had a different mission in mind. I sat down at my mum's white Victorian-style dressing table and pulled open the first drawer; it was filled with assorted colours of little sewing thread spoons and tiny plastic tubs of pins, needles and buttons.

"Nope," I muttered. I opened the second drawer and rubbed my hands together.

"Hmm, so many options!" Best to go with the simplest: I loved pink; it was my favourite colour. I picked up some pink eyeshadow and applied it to my eyelids.

"So far, so good." Admiring myself in the oval vanity mirror, I decided on some pink lipstick to match the eye shadow. I applied it and pursed my lips; it didn't look right so I walked into the en-suite bathroom to get some tissue paper and wiped off my first attempt but my lips just looked bruised. I dampened some more tissue paper and proceeded to wipe off every trace of the lipstick. The tissue paper left a trail of white residue around my mouth; I washed it off with some water and dried my mouth on the hand towel by the sink. Satisfied that my mouth looked normal, I went back to the dressing table, but no matter how hard I tried, I couldn't get the lipstick on without looking like a clown.

"Who knew putting on lipstick could be so difficult?" I gave up on the lipstick. "Hmm, what next? Ah, mascara!" I plucked out the wand and proceeded to give myself longer and more beautiful lashes.

A few minutes later, the door to my parents' room slid open. In haste, I screwed the mascara shut and tidied up the table top, throwing the makeup back into the drawer and slamming it shut.

"I thought I heard someone in here," Tayo said, striding into the room like Sherlock Holmes. I turned to face her, and she gasped.

"What did you do?" she exclaimed. Taking in my situation, she covered her mouth with her palm and chuckled. I knew I was a mess; I had managed to stab myself in the eye a few times with the mascara, and my eyes were red and runny.

"Help, please," I pleaded as a tear slid down my face. I swiped at it with the back of my hand, smearing my cheek with black mascara in the process.

"Why would I do that?" asked Tayo, walking into the store room and re-emerging with a packet of Okin shortcake biscuits and a bottle of Fanta. She turned back to me as she was leaving.

"Make sure you tidy up this mess and remember to lock up properly before Mum and Dad get back." She arched an eyebrow and pointed a finger at me. I nodded quietly, and my sister left me alone, humming to herself as she shut the door behind her.

I rushed to the bathroom to wash the makeup off my face. It took three attempts with a bar of Imperial Leather soap and elbow grease to get my face looking less like a child's workbook that has been scribbled on and erased too many times, and more like the face I was used to.

"That's the last time I try to put makeup on because of a boy," I swore to myself. I just had to find another way to get Josh to fall in love with me.

One afternoon, during a power outage, my brothers and I played 'go fish' at the dining table to while away time.

"Ben was here earlier; he was asking if we wanted to come over after dinner," Gbenga said to Timi and Femi. My ears pricked up on hearing Ben's name, and I glanced around at my brothers. If I could go with them to Josh's house, maybe he could see that I was cool, and he could let himself relax around me. I just knew he liked me. He had to like me; why else would he make such an effort to avoid me all the time?

"Erm, so are you guys going over to play a game?" I feigned nonchalance, paying my card more attention than was required.

"Yup," Gbenga responded

"What game?"

"Need for Speed, it's supposed to be this awesome racing game, Ben won't shut up about it, so we're going to check it out, see if it is as bad-ass as he says." Gbenga scrutinised his cards and then looked up at me with a mischievous grin. "I need all your threes."

"Go fish," I responded smugly, before adding, "Ooh, can I come? I love racing games."

Gbenga fidgeted; I saw him exchange a look with Femi and Timi. Femi scratched his head, and Timi avoided my eyes by staring at his cards. I could tell what they were thinking.

"Aww, come on," I said, scowling. "I want to play."

"Sorry, I don't think that's a good idea. Besides, it'll just be guys there; it'll be weird cos if you're there we won't be able to talk about guys stuff." Femi's tone was enough to tell me there was no point in trying to change their minds.

"Fine," I sighed, feigning defeat and noticing my brothers relax visibly. It wasn't over yet; I'd made up my mind that I really wanted to go, and I was about to unleash my secret weapon. "Timi, do you have any Jacks?"

Timi grunted as he threw down a couple of cards in front of me. I picked out two Jacks from my cards and added them to the two on the table. I looked at Gbenga and chuckled: maybe a little too dramatic.

"What's funny?" Gbenga asked, guarding his cards suspiciously.

"No, nothing, I just remembered the night you snuck out to go to Rachel's party, and I caught you trying to sneak back in through the window in the bathroom downstairs. I just thought that I should share that story with Daddy. I'm sure he'll find it amusing."

Gbenga laughed uneasily. "Yeah right, I'll make your life miserable if you even try."

"Or the time I caught you with that girl in the guestroom." I looked at Timi, my lips pressed together, like the last thing in the world I wanted to do was tattle on him. "Or the time you borrowed Daddy's new BMW." I pointed at Femi. "When Daddy got home, he knew someone had moved the car, and I covered your back and convinced him that no one had touched it." I turned back to Gbenga. "What about the time you sold a gallon of Daddy's emergency fuel so you could take that girl, what's her name, on a date and when Daddy asked what happened to it, you lied about how much fuel had been there in the first place and Daddy thought he was losing his mind..."

From that day on my brothers let me tag along when they went over to Ben and Josh's house and I was able to get closer to Ben and his mum, Sue, but I could never get to Josh. I would often go over to help Sue in the kitchen. It wasn't like she needed my help, she had a cook and a maid, but it was the only excuse I had for being there. The irony was that I avoided doing any cooking or cleaning at home, as much as this infuriated my mother. Most days I would run home from school, drop my books on my bed and run straight back out to Josh's house. At first, I think Sue had tolerated my presence; I didn't fool her even as I continually asked her if she needed me to help with anything, but with time she came to enjoy having me around. Some days she would send her maid to call me over. I would sit on a swivel stool at the kitchen island, watching Sue bake while she regaled me with stories from her childhood. She talked about the townhouse in Buckinghamshire where she grew up and how much she missed her friends and her family in the UK. Sometimes during the afternoons when there were power outages, I would go over to play Monopoly or Scrabble with Ben and Sue, but Josh never joined in, no matter how much fun we were having.

I decided to give Josh a taste of his own medicine and started ignoring him, not bothering to respond when he said hello, but he would just smile. When he smiled at me, my face would remain expressionless, but my insides would be burning up. I would lie on my bed all day thinking of how his face glowed when he smiled, savouring the warm feelings it infused in me.

CHAPTER 3

1998

By the time I was fifteen, Josh and I were going steady even though he was unaware of our relationship. I told all my friends about him and dropped his name into conversations at the slightest provocation just to feel the thrill of saying it. I carried a picture of him everywhere, telling any boy that asked me out that I had a boyfriend; if they didn't believe me, I would flash Josh's picture with a flourish, relishing the intimidation in their eyes as they realised that they couldn't compete with such beauty. On Valentine's Day, I sent myself chocolates and a pink teddy, with a card signed with Josh's name. Only Alexia and Tobi, my best friends, knew the truth about my relationship. Alexia was Ghanaian: tall, dark-skinned and popular for her amazing voice. Tobi was easily the prettiest of us, with a soft round face, big 'Bambi' eyes and long dark lashes. She walked as if she were moving to sensuous music and boys flocked around her like moths to a flame.

There was no giving up on Josh now, not when we'd become such good friends in the sense that he'd stopped ignoring me, and we now had conversations consisting of more than three syllables. No matter how basic and uninteresting our conversations were, I made up for it by re-enacting the scene once I was alone, embellishing our talk with the life and drama it deserved. His "Hello" meant that his day was all the more pleasant for seeing me, and his "Your hair suits you" meant that I was beautiful, and he would love me forever and ever.

Alexia and Tobi teased me constantly about Josh; they had met him the year before at Gbenga's birthday party.

1997

"So where is this Josh you're always going on about?" Alexia had asked with a twinkle in her eyes as soon as they arrived at the party. "I need to make sure he's not just a figment of your imagination; no one can be as amazing as you make him out to be."

I had laughed then. "Come on, let's go look for him, and then you can see for yourself." I grabbed her hand and pulled her through the party, eager to show off my Josh.

"Hey, Josh!" I called out when I spotted him by the drinks cooler. I heard Alexia catch her breath as she caught sight of him and I smiled, waving him over proudly. Tobi rolled her eyes at me.

"Easy, girl, be cool," she whispered. "You'll scare the guy away."

"Don't be silly, I *am* cool," I smiled at her and shrugged.

"Hi Josh," I said when he was within earshot, savouring the sound of his name on my lips. "I want you to meet my best friends, Alexia and Tobi. Alexia, Tobi, this is Josh."

"Hi," Josh said, shaking hands with Alexia.

"Wow, it's so good to meet you, I was beginning to doubt that you were real," Alexia said, giggling, and I elbowed her. She winced and grimaced at me before turning back to Josh.

"Nice to meet you," Tobi said, dropping his outstretched hand as quickly as she had taken it. I arched a brow in her direction, and she shrugged.

"This one will not shut up about you. Josh this, Josh that---ouch!" Alexia shrieked and shoved me away from her. I had put an arm around her and pinched her below her armpit as hard as I could. I aimed the sweetest smile I could muster at Josh; he wouldn't meet my eyes and he looked as if he'd rather be anywhere else. My heart sank. Would it have hurt him to pretend that he could at least stand me in front of my friends?

"Alright, Josh, catch you later. Enjoy the party." I turned to walk away, dragging Alexia behind me.

"Laterz," Tobi said, wriggling her fingers at Josh and walking away with Alexia and me. When I was sure that we were at a safe distance from Josh, I let go of Alexia's hand and faced her with my arms folded over my chest.

"Really? "This one will not shut up about you"," I said, mimicking her.

"Yeah, Alexia, what was that all about?" Tobi flicked Alexia on her arm.

"What?" she asked, rubbing her arm. "Okay, I'm sorry, I know I shouldn't have said that but it just slipped out. You're right, Josh is really cute, and I was nervous, I just couldn't think of anything else to say."

I tried to maintain my cross expression but couldn't resist the smile tugging at the edge of my lips.

"You think he's cute?" I asked, giving in to a grin that stretched the breadth of my face.

"Oh my gosh! Are you kidding me? Even a blind person can tell how cute he is. And his accent! I don't blame you for hiding him from everybody," Alexia said, winking at me.

"You girls are just pathetic." Tobi rolled her eyes at us.

1998

"What would you think if I asked Josh out? Do you think it would make me look desperate?" I whispered, leaning forward in my chair and glancing around to make sure that no one could hear. It was lunch period, and the dining hall was packed full and noisy, so I needn't have bothered. I saw a look pass between Tobi and Alexia.

"You're right; I can't ask him out. Forget I asked." I waved it off and sat back in my chair.

Tobi cleared her throat. "I think it's an excellent idea."

My mouth fell open; I hadn't expected them to agree so readily. If anything, I'd thought Tobi would try to talk me out of it.

"You do? Really?" I inched closer towards Tobi's face, and she pushed my nose away with her forefinger.

"Yeah, why not? What do you have to lose? Just go for it, he'll be a fool to turn you down."

"But what if he does?"

"What if he doesn't?" She waggled her fork at me, her lips turned up in a conspiratorial smile and winked.

"Hmm, I don't know."

"You asked for my opinion." Tobi shrugged.

I looked at Alexia, who was pushing her food around her plate with a distant look on her face. She started when she realised I was watching her.

"So, what do you think?" I asked, wrinkling my features in an anticipatory grimace. She shoved a forkful of food into her mouth and mumbled something incomprehensible.

"How should I do it?" Now that I had made up my mind, the thought of actually doing it was scary. "Should I write him a note? I'm not sure I can ask him to his face."

Tobi shook her head. "No, don't do that. You just need to walk up to him and say, 'Hi Josh, I like you, will you be my boyfriend?'"

I winced. "No, seriously." I looked at Alexia again. "Alexia, come on, why are you keeping quiet? I need your help. What should I do?"

"I'm the last person who would know anything about asking a boy out." Her lips curled in a weak smile, she shrugged and then continued picking at her food.

"Fine, you guys have been no help at all. I'll figure it out on my own."

Later that day

The car rumbled in through the gates of the house, and as soon as the engine died, I pushed open the car door and raced into the house, my mind on the task ahead. I changed into my home clothes and, with no concrete plan in mind, I made my way to Josh's house.

My face was burning as I rang the doorbell. I clasped my hands together to keep them from trembling.

Sue answered the door.

"Hello, Jade! You alright, love? I wasn't expecting you today."

"Hi, Sue," I said, wondering why she didn't invite me in. "I was wondering if I could speak with Josh. I need to ask him something."

"Erm, yes." She hesitated, glancing behind her, and then looked back at me and smiled. "Of course, honey." She stepped away from the door and let me in.

I followed her into the living room. I saw Josh on the sofa, next to him was a sight that made me stop in my tracks. Alexia sat next to him, her hands clasped in his. My blood ran cold as they exchanged a look.

"What are you doing here?" I blurted out. 'Oh please, let there be an innocent reason why my best friend is sitting with the boy I love,' I prayed.

I walked over to them and sat next to Alexia, my face frozen in a broad smile, not unlike the Cheshire cat in Alice in Wonderland, but nobody smiled back at me. Alexia bowed her head. I felt as if someone had reached into my body, ripped out my heart and then proceeded to smash it into a million tiny pieces with a sledgehammer, over and over again, until all the pieces were unrecognisable.

Josh's lips curled in a smile that didn't reach his eyes.

"Hey, erm, meet my girlfriend." He introduced us as if we were strangers.

My breath caught in my throat at his words. I looked at Alexia as if willing her to tell me that it wasn't true: that it was just an insensitive prank they'd cooked up. She refused to meet my gaze.

I decided to be calm, to pretend that it was nothing to me that my friend – someone I had shared everything with, someone I had trusted blindly – was dating Josh.

"Oh wow, you sneaky devil." I nudged Alexia's shoulder with my elbow. "When were you going to tell me? That's awesome! Well, I'll let you guys get on." My face throbbed from my plastic smile which stretched up to my ears. I turned around and walked out without a backwards glance.

Once I reached the road, I just kept walking. I didn't know how or what to feel; I felt too many things at the same time. I had given so much of myself to the dream of being with Josh, and now it was gone forever – and with it, my relationship with my best friend. I could never trust her after this. She of all people knew what Josh meant to me. How could she betray me like that? I felt like screaming, I felt like running, I felt like dying. I stared longingly after cars, wishing one of them would lose control and take me along with it, emptying me of all feeling and emotion. I'm not sure what hurt more, losing Josh or knowing that I'd been made a fool of by my best friend. They were probably laughing at me right now. I sat down by the side of the road and hugged myself, willing the tears to fall. But my eyes remained dry. I moaned his name over and over and over. A hand pulled me up; it was Ben. He held me in his arms, and I leant into him. The tears came then.

"You'll be okay," he said over and over again as he patted my back. He led me to a little shop in front of one of the houses where an elderly woman sold sweets, biscuits, cold drinks and household products. We sat facing each other on benches outside the shop.

"Can I buy you a drink?" he asked.

I shook my head.

"Well, I'm going to get you one; I don't think we can stay here unless we buy something," he said, getting up. I was no longer crying, but it felt as if my tears were only being held at bay by a weak dam: the slightest provocation and it would burst, causing my tears to flow once again. I stared at my hands as I waited for Ben to come back.

"Here," he said, placing a bottle of Sprite in my hands.

I looked up at him, shaking my head, and pushed the bottle back towards him.

"Go on, take it," he insisted, handing it back to me.

I took it, and as I held the cold, perspiring green bottle, I realised that I was thirsty. I lifted the bottle to my lips for a sip, but I didn't put it back down until I'd drained half the bottle.

"Thanks," I said in a small voice, and he nodded. We were both silent; he sat watching me as I sat staring at my hands. "Why did you follow me?" I asked, looking up into his face.

"I was in the living room when you came in and when I saw you walk out moments after, I just knew I had to make sure you were okay, and when you didn't go straight home..."

I nodded at his response and sniffed. Should I ask my next question?

"How long..." My voice caught in my throat. I shook my head and looked away. Ben took my hand.

"Jade, you need to get over Josh and move on. I don't know how long he and Alexia have been together, but does it matter?"

I bit my lip and stared at the sky, trying hard to keep that damn dam intact. The tears were threatening to fall again, and if they did my speech would become incoherent, and I really didn't want that to happen.

"I just want to know how long I've been walking around with a knife in my back, not even realising it. And that time I spent waiting for Josh to see that I really liked him and would have done anything for him."

Ben nodded.

"I think he saw that but, Jade, it was too much for him to handle. Don't you get it? Joshua is very shy, and maybe if you had given him time and space, he would have come to realise how amazing you are. You know, that first day you met, he'd told me about you. In fact, he wouldn't stop talking about you."

"He did?" My mouth fell open.

"He talked about you at any opportunity he got; it was annoying to listen to. Everyone could tell he liked you except him. You know, it was hard for us moving down here from London; we'd left all our close friends and to make it worse, Dad travelled a lot. Josh wanted to be friends but every time he tried to talk to you he choked."

I shook my head in disbelief. "I thought he couldn't stand me. It never crossed my mind that he was afraid to talk to me."

"Yes well, that was years ago. Now it's just..." He stopped and looked at me. I knew what he was going to say.

"I came on a bit strong sometimes, didn't I?"

Ben pursed his lips. "It was too much for him, yes. I don't think he could handle it."

"So you think his relationship with Alexia is his way of pushing me away?"

"I don't know, maybe. Josh may just really like her, although I don't know what he sees in her, she laughs like a hyena," he said, smiling at me in an attempt to make me feel better. I smiled back at him; I still felt broken and frail, but I had more clarity now. I was never meant to be with Josh. I had wanted him too much, so being with him would have hurt because there was no way he could love me half as much as I had loved him. I made up my mind that when I met a boy I wanted to be with, he would need me more than I needed him. It was the only way I could protect myself from being hurt again.

CHAPTER 4

A door creaked open, and I heard the click-clack of heels walking down the corridor towards my room. My door opened, and the room was infused with the sticky-sweet scent of my mum's perfume. I kept my eyes shut, hoping she would leave me alone even though I knew it was unlikely.

"No school today?" Mum asked, yanking the covers off me. I opened my eyes and groaned as I sat up.

"No, I'm not going. I have terrible menstrual cramps," I lied, saying the first thing I could think of. The thought of spending the day in the same classroom with Alexia shot painful darts through my chest. I winced every time I thought about her and Josh together. To make myself feel better, I pictured walking up to Alexia in class, the look of terror on her face, and her cry for help as I yanked her ponytail and dished out a few slaps across her annoying, backstabbing face. I wasn't much of a one for violence, but I couldn't help the sneer that crept across my face. I wouldn't really do that, but there was no harm in imagining it.

"I can see you're feeling better already," Mum said, misunderstanding my expression. "Get up and get ready quickly. Sunday will take you to school if you can be ready in twenty minutes. Otherwise, you'll have to find your own way there."

"Yes, Mummy," I mumbled. She waited until I managed to drag myself out of bed and then left, leaving behind a hint of vanilla perfume. I showered and got dressed. Skipping down the stairs, I tried to convince myself that today was going to be an awesome day. The thought that my classmates would know about my embarrassing crush and about the fact that I'd lied about actually dating Josh once Alexia decided to be open about her relationship crossed my mind and I cringed. "Shit."

When I got outside, I looked around for Mr Sunday. The car was parked in front of the house, but he wasn't sitting there.

"Mr Sunday, I'm ready to go!" I called out. Not getting any response, I went round to the gatehouse, and sure enough, I found him there, wolfing down a loaf of bread and fried bean cakes. I grimaced as the smell hit my nostrils. I hadn't eaten or drunk anything since the Sprite I'd had with Ben the day before, and the smell of food made my belly churn.

"Ah, Mr Sunday, we need to leave now, I don't want to be late for school." I glanced at my watch; it was already 7.30 a.m.

"Go and wait for me in the car," he said through a mouthful of bread and beans.

I turned away, disgusted, and headed back to the car.

In less than three minutes Mr Sunday jumped into the car and started the ignition, following the sound of the car engine with a loud burp. He flashed a grin at me in the rear-view mirror.

"Ehn, Lady J! You go late for school today o." And the award for stating the obvious goes to-.

"Thank you, Mr Sunday, please can we just go?" I turned away from the image of yellowing teeth protruding through pinkish-brown gums.

I prayed that the traffic would be light; it wouldn't do for me to be late on my first day as Head Girl. But the traffic was anything but light. I missed assembly and made it into class ten minutes into the first period.

Mrs Oye, the geography teacher, stood with her back to the class, writing on the chalkboard. She turned around when I walked in and glared at me, her hands on her waist.

"Good morning, Ma," I greeted, bending my knees in a curtsey. I scanned the classroom for somewhere to sit. My usual desk was next to Alexia's, and there was no way I was ever sitting there. Plus I risked losing control in the middle of the lesson and pummelling her in the face. Arrghh, her face was so annoying. I took a deep breath and headed towards the empty desk at the back of the classroom. I felt eyes boring into my back.

"Jadesola, I understand that you're Head Girl now so I will let this pass. You cannot be late for my class. It is unacceptable!" Mrs Oye screeched from across the room, an ugly frown distorting her face. Her left hand was still splayed on her hip and her right hand hung by her side. I could see it twitching as if aching to grab the long shiny cane lying on the desk in front of her.

"I'm sorry, ma," I said, sounding as remorseful as I could. "I was sorting out the appropriate punishment for the latecomers." It wasn't entirely untrue. I had snuck in behind fellow latecomers and had joined the other prefects meting out punishments as if I had been there all along.

"Okay, I will allow you." She addressed the class. "Only Jadesola can come into my class late. Everyone else will be flogged." My classmates grumbled.

My chair creaked as I fished my books from my knapsack. *Shit.* I swore under my breath as I realised the chair I was sitting on had a wonky leg. I shifted my weight to take the strain off the bad leg; the last thing I wanted was to end up on the floor if the chair collapsed. At the end of the lesson, I would have to ask someone to swap seats with me. This was torture, but it was infinitely preferable to sitting next to Alexia.

After Mrs Oye's class, I managed to persuade Yinka to swap seats with me; she was the only one willing, and under normal circumstances, I would never have taken her place, but I was desperate. I was the proud owner of the desk right at the front centre of the classroom: officially the worst seat in the class. But it was worth it.

During lunch period, I set off for Tobi's class; she was in a different class from Alexia and me. There was a small voice at the back of my mind saying that she'd known about Alexia and Josh, but it didn't seem plausible that Tobi would betray me. I trusted her. I glanced back at Alexia as I walked out of the classroom; she was putting her books away and locking up her desk. She looked up, and our eyes met for a fraction of a second. I turned away and kept my face resolutely forward. I heard her getting out of her seat, and I increased my pace, marching out of the classroom and down the corridor towards Tobi's class, resisting the urge to check if Alexia was following me. When I got to Tobi's class, I succumbed to temptation and glanced back over my shoulder.

"Oh." She wasn't behind me. I swivelled around, curious as to where she was, but I couldn't see her. In spite of myself, I felt a slight tinge of disappointment. A part of me had expected her to run after me, begging me to forgive her.

"...ripped it up and tossed it in the bin." I caught the tail-end of Tobi's conversation with one of her classmates, a tiny girl with a voice to match. Tobi was sitting on her desk, her feet on her chair; the girl threw back her head and let out a high-pitched crackling laugh. I winced and almost raised my hands to cover my ears, but I stopped myself. I stood between them and smiled at the girl, raising my hand in a half wave. She waved back.

"See you later," she said, patting Tobi on the shoulder before walking away.

"Hey," Tobi said, sliding off her desk. She put her arm around my shoulder and pulled me closer to her so that my shoulder jabbed into her armpit.

"You look like hell. Come on, let's go get lunch." She glanced behind me as if she was looking for something. "Where's Alexia? Isn't she coming? I swear that girl has been acting a little shady. Maybe she doesn't want to hang out with us anymore." She smirked, not believing for one moment that could be a possibility. Like, why would anyone not want to be friends with the most popular girls in school?

"Or maybe she has a new boyfriend?" I pursed my lips.

"No way!" Tobi exclaimed, her eyes wide, a big grin on her face. "Well, good for her. Why is she keeping it quiet, though? It's not like she has to hide it from us."

My eyes welled up and grabbing Tobi's hand from around my shoulder; I led her out of the classroom.

"Slow down, what it is? I need to get my purse," Tobi protested. But I didn't stop until we were by the side of the classroom block, where no one could see us. Tears trickled down my face, and I let them fall.

"Guess who Alexia's boyfriend is?" I smiled bitterly. Tobi's eyes widened at the sight of my tears. A second later she clapped her palm over her mouth.

"No!" she gasped. "Josh?" She narrowed her eyes.

I nodded, wiping my tears with the back of my hands and sniffing. Water dripped down my nostril, and I swiped at it with the side of my palm and dried it off on the skirt of my uniform. Tobi made a face.

"Here." She dug in her pockets and shoved a white handkerchief under my nose. I grabbed it and blew hard.

"Thanks."

"That little...! Just wait till I get my hands on her." Tobi gritted her teeth and clenched her fists. Then she looked at me and sighed, her stance relaxing.

"Come on, let's go and get something to eat."

"I'm not hungry."

"Will you feel better if I punch the living daylights out of our friend?"

I nodded, managing a weak smile at the thought. In my head, I could already see Tobi sitting on Alexia and punching her in the face.

"Yeah? Don't worry; my uppercut alone will have her scrawny ass running back to Ghana." We both chuckled. I wiped at the tears that were already drying on my face.

"You're going to be alright, yeah?" Tobi said, pulling me into a tight hug. "He may not have felt the same way, but I know how much you liked that idiot..."

"Don't..."

"But he is! Only an idiot would pass you up for that..." She paused, searching for an appropriate word. "Backstabbing bitch!"

CHAPTER 5

The rest of the school year passed by in a blur. Tobi and I became closer than we used to be but, as much as I hated to admit it, I missed Alexia. Losing her hurt almost as much as it had hurt to lose Josh. I tore up all the pictures I had of both Josh and Alexia. I cut her out of the pictures we'd taken together. It was easy to cut her out of the pictures of me, her and Tobi as I was in the middle in many of the pictures, so they just looked as if it had always been only me and Tobi all along.

I went to great lengths to avoid bumping into Josh. He rarely came to my house anymore, so that made it easier. I winced at the thought that he was probably spending more time with his new girlfriend. As much as I longed to get over him, I had to admit that I missed seeing him. My emotions were still raw and seeing his house every day, knowing that he was in there, only a few feet away from me, didn't help. What was he up to? Did he miss having me around him, practically stalking him? I guessed not. He was probably celebrating the fact that he had succeeded in getting rid of me. A part of me hated him. He had taken my best friend away from me. It wasn't enough that I wasn't good enough for him; he had to go and twist the knife in my chest? Every time I thought about the two of them together, my heart caught in my throat, and a feeling of self-hate crept through me. I felt useless and worthless. I must have been a terrible friend. Why else would I have been treated this way? Maybe I deserved it. Maybe it was my fault. If only I hadn't been so pushy. If only I had been a better friend. I was unwanted and unloved. Who would ever love me? What was there to love about me?

One morning I woke up with a heavy heart and lay in bed for a long time, just staring at the ceiling. It was a Saturday so I didn't have to get up... I never wanted to get up. I felt hollow and raw. My head felt like a boulder as I pulled myself up and propped my pillow behind my back. I leant my head against the headboard, shut my eyes and took a deep breath. I couldn't talk to anyone about what I was going through; no one took me seriously. Tobi had moved on, and she rolled her eyes whenever I mentioned Josh.

"Get over it already!" she had snapped the last time I tried to open up to her. But I knew someone who wouldn't ask me to be quiet.

"Lord, if you're listening. I just want to say that I'm sorry. I'm sorry for my obsession with Josh. I know that I'm not supposed to have any other God besides you, and it may have seemed like I worshipped him. Or... um... if I'm too young to be thinking about a boy. But Heavenly Father, please can the pain go away now? I don't know what to do, or how to feel or how to act. It hurts so much, and everyone makes me feel like I'm not supposed to be hurting. Why do I feel like this? Why won't the pain just go away? I just want it to end." I prayed through pursed lips, a stray tear squeezing through my shut eyelids. I had prayed many times before, but I felt as if this was the most important prayer I had ever needed to be answered. I feel a calm settle over me like warm fluffy arms pulling me into a loving embrace.

* * *

"You can't not come to prom. Have you ever heard of a Head Girl missing her own prom?" Tobi turned sideways, admiring herself in the full-length mirror. She had dragged me out to go shopping for a prom dress with her, and now she was trying to get me to buy a dress as well.

"I'll fake an illness. Or better still, I'll throw myself down the stairs. Anything would be better than having to sit through a night of watching Alexia and Josh together."

Tobi rolled her eyes.

"You can't still be stewing over that. You should be over this guy already." Her eyebrows knitted. "Tell you what; I'll hook you up with one of my friends from Uni. You can make Josh jealous."

"No! Okay, fine, I'll think about it. Just don't try to set me up with anyone." I planned to sneak in, make sure everyone saw me and then sneak back out again.

"So who are you going with? You can't come alone! Especially since it's likely that Josh will be there."

"I don't know. Fine, I'll think about it."

Tobi clapped her hands gleefully. "Yay! Wait here; I've seen a dress that would be perfect for you." Less than a minute later, she shoved a red dress at me. I held it against my body and admired it in the mirror.

"It's beautiful, but I'm sure I can't afford it." I turned the dress over, looking for the price tag, and gasped. "Okay, I definitely cannot afford this." I shoved it back at her quickly, afraid that I'd be made to pay for the dress if I held it any longer.

"Chill, it's only 15,000 naira..."

"That's a lot more than my allowance. How can you afford it?"

"Let's just say I have a very rich uncle. I'll pay for your dress as long as you let me set you up with my friend."

"Tobi, I'm not letting you set me up with your friend and I'm not letting you buy me a dress," I said, adamant. "I'll go to Yaba Market over the weekend."

"Ew, how can you even think of wearing a second-hand dress to your prom?"

"No one will know it's second-hand and even if they do, I don't care."

The next day I tramped through the market, but I couldn't find anything suitable.

"Who cares about a stupid prom anyway," I said to myself as I got back on the bus, empty-handed.

CHAPTER 6

2 0 0 0

"Great, just perfect, Jade. The first day of school and you're late." I muttered to myself as I half ran down a really long corridor trying to find my class. It was like a cruel joke.

"201, 202, where the hell is room 203?"

"Hey," someone called out.

I turned to face a guy in a black t-shirt, baggy jeans riding low with half of his boxers hanging out and a baseball cap worn backwards.

"Room 203 is over there." He said.

I looked in the direction he pointed. It was all the way on the other side.

"Just go up those stairs over there, turn right, walk right down the corridor then talk the flight of stairs down," he said, hiking up his jeans which fell back down to its original position when he let go of it. "Good luck."

"Thank you," I said over my shoulder, running in the direction of the stairs.

"Shit, shit, shit," the doors to the lecture room were shut. I debated whether to open the doors or skip the class entirely when I saw a girl running towards me. The girl wore a flowery summer dress and green open-toe wedges which made a loud slapping sound against the concrete floor with each step. Her long black braids had grey streaks running through them, and they blew behind her, away from her face which was covered in a light sheen of perspiration. She stopped in front of me and doubled over as she struggled to catch her breath.

"Hey," she managed, her chest heaving. "Why are you standing here? Are we not allowed to go in?"

"I..er. I actually don't know. I just got here."

"So..." She straightened up and gestured for me open the door.

"Why don't you go on ahead? I'll be right behind you." I offered, stepping away from the door.

"Ha-ha," she wagged a finger at me. "No way, I couldn't possibly. You were here before me."

"It's okay, I insist."

We faced each other in a standoff. If we opened the door, it could go either way, but I wasn't about to risk getting yelled at on my first day of Uni. If only this girl would volunteer to be the guinea pig.

"I think I'll give this class a miss. It's only the first lecture; we can't be missing much. Want to go get breakfast?" The girl asked.

"I already had breakfast, but I'll come with you." I looked back at the closed doors as we walked away. I had been looking forward to this day for so long, and I was disappointed in myself that I couldn't even make it to my first lecture on time.

"What's your name?"

"Jadesola, but everybody calls me Jade."

"I'm Monica. Pleased to meet you." She extended a hand to me, and I grasped it in a handshake.

"Likewise."

"I completely overslept this morning. I couldn't sleep until 4 am, my bunkmate's snoring kept me up. And then the queue to use the bathroom...!"

"I know!" I threw my hands up in agreement. "What about the queue to get water? I spent over an hour in the queue."

"No, you have to fill your bucket the night before."

"Huh? Where do I keep it? In the bathroom?"

Monica burst into laughter. "Are you for real? Didn't you go to boarding house?"

"No," I said, my brows coming together in a frown.

"You keep it under your bunk or in your corner. But be careful, people will steal water if they can."

We walked into the cafeteria, and I went to find a seat while Monica went to the counter to get some food. She came to the table bearing a large plate of Jollof rice with plantain and small pieces of meat fried in pepper.

"Whoa, I thought you were getting breakfast."

"Allow me, please. I'm in Uni now, and if I want Jollof for breakfast, then that's what I'm having." She swept her hair away from her face and over her shoulder as she sat down. "Come and join me."

"Sure, I just get a spoon." I started to get up but sat back down when I clocked her clenched jaw.

"Actually, no thanks. I just had breakfast."

"Cool, cool." She said, tucking into her food.

I shook my head in wonder as I watched her eat.

We talked some more as she ate, Monica covered her mouth with her palm as she spoke with her mouthful. I resisted the urge to wince, the sound of her chewing set my teeth on edge. It turns out we had a few things in common. We were both born in April, and we were both the last born children of our parents. We also discovered that we had mutual friends.

My day was turning out a lot better than it started, it was only my first day, and I had already made a friend, I thought as we walked to our next lecture.

"No way," I said, spotting a familiar figure at the back of the classroom. "Gimme a sec, I've just seen a friend from secondary school, please save me a seat," I said to Monica.

I tried to mask the shock on my face as I approached Deji, he'd been more famous for his escapades with girls than he was for his intellect. I wondered how he'd achieved the high exam results required in JAMB and WAEC to get into law.

He was engrossed in the conversation he was having with a slim, beautiful, dark-skinned girl with long, neat copper tinted dreadlocks swept to one side of her face, revealing the bare skin of her neck on the other side.

"Deji!" I exclaimed a few feet away from him, clapping my hands together.

He looked up, and a wide grin spread across his features. "Jade!" He got up and closing the gap between us; he enveloped me in a bear hug. The girl with the dreads was looking at us with interest, but Deji ignored her. She sighed and stuck her head into the book she had open on her desk.

"What? Are you stalking me now?" He asked. "Six years of that shit-hole and I thought you would be sick of my face."

"Yeah, you wish. We both know you're the one doing the stalking. And St. Andrews wasn't a shit-hole."

"I knew you would say that Miss Headgirl, by the way, what happened to you at prom? I looked everywhere for you. I can't believe you didn't show. And where are Tobi and Alexia?" He asked, looking around like he was expecting them to appear over my shoulder.

"Well, let's see," I tapped a finger on my lip. "I didn't have a date to prom so..., yeah. Tobi has to retake JAMB next year, and Alexia can go to hell for all I care."

"Whoa! Boy drama?"

I gasped. "How...?"

"I have a sixth sense about these things." He tapped a finger against the side of his forehead, and I laughed.

"I'm sorry, I forgot who I was talking to."

"Ah, this is incredible. You and me! In the same class!" He paused to look me over. "You're looking good."

"You're not looking bad, yourself." I had never noticed just how good looking Deji was until now. I guess I had never taken much notice of him because I'd been so much in love with Josh.

"Let's catch up after class." He said as the lecturer walked into the room and addressed the class.

"Cool, see you after." I walked to the desk Monica reserved for me, conscious that Deji was watching me.

CHAPTER 7

2 0 0 1

"When does your mum get back from work?" Tobi asked, looking up from her phone.

Her face had been buried in it for over ten minutes, and she had been hmming and heehawing to herself the whole time. It was the school holidays; I'd just completed my first year of university, studying law. Tobi had had to re-sit her JAMB exams; she had chosen Breamston as a first choice but was only accepted into her second choice, the University College Oyo State. The two schools were approximately 180 kilometres apart. It was hard on our friendship, but we were determined to keep in touch, so Tobi came to spend a few weeks with me during the school holidays. As much as I knew she stayed with me because we were best friends and loved one another, I also suspected that she just dreaded going back to the village where her parents and two younger brothers lived. Her parents had sent her to Lagos when she was nine years old so that she could attend secondary school. I had never met her parents or any member of her family. She stayed with an aunt when she was in Lagos, but she never allowed me to visit there, either. As far as I knew, she spent as little time there as she could; apparently, her aunt had four children, and she always had a pile of chores waiting for Tobi. Sometimes our relationship felt a bit one-sided; she knew everything about my family and me, but I knew almost nothing about hers; she just refused to talk about it.

We sat in the living room; there was no electricity, and the heat was stifling, so we'd opened all possible windows – not that it made much of a difference.

"I don't know, 5.30, I think," I said, without looking up from my book.

"Hey!"

I tore my eyes away from the book reluctantly. I knew that tone; it was her 'I have something really exciting to tell you' tone.

"Do you want to take a trip to the island? You know my uncle John who lives in Parkview Estate?"

I nodded. She'd mentioned him to me a few times. I know that he was rich and that he gave her money from time to time. Every time I asked about how she could afford a particular outfit or an accessory, the answer was always the same. I did wonder why she didn't just live with her rich uncle on the island, but she said it was because he had a cruel wife who didn't like any of her husband's relatives living in her house.

"Anyway, he wants me to come and pick up some money this evening. You should see his house – it's amazing! You can fit yours in it five times." She stretched out her arms to emphasise her point. I sucked my teeth: surely it must be an exaggeration; my house was big by anyone's standards. I knew she didn't mean any harm, but I felt offended.

"Can you ask your mum to lend us her car?" she continued in her excited voice.

"I don't know. I'm tired. Why don't you take a cab?" Even though I was curious to meet this rich uncle and to see how wealthy people lived, Tobi's statement had stung, and I didn't want the opportunity to find out that she was right.

"Aww, it's not like you're doing anything. Okay, I'll buy you dinner from Blue Lagoon."

My eyes widened; now she had my attention.

"That's a very expensive restaurant. How will you pay for it?"

"Come on now; my uncle is bucks-ed. Will you come?"

"Er, yeah! Like you have to ask me twice."

"Awesome!" Tobi resumed her texting and heehawing and left me to my food daydream.

When my mum got home from work, I borrowed her car and drove Tobi to her uncle's house. It looked beautiful on the outside, but nothing prepared me for the opulence inside. It was pure luxury from the moment we drove through the automatic gates. The house had a winding driveway and imposing Corinthian-style columns by the entrance to the main house. There was a huge fountain in the centre of the grounds, and I was amazed that it actually worked; it was more commonplace in Lagos to find facilities – even essential ones like lifts, escalators, air conditioners and light switches – to either be out of service or not functioning properly. The fountain was a sculpture of a voluptuous maiden in all her naked glory with a calabash over her shoulder from which water flowed, mixing with the pool by her feet.

I took in my surroundings and was glad I had come; it was worth it just to stare, taking notes on what I wanted my future home to look like. We rang the bell, and the door was answered immediately by a young man in uniform.

"Who you come to see?" he demanded in broken English.

"My friend, tell your Oga that Tobi is here and stop being a nuisance," Tobi spat back, equally rudely.

The man hissed and shut the door in our faces.

"Isn't your uncle expecting you?" I asked, startled at our reception.

"He is, but you know how help is; always taking liberties whenever they can. I'll be reporting his insolence to my uncle. This is unacceptable behaviour," Tobi fumed.

A few minutes later the door swung open, and I did a double-take; the same man had opened the door, but his demeanour had changed so much that he could have been a different person.

"Ha, Aunty Tobi," he greeted, his corn-yellow teeth exposed in a smile. "I no know say na you now. Abeg no vex, welcome. Oga say make you come upstairs. Oga don dey wait for you tey." He bowed and stepped aside to let us in.

"Idiot," Tobi mumbled under her breath as we sauntered into the house.

The interior of the house literally took my breath away.

"Wow!" I exclaimed. "This place is lush."

"Didn't I tell you?" Tobi smiled, looking pleased.

"Yeah you did, but wow!" I spun round slowly with my mouth open.

"Wait till you see the rest of the house." She took my hand and walked me toward the curved staircase.

"Where are we going?" I asked her.

"To look for John."

"Who? Your uncle?"

"Yes, whatever."

"What do you mean 'whatever'?"

"Wake up, sweetie; he's not actually my uncle." She rolled her eyes.

"But you said…"

"I know what I said," she interrupted. She turned to face me, a stern look on her face. "Did you really believe an uncle would give me as much money, or as many clothes, as I get from John?"

"Yes, I did, there's nothing..."

"Oh please, spare me, there's nothing like a free lunch. Something always goes for something; remember that, if it's the only thing you ever remember. I have uncles that have sexually harassed me and haven't even given me one kobo when I go to them for school fees. Their wives turn me into a house-girl, doing menial tasks and slaving away just to get a roof over my head and food to eat."

I gasped and pulled her into my arms.

"Oh, Tobi, why didn't you tell me things were so bad?"

She pushed me away.

"Because they're not bad anymore. Now I have John."

I nodded mutely. "So is John, like your boyfriend?" I don't know what was so funny about my question, but she burst out laughing as if she had never heard anything so ridiculous.

"Boyfriend! Ha! He's married with four kids. His family is based in the UK. Don't worry; he's not my boyfriend."

"So what exactly is this, Tobi?" I was worried. "Are you a prostitute?" I asked in a small voice, fearful of her response, but she just laughed at me.

"Really, you crack me up, I'm not a prostitute. It's a little complicated; that's all. I know John; I wouldn't just go around sleeping with men I don't know. But I'm more of a freelancer if you get my meaning."

"Isn't that just another word for 'prosy'?" I raised an eyebrow.

"Babe, you're really beginning to annoy me. If I knew you were going to be like this, I wouldn't have brought you here. I wanted to show you that there are other ways of making money instead of burying your head in books all day. You keep wearing your cheap, fairly used clothes from Yaba and Tejuosho market, and it is just embarrassing." She raised an eyebrow and wrinkled her nose.

I felt insulted and ashamed at the same time. It was true that I got most of my clothes from the local markets, and while I was in the habit of looking over and admiring Tobi's designer bags and lovely clothes, I had never thought I seemed desperate for nice things. I was satisfied with everything that I had.

"Tobi, I don't know what to say. I guess thanks for your concern; I'm really sorry if I embarrass you." I was pained, and it was hard for me to be civil, but I took deep breaths and continued. "But I can't condone what you're doing. Everything about it is degrading to women all over the world. How can you let some fat, ugly man use you just because he can give you some money? Don't you think you're worth much more than that? What is the point of all your education?"

Tobi's eyes widened, and I could see that I'd hit a nerve, but I refused to back down.

"Listen, this is neither the time nor place..."

"Yes, I agree. I'm going home. See you later." I turned around and stomped down the stairs.

"Okay, come on, don't do this. Just wait for me, alright? We'll talk about this later, I promise." Tobi sighed. "I'm sorry I lied to you."

On one hand, I was furious and disgusted; on the other hand, I wouldn't be able to live with myself if I left her alone and something bad happened to her.

"Okay, I'll stay," I decided.

She looked relieved. "Thanks, babe."

"But only to make sure you're safe."

"Cool, come on." She took my hand, and we walked back up the stairs. When we passed a windowsill with the loveliest vase of flowers on it, I stopped to inhale the scent; the flowers were fresh. The stairs led into a large living room area decorated in subtle tones of orange, beige and gold.

"Just wait here," Tobi said, nudging me in the direction of a plush armchair. "I'll be right back."

I slipped off my pumps and buried my feet in the thick, soft rug. Then I walked around the room, admiring the soft velvet cream and gold curtains and running my hands over the spines of books arranged on the shelves. I leant closer to peer at the titles. Pfft, boring books; I didn't know any of the authors. They were mainly autobiographies. Why would I want to read another person's version of their life? I sat sprawled in one of the armchairs and tried to imagine that this was my house. Closing my eyes, I took a deep breath, snuggling into the soft embrace of the armchair. Ah, if I had a chair like this in my house, I would never get up. I sighed as I opened my eyes, and I pulled my book from my bag. It was a Stephen King novel called *Thinner* about a man cursed by a gypsy. I settled into the book and proceeded to while away time.

After an hour and a half, as absorbed as I was in my book, I was beginning to toy with the idea of going to look for Tobi. She had said she'd be right back. I was uncomfortable. In the time I had been here, I hadn't seen or heard anyone or anything. Just as I was debating whether to go home or go in search of Tobi, I heard a movement behind me.

"You idiot, you said you would be right back," I said, not looking up from my book.

"Not very nice, are you?" The reply came in a smooth male American accent.

I turned around sharply and was horrified to see a tall, dark-skinned man. He was clean-shaven and even though he was only wearing a polo shirt and jeans, he wore them like an Armani suit. I figured he was in his early thirties.

"I didn't mean to sneak up on you," he said, flashing white teeth in a dazzling smile and extending his hand to me. "Alex."

"Jade," I muttered.

"So I take it you're Tobi's friend."

"Yes, but don't think that will stop me from killing her."

He laughed.

"You don't like being left on your own, then? Actually, I prefer my own company, so I don't know what you're upset about." He came around and perched on the arm of my chair. I shuffled to the edge of the armchair to give as much distance as I could manage without seeming awkward.

"Yeah, but not left alone in someone else's house. Who knows what might be lurking in the shadows," I huffed.

"You're strange, a lot of girls wouldn't mind being in a house like this. Just yesterday a girl came in here, and I met her feeling right at home and using the landline to call her boyfriend in London."

"Hmm, do you get a lot of girls here?"

He laughed again.

"Women! So was that what you got out of everything I said?"

"Just curious. A house like this, I can imagine girls walking in and out. So do you live here?" I leant back to see his face better. He was good-looking, with long eyelashes and a straight nose.

"Sort of. I live in the States, and I stay here whenever I'm in Lagos. John and I go way back; we went to secondary school together."

"And your wife and kids...?"

"Are non-existent. Now tell me about you." He folded his arms and smiled at me. I relaxed, finding myself drawn to this stranger I'd just met.

"What would you like to know?"

"What do you do? Are you in university?" He picked up one of my braids and tugged at it playfully.

"Yep, Breamston Uni, studying law."

"Wow, Breamston. So, beautiful and smart."

I was pleased to hear the admiration in his voice; I wanted him to like me.

"I went there myself," he said. "I read Chemical Engineering, but that was years ago."

"So what is it that you do now?" I looked up at him, my lips curled in what I hoped was an intelligent-looking smile. A second later my smile disappeared as his hand settled on my thigh. My first instinct was to brush it off, but I hesitated when I saw the expression on his face; no one had ever looked at me like that before. I was like a deer caught in the headlights, unable to look away. I ignored the tiny voice in my head as a warm sensation engulfed me, and I felt an uneasy moistness between my thighs. What was wrong with me? I had just met this guy five minutes ago, but there was something about him, he seemed so sure of himself. The way he looked at me made me feel desirable and sexy. No man had ever looked at me that way before. My first instinct was to slap his hand off, but I didn't.

Emboldened by my lack of indignation, that hand crept slowly forward. I stared at a little spot on the wall, trying to keep a straight face.

"I'm an IT consultant for British Petroleum, but I always wanted to be an architect."

"That's nice," I gasped, not entirely sure which I meant: what he was saying, or what his busy hand was doing. We were both silent for a few minutes while I continued to pretend that his hand wasn't up my skirt. I swallowed, feeling a little light-headed. This was bad; this was really, really bad. I had to stop him now. But I knew I wouldn't. I couldn't. I had never experienced anything like this before, and I didn't want it to stop. I glanced around; there was no one there; no one would know.

"Come with me." He stood up, holding his hand out to me.

Oh boy, oh boy, oh boy, I should just refuse. I should stay here.

"I should stay here and wait for Tobi," I said out loud. Where was that stupid girl? I was so going to kill her if I ended up doing anything stupid. How was I supposed to control myself when I was being barraged by all these powerful and confusing emotions?

"Trust me; she won't miss you."

"Erm, but still, I don't think I should. Thanks," I said, faking a smile. I couldn't have sex with Alex; I was a virgin, and I wasn't going to lose my virginity to a stranger. My mother's words of advice rang in my ears; she always warned me to be wary of the games men played. If they got what they wanted too easily, they moved on quicker. Easy come, easy go.

"Don't worry. We won't do anything you don't want to. Come on; I want to show you something." I hesitated before taking his outstretched hand, and he pulled me up from the sofa. He led me through the living room and up another flight of stairs into a large and modestly furnished room; cold air flowed around the room from the air conditioning hung high on the wall adjacent to the door. There was a queen-sized bed against the wall opposite the door. The floor was carpeted in beige from wall to wall, and a bright red rug lay in the middle of the room. A TV hung on one of the walls and below it was a table with a glossy hi-fi system and a tower of CDs on it.

"Make yourself comfortable," Alex said, gesturing towards the bed. I walked to the bed but decided at the last minute not to sit on it. I looked around for a chair, but there was none. Alex was looking through his CD collection and humming to himself. He finally found whatever he was looking for, and he inserted the disc into the CD player. I groaned when I recognised the cheesy song.

He swung his hips back and forth to the music like an amateur stripper, and then he undid his zipper with a flourish. "Look what you're doing to me," he announced, brandishing his manhood proudly as if it were a magician's wand. He pushed his trousers off his hips and stepped out of them.

"Erm... what are you doing?" I had never seen it in real life before. It was massive and throbbing. Oh hell, no! No way that thing was coming anywhere near me. My lust was fast turning into dread. Gosh, it would be painful. I was so not ready to die.

"I can't do this; this is a big mistake. I'm sorry, but I have to go."

"We'll see about that," he said, blocking the door. "Come on, baby; I won't hurt you." He came closer, and I allowed him to unbutton my blouse. My bra came off next, and I felt my nipples harden as they were exposed to the cold air in the room. I stood still and closed my eyes as he groaned and reached for my breasts. He touched one, his hands soft and reverent; then, bending down, he put his lips over one nipple and fondled the other. His lips felt hot and soft, and his tongue flicked expertly around my never-been-touched breast. My knees buckled, and he lowered me gently onto the bed. He continued licking my swollen breasts while his hands roved all over my body, leaving trails of fire behind. I was burning up, fear and desire, a dangerous cocktail, running through my veins. I moaned and was surprised that the sound had come out of me. It sounded so amoral.

Emboldened, he pushed his hands under my skirt and yanked my panties to the side. He stuck a finger inside, and I jerked from the discomfort.

"Wow, you're so wet. It feels so nice," he whispered in my ear. I knew I should stop him; I had to. On the one hand I had explosives going off all over my body, in places where I had never imagined possible; on the other hand, I knew that this couldn't be right. If I was going to have a relationship with him I knew that this wasn't a good place to start. If he got what he wanted now, he would think I was easy.

He lifted himself up to lean on his elbow and slid my skirt up. I didn't need a crystal ball to tell me what he was going to do next. "No!" I said, almost shouting. I pushed my skirt back down and struggled to get up from beneath him. He rolled to the side and allowed me to sit up.

"What's wrong?" he asked. I could see him struggling with himself. It wouldn't take much to overpower me if he wanted to. I was aware of my precarious situation; I was in bed with a stranger, and if anything happened to me, no one would believe I had been the victim. I decided it was time for me to end this.

"Come on, what are you scared of?" Picking up the hand closer to him, he traced circles in my palm.

"I've never done this before, and I'm not ready," I admitted. It felt weird saying the words out loud as if I was watching a movie: watching myself say it to Alex.

"No way, you can't be serious!" he exclaimed.

I grimaced.

"I'm sorry, I can't do this. I really need to go, now!" My voice trembled, and I wrapped my arms around myself.

He jumped off the bed.

"Come, I want to show you something."

I thought I had just seen the biggest shocker of my life. What else could he show me that could surpass it? I couldn't help stealing glances at it. It was massive and scary: proud-looking, even. He didn't seem to be embarrassed that he was stark naked from the waist down. I got off the bed and picked my bra up from the rug. I put it on and adjusted my skirt. I was worried that I would get a rash from my underwear; it was a damp and uncomfortable.

He pulled a wardrobe open, and my eyes nearly popped out of their sockets; half filling it, were bundles of money in stacks.

"Wow," I said. "I've never seen so much money in my life. Why are you showing this to me?"

"I was hoping it might be a bit of incentive, help you make your mind up," he said, grinning. I walked back to the bed and sank into it.

"Did you think that would make me have sex with you? Look, I'm not like Tobi, okay! I will not sleep with you because of your money!" I said in a low, furious tone and I saw confusion flicker across his face.

"I'm sorry, I didn't mean to offend you, I just thought..."

"Well, you thought wrong." I folded my arms across my chest and shook my head. I couldn't believe I had considered dating such a rude and arrogant man. Not that I could blame him. I mean, a minute ago I was half-naked in his bed. Stupid, stupid girl, I berated myself.

"It's not like that at all. You've got it all wrong."

"What then? Why did you show that to me?" I gestured towards the cash-filled wardrobe.

"I just wanted you to know that you have nothing to fear. I can take care of you. I don't do this with just anybody, but you look like a good girl, someone I can trust."

"I'm going to leave now. It was nice knowing you." I pushed myself off the bed and picked up my blouse, shoving my arms into the sleeves angrily. I tried to do up my buttons in a hurry but it was futile; my hands were shaky. I took a deep breath to calm myself down, and I was going to try again when I felt his arms around me. He was standing behind me, and I could feel his manhood pressing into my back.

"Stay, don't go. We don't have to have sex. We can do other things."

"Look, Alex." This had gone too far.

"Ah," he groaned. "You're killing me."

"I'm sorry." I pushed him away.

"Look at me, how you can leave me like this?" He put on a mock-hurt expression.

"I'm sorry," I repeated.

"Come on, just give it a little kiss," he pleaded.

Eww! No way! I screamed in my head. Of all the disgusting things, I wasn't putting that thing in my mouth. My lips curled in disgust.

"Alex, I'm really sorry, but there's no way that is going to happen. Plus I don't know where it's been." I put up my hands and leant as far away from it as I could get.

"It hasn't been anywhere. Come on; you'll enjoy it."

"Er... no, I don't think so. Sorry."

"Please, come on, just one little kiss," he pleaded desperately. "I really need you."

"No," I replied, looking him squarely in the face. Surely he could see that I meant it.

"I'll give you anything you want." He held my hand.

"Oh, for heaven's sake, please just let me go."

My mouth fell open as I watched Alex drop to his knees. I looked down at him, and all I saw was a pathetic man.

"No, get up!" I yelled, snatched my hand from his grasp and ran out of the room. I prayed Tobi would be in the living room, but she wasn't there. I went to wait for her in the car; there was no way I was staying another minute in that house.

I debated with myself whether to tell Tobi what had happened but I decided against it. I always believed that I possessed some form of self-control, and I wasn't proud of what had just happened. It didn't help that, as I went over the events in my mind, I felt thrills of pleasure course through me. I had been in the car for almost half an hour when Tobi walked out the front gates with a huge grin on her face.

"Here you go, that's 25k," she said, sliding into the car and pushing a wad of 100 naira notes at me.

"What's this for?" I grabbed it from her quickly, just in case she changed her mind.

"That," she said, pointing at the money I was stuffing into my bag, "is for being a 'goody two-shoes'."

"I don't follow."

"Alex was with John when I went in, and he asked me if I brought a friend for him. And I said, 'No, of course not, what do you think I am? A pimp?' Then I said, 'I'm here with my friend, but you're not her type.' And then he said, "I'm every girl's type, just you wait and see." And then I said, "Why don't you put your money where your mouth is?" So he bet that he would give me 50k if you didn't sleep with you." My blood ran cold as I listened to her narration.

"So it was all a bet. I'm such an idiot." I buried my face in my hands. "Tobi, how could you do that to me? I thought you were my friend?"

"What are you talking about? I know you too well, and I knew there was no way you were going to put out for Alex."

"But what if I had?"

"I don't know. You would have earned yourself a rich Aristo, I guess." She chuckled. "That you would sleep with him didn't even cross my mind; I was so sure of you, and you proved me right. What I wouldn't give to have been a fly on the wall when you told him off. Did he show you the wardrobe full of money?"

I nodded.

"Ah, classic move!" She laughed again, slapping her hand on her thigh.

What was so funny? I didn't get the joke.

"What exactly happened? Give me details!" she said eagerly.

"Didn't he tell you?"

"Nope. He just said nothing happened. You must have really done a number on him; I think he might be in love with you."

"Yeah, right," I snorted. "As if." But even as I denied it I found myself feeling something close to hope that Alex and I could end up together as boyfriend and girlfriend. It was a long shot, but we could start over, take things slow. I smiled to myself. I turned the key in the ignition and was pulling out when I remembered something Tobi had said earlier.

"Remember when you said I could have had a rich Aristo if I had slept with Alex?"

"U-huh."

"Why did you call him that?"

"Didn't he tell you he was married? His wife and his five-year-old son are in the States."

"No, no, he didn't," I murmured, my hopes crashing into a million pieces.

56

CHAPTER 8

2 0 0 1

"That guy is completely checking you out," Monica said, nudging me with her elbow.

It was the first day of our second year at University, and Monica and I were in line outside the Head of Department's office to register for our courses for the year.

"Where, where?" I whispered, whipping my head from side to side. "Wait..." I paused and held up my palm hand as if to stop her, even though I was the one doing the head-whipping. "My 3 o'clock or yours?"

"Hrgh." she rolled her eyes and angled her head.

I looked in the direction of her angled head, and my eyes met his. I felt my heart beat quicken, and I slid my eyes to the ground. He had soft eyes and a strong jawline, a short haircut which faded at the sides and a shadow of a moustache which framed his full peach-like lips. He was tall with skin like milk chocolate, he wore square black-framed glasses, and his pink shirt was tucked into his jeans. His shirt wasn't buttoned all the way to the top, and I caught a glimpse of dark, smooth chest. He was gorgeous; he looked like he'd walked right out of the pages of a GQ magazine.

"Oh my God! He is cute," I gushed. I turned to check if he was still watching me when I saw a light skinned girl run towards him.

"Wale!" She squealed as she leapt into his arms. He staggered from the impact and looked uncomfortable. I felt a pulling sensation in my gut; she was beautiful. My heart sank.

"Hi Sade," he said, disentangling himself from her embrace.

"It's so good to see you! Come, come, come." She said, pulling him by the hand. As they walked away, he put his arm around her shoulders and she snaked her arm around his waist.

"Maybe they're related." I swallowed.

"Yes, of course," Monica said, her tone lacking any conviction.

A few months passed and I tried to forget about the moment I had shared with Wale. We took Philosophy 201 together, but we had never exchanged a word. I wanted to keep it that way, I tried to convince myself that the last thing I wanted was to harbour a crush on another boy who wanted nothing to do with me, but a part of me knew that it was too late. I hated to admit it, but I looked forward to this class. Every Monday and Wednesday, I took my time getting dressed. Knowing that I would see him got me skipping out of bed on those days. Unfortunately, it was torture to watch him with Sade; she was always stuck to him like her skinny jeans clung to her long longs.

I could stare at Wale forever and never get bored: the way his beautiful long fingers held his pen as he scribbled on his notepad, the way his head hung to the side and he stuck his tongue between his teeth when he wrote. And his face, so smooth and handsome! I wanted to shower it with kisses, all of it, including his beautiful eyes and his breath-taking smile that exposed his near-white and even teeth. His glasses reminded me of Clark Kent; I liked watching him push them up with his finger whenever he spoke. He was perfect — maybe too perfect for me — but if I couldn't have him, at least I could dream.

"Hey, quit staring. You're drooling," Monica scolded.

"Sorry, what?" I blinked back into focus and shook my head to clear my thoughts.

"You've been staring at Wale for the last five minutes."

"Yeah, right. Pfft, I wasn't staring." I sighed, my eyes settling back into their previous position. The lecture theatre was stuffy and packed with second-year students so that the stairs were being used as seats. Bags and books were tucked under bums to protect said bums from the dusty floor and also to give the tiniest relief from its unyielding hardness. The whirring fans, blowing cold air around the theatre, did nothing to alleviate the heat. Sweaty faces were being mopped by bare palms, tissues or handkerchiefs. The room around me melted away as my mind drifted: soon all that remained was Wale and me. We sat down face to face; he took my hands in his and smiled at me. I must have said something funny, for he threw back his beautiful head and laughed, it rang like music and dragged forth a burst of light from within me. I was glowing. He toyed with one of my braids as he stared into my eyes. He was just leaning towards me; his eyes locked on my lips when Monica nudged me out of my reverie. I sighed, disappointed to be back in the miserable lecture theatre.

"You have a huge crush on this guy; it's so pathetic. Just don't let Sade catch you."

"Me? Crush? Never!" I protested, looking her in the face in an attempt to appear believable.

She raised one eyebrow and wrinkled her nose in mock disgust.

"Besides, he has a girlfriend." I sighed again.

When class was over, I spotted Deji coming up the stairs towards the exit of the lecture theatre, and I waved to him. He waited for me on the steps at the end of the aisle where Monica and I had been sitting, a big grin plastered on his face.

"My main person!" He swung his arms around me, enveloping me in a big hug that lifted my feet off the ground. I grinned back at him.

"What do you want?" I asked when he let me go.

"Haba, come on. Can't I just be happy to see you?"

"Aww," I cooed.

"Fine, whatever. I'm having a pool party tomorrow night. I need you to invite all your girlfriends."

"Why? I'm sure you can find girls for your party without my help. The greatest gigolo in Lagos?"

"You've got to stop calling me that." Deji looked offended.

"I'm sorry, it's just... dude, I'm not exaggerating, but you tend to change girlfriends as often as you change your shoes. I've given up trying to keep up with who is just a fling and who is a sure thing — meaning that she'll last up to a week."

"Ha, it's not like that. They're just my friends."

"Can I come?" Monica asked from behind me.

"Of course, the more, the merrier." Deji patted her on the shoulder. "Don't forget, tomorrow evening, my place. Bring all your girlfriends, and please, only bikinis allowed."

"I don't own a bikini." I pursed my lips and shrugged with resignation. "Sorry".

"Don't be sorry, come without it," he said in a husky voice. He winked and then turned and bounded up the stairs.

"Eww, perv," I said to his back. Monica and I followed him up the stairs. FRC 205 was just about to start, and it would take us at least five minutes to get there. However, we took our time — knowing Mrs Olayinka, she was going to be late.

We were at the door of the lecture theatre when Monica swung her arm around me. "Ooh, guess who's coming this way?" she whispered in my ear. "You might want to slow down."

My heart quickened. I could feel his presence. I swung around and saw Wale walking towards us. "Stop smiling like an idiot!" I told myself, even as I felt my grin inch wider.

"Hey!" I half-waved and half-skipped, a braid escaped and fell into my face, and I tucked it behind my ear.

"Hi." He hesitated. We were in his way. He walked around us, and my body swivelled with him. My cheeks were beginning to ache from smiling. Shit, I needed help. Surely I'd learnt my lesson about Crushes by now.

"You're gorgeous," Monica said breathily.

I frowned slightly and turned to look at her. She had a broad smile on her face. Great, now we looked like a pair of gushing teenagers or groupies. I eased my Cheshire grin into a more self-respecting and comfortable smile. I tried to brush off the sense of déjà vu; my friend, stealing my crush before I'd even had a chance.

"Er…" Wale stopped and turned to us, a look of confusion on his face.

"I'm sure you get that a lot," I said, trying to make an excuse for Monica's outburst. This was the first time I was having an actual conversation with him, and I hated the fact that it was about how good-looking he was: first impressions and everything. It would have been better to play it cool —damn it, Monica!

"Erm, no, actually. I've never been complimented in such a manner before, so thank you." He addressed Monica. "And so are you... both of you," he added quickly, looking as if he'd just dodged a bullet.

"Oh, I know that already." Monica flipped her long black hair back over her shoulders.

Wale glanced at me as if asking for help. I smiled apologetically.

"I'm Monica; this is my girl, Jade."

"I'm..."

"I know who you are." She cut him off. Wale glanced at me again. Oh boy. "Do you go to parties?"

"Well..."

"I was wondering if you wanted to come to this awesome pool party tomorrow night. It's going to be banging. You know what? Gimme your number; I'll text you the address." Monica grabbed her phone from her bag.

"Erm, I'm not sure I can make it. I've got this thing..." Wale smiled as Monica interrupted him again. Our eyes met, and we both smiled. It was a little awkward.

"It's fine if you're busy. It's on till late so you can come anytime." She handed him her phone. He took it from her and punched some buttons; he looked at me again as he handed the phone back to Monica. I smiled, but this time a little sadly. Once again I was losing my crush to a friend. I hadn't even decided if I wanted to go for the stupid party, but now I definitely wasn't going, if only to avoid seeing them together. Ooh, the nerve of her. I made up my mind then that if I ever got myself to like a guy again, I would never tell a soul. I would have secret crushes... or better yet, no crushes! I would only start liking a guy after he'd asked me out and we started dating. No, wait, that was boring. I hated getting asked out: the courting, having to play hard to get, the song and dance that a guy expected or the risk of being called 'easy'. I wasn't willing to let go of my dreams of how I would meet my first love: there would be an instant connection and an intense chemical attraction, and we would both know that we were meant to be together. We wouldn't be able to fight it. Everything would happen naturally: no pressure, no games.

"Are you going to wear a bikini?" Wale asked, looking at me.

Jeez, what was it with men and bikinis? Monica and I exchanged a look.

"I don't know, are you?" I asked, a teasing smile playing at the corner of my mouth.

"Hey, I look awesome in a bikini!"

We all burst out laughing. Now I had an image of Wale strutting around the pool in a bright yellow bikini and high heels, and I laughed even harder. Wale and Monica looked at me in concern.

"Sorry, it's just... now I can't get the thought of you in a bikini out of my head," I said, struggling to breathe from laughing so hard.

"So, maybe see you tomorrow?" He looked at me, and then Monica, and then back at me. Monica and I nodded and watched as he walked away.

"You're welcome." Monica handed me her phone.

"Wait — what?" It clicked then; Monica had been playing Cupid!

"What?" She looked at me in mock horror. "Did you think I wanted him for myself?"

"Well..."

"Seriously, he's not my type."

"What do you mean he's not your type? He's hot!"

"Do you want his number or not?"

I hesitated. Although I felt that I had a lot of self-control, I didn't want the temptation of Wale's number, begging to be dialled, knowing that it was only a matter of time before I gave in. Sure, I didn't want a relationship where I had to play games — but I still wanted romance; I wanted the guy to call first.

"Nope, I don't want it, but thanks."

Monica shook her head in disbelief. "I don't get it, you like him, don't you?"

"Yes, but I'm not calling him first."

"Well, I couldn't have given him your number; that would have been too obvious."

"Fine!" I snatched her phone and texted Deji's address to Wale, and then I deleted both the text and his number from Monica's phone. I was pleased with myself for thinking to delete his number. The last thing I wanted was for Monica to have it.

"There you go! Thank you!" I handed her the phone.

"Whatever." She took her phone back. "But guess what? Now he has my number! In your face!" She chuckled.

I gasped. I hadn't thought of that.

"Oh, well," I shrugged. A tinge of fear settled behind my spine, and I sighed. What if Wale called Monica, wanting to speak to me, and then they started talking, and she changed her mind and decided that he was her type after all?

"Relax; you need to learn to trust your girl. I would never do that to you."

""I know," I lied. "Come on, let's go in, before Mrs Olayinka catches us outside."

I went from not caring about Deji's party to being a nervous wreck in less than an hour. If I'd had the power to make the day go faster, I would have brought Friday night on in a heartbeat.

"Can you just relax," Monica admonished me after I'd asked her for the fifth time what we should wear to the pool party. "It's just a stupid pool party; nobody cares if we show up in t-shirts and flip flops."

"I wonder if Wale will get in the pool." I pictured him in swimming trunks, six pack glistening, chest and arms rippling, flawless brown skin. I would pretend I was drowning, and he would dive in the pool to save me. Strong arms, slicing through the chlorinated water, rushing to my rescue, encircling me, drawing me to safety, laying me down to administer the kiss of life.

"You're away with the fairies again." Monica said, shaking my shoulders.

Just then, my phone rang. It was my sister. Typical, trust Tayo to always ruin my mood. But this time, I wasn't going to let her get to me.

"Hi sis," I greeted her in a loud, cheerful voice that made Monica wince. I was living in my own fantasy, and I was going to stay there as long as I could.

"Are you coming home tomorrow?"

I hesitated. I racked my brain for any reasons why Tayo would ask me this question. One thing I knew for sure — it wasn't because she missed me.

"Why? Is anything wrong?"

"Of course not. Why would I call you if anything was wrong?" Tayo snapped.

I grunted, feeling frustration begin to invade my happy mood.

"Anyway, we're going out for dinner tomorrow night for Mum's birthday, so you need to get your ass home before 6 p.m. Do you want Mr Sunday to come and pick you up?"

"Erm..." I couldn't believe this was happening. It was as if there were forces were at work to keep me from getting my happily-ever-after. I tried to think of an excuse, but I couldn't come up with anything. It's not that I didn't love my mother — of course, I did. It was just that birthdays had never been a big deal to her; in fact, she hated celebrating her birthday. Why, oh why did she have to want to celebrate this one? I moaned as I waved my fantasies goodbye.

"Okay, I have to go, I can't be wasting my credit on you."

Wow, thanks, sis!

"Call or flash me if you need a ride home." And she hung up.

"Oh shit!"

"Everything okay? What did Tayo want?"

"It's my mum's birthday tomorrow, and she's decided she wants to do something," I said in a whiny voice. "I have to go home, and that means I can't go to the party." A heavy weight settled on me as the one chance I had to hang out with Wale faded away.

"No!" Monica had been texting on her phone, and she dropped it on her bed. "You have to come to the party!"

"Why me?" I wailed. "Why tomorrow?"

"There has to be a way. Don't you live close to Deji's house? Surely your folks will let you go?"

"Seriously? There's no way my parents will let me out of the house. Curfew is 8 p.m."

"Come on! You're pulling my leg." Monica's mouth dropped open in disbelief. "You're eighteen years old! Surely that must be illegal."

"Yeah, well, according to them, 'their house, their rules'. This sucks." A thought occurred to me, and I narrowed my eyes at Monica. "You know, this is all your fault." I waggled my finger at her. "If you hadn't invited

Wale, I wouldn't be in this mess. I wouldn't even care about the stupid party."

"How come you're blaming me all of a sudden? I was only trying to help."

"Well, next time stay out of it." I knew I was being ridiculous, but it made me feel a little better to take it out on Monica.

"He did say he had a 'thing', so he might not even go to the party, so you won't be missing much."

"Oh yeah, call him now!" I perked up a little. "Ask if he's definitely coming."

"Sorry, babe, I can't. You deleted his number."

"Shit, I forgot about that." I sank back into Monica's bed and sulked.

"Just forget about the party, there'll be more opportunities for you guys to hook up."

"Easy for you to say — you're the most confident chick I know. I'll most likely just go back to staring at Wale from a distance." I felt as if someone had snatched my favourite toy from me and I spent what was left of the evening in a sullen mood. The night dragged on into the next day. There was nothing to look forward to anymore, except my mum's birthday, which I had to admit I wasn't looking forward to in the slightest.

"Can't you find a way to come?" Deji looked distraught when I told him I couldn't make it to his pool party. It almost seemed as if he didn't believe I couldn't get out of my mum's birthday dinner. The only way I was able to attend a night party was if I stayed in school or over at a friend's house. Deji knew the drill; my parents were strict.

"Trust me; I would come if I could."

We had a free period and were sitting in the half-empty classroom where we'd had our last lecture. It had just stopped raining, and a cool breeze flowed through the open doors and windows. Deji sat on the desk in front of me, his long jean-clad legs on either side of the chair I sat in, his fingers drumming on the desk space between his legs as he looked down at me.

"Dude, you only live a few minutes away, you've got to find a way to come." Ever since Deji had seen the movie *Dude, Where's my Car?* with Aston Kutcher, he called everyone dude.

"I'm not a dude, please don't call me that."

A smile played around Deji's lips. "I couldn't mistake you for a dude, even if I tried." He stared openly at my chest, and I slapped his arm.

"But seriously, call me after your mum's thing, yeah? And I'll come get you — how about that?"

"You'd leave your party to pick me up?"

"Yes, why not? It's not like you live far away."

"I don't know. I've never thought of sneaking out of the house. My dad would kill me if he found out." I shook my head, but now that I was thinking about it, I couldn't get the idea out of my head. There had to be a way. I perked up a little; maybe there was hope after all.

CHAPTER 9

It was 11 p.m. by the time we returned from the restaurant. I had gotten home from school just before 6.30 p.m. to find my mum dressed in a beautiful lace Iro and Buba, with a glamorous head tie. My dad was dressed in a flowing Agbada in the same lace fabric as my mum's; his cap tilted loftily on his head. I wondered if these people knew we were going to a restaurant.

"Mum, is that really what you're going to wear?" I'd asked, fearing their response.

"Yes, don't you like it?"

"Jade, just leave Mummy alone. I've tried to talk her out of it, but she won't listen," Tayo chimed in. "Hurry up and get dressed so we can leave on time."

I left them in the living room to go and get ready. When I rushed out fifteen minutes later, wearing a purple off-the-shoulder blouse and my favourite pair of jeans, my parents stared at me.

"Go back upstairs and change into something more appropriate," my dad said, scowling. I eyed him and my mum in their gallant traditional attire and looked to my sister for support. She was wearing a flowery summer dress and she looked amazing; her hair was parted in the middle and done up in braids, which fell to her shoulders. I didn't have any dresses that were half as beautiful as hers. She didn't look up at me; her attention was on her mobile phone, a half-smile on her lips, her thumb flying over the buttons. I groaned.

"I'm not wearing trad! Why are you all dressed up anyway? We're only going out to dinner."

My mum marched me up the stairs to my room.

"Muuum!" I moaned as she fished out a dress hanging at the back of my wardrobe. There's a reason that that dress was hanging way, way back there. I glared at it in disgust. It was one of the dresses my mum had gotten her tailor to make for me. I hated it. I had given the tailor my designs and told him exactly how I wanted it: nice and fitted in all the right places, showing just the right amount of cleavage. But somehow the dress had evolved into this monstrosity. I just knew my mum had had something to do with it.

"No one wears shoulder pads anymore; there is no way I'm wearing that! I'd rather stay at home by myself." I was tempted to throw myself on the floor and start kicking and hitting it with my fists.

"Okay, just try it on for me, dear. We'll take it off if you don't like it," my mum said in a placatory voice.

"Fine, I already know I'm going to take it off so this is just a waste of time, but if it makes you happy..."

My mum smiled and held out the dress. I grunted as I stripped. I put on the dress, and she pulled me to the mirror.

"Ugh." I wrinkled my face. "It's even uglier than I remember."

"Really? I think it's beautiful. A lot better than the rags you wear that put your whole body on display. In this dress, you look lovely, like a decent girl from a good home."

Realisation dawned, and a feeling of dread crept through me. I looked at my reflection in horror. I couldn't believe that I'd fallen for my mum's trick. There was no way she was going to let me take the dress off.

"Okay, Mum, thanks, but I hate the dress, so I'm taking it off now," I said quickly, grasping the hem and yanking it up. Even as the words left my lips, a part of me knew that it was futile, but I couldn't give up without trying.

My mum smiled, walked to my bed and sat down. She patted the space next to her. I let go of the hem of my dress, sighed with resignation and sat next to her.

"You know, when you expose your body to a man, you narrow everything he might want from you down to just one thing." She raised her eyebrows and looked me in the eye, trying to drive her point home without having to spell it out completely. "This dress makes you look sophisticated. I'm your mother; would I lie to you? Any man that looks at you now will know that you're a treasure and that you respect yourself." As I listened to my mum's words, I thought of the pool party and the scantily dressed boys and girls; I couldn't help the teasing smile that broke out on my face. If only my mum knew the half of it! I looked at her hands clasped on her lap and I placed a hand on them in what I hoped was a reassuring gesture.

"First of all, Mum, I know what you're doing, and I'm not falling for it. Plus, I've never exposed my body to any man. The way I dress is actually conservative compared to a lot of girls on campus."

My mum nodded and smiled. She grasped my hand and patted it, and then she got up and walked to the door. My heart lifted: I had won! Wow, I couldn't believe it, and it had been so easy! My mum opened my door and stuck her head out.

"Baba Tayo, please come in for a minute." My heart sank as I realised my mum was pulling out the biggest gun in her arsenal. My dad walked in as if on cue. Come on! He had been sitting downstairs; how had he gotten upstairs so quickly?

"Oh, my beautiful baby girl," my dad cooed, his eyes wide with admiration. Come on, who was he fooling? The whole scene felt rehearsed. "Oya, let's go, the boys have already left, and Tayo is getting impatient."

"But I'm not ready yet," I moaned as my mum led me out of my room. Short of throwing a tantrum, I couldn't see a way out.

Apparently, my sister, Tayo, was footing the bill for the meal. Now it made sense that my mum had agreed to celebrate her birthday. Tayo had started her first job after her youth service a few months ago, working in a bank in Victoria Island. I didn't know how much she earned, but I envied her. Tayo had all her earnings, and she didn't even have to pay rent. Plus she'd just bought a new car: a Golf. Well, it was second-hand, but it was still newish-looking.

The meal was lovely and half an hour later, I'd completely forgotten about my dress. My sister had ordered a cake, and we sang Happy Birthday to my mum; the restaurant staff and other diners joined in. Tayo beamed throughout the evening as everyone commented that she had done well and was indeed a good daughter. My brothers joked around the table, keeping everyone in stitches. I was having a great time with my family but, thanks to Monica, my mind was also somewhere else. She sent me constant updates about the party. By 10 p.m. I was aware that the party was in full swing; there were loads of food and drinks, but still no sign of Wale. I was relieved; his absence meant I wasn't missing much. By 10.30, people had started taking off their clothes and jumping in the pool — and still no Wale. We were on our way home when my phone rang. I answered it, all too aware that my mum and dad were in the car. Tayo was driving, and I was sitting in the passenger seat.

"He's coming! He's on his way!" Monica shouted, and I turned down the volume hastily. I glanced back quickly to check if my parents had heard, but if they had or if they could hear the loud music coming from the other side of the line, they didn't show it.

"You don't have to shout; I can hear you. We're on our way home from dinner," I whispered into the phone, my heart sinking into my belly.

"Oops, did Momsie and Popsie hear?" she whispered back so that I had to struggle to hear her.

"I don't know. It's fine."

"Wale just texted me. He's on his way here. Said he'll be here in thirty minutes, and he wanted to know if we were still at the party. I said yes! Babe, you have to come! Lie, sneak out, bribe your gateman, do whatever you need to do. If you get caught, you'll pay the price tomorrow, and it will be so worth it."

"I'm sorry, I can't."

Monica sighed. "Chicken, I'll keep you updated. Don't worry; I've got your back. I'll spend the night selling you so bad that he'll be practically falling at your feet the next time you see him." And she hung up.

I settled back in my seat and shut my eyes. I had an immense feeling of loss as if something was slipping through my fingers and there was nothing I could do to stop it. If it had just been an ordinary crush, it wouldn't have hurt so much. This felt like so much more; a part of me was sure he liked me back. I had tried not to read much into it and to be content just staring at him from a distance, but sometimes I'd caught him staring back at me. He always looked away quickly when our eyes met, but I couldn't believe it was just a coincidence.

"What's up with you?" Tayo asked as we were getting ready for bed. "Your phone keeps beeping and you sigh every time you check it."

"Tayo, please leave me alone, I'm all right." I walked to the bathroom to brush my teeth and wash off my makeup.

Tayo followed me. Why wouldn't she leave me alone? She leant on the doorframe while I brushed my teeth, staring at my face through the bathroom mirror. After a few seconds, I couldn't take it anymore; I stopped and confronted her with the intention of asking for some privacy.

"Who is Wale?" she asked, a teasing smile on her face.

"How..."

"I heard your friend on the phone." She waved my question away with a flick of her wrist. "Here's what I have deduced. From the loud noise in the background, your friend is at a party; from the face you've been carrying around all evening, I can tell that you really wanted to go. And because I'm a very perceptive person," her voice softened, "I'm guessing you like this Wale boy."

CHAPTER 10

I'd made it! I was at the party! It felt surreal. Tayo had helped me sneak out of the house; she gave the gateman some money in return for his silence and - I'm pinching myself about this last bit — she let me drive her car! She handed over the keys with the threat that she would break my legs if I so much as put a dent in her car. I believed her.

Monica shrieked when she saw me.

"I can't believe you did it! You actually snuck out of your house! We need to toast this occasion."

"I can't drink; I'm driving," I proclaimed, twirling my sister's car keys on my finger, a smug grin on my face.

"No way!" Her eyes almost popped out of her skull.

"I know!"

I looked around the party; the place was packed. Surely it must be a hazard to have this many people in one place. Music blared from a couple of massive speakers placed at opposite ends of the pool area. I could smell grilled chicken and my mouth watered, but I was too full from dinner to want to eat.

"He's here, and you should have seen his face when I told him you couldn't make it," Monica shouted in my ear.

"Where is he? I can't see him anywhere."

Monica shrugged. "Sorry, I lost him. Maybe he left."

My heart sank; I couldn't bear to think that I had just defied my parents for nothing.

"But hey, you never know, come on, let's look for him together." Monica linked her arm through mine, and we trudged around the party. Initially, we were polite. Asking people to 'excuse us' we soon found that it was quicker and easier to nudge them gently out of the way.

"Jade!" I heard a familiar voice, and a feeling of dread crept up my spine. My head whipped around to face my brother, Gbenga.

"You naughty girl, how did you get out of the house?" Gbenga leant against the railing of the stairs that led into the main house, nursing a cold beer. Apparently, he had crept out of the house too — so he couldn't expose me without exposing himself, I reassured myself.

"How did you get out of the house?" I threw back at him, my arms folded. We both burst out laughing. "Tayo helped me," I offered.

"Nice."

I introduced Monica and Gbenga to each another, and they shook hands.

"What are you doing here? I didn't know you knew Deji."

"What? Deji is my guy. How do you know Deji?" he asked, his eyes narrowed.

"He's my guy too," I teased. "Just kidding; he's in my class," I added quickly before Gbenga's eyes could turn red, figuratively speaking. "So you came by yourself?"

"No, actually Josh gave me a ride; you just missed him, he went to get some barbeque."

"Oh, right. Well, maybe see you around." I waved and turned around, Monica in tow.

"Ooh, your brother is cute," Monica said as we walked away and I threw her a look of disgust.

"You don't think Wale is hot, but you think that is?" I jerked a thumb over my shoulder in Gbenga's direction.

"We need to get your eyes checked... or your head." We giggled.

"So, the famous Josh is here. What are the odds? Your present and past crush together in one party. I wonder if he's still with Alexia. Oh, I wonder if they came together." I had told Monica about Josh a while back, but she had never met him.

"It's sort of put a little dampener on my night," I admitted.

"But why? Surely you're over him by now."

"I am... I just... I don't know; I feel weird around him. He reminds me of my clumsy fifteen-year-old self, and I feel like I revert back to her when I'm around him. I can't control it; he just has like this power over me. Argh, it's so annoying."

"You're such a mess," Monica said, laughing.

"Aaaaahh!" I shrieked as strong arms lifted me up from behind and pulled me into a tight hug. I thrashed and broke free. I turned around ready for a fight, but my face softened when I saw who it was.

"You came!" Deji squealed with delight, his eyes were bright, his smile was broad, and his arms were outstretched. "Hi, Mon." He nodded at Monica and then looked back at me. Monica responded with a half-smile. She took out her phone and started texting.

"Dude! No back hugs, come on! You frightened me."

"Sorry, just so happy to see my main person. So what happened? How was your mum's thing?"

"It was good; I'm stuffed." I rubbed my tummy. "But wow, awesome party, I had no idea it was going to be this huge." I looked around, spreading out my arms to emphasise my point. I felt my heart skip a beat as I caught sight of Wale looking at us from the other side of the pool. I smiled, but he turned away as soon as he saw that I had spotted him. My smile faltered. I felt as if a bucket of ice-cold water had been emptied over my head. I looked back at Deji and made an effort to hold onto my smile.

"Yeah, neither did I," he said. "Did you invite your girlfriends?"

I gave him a look. "Really? I think you have enough girls here."

"I know, I know. I'm just glad you could make it." Some girl was trying to catch Deji's attention. She was slim and tall, with long hair which she tossed every few seconds, so much that it looked as if her neck was made of rubber. She looked me up and down and gave a caustic smile. I ignored her.

"I have to go; I'll see you around. Make sure you find me before you leave." Deji put his arm around the girl and walked away.

I looked around again, searching for Wale; surely he couldn't have gone far. Maybe this was a bit desperate. Clearly, he wanted nothing to do with me; if he did, he would have waved or something? A part of me wanted to keep looking for him, but another part was beginning to feel that maybe looking for him might come across a bit stalky. Monica looked up from her phone and spotted him immediately.

"Wale!" she shouted, jumping up and waving her hands over her head like a survivor on a deserted island. My heart raced as I watched Wale walk, somewhat reluctantly, in our direction. I was nervous all of a sudden, a thousand thoughts running through my head. What if he didn't like me? Or he had a girlfriend? Or I found him annoying and couldn't stand him? I liked staring at Wale from a distance; why ruin a good thing? What if he was a terrible person up close? What if I said the wrong thing?

"Hey! There you are!" Monica said to Wale, raising her voice because of the noise and his height. "She made it after all! I need to go; I'll see you guys around."

"Hi," I said, a little shy. I couldn't look at him.

"Hey, you made it!"

"Yeah, I... erm." How much detail to give? Having an 8 p.m. curfew was lame, and I wanted him to think I was cool. "Yes, I did. How did your other thing go?"

"Good, really good." He spoke in a loud voice to be heard above the din of the music. "Thanks for inviting me."

"Well, technically Monica invited you." As soon as the words slipped out, I wished they hadn't. I watched him deflate, like a punctured football.

"Yes, of course."

There was an awkward silence. As much as I had looked forward to this, I hadn't thought of what I would say to Wale and was worried that I would say the wrong thing again. What was wrong with me? Why wasn't I twirling my hair and swinging my hips? Perhaps some eyelash batting wouldn't be out of place. My hands were practically clasped behind my back. I convinced myself that it was to keep me from reaching out and stroking the cute stubble along the side of his face, rather than that I felt shy and inadequate.

"So, you and Deji...?" He trailed off. He seemed to be focussing on something on my head. I swiped my hand over my forehead, thinking perhaps there was something there.

"Deji and I...?" I urged him to finish his question.

"Are you guys together?" He cleared his throat, and his eyes met mine. He had a look in them that I couldn't place.

"What?" I wasn't sure I heard him correctly. "As in, are we dating?" I chuckled.

A pained look flashed across his face, and his shoulders tensed.

"Sorry," I laughed, "it's just, the thought... eww, he's practically my brother."

His shoulders relaxed visibly, and he smiled. I smiled back, a warm feeling enveloping me as I realised that he had been jealous. That only meant one thing. He liked me! He actually liked me back!

"It's loud in here. Do you want to go somewhere quiet?"

I nodded, and we walked out of the front gates of Deji's house, as far away from the noise as we could. Outside the air was cool, there was a slight breeze, and it felt as if it was going to rain. The trees swayed softly in the wind and the air smelt fresh and clean.

We walked together, side by side, in comfortable silence. I was feeling so many things at the same time; it felt so surreal that I could be with the boy I had dreamed about so many times. I stole a glance at him and smiled to myself. "Wait till I tell Monica," I thought.

"I can't believe this is actually happening — that I'm here with you," he said, breaking the silence. He looked at me and smiled. We were standing a couple of houses down from Deji's house; parked cars lined the streets, and we sat down on the boot of a Peugeot saloon, him sitting with poise while I opted for a graceless hop which caused the hood to bend and creak.

"Why do you say that?" I asked, bracing my palms behind me on the car and tilting my chin towards him.

"Well..." he started. "I've had a crush on you for so long, but of course, you know that." He looked into my eyes and drew circles on the back of my hand. I feel a rush of hot and cold at the same time.

"No way! You're just saying that" I gasped, shoving him playfully with the tips of my fingers.

"No, it's true. You always seem to be mocking me," Wale smiled.

"What, me? I would never mock you."

"Then why do you do that thing with your eyes when you see me, like 'Oh gosh, here comes this clown again'. You always make me feel so clumsy."

"Er, are you for real? There is no way I would think you're a clown." I took a deep breath. "I have a crush on you too," I said in a rush as if I was ripping off a Band-Aid. I glanced at him and saw he was smiling. It was a very broad smile, and I shuddered at the rush of adrenaline from my boldness. "I remember the first time I saw you. It was just outside the Faculty. You wore a pink shirt tucked into a pair of jeans. I remember because Monica thought you looked like a nerd. Not many guys can pull off wearing pink in the piercing heat." I laughed.

"So, I'm a nerd, and I can't pull off pink; Roger that." He chuckled. We settled back into silence. It was nice. I wasn't struggling to think of what to say; I was just content to have him there next to me. To know that that was where he wanted to be as well. I watched the stars flicker in the darkest blue sky, and I took a mental picture of that moment, wishing I could hold on to it forever.

"You know, I was afraid that you liked Monica." I turned to look at him. I studied his face. The way his full eyebrows knitted together when he was thinking, the way the tip of his tongue lightly flitted across his bottom lip. His teeth grazed his lower lip, and I wished it were my lips instead. I shook my head to get rid of the image in my head.

"What made you think that?" He studied me too. His eyes flitted over my face as if he was searching for something.

"Nothing really..." I paused. "I had a bad experience once." I shut my eyes and cursed myself inwardly. Why didn't I keep my mouth shut? The last thing I wanted was to bring Josh into this conversation. But I felt like I couldn't help it. Ever since Gbenga had mentioned that Josh was at the party, he had been stuck in my subconscious. It was only a matter of time before I told Wale about him. Would he think I was a loser? Would he wonder what was wrong with me? Why hadn't Josh wanted me? Would it make Wale not want me too? I felt a soft breath on my face, and I opened my eyes slowly. Wale's face was less than an inch away from mine. I shut my eyes again and waited for the crush of his lips against mine.

"What happened?" he asked. I opened my eyes, and he was back on his side of the car.

"It was a silly schoolgirl crush. I shouldn't have brought it up." I flicked my wrist in an attempt to brush it off.

"I can tell that whatever it was, it really affected you. You can tell me, I won't tease you about it, I promise. You know what? Let's make a deal. If I tell you a really embarrassing story about me, will you tell me then?"

"Yes!" I sat up to give him my full attention, eager to glean as much as I could about him. He knitted his fingers behind his head and brought his knee up on the bonnet of the car. I was facing him fully. I pulled my knees up, tucked them under my chin and wrapped my arms around them. He cleared his throat and gazed up at the sky in mock seriousness.

"Once upon a time, there was a boy... that was me, by the way."

I slapped his arm playfully. "Just continue."

"Okay, so this boy had a best friend, and it just happened to be a girl; her name was Anita... You know what? I can't tell you this story. It doesn't reflect me in a good light." He grimaced.

"No, tell me — what happened?" I said in a soft voice. He looked at me for what seemed like ages, and then he sighed and continued.

"Well... like I said, we were best friends. There's something you should know about me; I'm an orphan. Gosh, I hate that word." He broke off, and his eyes moistened.

I didn't know how to react. I'd never met anyone that had lost someone they were close to. I touched Wale's arm, and he pulled his hand out from under his head to grasp my hand. He held it to his chest.

"My mum and dad died in an accident three years ago. I'm an only child, and my grandma moved in with me. I completely withdrew into myself. Anita, bless her, tried hard to cheer me up. One day she had an idea. I'll give you a hint; it involved us being naked. At first, it seemed like a good idea, but in the middle of fumbling to get our clothes off, I must have come to my senses. I just knew that if I let it happen, I would lose my best friend forever. What I didn't know was that by not doing it, I'd lose her altogether. In my defence, I was a stupid, clumsy boy and instead of letting her know I was freaking out, I literally shoved her away and ran out of her room. She was hurt and refused to speak with me since."

"Wow," I said, trying to suppress the tiny part of me that was jealous of Anita, wherever she was. It was evident that he must have cared about her. "I'm sorry about your parents." He smiled and patted the back of my hand that he still grasped.

"Now, your turn."

"I don't know; your story is going to be hard to beat."

"Hey, a deal is a deal. Now spill."

I told him about my crush on Josh, trying to tone down anything that might make me come across as stalkerish.

"So Josh and Alexia are still an item?"

I shrugged. "I try not to keep up with whatever is going on in their lives. To me, they've both ceased to exist."

"But he lives next door?" Wale's brow shot up.

"Yep, why?"

"I just want to know what I'm up against; that's all. So far, I have to watch out for Deji and Josh."

I threw back my head and laughed. I loved that he made me feel as if I had a whole trove of men vying for my affection. He looked pleased that he'd made me laugh.

"What do you like about me?" I asked. I felt my heart quicken, and my belly churned.

"There's just something about you; you carry yourself like you don't care what people think about you. You're so different from all the girls I know, and I find that refreshing. It doesn't hurt that you're absolutely gorgeous," he said, grinning. "I kept wishing that I would one day have the courage to ask you out, but you're always surrounded by guys. I'm glad you... sorry, Monica invited me to this party." He brushed the back of my hand with his thumb, and my whole body tingled. His touch sent currents running through me; I had never experienced anything like it.

"Don't get upset," he said, "but I need to ask you something."

"You can ask me anything," I acquiesced, wondering what it could be that would upset me. Wale could run over my foot, and I would still think he was fantastic.

"You and Deji... I know you said he's like your brother but... did you ever date or like, did he ever ask you out?" He looked into my eyes as if to be able to detect if I was going, to be honest with him. I smiled at the nervousness I could hear in his voice. So that's what he was worried about.

"No, Deji and I are just completely friends," I said, making an effort to stop a massive grin from spreading across my face. Surely it was a good sign that he wanted to be certain I wasn't in a relationship...

"But you know he fancies you, right? I see the way he looks at you."

"Oh please, like that could ever happen! You don't know Deji like I know him. He literally has no capacity to hold onto a relationship. He really is just my friend," I stressed. Every fibre of my being knew Wale was wrong. Besides, I was so not Deji's type. He usually went for glamorous, beautiful, more-legs-than-brains kind of girls.

"Yeah," he smirked, "not if it was up to him."

"Oi." I poked him sharply on his shoulder. "Let's not even go there. What about Sade?"

"What about her?" he frowned.

"Well, everyone can tell she has the 'hots' for you."

"Yeah, I... there's nothing I can do about that." He spread out his hands in surrender. "She tried to ask me out once, but she's just not my type."

"Wait — so she asked you out, you said no, and you're still friends?"

"Did I say 'ask me out'? I meant more like she hinted it."

"So you never took advantage," I mocked.

"No, I would never do that. I told Sade I appreciated her as a friend, and that was all I could be to her." He said.

"Maybe she doesn't believe you," I said in a small voice. I knew what unrequited love felt like. I still had my memories of Josh, and although I'd have liked to believe that I'd moved on, it still hurt. There was no way he didn't know that I loved him: okay, maybe love was a strong word, but I honestly felt that I would have done anything for him.

"You need to let her go. Whether you know it or not, you're leading her on by continuing to be her friend.

Imagine how she'll feel seeing you date other girls: always wondering what you see in them that you don't see in her, always trying to make herself good enough for you, even indispensable to you. Allow her to move on. Sade is stunning; I bet she'll be hooked up before long, but not if she thinks she still has a chance with you."

"I never thought of it that way." He rubbed his palm over his forehead. "I never meant to lead her on. I guess it's a bit like you and Josh, isn't it?" He ran his hands through my hair, and I didn't care if he messed it up; it felt good, and I didn't want him to stop.

"Yeah well, Josh and I were never and will never be friends," I corrected.

I looked at my watch; we'd been talking for hours. "Can you believe it's 3 a.m. already?" I exclaimed. Without saying a word, he gently pulled me to him. I don't know why he did what he did then — maybe to make the time we had spent together seem more real or out of fear that if we parted things would go back to the way they were before. Whatever his reasons were, I was glad he did it. It felt so intense that I forgot how to breathe. His fingers held my face so gently. I was fire and water and molten lava all at once, my head exploded into a million bright lights, and I sighed into his mouth. My first kiss.

CHAPTER 11

It seemed to go on and on. We clung to one another on the bonnet of a strange car. I felt as if I could see into his heart and soul. He was gentle and firm at the same time. His teeth lightly teased my lips, and his tongue pushed buttons in my brain that I hadn't known existed. When it ended, he wrapped his arms around me in a warm embrace that made me feel safe and deliriously happy. I could feel his heart beating fast beneath his shirt, and his warm breath soft on my forehead.

"We need to get back inside, Monica will be worried," I said, breaking the silence. I felt intoxicated; the whole experience was surreal. My mouth was less than an inch away from his smooth neck, and I couldn't resist pressing my lips against it; he felt incredible, but it wasn't enough. I wanted to taste him, so I ran the tip of my tongue lightly over his skin and sucked on it. He groaned, a low guttural sound deep in his throat, and he let me go. His eyes were slightly glazed, and he shook his head.

"That is just playing with fire."

"Sorry." I peered at him through my lashes. "I don't know what came over me."

He looked amused. "Don't apologise for doing that, ever." He chuckled and then his face became serious. "Don't freak out, but I think I might be crazy about you." My face broke out into a broad smile and my toes tingled.

"Come on, let's go find Monica." He got off the car and held out his hand to me; then we walked arm in arm back to the party which still seemed to be in full swing. I checked my watch; it was 4:05 a.m. Wale and I walked around looking for Monica, but we couldn't find her anywhere.

"Maybe she left," Wale suggested.

"Yeah, but she wouldn't leave without saying goodbye, would she?"

"Or, she could have thought you left... you know, with me?"

"Argh," I groaned. That was the last impression that I wanted Monica to have of me. That I would ditch her at a party with a guy I barely knew — well, a guy I'd barely known a few hours ago. I spotted Josh sitting by himself, nursing a can of Pepsi.

"Hey," I called out to him.

He looked taken aback.

"Josh, this is my friend Wale. Wale, this is my brother's friend, Josh."

Josh's eyebrows shot up at my introduction.

I watched them size each other up as they shook hands. Wale's arm tightened around me.

"Where's Gbenga?" I asked.

Josh sighed. "I have no idea. And he's not picking up his phone. I'm going to have to leave without him. How did you come? Do you need a lift?" His eyes kept flickering from Wale to me. I could feel Wale tense up next to me.

"No, it's fine, I drove," I smiled as I felt Wale relax.

"Good, so you can take him home."

"Yeah, actually, I can't. I have to leave now." I felt as if I needed to explain, to avoid coming across as a mean sister. "Before Dad realises I'm not in bed." I grimaced. Wale and Josh burst into laughter.

"You snuck out?" Wale asked, looking at me with something close to admiration.

I shrugged.

"Fine, I'll wait for half an hour; after that good luck to him trying to get a cab at this time of the night, because I need to go to bed. I have tennis in the morning." Josh said.

"Wow, so you sneak out of your house?" Wale asked when we left Josh.

"No, this was my first time. And I hope I never have to do it again." I was actually terrified that my parents had realised I wasn't at home. I could picture my dad waiting for me in the gatehouse, brandishing a long thin whip. I tried to reassure myself that it had all been worth it.

"How much trouble will you be in, if your dad finds out?" Wale looked genuinely concerned.

I shrugged. "What about you? Did you have to sneak out?"

"No, my grandma lets me do whatever I want. She trusts me."

I stuck my tongue out at him.

"Right, let's get you home." He walked me to Tayo's car.

"I had a really amazing time," I said.

"Me too," he responded.

I hugged him tight, not wanting to let him go. I didn't want the night to end. He released me reluctantly.

"See you on Monday," he said, and it sounded like a promise.

CHAPTER 12

The next day, I woke up with a smile on my face. I was tired and groggy but I'd never been happier in my life. I couldn't wait to tell Tobi and Monica. Hmm, maybe not Tobi —she might put down my newly found status. I'd gone from never-been-kissed to being very thoroughly kissed! I called Monica.
"Mon!"
"What happened to you yesterday? You went completely AWOL!"
"I'll tell you all about it on Monday." I didn't want to give details over the phone. I wanted to watch her expression when I told her about the most magical night of my life. I spent the weekend in a bubble. I was so grateful to my sister; it felt like our relationship had done a complete 180 degree since Friday night. I skipped around the house doing chores without being asked. If anyone noticed, no one said anything; I think they were all just glad to have someone cleaning up after them. I kept checking my phone to make sure it was turned on. Wale didn't have my number so I'd asked Monica to let me know if he called her to ask for it. Briefly, I wondered if I'd imagined Friday night. He had said he was crazy about me; was it naïve of me to believe him? Mr Sunday dropped me off at my hostel on Sunday evening. It rained heavily that night, and I didn't sleep very well. My dreams were a repeating pattern of falling petals; chants of "he loves me, he loves me not" tortured me as each petal

peeled away from a rose, to fall into an abyss of despair and lonely desperation. Did he think we were moving too fast? Was I easy for letting him kiss me? For enjoying it?

My first class wasn't until 11 a.m., so I stayed in bed a little longer than usual, playing the events of Friday night over and over in my head. Monica came to my room at 10.45 a.m. I packed up my books, and we set off for the lecture theatre. On the way, I told her about the kiss.

"Wow! That was fast! So how was it?" she asked.

"I don't know, it was a little weird at first, but it was nice when I stopped thinking about it and just let go."

"Hmm, just 'nice' eh?" She sniggered. "So give me details, did he use tongue?"

"We kissed for ages — of course, he used tongue." I wanted to tell her everything, to confide in her, for her to reassure me that he wouldn't think I was easy for kissing him even though we weren't dating. I wanted her to tell me it was okay and that people did it all the time. I wanted to tell her that I thought I was in love, and about the things we had shared, the way he'd looked at me and held me in his arms. But for some reason, I couldn't bring myself to give her any more details. It felt too private as if she would be intruding, and if I told her every last detail, it would no longer feel as magical. Also, I was scared, and so I thought that if I played it cool, it wouldn't be so terrible if it turned out that he didn't want me; I could pretend that I didn't want him either.

"So did he know that you know... he was your first?"

"Jeez, Mon, you make it sound like we had sex." I laughed.

"Well, in a way he dis-virgined you." She hee-hawed. "He popped your kissing cherry," she said making a popping sound by smacking her lips together.

"Haha, hilarious. In any case, there's no way I would have told him it was my first kiss; he would have thought

I was either weird or lying." We were close to the classroom when we spotted our lecturer coming from the opposite direction.

"Oh-oh, quick, Mr Adagu is coming," I whispered to Monica. Was it my imagination, or did he take faster, longer strides as soon as he spotted us? If he got to class before us, he would either make us stand outside for a long time or come up with some form of insult, making the rest of the class laugh along with him, grateful that it wasn't them under attack. We ran down the corridor and into the classroom, panting, and we found empty seats to slide into.

After the lecture, just as I was about to rush to the bathroom, my classmate, Yomi, accosted me. Yomi was good-looking, but he seemed to have a one-track mind, and I always tried to avoid being alone with him. It didn't help that he was part of a campus fraternity. I found him arrogant; he seemed to think he was the answer to every woman's dreams. He reminded me of Gaston from *Beauty and the Beast.*

I cringed inwardly and looked around for an escape route.

"I saw you at Deji's party yesterday," he said with a sneer. He was leaning against the desk at the end of the aisle, and he'd put his feet up against the wall, thereby barring my exit. His eyes avoided mine and settled somewhere below my neck. I sighed impatiently.

"That's nice," I smiled, deciding to patronise him. "You should have said hello."

"Well, you looked really preoccupied; I didn't want to disturb you. So who was that guy? Your boyfriend?" His eyes still hadn't shifted from their primary position.

"You know, my eyes are up here. You have to stop addressing my boobs every time you talk to me; it makes me feel like you're only interested in them," I admonished him.

That threw him off, and he straightened, lifting his feet from the wall.

"No... I, no, of course not..." he spluttered, gesticulating with both hands. "I wasn't looking at your boobs — is that what you think?"

Quickly, I slipped past him. But I knew he was going to follow and sure enough, in less than five seconds, he was walking by my side. Where was Monica when you needed her? I looked around and noticed her walking behind us, smiling. "Help me," I mouthed to her but she just shook her head and continued smiling. She believed that Yomi and I would get it on eventually; according to her, there was a strong chemistry between us. Yeah, more like physics — he repelled me in a similar manner as "like" magnetic poles.

I'd never been attracted to Yomi — or maybe I'd never allowed myself to be. He had "I'll break your heart and suck the life out of it if you are so stupid as to give it to me" written all over him. I could bet my last naira that as soon as he left me, he moved on to another girl, stroking her neck and arm with his finger and watching to see if her nipples hardened and strained through her blouse.

"You haven't answered my question," he said, matching my walking pace.

"No, he's not my boyfriend," I sighed. Oh, how I wished he was!

"Nice. So when are you going to come and see me?" Yomi lived in a boys' quarter just off campus, and his hobby was trying to get girls to come and see him.

"I'll think about it," I replied, batting my eyelids in an attempt to get rid of him.

Convinced I was sincere; he gave a quick peck on my cheek and buzzed off.

I looked back wide-eyed at Monica.

"Woohoo, what's with the kiss?" she asked, catching up with me.

"Don't be silly, you traitor. There is no way I am hooking up with Yomi." I punched her playfully on her elbow.

"Yeah, you say that now. Yomi is *so* fling material. You know, if it doesn't work out between you and Wale."

"Why don't you have him?"

"Eh... he's not my type."

"Hmm? Come on; he's hot! Quit it with the 'he's not my type' line."

"Jeez, you're like a broken record! Just because a guy is hot doesn't mean he's anyone's type. You just need to tell him to back off."

"I can't, I don't want to hurt his feelings."

"Aww, you're so sweet. I know all your moves. When a guy likes you, you either pretend not to know he likes you, talk around him asking you out to avoid saying no, or — and you know this is by far the most hilarious thing I've ever seen in my entire life — you go to ridiculous lengths to avoid the guy."

"That's not true!"

"You know I'm right."

"I don't know, it just seems so final, like getting married." I grimaced.

"Do you remember Gabriel?" Monica asked, on the verge of laughter.

"Ah, Gabriel, how could I ever forget?" I was in my first year when I'd met Gabriel; he was the epitome of the hero of all my romantic novels, and he embodied the tall, dark and handsome label. He was a really nice guy, and I had a massive crush on him until the day he asked me out. I so wish he hadn't. From that moment onwards, he became so boring, and I couldn't stand the sight of him. One particular day, Monica and I were walking to class when she spotted him. "Angel Gabriel, 2 o'clock," she whispered urgently. I'd disappeared before the words were even out of her lips. According to her, one second I was right next to her and the next she was talking to herself.

I wrinkled my nose at the putrid stench as I pushed open the door of the Law Faculty bathroom.

"I'll wait for you here," Monica called from behind me.

"Thanks." I tiptoed in, poking my head into each stall to find the least dirty toilet. There were a few pools of water, and I hoped it was rain from a leaky roof. I rushed out when I was done, thankful to be able to breathe properly once again and to be rid of the pungent smell.

"So when are you next seeing Wale?" Monica asked as we headed in the direction of our next lecture.

"I don't know; I haven't spoken to him since Saturday morning."

"And you're not going to call?"

"That's right." I smacked my lips to indicate that I didn't want to discuss it anymore. I had decided that I was going to wait for him to call; even if it took weeks, I was going to ignore him until he spoke to me first.

"Don't you think that's a little childish?"

"Old-fashioned, maybe, but I don't think it's childish. I'm just trying to protect myself. Okay, maybe a little bit insecure but I'd rather err on the right side. I don't want it to seem like I'm chasing him."

"Okay, I can't argue with that," Monica laughed.

Just then my phone rang. I didn't recognise the number, and I held the screen out to Monica with a raised eyebrow. But she just shrugged.

"Hello?" I answered.

The person on the other end hesitated as if making a decision to hang up or remain on the line.

"Hello, who is it?" I sang into the phone.

"Erm... hi, it's me."

It was him! My heart stopped for a fraction of a second.

"Oh, hi," I answered, trying to play it cool but unable to stop the wide grin that broke out on my face. "How did you get my number?"

"A gentleman never tells, do you mind?"

"No, I was just curious, since I don't recall giving it to you."

"Are you busy?"

Why? Like I wouldn't drop everything and run to him even if I was.

"Er, no, I'm just whiling away the time till my next lecture — what's up?"

"Can you meet me in the car park?"

"Now?" I took a peek at my watch; I had twenty minutes until my next class.

"Yes, please. If you're not busy."

"Okay, see you in a sec," I said, flipping my phone shut.

"Wale wants me to meet him in the car park," I said to Monica.

Monica grinned. "Rendezvous in broad daylight. Way to go, Wale."

"Okay, calm down, Monica. I'll see you later, yeah?"

"K, have fun, don't hurry back!" she called after me as I skipped down the long corridor and into the sunlight. It was a lovely August day, cool from the torrential rains the night before. I skipped across puddles of water on my way to the car park. I searched for him as soon as the row of cars came into view. I could sense him before my eyes rested on him. He leant against his Golf in a yellow t-shirt and a pair of jeans tucked into Timberland boots. And he was holding a bouquet of flowers! What the...?

His eyes lit up when he saw me. I ambled over to him, taking care not to trip or fall into any puddles, conscious the whole time of his eyes on me.

"Are those for me?" I asked, half-dreading the answer. On one hand, I was flattered that he'd bought me roses. They were a gorgeous pink and beautiful. No one had ever given me flowers. On the other hand, I would have to carry them back to class with me. I wasn't looking forward to the staring and giggling... plus the guys in my class were going to rip him apart figuratively speaking. I could already hear their taunts and jeers; they would call him an idiot for giving a girl flowers. I had heard the boys in my class boast that they could bag a girl with minimal effort, and they despised or made fun of any form of chivalry.

He handed the bouquet of roses to me.

"I was just passing by a flower shop, and these caught my eye."

Yeah right! I smiled. "They're gorgeous; I love them. Thanks. So..." I tilted my head to the side. "Do you buy flowers for every girl you kiss or is this special?"

"You tell me." He smiled back. "Is this special?" He leant forward and dropped tiny kisses around my mouth. His tongue traced the outline of my lips and drove me crazy. My belly was getting warm with all the fluttering butterflies, and I wondered how long this feeling would last.

CHAPTER 13

"Mr and Mrs Wale Becker," I enunciated under my breath as I scribbled in my notebook. I was in class, waiting for the Philosophy lecturer to come in. Monica sat next to me. She had just signed onto this social networking site, Hi5, and the thing was like a drug; she was always on it. She'd tried to get me to join, flooding my rarely used email account with "friend" requests. I spied Wale in the front row. I couldn't help but feel a slight twinge of... I don't know, shame. Sitting in the front row was just such a nerdy thing to do.

"I'm short-sighted, so it helps," he'd explained when I asked him about it.

"Yeah right," I had replied. "That's not why you sit in front; you have glasses for your short-sightedness. I think you just like being the teacher's pet!"

The lecturer walked into the lecture theatre fifteen minutes late and started the lesson on René Descartes before he reached the podium, not giving the students in the theatre enough time to compose themselves. Pens and notebooks flew out from bags. I already had my book open, and my pen was in my hand, but I couldn't keep my mind from wandering. I found the lecture boring; it was on the "Passion of Souls", about how the soul is not just found in the brain but in the innermost part of the brain, and something about the soul being attributed only to our thoughts. How do people come up with stuff like this? If I was born in the eleventh century and came up with something like "The sky is blue, so therefore the spirits that hover around us must take the form and colour of the clouds", would that have made me a famous philosopher? It's like these people retire into their chambers and think, "Umm, what shall I dazzle them with? If I think it is, then so it really is."

"I'll be right back," I said to Monica after the lecture, throwing my books into my bag.

"Where are you going?"

"I'll see you later." I avoided answering her question as she never passed up any opportunity to tease me about my eagerness to always be with Wale. I shot off my seat, and it flipped upright with a loud bang, startling Monica.

"Alright then, sha take it easy, love nwantintin. You don't have to break the seats now."

"Yeah, sorry. Catch you later." I had to hurry before Wade left the hall. I made my way across the seats on my aisle, to the stairs.

"Aren't you coming for GST?" Monica called after me.

"Erm, yes, keep me a seat, yeah?" I skipped down the stairs and shuffled my way across the seats to where he sat; his head bent in that oh so charming manner. I plonked myself on the seat next to him; Sade sat next to him on the other side. I wished she wouldn't follow him around like a sad puppy. It was just pathetic. In his defence, she always clung to him, and he didn't want to hurt her feelings by asking her to back off. I'd offered to do it for him; I didn't give two hoots about her feelings. And what about mine? I gave her a half smile; she looked back at me as if she would have liked to bite my head off. I ignored her.

"Hey, so what does this really mean?" I pointed to a section Wale had highlighted in his book. His face lit up, and he smiled. I melted right off the seat.

"You think it's rubbish, don't you?" He tucked his fist under his chin.

I shrugged.

"Well, Aristotle also believed that René Descartes was wrong."

"Did he? I guess I would have to rely on Aristotle then."

We were both in our own little world as we argued the logic of Plato and the works of the great philosophers. The words were coming out of my mouth, but my mind was somewhere else. At some point, I looked around and noticed that the room was almost empty. When had Sade left? I hadn't noticed. From the works of the philosophers, we'd moved on to the tragic love affair between Abélard and Heloïse.

"I can't get over Heloïse — for a woman to have been schooled by one of the greatest minds of her time. I try to imagine what life was for her," I said. "She had known no other man and was still in love with a man who had seemingly abandoned her, she hadn't seen him in years and even knowing he had been castrated, she still loved him."

"A sharp contrast to what we see nowadays, don't you think?"

"Hmm, in what way?"

"Well, in our culture the tradition of a woman keeping herself pure for one man is slowly dying. There are statistics to prove that a lady who has only known one lover will become curious at some point in her life and will want to experience intercourse with other men. The advice is to get the sexual promiscuity out of one's veins before marriage."

Ah, I wondered if it was a coincidence that we were on the topic of Heloïse.

"I don't know; I'll have to see proof of those dodgy statistics." I had confided in him the evening before that I was still a virgin. I'd thought that it would make him happy, the fact that I'd never been touched by another man. Well, Alex didn't count, I convinced myself. And Wale had seemed happy enough — until I mentioned that I wanted to remain that way until marriage. It wasn't something I had given much thought to, but my mum was forever going on about maintaining my purity, and so I'd decided to try for as long as I could. If Wale and I were going to be together, it was only fair that I was completely honest with him.

He leant forward and brushed my cheek softly with his fingers. I inhaled sharply.

"An eyelash."

The electricity crackled between us and I restrained from throwing myself into his arms there and then. I could have sworn that he'd felt it too; his fingers had hesitated just a second longer on my skin. I wondered how long it would take before I lost my reserve.

I looked up then and noticed students I didn't recognise filing into the lecture theatre.

"Where's your next class?" asked Wale, and suddenly I realised that I was fifteen minutes late. The weird thing was that I wasn't bothered. Nothing else mattered as long as I was with Wale.

CHAPTER 14

It was six weeks since that fateful pool party. Six amazing weeks, during which we'd spent as much time as we could together. Time apart just seemed like wasted time. Six weeks of talking on the phone every night, of trying to keep our hands off each other — and the heady feeling intensified every day. Six weeks of bliss.

I felt as if I could never get enough of Wale. He had a funny anecdote for everything, and despite his geeky appearance, he was anything but a geek. He was intelligent and knew something about everything. Before I met him, I'd spent every weekend at home, but now I rarely stayed the night at home. I went there on Sundays, had lunch with my parents and then went back to school, after extorting money for some excuse or the other. I may not have admitted it to myself, but I had begun to see a future with Wale. Sometimes I couldn't imagine what would happen if we broke up but the idea of it happening was so painful that I couldn't dwell on it. He was my own personal heroin; I needed him to keep me high, I needed him to be happy. I counted my day as an excellent one if I saw him. He became the defining item in my life. I had never felt this way, and I was confident that I could never feel the same way about anyone else.

I had a boyfriend now, so I paid more attention to how I dressed. I wore jeans and trainers less; now I wore dresses and high heels. At first, I felt ridiculous; I almost twisted my ankle more than once. Trying to walk confidently in high heels is one thing, but manoeuvring high heels on uneven pothole-intensive roads was just plain insane. I stuck to it, though, and with time I got used to it. I swapped my backpack for a handbag, and I borrowed Monica's Mac makeup while saving up to buy my own. I began to notice other girls, more beautiful and shapely than I was, and better-dressed. I saw how they said hello to Wale, drawing out their "hi's", batting their eyelids and swinging their hips. I saw the way he smiled back, that smile that to me said: "you know I would, only it's a shame I have a girlfriend". It was pain, and it was torture. What a horrible feeling love is! I had expected total bliss with minimal effort, but it seemed the more I tried to make myself look better, the more beautiful girls tried to poach him off me. And the worst part was that he appeared to glory in all the attention. But when we were alone together, I forgot about anyone else; nothing else mattered. The energy between us was incredible; I could feed off it and never be satiated. I loved it when we just lay in each other's arms, not speaking, just content to be. I loved his scent and even without seeing him, I could tell when he walked into a room. Every cell in my body was alert with anticipation whenever I felt his presence and was never wrong. I had never felt anything like this, and I imagined that he felt the same way, for I noticed how his eyes lit up when I came into the room, and could glimpse the disguised hurt in his eyes when I flirted with other guys while ignoring him. I wasn't trying to hurt him; I just wanted him to be a little jealous. I figured that if he saw other boys found me desirable, he would never take me for granted. The way he watched me as if he was trying to fix my every move into his memory — I knew he liked me.

 I knew it was irrational that I flirted with other guys and still felt insecure whenever he did the same with girls, but even as I flirted my eyes would always dart to wherever he was, to make sure he was looking, to check that he appreciated the effect I had on other boys. I was thinking about him when I twirled a braid around my fingers and peered at the boys through lowered lashes. I thought of him when another boy's eyes widened, and he stuttered out his words – but when Wale flirted with other girls, how could I be sure he was thinking of me? I knew I would never leave him for anyone else, but I needed to know that he felt the same way.

One Saturday, while we lay on his bed in his room, I brought up his flirting.

"That girl Tasha seems to spend an awful lot of time around you. What is it you guys do together?" I asked, trying unsuccessfully to mask my insecurity.

"Tasha? Come on, you know she's just my friend. Besides, she has a boyfriend, and is really into him." I was lying in his arms, studying the ceiling so he couldn't read my expression.

"She seems to think you like her, though."

"Why do you say that?" He was looking at me, but I kept my eyes trained on the ceiling.

"Apparently, Tasha boasts that you would dump me in a heartbeat if she were available. She seems to think you have a crush on her."

"What? That's ridiculous…"

"I've seen the way you look at her," I countered, looking in his eyes, and he flinched.

"Okay, fine," he admitted. "I used to have a crush on Tasha but all that's over since you and I started dating. You know the way I feel about you, I can't jeopardise this for anything." He hesitated before adding, "I can't promise to stop talking to her, it would be too weird as we take the same classes but I can tone it down a little and try hard to discourage any ideas that I might still have a crush on her. Would that make you feel better?" He stroked my face. I smiled and waited for him to bring up my flirting with other guys, but he just snuggled closer to me and kissed my neck. And instead of relief that he conceded to my feelings, I wondered if he didn't care enough about me.

A few days later, during a free period, I was hanging out in the car park with Deji and some of his friends. It was a pleasant afternoon with a cool breeze bringing some respite from the torturous heat of a September afternoon. A small crowd had assembled around a dust-covered BMW 3 series, the volume of the car stereo was turned up high to a rap beat. There was a space in the middle of the crowd where two boys faced each other in a freestyle battle. One boy was tall and slim while the other was a few inches shorter and a little on the chubby side. They were both familiar faces: the faces of people you come across every day but never speak to unless you meet in the company of mutual friends or outside campus. The faces that make up the faculty, the ones that will always be there, the predictable ones, the faces that are always in a particular spot at a given time; be it staying in class after a lecture to read or muck about loitering around the kiosk near the car park where you could get snacks, cold drinks, and shelter, and where, later in the evenings, the slight aroma of marijuana could be perceived in the air.

With chants of "go, go!" the crowd urged them on. It felt as if the atmosphere picked up the lovely melody and suddenly everything was beautiful and everyone that passed by felt their mood lifted by such a happy crowd.

"My mic is tight, and my look is fresh, I step to your lady in the lime green vest, and I must confess it cost me nothing, that's why I know your game must be wack!" The chubby guy finished with gusto, the crowd cheered, and the tall boy and his friends jeered. He reached into his pocket and fished out a handkerchief that had probably been white at some point but was now what could only be described as mocha and wiped his sweaty face. He raised his arms, turning around slowly with a huge grin as if asking for more applause, and then took an elaborate bow. The tall guy stepped in with his defence.

"One, two, buckle my shoe, oops, my bad, you're so fat, I bet you can't see your toes. I saw you last night talking sweet to a burger. You wouldn't know a hottie unless she's shaped like a doughnut." He finished to screams of laughter and cheers. Another boy strode into the middle of the crowd and started freestyling, and it continued in this vein, when one person finished, another one started. At one point, someone pushed me into the centre and began chanting my name, and in two seconds everyone else had picked up the chant. I knew I sucked at rapping, and there was no way I was going to humiliate myself. I looked around frantically for the idiot who thought it was funny to push me in and caught Wale's huge grin. I was going to kill him for doing this to me. Just the other day we'd been playing around singing to TLC's Waterfalls, and when it came to Lefteye's rap, I did it with so much energy that I had Wale cracking up. I knew I sounded horrible but that was part of the fun, wasn't it? So there was no excuse — he definitely knew how bad I sucked. I smiled — a smile that I hoped said, "Thanks, but no thanks" — and tried to slip back into the crowd, back into obscurity. But the crowd was having none of it. All this while, my name was still being chanted, and I decided I might as well put myself out of my misery and get it over with as soon as I could. What angle to take on this one?

"Um, yeah, now check this..." I started, trying to get my bearings. "They say Mary had a little lamb, its fleece was white as snow, and everywhere that Mary went the lamb was sure to go." I delivered my rap with all the attitude and confidence I could manage and the crowd was silent for a second before they burst out laughing, Whatever they were expecting, I bet they weren't expecting that. I smiled and took a bow, and this time, when I tried to push back into the crowd, I didn't experience any resistance. I pushed my way to where Wale stood and grabbed his ear; I pulled him out of the crowd.

"Wow, that was a new level of suckiness, even for you. How very original. Seen Sister Act lately?"

He burst into fresh laughter, doubling over and grabbing his waist in mock agony. "Oh my word, but that was so worth it. You should have seen your face."

"Yes, laugh now, for your punishment awaits." I stood with my arms folded and waited for him to recover from his laughing fit.

"And what are you going to do to me."

"Ah, that you will have to wait to find out. I will pounce when you least expect it and trust me; it will not be nice."

"Oh, look at me; I'm shaking in my Tims," he said, simulating a shudder.

"And so you should, darling."

"No matter what the punishment may be, it would have been worth it," he said, drawing me into his arms. "Mary had a little lamb." He mimicked me, chuckling softly. "It was unbelievable; I don't know any girls that would have been camp enough to go through with that. I was half-expecting you to stamp your feet and demand the crowd let you through, but you stood there and fought like a man."

"Yeah, I brought it, didn't I?" I smiled and flexed my non-existent biceps.

"Erm... yeah," he responded with exaggerated sarcasm.

CHAPTER 15

It was Thursday evening, and I was in my room which I shared with three other students. The room was divided into four equal spaces with small pockets of privacy provided by the wardrobes in each corner. My roommates and I had pooled some money together to buy a rug; it wasn't an expensive one, but it was nice. It was beige; we figured it was better than having the floor covered with four different rug designs like most of the other rooms. We had painted the walls bright yellow to add some colour.

My wardrobe was covered in a pink and green flowery wallpaper; I had met it that way when I moved into my "corner". I had my clothes both hanging and folded in one section of the wardrobe, at the bottom; I had arranged my spare collection of shoes neatly. The other section was divided into three shelves; I had my toiletries on the topmost shelf, foodstuff on the middle shelf and my books and stationery at the bottom. My wardrobe faced my bed so that I could access it without having to get up from my bed. A couple of my roommates were in their corners eating; whatever they were having smelt really good, and it made my stomach rumble. There were only a few days to go until the end of the month, and I was broke. I would have to make do with whatever I had in my wardrobe. I sat on my bed staring at my few choices. There was a half-eaten loaf of bread that was tempting, but I'd planned to have it for breakfast the next morning.

"I could have some Indomie noodles," I thought as my eyes fell on five yellow packs stacked in a corner. But that would mean soaking the noodles in water as I only had a hot plate and there was a power outage. "I think I would rather soak Garri," I thought, contemplating the big five-litre see-through tub of roasted cassava grains sitting proudly in the centre of my cupboard. I sighed as I picked up my "garri" bowl and scooped four handfuls of grain into it. I was just about to add sugar when my phone rang. I checked the caller ID; it was Tobi.

"Hey girl," I sang into the phone.

"Yo, I'm in Lagos. Are you busy? I'm coming to pick you up. This Mugu is taking me to dinner, and he asked me to bring a friend."

Yes, yes, yes! Inside, I was jumping for joy. I picked up my bowl and emptied its contents back into the tub.

"I don't know, I was just about to have dinner, besides I already have plans for the evening," I said with a smirk.

"Which kin yeye plans? Okay, fine, since you're playing hard to get, I'll let you pick the restaurant..."

"And I can order whatever I want?"

Tobi always ordered the less expensive meals when she went out with men for the first time, giving them the impression that she was low-maintenance which in turn caused them to let down their guard. I think it did something to their egos, made them feel they had to persuade her that they could afford whatever she desired and that she could feel free to spend their money. When that happened, then she had them right where she wanted, and that was when she hit their pockets, hard. The last time I had gone out to dinner with her, I had been so hungry and excited that I had ordered as much as I could get away with but she had made a big thing out of it, asking the waitress to ignore half of my order to the embarrassment of our patron who had insisted that it was okay and that he was happy to pay for it.

"You this girl, you're a thief o. Fine, you can order whatever you like, and I promise I will not say anything."

"I don't understand what your problem is, it's not like you're the one paying for the food."

"Whatever, I'll be there in an hour. Make sure you're ready, don't keep me waiting – and please whatever you do, do not wear those jeans!" She hung up, and I frowned at the phone. What was wrong with my jeans? They were perfect. I had half a mind to put them on just to spite her, but then I decided it wasn't worth the trouble. Tobi was unpredictable, and I could actually picture her refusing to let me into the car in those jeans.

I put on a blue silk halter neck blouse I had "borrowed" from my sister a few months ago with a pair of brown trousers. I was strapping on a pair of blue sandals when I heard a knock on the door.

"Come in," one of my roommates called out.

The door slid open a few inches and Wale's handsome head poked through the opening.

"Are you sure everyone is decent?" he asked with a grin and a wink in the general direction of the room, causing my roommates to break out in giggles.

"Hey, it's fine, you can come inside." I was only half-pleased to see Wale; I wasn't happy that he hadn't called to let me know he was coming. I would never show up at his room unannounced; it just wasn't polite.

He was wearing a yellow and purple LA Lakers Swingman jersey and shorts. He swaggered over to where I sat. I sucked in my breath as I ran my eyes over him, and his long smooth arms. He had never looked so sexy. I stood up in my heels and wrapped my arms around his neck, giving him a quick kiss on the lips. I slid my hands down over his body and let them linger over his chest before bringing them down slowly over his toned midsection, stopping just above the dip below his belly. He grabbed my hands before they left his body and pulled me back to him, wrapping my hands around his waist. I laughed and tightened my hold around his waist. He bent his head towards mine and dropped tiny butterfly kisses around my face and my neck. I closed my eyes and gave in to the shivers playing havoc with my nervous system as he blew gently into my ear.

"You look good enough to eat," he whispered, before tracing my earlobe lightly with his tongue. I moaned, and my knees buckled slightly, causing me to lean into him even further. I was conscious that we weren't the only ones in the room so, despite the waves of pleasure crashing through me, I opened an eye just to make sure that no one was looking at us. I caught one of my roommates staring at us as she chewed her food; she looked away in haste and pretended to be studying something in her polystyrene food pack.

"Erm... we should stop," I suggested without conviction, loosening my hold around Wale's waist. He tightened his grip around my waist, and his soft lips met mine in a slow and sensuous kiss. I tried to push him away. His tongue darted around my lips, and I felt a current jolt through my body and linger at my toes, causing them to tingle with a sweet sensation. Despite myself, I let his tongue push my lips apart, my eyes closed again, and a sigh escaped my lips as my tongue linked with his like a woman reuniting with her lover after a long separation spell. By the time our lips parted we were out of breath.

"Wow," he said, looking around him as if realising where he was and why he had come. "Hey, I'm going with some of the guys to shoot some hoops, do you want to come?"

"Aww, I wish I could, I've never seen you play."

He boasts about his prowess on the court, and I'd pestered him to let me watch him play, but his timing was just off. I was starving, plus I couldn't break my promise to Tobi.

"Yeah, come on, you look dressed already." He ran his eyes over me and grinned. "We have to leave now, though. The guys are waiting for me downstairs. I literally had to beg them to let us stop here. You're lucky they like you."

"But why didn't you call to tell me? I already made plans with Tobi." Wale had never met Tobi, but he felt as if he knew her already because I talked about her a lot. He questioned how she could afford to do the things I told him about, and he'd come up with his conclusions about her all by himself. He stiffened when I mentioned her name, and wondered if I would have been better off lying about who I was going out with.

"Call her and cancel, I'm sure she'll understand," he said, sounding as if he knew it was futile.

"I can't do that; you know how she gets. Besides, I already promised. The last thing I want is for her never to believe me when I give my word." My phone rang. "That'll be her now; I bet she's here already," I smiled sympathetically at him, hoping he would understand.

"Hey babe, I'll be right down," I said into my phone. I didn't have to look at Wale's face to feel his disappointment.

"Where are you guys going? Who are you going with?" he asked, his hands hanging limply by his side. I gave myself some time to think about my response. If I told him I didn't know, he could state a case about how dangerous it was to go out with men, even if your friend claimed to know the man. I could lie to him and say it was

Tobi's cousin, but I was a dreadful liar, and that would only make things worse.

"Wale, do you trust me?" I looked into his eyes, my face sombre.

"Yes, of course, I trust you."

"Then you have to trust me to make the right decisions. I really care about you, and I would have loved to go with you. Think about it; I've been pestering you for ages to let me watch you play and now that I can actually go with you, do you think I wouldn't drop everything if I could? But Tobi is my good friend, and I gave her my word. She's come all the way from..." Where was Tobi coming from? I had no idea. She was at the University College Oyo, studying accounting, but she was in Lagos so often that I wondered how she managed not to flunk her exams. I shook my head. "From Oyo, and I can't just tell her that I can't go because my boyfriend showed up at my door. What type of friend would I be?"

"I see where you're coming from," he muttered. "I'll walk you downstairs." He held out his hand to me. I took it and beamed at him. This was not my ideal scenario. The last thing I wanted was for him to walk me to another man's car; knowing Tobi, it was likely to be a very flashy car with her sitting in the back with a middle-aged pot-bellied slightly balding man. We were barely out the door when Tobi rushed towards us.

"Babes, I need a fucking tampon, like right now. Can you fucking believe I'm stained?" She clocked Wale holding my hand and grimaced. "Oh hi, I would shake your hand, but I'm kind of freaking out here," Tobi said, not in the least embarrassed that she had just announced to my boyfriend, whom she had never met, that she was on her period. She grabbed my free hand and proceeded to march back into the room. I looked apologetically at Wale. "I'm sorry, I have to go. I'll call you." I expected him to let go of my hand, but he didn't. I was beginning to feel like a tug-of-war rope, Tobi yanking persistently on one arm and Wale with an iron grip on the other.

"No fucking way," said Wale.

I was stunned; I had never heard him swear before.

"Tobi, I presume," he said, "can you give my girlfriend and me a moment? She'll be right in to help you with your emergency." I had never seen him look so serious. Tobi's mouth fell open; she let go of my hand and glared at Wale. With a "humph" she swivelled around and stormed into my room to wait for me. I wondered if this was the first time a boy had told her off. She seemed to be able to get away with anything.

"What the hell was that?" I said as I realised the enormity of what had just happened. I had always hoped that when Tobi and Wale eventually met, they would get along, but now the chances of that ever happening were very slim.

"I should be asking you the same question. Is that the friend you're always raving about? She's rude and obnoxious and–"

"Don't speak that way about my friend."

Wale let out a deep sigh. "Look, I don't want to fight with you, and I'm sorry I reacted the way I did. Tell her I said sorry. I'll catch you later." He dropped a kiss on my lips and brushed the skin of my hand with his thumb before letting go and striding off, his yellow jersey rustling around him as he walked. I stared after him for a moment, hoping things were alright between us, before going in to face Tobi.

I found her sulking in my corner, arms folded across her chest and right foot tapping impatiently against the floor. She looked as if she was spoiling for a fight.

"What's wrong with your boyfriend?' She said the last word with a scrunched-up face and a mocking tone. "That's why I don't date little boys; they're too sensitive."

I rolled my eyes at the ceiling. "Shut up and let's get you changed before you bleed all over my rug."

CHAPTER 16

2003

I woke up with a skull-cracking headache. I groaned inwardly. It was Monday morning, and I had a lecture in half an hour; I needed to get up immediately if I intended to make the class. The thought of skiving deliberately had never seemed an option to me before. Wale and I had been together for almost two years now. Before Wale, I'd been the perfect student, albeit noisy and always picking arguments with lecturers; now I skived at every opportunity and was fast on my way to becoming one of the 'unserious' students – and the last thing I wanted was for my lecturer to perceive me as one.

Damn Tobi; she had come into town yesterday from the Oyo and persuaded me to accompany her and her "friends", Ian and Terry, out for dinner on the Island. Wale had gone out with his buddies, and I wasn't doing anything so I'd agreed. After dinner, we'd gone to a karaoke club. Ian and Terry must have been in their mid-thirties and, compared to the men I usually saw with Tobi, they were actually good-looking. It was getting easier to turn a blind eye to the fact that Tobi slept with married men for money. They treated her well and showered her with gifts. Often she barked orders at them, and they scurried to obey. Interesting to watch, actually, like a dog chasing its tail to amuse the self-absorbed cat.

Tobi always had ready cash; although she rarely needed to spend it, so a night on the town with her was always fun – and last night had been no exception!

We arrived at the club before 11 p.m.; the place was packed, and so we ended up sharing a table with a couple of celebrities. At first, I was a bit star-struck, but they were so nice and down-to-earth, soon we were all chatting and trying to decide what songs to do when the microphone reached our table. One of the celebrities, Ruka and I flipped through the song list while Terry proceeded to order three bottles of champagne for the table. Ian and Tobi were eating each other's faces, and I made an effort to avert my gaze. My lip curled in distaste: not that I had anything against PDAs, but the guy was married, for heaven's sake! Here we were in a room full of random people; how could he be so sure that there wouldn't be someone who knew his wife in that room? I mean, I can kind of understand if a guy is weak and feels the urge to sleep with someone else for whatever reason, but this was a blatant disregard for the sanctity of marriage, for his wife, and for his kids, if he had any. I wondered briefly where his wife was and what she was doing while her husband was out getting ready to have sex with a nineteen-year-old.

When the mic finally made it to our table, I sang *Turn the Lights Down Low* by Lauren Hill and Bob Marley, with Ruka totally killing it when it was her turn to do the rap. It felt amazing when people got up and danced to our song. When our song ended, we received a deafening applause. I passed the mic to Terry, who sang *Lady in Red* in a deep baritone, all the while looking at me. So yes, I was wearing a red top – but *ugh*, it was so irritating! Even if I weren't already in a relationship, i.e. so not interested, singing that song to me would still have been off-putting. I kept my eyes glued to the screen the whole time, pretending he wasn't singing to me, while everyone looked at me and smiled indulgently: that "Aww, aren't you the lucky one" smile. As the night progressed and inhibitions slowly dissipated due to the increasing flow of alcohol, we were all singing and dancing to every song, even the Chinese ones. I sang so loudly that I lost my voice and at one point Ruka, and I may have danced on the tables. Now I was paying for it.

   I lifted my head off the pillow with some effort. Swinging my legs off the bed, I reached under my pillow for my phone; it was off: dead battery. I plugged it into its charger and stuck it back under my pillow. Dragging my bucket and shower bag from under my bunk, I fled to the bathroom, praying that the taps would run today. It took me twenty minutes to get dressed and rush off to my class. In my hurry, I forgot to take my phone with me.

   I was glad not to miss my morning lecture as only a handful of students had made it there, and the lecturer was only too happy to give an impromptu test. Monday is typically a hellish day for me; I was now in my fourth year, and on Mondays, I had lectures all through the day with a thirty-minute break around noon. I didn't get back to my room until half past six where I found Wale stretched out on my bed. I reacted the same way I did every time I saw him. My legs felt a little weak and I was overcome by a warm and fuzzy feeling. My face broke out into a huge smile, but he didn't smile back.

   "Hey, what's up?" I asked, racking my brains for what the problem could be. I wondered if he was going to make a habit of showing up in my room unannounced.

   "Can we talk somewhere private?" he asked, looking at me for the first time since I came in. Without waiting for my response, he stood up and walked out of the room.

   My roommates were in and regardless of the demarcated corners for each student, privacy was an issue. At that moment I could feel three pairs of eyes watching me; I looked at one of my roommates, needing some reassurance or clue as to what I was missing, but she shrugged and mouthed "Sorry". I squared my shoulders and threw my head back. I feigned indifference, but Wale's demeanour was so dark and cold that I quaked inside, afraid that whatever he had to say to me was not going to be good.

"Erm, sure, I just need to get changed first," I said to buy myself some time.

"That won't be necessary, what I have to say won't take long. Come on, let's go." He snapped his fingers.

Did he just snap his fingers at me? Anger was fast replacing fear. I marched to the door, but he was already walking away, and my first instinct was to walk faster – to run, even – to catch up with him, but I decided that since he was beginning to piss me off, I would enjoy doing the same to him. So I took my time and walked as slowly as I could, even stopping to say hello to a couple of people. I saw him stop a few times, a look of helpless frustration on his face, and I walked even more slowly.

"Yo!" a familiar voice called from behind me. It was Deji. I had been so preoccupied that I had walked right past him. "Hey!" I called out, wincing at how high-pitched my voice was.

"What's up, baby girl?" He grabbed me in a bear hug, lifting me off the ground, and then planted a fat kiss on my cheek. "You look like you need a drink. Come on; I've got a bottle of Baileys in my room – I know that's what you like."

I smiled. At that moment I wished I could drop everything and follow Deji to his place.

"Tempting, but maybe some other time." I disentangled myself from his embrace. "Aren't you visiting some chick?"

"Yeah, but you're better company any day," he replied, tickling me. From the corner of my eye, I could see Wale storming towards us, looking for all the world like a volcano about to erupt. I could imagine how this scene must look to him, although he'd met Deji a few times and he knew we were old friends. Deji spotted Wale approaching and took a step backwards, holding his hands in the air, smiling sheepishly.

"Later, I have to go," I smiled apologetically and rushed to ward off Wale. "Hey, sorry," I muttered and walked past him, down the two flights of stairs from my floor to the ground floor and along the corridor that led to the hall gate. When we got outside, he led me to his car, and we sat in silence: me, wondering what was up and in a turmoil inside, and him kneading his forehead with his knuckles.

"I understand your need for independence and I love that you have a carefree attitude – I mean, that's what attracted me to you," he started slowly. "But the fact that I'm so accepting doesn't give you the right to treat me this way."

I looked at him, puzzled. What?

"Where is all this coming from?"

"I just feel like I'm hanging on to you; it's almost as if you don't want to be with me."

I swallowed. "Okay," I said slowly, "please answer my question."

"You want to know where this is coming from?" He sighed. "You never put me first. It's always Tobi or Deji or Monica, there's also the way you are with other guys. If I treated any of my female friends the same way, you'd scream my head off, but just the other day I saw you jump on that idiot's back, prancing around the place like kids." He gesticulated angrily.

"Who? Deji? Please don't call him an idiot; this is between you and me."

"See, you're defending him now, even though our relationship is at stake."

"Is it? I thought things were fine with us until you showed up spewing fire and brimstone."

"So you think things are fine when you act as though you're not in a relationship? Like your actions affect no one else. Do you even consider how I feel?"

"I'm slightly confused here. We spend almost every day together, and we're always happy, we have fun, so yes, I think things are fine."

"Okay, just answer one question. Where were you last night?"

I paused for a second before answering; I wondered what he was getting at, how much he knew and how much information to give.

"Tobi and I went to a karaoke club," I answered, looking him in the eye.

"By yourselves?"

"We always go by ourselves," I lied, a little awkwardly.

"Why didn't you tell me you were going out then?"

"I'm sorry, I didn't know I had to inform you of my every move; it was a spur of the moment thing. Tobi came over, and we were bored so we went for a drive and ended up there." I noticed that his breathing was beginning to slow down; he looked convinced. He took off his glasses and wiped his palm across his eyes.

"That makes sense. What I don't get is why you didn't pick up your phone. I called you several times, but your phone kept ringing off and then today I simply couldn't get through to you. I was going crazy with worry. What happened? Why weren't you picking up your phone?" His voice was gentler, but I could sense his agitation. How would I feel if I tried calling him once and he didn't pick up or call me back within the hour? I could imagine what he had been through, waiting for me to call him back, repeatedly trying to reach me. With my overactive imagination, I would imagine all sorts of scenarios. I would have shown up to his room with a machete expecting to find a bevvy of naked ladies feeding him grapes and strawberries dipped in chocolate while he lay – naked, of course – on a chaise longue glorying in all the nudity and attention. I mean, what else would keep him away from me?

"Oh, no." I covered my mouth with my palm. "I'm so sorry, I didn't hear my phone ringing in the club, and I forgot to take it to class with me this morning."

He sighed. "Even if you didn't hear your phone ring, didn't it occur to you that I would have been trying to reach you? The least you could have done was call me. This just proves how little my feelings are worth to you."

We fell silent. I totally got why Wale was upset but wasn't he milking it just a little bit? Even after two years, I would be the first to admit that I don't have a great handle on the relationship etiquette, the "what not to do's". I thought the whole point of a relationship was to have fun, to enjoy each other's company and make out a lot. When had it become so serious? I fidgeted; this wasn't what I wanted to be doing right now. I had had a long night and slept very little. I wanted to be cuddled up with him, laughing and joking, not arguing just because I hadn't called him last night or this morning.

"I really am sorry," I said, making an effort to bridge the gap that was yawning between us; I stroked the side of his face and tickled his ear. "I'll make an effort next time."

"That's the thing," he said, halting the hand that was stroking his face and pulling it down to my lap. "I shouldn't always have to try and get you to make an effort; it should come naturally to you. You should be attuned to my feelings by now. I think that maybe we should take a break." He paused, just in time to hear my heart shatter into several unidentifiable pieces. "Just for us to put things in perspective. I want to be in a relationship with someone I know feels the same way about me, not someone who treats other guys with more consideration than me. I thought we were made for each other, but now I'm not sure."

I didn't want to believe that he thought this was the solution. I was convinced he was only doing this to get back at me for what he must have been through last night. How did we go from intense bliss to this? I couldn't imagine my life without Wale, and I couldn't accept it. This wasn't right.

"Just like that?" I asked. "How can you throw away what we have because of something so little?"

"I couldn't sleep a wink last night. Look at me. I'm a wreck! And all the while you were too busy having fun to think of me even once. I can't keep putting myself through that! You don't have the right to keep doing that to me." His eyes were bulging from their sockets. I shook my head. Nothing was right; it couldn't just end like this. I struggled to pull myself together. No matter what happened, he was not going to see me cry.

"Okay," I said, taking a deep breath. "So what happens next? Do we date other people?"

"Oh gosh," he muttered, and a couple of stray tears rolled down his face. He wiped them away angrily. "Do you want to date other people?"

Stupid question, I would die before I saw myself with someone else.

"I just want to know where we stand now," I said, my voice catching.

"We're on a break; you can do whatever you want. It's up to you."

I nodded, waiting for it to sink in. I wished I could turn back time, go back to last night. I would have stayed in my room if I had known this was going to happen. It just didn't seem real; I felt as if I were watching us, detached from the heartrending pain I should be feeling, from the tears that should have blinded me, the pleas that should have been flowing from my lips. I would promise never to leave him, to stop going out, even, to stop talking to any other man apart from my family: anything to make him take back the words he had spoken. I knew that sooner or later the pain would be excruciating, but the most important thing now was that I delayed the pain, that I leave with my dignity. I had made a promise to myself never to love a guy more than he loved me and even if I did, to never show it. He would never know how much he was hurting me right now. It crossed my mind that maybe he wanted me to plead, that he didn't really mean for us to go our separate ways, that he just wanted some kind of reassurance, some sort of sacrifice. Maybe even to gain the upper hand in the relationship, to be the man and not the one always pining for attention, always seeking me out. He could still take back those words, spoken with casual pretence; it wasn't too late. But what if he didn't? What if I begged and pleaded but he remained adamant? Or worse, if he listened to my pleas and we didn't break up, but he treated me with less respect and criticising everything I did, always threatening to end the relationship? If this was a bluff, then I was going to see it through, in the same way, you shouldn't give in to blackmailers and terrorists. I knew that if Wale was bluffing and I fell for it, he would always hold the power, the axe, always threatening to let it drop to keep me in line. I wasn't sure I wanted to live like that. I sighed heavily and took hold of his hand.

"Is this what you want? I want you to look deep down; don't you think this is a bit extreme?"

He was silent, reflecting on my question; I was giving him a chance to take back his words.

"I've had a long time to think about it. I'm not doing this to punish you, I just need to regain control over my life and set my priorities in order, and I think you need to do the same."

"I see." I let go of his hand and got out of his car, not knowing if my legs would function properly but needing to get somewhere private, where I could wail, and no one would hear me. If I went back to my room, I would be bombarded with questions, and I wouldn't be able to cry in peace. I walked, tired and dejected, in the direction of the hall and at the back of my mind I registered that Wale had started up his car and was driving away.

"Hey!" I heard, in a familiar voice. I turned round to see Deji walking behind me; he caught up with me and tugged my arm. "Come on," he said, nodding his head in the direction of his car.

"Look, Deji, I'm not in the mood, I just want to be alone." I tried to pull my arm away, but he wouldn't let go.

"I know," he said.

"What? What do you know?" I was beginning to lose control, and the tears were threatening to free-fall.

"Come on, I'll take you to my place, I can leave you alone there if you want but you don't want to stay here, and I know you don't want to go back to your room."

I nodded and allowed him to lead me to his car, and as soon as I sat down in the creamy soft leather interior, the dam burst, and I broke down in tears. He let me cry and didn't interrupt my wailing.

"Would you like me to leave?" he asked when we got to his place. He lived in the boys' quarters of his parent's house.

"No, please don't." I didn't want to be alone.

"How did you know?" I asked while he poured me a large glass of Baileys with ice.

"Hmm, know what?" he asked distractedly, handing me my drink and settling into the sofa beside me.

"How did you know to show up when you did? How did you know what I needed?" I turned my head sideways to look at him. I could just imagine how I looked, with tears and snot smeared all over my face.

"I was about to leave when I noticed that you guys were sitting in the car. I mean, I'd seen his face in the corridor, it looked like trouble was brewing, so I decided to wait to see if you were okay."

"Well, thank you," I said, more than a little taken aback. "My hero." I sniffed. I sipped from my glass and put it down. "Do you mind if I just lie down?" I got up and walked to his bed, curling up on it like a ball and hugging my knees.

"So do you want to talk about it?" Deji asked, coming to sit by me on the bed. He rubbed my back in a circular motion.

"It's over; he broke up with me." I rocked myself back and forth, staring into space.

"No! Why?"

"He feels I don't love him enough," I said, shrugging.

"That's just stupid; anyone with eyes can see that you do," he said.

"I know." I was glad to have Deji on my side. "Thanks again, you're the best," I told him before I tucked my head into the crook of my arm and a fresh batch of tears flowed down my face.

CHAPTER 17

I spent the night at Deji's place, sleeping in the same curled-up position. It stopped being comfortable at some point, but I didn't have enough strength to change position. I dreamt that I was at a wedding – then I realised that it was my wedding. I looked resplendent in a figure-hugging champagne lace and satin wedding dress with a lace halter-neck collar; I had fresh orange blossoms in my hair and wore lovely pearl earrings. The church was decorated with beautiful white flowers, and the sun was shining brightly through the massive church windows. My dad was walking me down the aisle, and I was euphoric. However, when we got to the altar, I tried to look into my groom's face, but I couldn't see who it was. He was protesting that he had been given the wrong bride. I glanced around, confused, and when I turned back around, my groom had morphed into a Billy goat and was trying to eat my dress. I screamed and turned around in panic, with the intention of running into my father's arms, but he had also transformed into a goat, as had the congregation who were bleating serenely through a hymn. I opened my eyes slowly; my head was groggy from the dream, and it throbbed from crying too much. My body ached from sleeping in the same position for nine hours. Deji had slept on the couch in the living room and from the snoring coming from that direction clearly he was still asleep.

I got up and stretched; our first class was at 10 a.m., and it was now 8 a.m. I walked on bare feet to the living room and nudged Deji with my knee. The snores stopped immediately, and he opened one eye and smiled at me, but then he turned over on his side and resumed sleeping.

"Hey." I nudged him again. "We have Dr Williams this morning, and I need to get to my room so I can have a shower and get changed."

He groaned and turned to face me. "Why don't you have a shower here? Then I'll take you to get a change of clothes. Wake me up in an hour, not a minute before. I need my beauty sleep." He pulled the pillow from beneath him and placed it on his head, keeping it in place with both arms.

I made my way back to the bedroom and fished out a towel from his wardrobe. I sniffed it just to be sure. I had a shower and put my old clothes back on, feeling a little out of sorts and uncomfortable. I picked up Deji's Bible from the bedside table and read it until I decided it was time for Deji to get up. This time, I didn't give him any chances of going back to bed. When I got to my room to change, I was relieved to find that none of my roommates were in; I wasn't in the mood to answer any questions about Wale's strange behaviour last night. I changed into my favourite pair of jeans, tight and low –slung, with a flowery off-shoulder blouse that showed a small line of flesh between the bottom of my top and my jeans. I put on makeup and perfume and hurried outside, where I jumped into Deji's car. I could hardly concentrate in class. I felt as if my life was over and I was only just existing; it wasn't possible to live like this, with this much pain. The worst part was that Wale and I were in the same faculty, and we took a few lectures together, so I knew I was going to bump into him regularly. I could imagine the smug look on Sade's face, the superior attitude that she had outstayed me, albeit as a friend rather than a girlfriend, and I envied her that position, the same one for which I had pitied her. At least she got to be with the one she liked even though he didn't feel the same way about her. I would have gladly taken that position with Josh then if I'd had the chance. Feeling the pain from my break-up with Wale blurred any kind of feeling I might have had for Josh now. Wale! Oh, my Wale! Why? Why didn't you just hold on a little longer, why did you have to be so bloody insecure? I knew it was my fault that he had broken up with me; if I only I had been a better girlfriend.

After the lecture, Monica cornered me.

"What's up with you? I've been calling your phone, and it was switched off. Then I tried calling Wale, and he said he hadn't heard from you either – and he didn't sound too bothered about it. And then this morning you walk in with Deji. Deji!" she stressed, her eyes wide and assuming. "Can you tell me what the hell is going on?"

I didn't know how to respond. I cast my eyes down, trying not to cry, but a few stray tears struggled free.

"What did you do?" Monica grasped my shoulders and peered more closely into my face. "No," she exclaimed. "You didn't?"

"What? No, of course not." I sniffed, brushing her hands off my shoulders. I didn't have to be able to read Monica's mind to know she meant had I done anything with Deji. As if!

"Then what is it? What happened?"

I wanted to tell her, but I couldn't. In the light of day, it was easy to ignore the pain, to pretend that it hadn't happened – but to give her the details now was to bring it all crashing back in. I shook my head and brushed the tears from my face. I took a large breath and blurted it out. "Wale broke up with me, and I don't really feel like talking about it right now, please, I hope you understand."

Monica nodded, but I knew she was far from satisfied; I could sense a million questions bubbling beneath her inquisitive eyes.

"But you didn't cheat on him right?"

I knew she couldn't help herself, but I had to resist the urge to punch her. I shot her a sharp look, and she held up her hand in surrender. Just then Deji walked up to join us, and I was relieved; I really liked Monica, but she wasn't the sensitive type.

"Hey, Mon, looking good as usual," he said in a husky tone, eyeing her suggestively.

Monica smiled and slapped him playfully on his arm; then she lowered her eyes and peered at him through her eyelashes. "You're not looking too bad yourself; I see you've been taking care of my friend." I pinched her in her side to shut her up, but she ignored me. "You guys just be careful. He's a male prosy, and she's on the rebound." She said this pointing to each of us respectively as she spoke, with emphasis on the pronouns. I smacked her on the back of her head, and she tackled me playfully.

"Come on, girls, stop fighting over me, there's enough of the Love Doctor to go round." Deji picked me up and flung me over his shoulder, ignoring my loud squeals and kicks.

"Miss Heartbreaker here and I have to go get some breakfast; we haven't had anything since last night. Damn, I'm hungry. You're welcome to join us if you want," he called to Monica over my bum, but she just laughed and shook her head.

"Okay, put me down, you monkey," I protested, conscious that the entire faculty had a good view of my behind.

"I have a good mind to take you round campus like this," he joked, his hands holding onto my thighs, dangerously close to my bum.

"You wouldn't dare," I gasped.

"Suit yourself." He walked down the corridor, and I resorted to pleading, knowing from experience that mock anger wouldn't work. A cluster of guys sitting on the field facing us whistled and cheered, and a couple of girls stared openly at us, hissing and shaking their heads. Thankfully Deji put me down before we left the faculty.

We had breakfast in the small eatery lodged between the cyber café and the stationery shop in the mini-shopping complex on the other side of the Arts Theatre. When we had eaten, we walked to my Hall, and I ran to my room to get my phone while Deji waited for me outside the gates. But when I got to my room I couldn't find my phone. None of my roommates were in so I assumed one of them had unplugged it and was keeping it safe for me. I didn't think any more about it as I ran back out to join Deji and we walked to our next class. I struggled to push my relationship break-up to the back of my mind and tried to pay attention during my lectures that day but at one point I lost it completely, and I had to hide my face with my notebook as the tears trickled silently down my face. I bit my lip hard to bring my tears under control, but I only made it worse as my brain played back the events the night before. Deji patted my back; he looked at me with so much concern and it took a lot of willpower not to burst into loud sobs of self-pity. I had one more lecture before I was done for the day but I didn't have the strength to sit through it. When class ended, I left for my room where I lay on my bed staring at the ceiling, my stomach churning at the thought of going through another day without Wale.

When my roommates got back in, I asked them about my phone, but none of them had any idea where it was. I was frantic; I only had a vague idea about how much phones cost and I knew I couldn't afford one. Crap, who could have stolen my phone? I had lost my boyfriend and now my phone was stolen; what more could go wrong? I lay on my bed and cried my eyes out. My roommates tried to console me that the phone would turn up. Yeah right! I wasn't sure if I was crying because of Wale or because of the phone; I just felt downright miserable and alone. With my phone, I could have called someone if I needed to talk, but now I had to go and look for someone to talk to in their rooms where they could either have guests or have gone out. The unfairness of my situation was overwhelming, and it caused me to cry even more. If I told my father, he would get me a new phone –but even this thought didn't cheer me up. He had enough on his plate without having to worry about a careless daughter.

Around 8 p.m., there was a knock on the door. A part of me wanted to ignore it; I was the only one in, and my roommates had left me wallowing in self-pity. I opened the door, and my heart stopped. It was Wale, looking as if he had never left. What did he want? Did he want me back? Had he come to apologise? For all the emotions I experienced when I opened the door, I wished he'd come at a better time. My eyes were probably red and swollen from crying and I could just imagine the smudges around my eyes; it was very likely that my tears had succeeded in painting my face with the mascara that had been intended for my lashes. I pursed my lips and held my head up; I was crying because I had lost my phone, not because he'd broken up with me.

"Hey, can I come inside?" he asked, avoiding my eyes. For a wild second, I felt hope bubbling up within me and it took all I had to suppress a smile. He'd realised that he couldn't live without me and had come to ask me to take him back, to forget about the indefinite time-off period he had proposed barely twenty-four hours earlier. I nodded and moved aside to let him in. My eyes fell to the bag he carried slung over his shoulder and the hope bubbling in my chest burst, releasing a coldness that spread through me, numbing my limbs so that for an instant I stood frozen. I stared in disbelief. So this was it: he had cleared out my things from his room. For some reason, this hurt even more than when he had told me he wanted a break. How hard had it been for him to clear me out of his life, to erase what we had and pretend it was just one of those things? Maybe it was easy for him to move on, but it was the first time I had truly had my heart broken, and to make matters worse, I couldn't help feeling like I could somehow have avoided this. My stomach twisted with guilt; it was all my fault.

"Erm, I just wanted to drop this off," he said, handing me the bag. "Don't feel like you have to return any of my things."

"No, no, it's fine," I insisted, my voice breaking. "Thanks for bringing them over; I'll get your things, just give me a minute." I took the bag with shaky hands and turned my back to him to hide the pain reflected in my eyes. I was choked up, and I resisted the urge to gasp for air. "Breathe, Jade, breathe," I willed myself. I emptied the bag of my things and proceeded to fill it with the little bits and bobs I had borrowed from him over the years. I picked up his green t-shirt from among my pile of clothes and resisted the urge to sniff it. I had worn it the last time I had spent the night in his room. I shook my head to get rid of my memories from that night; the t-shirt in question was hiked up to my neck as his wet tongue flicked around my erect nipples, and I was arching my back and moaning as I stroked his beautiful, clean-shaven head. I felt his eyes boring into me, and I wondered if he was thinking about that night as well. I sighed as I picked up his big black and red headphones and stuffed them in the bag, along with his socks, a Tom Clancy book... I was startled out of my reverie by the sound of someone clearing their throat. I was so engrossed that I hadn't heard anyone come in. I looked up to see Deji hovering in the doorway.

"Hey," he greeted us.

"Hey," I responded in a low voice, smiling weakly at him. I felt a little relieved. Even though I was glad to be near Wale, it was too much of an effort pretending that I didn't want to leap into his arms.

"Do you want me to come back later?" Deji asked, half-turning away from the door.

"Yes," Wale answered.

"No," I said at the same time, while Deji stood there, looking from Wale to me. I could see the question in his eyes; he was wondering what was going on and if it would be safest not to interfere. Wale narrowed his eyes at me; annoyance and irritation at Deji's presence were written clearly on his face.

"Okay," Deji said. "I brought food; I figured you hadn't had anything to eat since breakfast, but I wouldn't want to interrupt anything. I'll just leave these here and see you later." He held up a bulging plastic bag and even though the last thing on my mind was food I welcomed the distraction.

"No, stay, please. Wale brought my stuff back and is just leaving with his," I said, relieved that Deji's presence would prevent me hurling my dignity out the window by begging Wale to come back to me. A part of me wanted to hurt him as much as he had hurt me. I looked at him, his eyes narrowed, and he looked from me to Deji and back again.

"Thanks again for taking the time to drop off my things," I said as if I were talking to a stranger. My smile didn't reach my eyes as I zipped the bag shut and handed it over to Wale. He looked at me for what seemed like a lifetime but which was in reality probably less than ten seconds, nodded, took the bag from me and left without a word. I stared after him longingly, wishing I could call him back, but it was too late. Even if I did, he wouldn't come back. I loved him, and I had lost him.

"Sheesh, you could have cut the tension between you two with a freaking knife. What the hell was that about?" Deji came to sit at the desk by my bed.

"Why does love have to be so hard?" I sighed, and Deji threw his head back, laughing.

"You're just a pair of horny teenagers. Don't worry; you'll get over it soon enough. Trust me, I know." He pulled out a couple of large sausage-shaped foil-covered wraps from the plastic bag. "You know the saying; the best way to get over a guy is to get under another one? Well, it's kind of true." He winked at me.

"Wait a minute." I laughed dryly as his words finally sank in. "Don't tell me you're offering your stud services? Dude, that's low, even for you." I grabbed one of the wraps and peeled off the foil, letting the delicious aroma waft through the room. I still wasn't hungry, but the shawarma smelt really good.

"Well, a guy can only dream," he replied grinning.

"You should be ashamed of yourself. I'm not even single for a second, and you're already trying to get in there." I tutted at him. "Anyway, I was never under Wale, so that saying doesn't apply to me." I blurted out before taking my first bite of the heavenly shawarma: hmm, yum. I felt a trickle slide down the side of my mouth, and I reached for one of the paper towels that had come with the food and dabbed it off quickly. I noticed Deji staring at me.

"What?" I asked, wondering if I had anything on my face. I dabbed my mouth again to make extra sure that I got all the shawarma juice.

"You know, you don't have to tell me anything, that's your business, but I'm surprised you feel the need to lie about that. It's the twenty-first century; nobody will judge you."

"Hmm?" I still had some food in my mouth so I held up my hand as I swallowed. "Oh, of course not. It's alright; I don't have to prove anything to you. We just never got to that stage, you know. We were taking things slow."

"So you never... you know, did it?"

"Nope." I shook my head, taking another juicy bite.

"Wow, you guys are like always all over each other, I just assumed... good on you then." He smiled. "You can start over with a clean slate."

I took a break from my chewing and swallowed hurriedly.

"Yeah right, like there is such thing as a clean slate," I argued. "Everyone has some sort of baggage. From the moment we come into this world, other people's thoughts and opinions are imposed on us. We all carry around some form of hurt, from our parents or from some other person's experience. I will always carry around this bruised heart. The reason this happened is entirely my fault! I just keep thinking, you know, what if I hadn't been too cautious, too afraid to show him and tell him how I felt? And all because some silly crush I had a long time ago." The words were flowing freely, and I was afraid that the tears would follow. Deji knew about Josh.

"You're way too hard on yourself. You can't blame yourself for what happened: Wale broke up with you, remember? He could have tried to work things out with you, he could have tried to get to the bottom of the matter if he really wanted to make the relationship work, but he chose to let you go, for whatever reason he conjured up in his thick skull. Let me ask you this. Before last night, did he ever raise an issue about how you felt for him?"

"Um... no, I don't think so." I sniffed.

Deji raised his hands and dropped them again as if I had just proved his point. "I mean, who does that? No warning, no indication that he was unhappy and then boom, out of the blues, he wants a break. Please, you deserve better than that."

I sighed. "I wish there was some way I could turn back time. I keep thinking I could have done things differently..."

Deji got up and paced the small length of my corner.

"I'm just going to stop you there. You shouldn't change the way you are for anybody; I know there's someone out there who will respect the fact that you've been hurt before and is, therefore, cautious instead of punishing you for it. Someone who will be able to communicate his feelings better seeing as you have a hard time expressing yours."

"Wow, Deji, I really appreciate the pep talk, but I still feel it's up to me to make it better." I pushed my food away, slightly frustrated. "Maybe I can convince him that I can change. You know, I need to stop flirting with other guys, and I need to be less afraid of showing my feelings. I mean, what's the worst that could happen?" I laughed mockingly. "You show your feelings and get heartbroken, but you still get heartbroken when you hide the way you feel." I looked up at Deji, and he looked just as frustrated as I felt.

"You know what? Fine! Do whatever you want. You can call him right now and ask him to take you back. Let me know how it goes and I will be glad for you but be sure that you'll be okay for him to have all the control. All he has to do next time is threaten that the relationship is over, and he'll have you hopping on one foot," he said, glowering at me.

I shook my head slowly. "I'm sorry; I didn't mean to upset you. It's just so painful, I didn't think it possible to feel this much pain and still be alive." I choked back the tears that were threatening to fall. They were in constant supply these days, always showing up when they weren't needed. I looked up at Deji hoping to get some sympathy, but the look he gave me was more irritated than anything else. I knew he was right, but his attitude was beginning to annoy me. At that moment I just wanted to be alone. Deji had always been my fun buddy, someone to make jokes and get slightly tipsy with; I didn't like this serious side to him.

"You look tired, maybe it's unfair of me to go on about this now, but trust me, you'll get over him soon enough." He gathered up the leftover food and wrappings and chucked them in the bin by my wardrobe. "You should get some rest; I'll see you in class tomorrow." He dropped a kiss on my forehead and left me to my pain and self-pity. I lay down on my bed and pulled my pillow over my face. "Please let this pain pass quickly," I prayed silently. Now that I was alone, I wished that I had someone to talk to. And then I remembered that my phone was missing; I couldn't have felt more alone.

CHAPTER 18

"Oh no, that's a shame," Tobi said, her lips curling up into a small smile when I told her about my break-up with Wale. It was Friday evening, four days since the break-up; the pain was still as sharp as ever. Tobi had come to spend the weekend with me on campus. She had been worried when she couldn't reach me on my mobile and had rushed down to Lagos as soon as she could, or so she said. I was always happy to have her around; she had such a joie de vivre that it was hard not to get caught up in it.

"Yeah, don't sound too sad about it!" I said.

"Oh, honey, I'm sorry, but Wale always rubbed me up the wrong way. I know you can do better."

"Ugh, not you too. Anyway, you never liked Wale cos he thinks you're a bad influence on me."

We were sitting on the raised platform in the middle of my hall. It looked more like a concrete stage, and this was where all the hall activities took place: the beauty pageants, award and music shows, or promotions. I preferred staying in bed with a good Marian Keyes or Fiona Walker book or making out with my boyfriend... sob, ex-boyfriend but since I didn't have a TV in my corner, this was Tobi's favourite spot whenever she came to visit. It was the ideal place for people-watching and Friday evening was the best time for it. We'd sat in this spot on countless occasions, watching boys loitering outside particular girls' rooms for ages before being allowed to come in, or watching barely clothed girls run outside to rendezvous with their married lovers waiting outside in their cars. On a few occasions, we'd caught the odd fight between girls who just found out they had the same boyfriend or best friends fighting over money or borrowed clothes; it could be anything, and it mostly happened on Friday nights.

Music blared from every corner; giving off a bubbly and carefree vibe. The weather was beautiful that evening: not so cold that you would need a sweater, but not too warm: just perfect. A handful of stars outshine the artificial lights and can still be seen twinkling beautifully in the sky.

"I saw that girl, Aisha, in Chief Okosu's hotel last week," Tobi said, pointing at a beautiful girl with flawless caramel skin and long black hair which fell in waves around her shoulders. As she strutted past us, her hips swaying with calculated rhythm, I spotted the designer label on her bag: it was Chanel, and she was wearing a pair of black high heels with the signature red Louboutin soles. She drove a shiny black RAV-4 and even though I would never admit it, I felt something close to envy when I saw her driving around campus. I imagined myself with a car like that someday.

"Really?" I said, interested in any gossip I could glean about her.

"Yup and boy, is she a dominatrix," Tobi smiled when she noticed my jaw on the ground.

"No way! How do you know? Give me details."

"Well..." She arranged herself in a conspiratorial position. "She came in with the Chief's friend, a high-ranking naval officer o, hmm and you should have seen the way she ordered him about the place. The guy was literally hanging on to her every word."

"Wow, to think that this man probably has a wife and kids at home, such a shame." I waited for a reaction from Tobi, but she was too caught up in the gossip to pick up on my sarcasm.

"Yeah, she really had this guy wrapped around her finger..." She had a gleam in her eye. "It got me thinking; maybe I need to find out who her guy is? Do you think I should go and ask her?"

I didn't really understand that statement; it sounded a bit odd. Maybe Tobi was joking.

"Wouldn't that be a dumb thing to do?" I said hesitantly. Maybe there was some kind of freaky Tobi I hadn't been introduced to.

"What?" She had a faraway look in her eyes, but then her eyes widened, and she jolted out of her reverie. "Oh, yes. Of course." She blinked as if she'd suddenly realised who she was with. "Yeah, idiotic." She smiled, looking like someone who had just narrowly dodged a bullet. She was hiding something, but I let it go.

"So you and Wale are like, totally over?" she asked, changing the subject.

"Um, well." I twiddled my fingers. "He said he wanted a break, just to get things into perspective." And I had been doing just that, trying to figure out ways to change to please him.

"Yes, perspective... always a handy thing to have." She chuckled, slapping her palm on her thigh. "The reason I ask is that Ian and Terry are coming to take us out. Are you up for it?"

"Nope, that's what got me into this mess in the first place," I said, alert. Knowing Tobi, she was going to find a way to make me go, and I wanted to ensure I could smack down any points she raised.

"I dig that, but it will be fun; you need to let your hair down a little."

"I always let my hair down, and I like having a good time, but I'm just not in the right frame of mind for hanging out with your Aristos."

"You don't have to do anything you don't want to do; I just don't want to leave you alone. I'll feel horribly guilty if I go without you." She thrust out her bottom lip.

"Don't go then, stay with me," I said, knowing it was futile. I realised with disappointment that Tobi hadn't really rushed down to Lagos because she was worried about me; she had come to have fun and make money at the same time. "We can talk all night and play cards or something."

"Yeah? So you can bore me to death talking about Wale? No thanks." She grimaced.

"No, I won't bore you, I promise, although that's all I seem to be able to think about right now." I cringed inwardly as my mind drifted back to Sunday night after we'd left the karaoke bar. Ian had refused to take me back to campus and had insisted on taking us to his hotel first. Obviously, that had been Tobi's plan all along, but I hadn't been aware. I couldn't afford a cab, so I was stuck with them. The cheapskate had got only one room, and I had to listen to them shagging on the bed while I suffered the humiliation of even being there in the first place and sleeping on the floor. I couldn't look either Ian or Tobi in the eye afterwards when they woke me up at 4 a.m. to drop me back on campus and to drop Tobi at the bus station to catch her bus back to Oyo in time for her lectures.

"I was only joking; you could never bore me, that's what I'm here for. I just think a few hours of escape from that over-analytic head of yours will do you some good." Then she grinned at me, that mischievous grin, signifying that she had something up her sleeve. "By the way, Terry has got the hots for you, like, really bad. Ian said he hasn't stopped talking about you after the other night. What did you do to the poor guy?"

"Me? Don't be silly."

"Well, you must have led him on in some way."

"What? Never!."

Tobi rolled her eyes. "So you say, Jade. You lead men on all the time." She laughed at me. "What with twirling your hair and jumping on their backs for a piggyback ride." She sniggered.

"I'll admit it's a little playful, but surely there's nothing sexual about it... is there?" Were my flirting and playfulness really that bad? I mean, I loved flirting with guys to make Wale jealous but did that also count as leading them on?

"What would you call what you did with Alex?" she quizzed me.

"Who is Alex?" I wrinkled my brows and pretended not to remember; I hoped Toby would let it go.

"The guy you met in Uncle John's house. You know, the Yankee that got down on his knees and begged you to touch his peepee," she said, giggling.

A long time after the incident with Alex, I had finally been comfortable enough to relate the incident to Tobi, but I'd left out some of the details I'd felt she didn't need to know. Like the part where I let him undress me.

"Okay, so I let myself get a little carried away," I said, shrugging. "But that was different. I let Alex know from the onset that nothing was going to happen." I cast my mind back to that day, and I distinctly remember uttering a "no" in the midst of all the cobwebs that clouded that particular scene.

"Uh, and at what point did you let him know? When you followed him into his room or when he was fondling your tits?"

"Okay, fine, can we just not talk about that day? I didn't mean to lead him on; I don't even understand how it happened.."

"You've just proved my point. You may lead guys on without meaning to, but it doesn't change the fact that you do lead them on. So you may have led Terry on without meaning to," she finished smugly.

"Okay, maybe I did. So do you think it would be wise for me to hang out with Terry again, knowing full well how it's going to end?" I folded my arms across my chest. She was clearly enjoying pissing me off. I mean, I had come to accept what she did for money, but was it really necessary for her to try and drag me into it?

"It's okay, Jade. Like I said, you don't have to come. In fact, I'll let Ian and Terry know that I changed my mind, that I'm going to stay here with you," she said, making an effort to placate me.

We sat in silence for a while, my mind wandering back to that afternoon with Alex and how it had felt to be wanted. A man had gotten on his knees begging me to touch him: a rich, good-looking guy at that... It had felt really good. It had made me feel like. Surprisingly, I hadn't felt any shame that I had gotten to third base with a man I didn't even know. It had felt good just to know that I had that much power over a man, albeit sexually. Maybe it wouldn't hurt to feel like that again, as long as I didn't let things get out of hand.

"You know what?" I started, and Tobi's face lit up with anticipation. "You're right. I need to get my mind off Wale, if only for a few hours."

"Atta girl!" she exclaimed, jumping up. "I knew you'd come around." She bared her teeth in a grin. "Come on; I have just the outfit for you." She waited for me to get up. I laughed, already getting caught up in her excitement.

"It's alright; I'm just going to wear my jeans and a ..."

"No way, you're not coming out with me in those jeans. Come on, get up, quickly, they'll be here any minute now."

CHAPTER 19

I was glad I'd gone out with Tobi. I was having a lot of fun. Maybe the fact that I was now single, and so I didn't have to look over my shoulder to see if any of Wale's friends were around helped. We went to Club 58, one of the "happening" clubs in Ikoyi. I was wearing a pink blouse with straps that wound around my waist, exposing my belly button, and a pair of skin-tight jeans that clung to my hips and was in danger of revealing my "builder's bum" when I walked.

Tobi had on a red ribbed boob tube that hiked up her considerably large chest, a pair of three-quarter-length black trousers and red high heels. She looked sensational and men stared at her as she swayed into the club.

We went right up to the VIP section; the men there were much older than we were and I spotted only a handful of boys around our age. The rich older men lounged about, talking to the young girls milling around the place as if they belonged there by right and not because they had come with men old enough to be their fathers. The VIP section was much nicer than the main club downstairs, which was overcrowded with sweaty bodies of teenage boys and girls humping, grinding and pushing each other to get some dancing room, the smell of cigarette smoke, perfume and body odour clinging to one's hair and skin. I wished I was down there, dancing senselessly to the music and not caring who saw, to do the Harlem shake and not worry that anyone would look at me funny. The people in the main club were there to have some fun while the VIP section just seemed superficial. The lights were on, albeit low, but you could see everyone in the large, plush room.

The girls who were brave enough to dance were being eyed by the other girls as if they were committing a faux pas. I recognised a few girls from my hall and smiled at one girl looking in my direction, but she turned away, blanking me.

Ian and Terry went to the bar to get drinks while Tobi and I sat on a sofa. I looked around, wondering how long it would be polite to wait before I could bolt downstairs.

"Hey, relax, you look like a deer caught in headlights," Tobi whispered. This was my first time in VIP, but I could bet N1000 of my meagre allowance that Tobi sat in VIP rooms all the time.

"Really?" I asked in mock surprise. "I thought I disguised it well."

"Just relax, okay? You have nothing to be worried about," she reassured me, patting my hand. "We'll leave whenever you want to; just say the word." She pursed her lips and raised her eyebrows, nodding her head. This was the look she gave whenever she was trying to be convincing: her "You can trust me, I'm in control" look. It might have fooled someone else, but I knew it was just an act. We would leave when she wanted to and not a minute sooner.

"Okay, thanks," I smiled at her. "So how long do we have to sit here?"

"What do you mean?" She narrowed her eyes at me. It occurred to me that she'd assumed I meant how long we had to stay in the club.

"This place is dull; I want to go downstairs."

"Oh!" Her face relaxed. "Let's wait till they get back from the bar. As soon as we've had a drink, we can ditch these old men." She winked.

"Nice." I sat back and tapped my heels on the carpet to the music, letting go for the first time since entering the club, relieved that we wouldn't have to wait too long in the stifling room.

As soon as Ian and Terry returned, bearing champagne bottles and glasses, we informed them of our plan. They didn't seem enthusiastic about it, and Terry insisted on coming along.

"I don't think that's a good idea, have you seen the state of that place?" I said. "Plus, you wouldn't be able to keep up with us."

I jumped up from the sofa, hitching my jeans up quickly to avoid exposing my builder's bum and Tobi got up gingerly; we blew kisses at the guys and left them nursing their champagne glasses.

Tobi and I went down the stairs to the club below; the music was so loud and enthralling that we moved to the beat, dancing with each step we took. This feels more like it, I thought, as we pushed our way onto the dance floor. Flashing lights picked up random movements and parts of bodies thrusting to the music. I glanced around, smiling to myself; on my left was a young couple trying to outdo each other, twisting, turning, stepping to the beat. Tobi and I danced together; Beyoncé's *Baby Boy* was playing, and half the girls, myself included, struggled to execute the moves she had displayed in the music video, twisting and wriggling our hips. Even the guys weren't left out; one on my left turned his back to his dance partner pushing his bum out, and wriggling his waist from left to right while his partner spanked his bum playfully.

"This is my song!" I shouted when Wyclef's *Perfect Gentleman* came on, amidst cheers from the crowds. I threw my hands in the air as I gyrated and sang along to the music. A guy in a green Ralph Lauren polo shirt snuck around Tobi, slyly elbowing her out of the way, and tried to sneak his arm around me. I shrugged him off.

"This isn't a slow song; keep up with me or get the hell out of the way," I screamed into his ear.

"Come on, baby. You can wriggle even better closer to me," my guy shouted back, and I got a whiff of his cologne. It was Hugo Boss, the same one Wale wore; the smell swirled around my brain, dulling my senses for a second. The second passed, and I felt the pain which had been absent all evening return in full force. I hesitated as the feeling of extreme loss reached out to me, pulling me slowly into the pain-induced state I had been in since Wale broke up with me. No, no, no; enough was enough. I was stronger than this, and I was going to push my heartache right out through my shoes. I smiled to myself as I resumed dancing. I took a closer look at my intruder. He wasn't bad looking; on the contrary, he was handsome, but I hadn't come to the club to get a man. I had come to get over one and to have fun. I wasn't ready to get tangled up in any relationship palaver. He persisted with his moves, trying to get really close, and at one point I could swear I felt something poking at me through his trousers. I continued shrugging him off as if it were part of my dancing.

"What's your name?" he asked. I guess the fact that I hadn't stormed off after having his "thing" brush against me might have seemed like a green light to him.

"Dude, I just want to dance, okay?" I said in between my hopping and stepping.

"That's okay," he shouted, to make his voice heard over the loud music. He leant into me once again and wrapped his hands around my waist, his fingers brushing against my bare midriff. "I really like you; you're not like any of the girls here. You look like you just want to have fun, and I dig that."

"Dig it a little farther away." Not that I minded the flirting, but he was really ruining my groove. I yanked his hands away roughly. This guy was not going to take no for an answer, and there was no point trying to dance while he continued harassing me. I decided to go look for Tobi so we could go back to Terry and Ian. "Excuse me," I said as I stepped around my harasser.

I found Tobi back in VIP.

"What happened to your boyfriend then?" she asked, laughing at me. From the amused expressions on their faces, I could tell she had told the guys about my persistent dance partner. I made a face.

"I don't understand," I said, laughing along with her. "The guy just refused to leave me alone; he was literally trying to hump me on the dance floor. I feel violated." I settled into the sofa next to Terry.

"You should have called me to save you," Terry said.

"Yeah, I should have; someone needs to kick his ass." I didn't know if I was more upset about the guy interrupting my dancing or his attempts to rub up against me. I hated the fact that I had had to cut my sojourn to the club downstairs short. Now I was stuck up here in the boring and pretentious section with guys I had nothing in common with. Would they think I was flighty if I decided to go back? If not, how much longer did I have to stay up here till it was less rude of me to take off? After a few minutes of half listening to Ian jabbering on about something, I decided I couldn't stand it any longer. If I'd wanted to sit down and listen to someone talk, I could have stayed in my room and listened to myself whine and moan about how much I missed Wale.

"Would you like to dance?" I asked, turning to Terry. I could avoid being rude and still enjoy myself. Terry looked surprised; I hadn't exactly been flashing the green light all evening.

"I don't know if you want to do that; I'll wipe the floor with you," he said, smiling.

"Is that so?" I grinned, loving the challenge. "Let's go; it is *so* on." I jumped off the sofa and pulled him up. Terry was tall and well-built, and he wore glasses which gave him a slightly dorky look. I'd never noticed how good-looking he was; whenever I'd looked at him in the past, all I had seen was a cheating disgusting man. Not like I was interested in him now, but being apart from Wale (and our overwhelming hormone-infused desire for one another) made me see things and people in a slightly different way. For instance, the girls I had viewed as evil, scheming bitches trying to steal my man away from me, I now saw as nice, fun-loving young girls just trying to get through life and having it no easier than I did.

I dragged Terry to the centre of the room where a handful of people were dancing rather self-consciously. There was no delegated space reserved as the dance floor, but it just seemed to make sense to me to move closer to the people dancing. Shine's *Get Out* was playing as we settled into our paces. I danced self-consciously, but Terry made it easier for me to let go. For an old guy, he really could move. He wasn't exactly doing a break dance or the Crip walk, but he moved in tune with to the beat. I slowly loosened up, becoming less aware of the glares from girls who I bet wished they could let go enough to have fun. We continued dancing until Tobi and Ian came to inform us that it was time to go. I was having so much fun dancing with Terry that I didn't notice that we had been dancing for almost two hours. My top was damp with sweat and my exposed skin glistened. Terry smiled at me, fanning himself with his palm.

"Wow, that was fun!" he exclaimed. "We should do that again."

"Not bad for an old man," I said, smiling. Tobi handed me my purse, and we proceeded to leave the club.

"Who are you calling an old man," Terry asked in mock horror. "Am I as old as your father?"

"You could pass for my father," I teased.

"Can you imagine? You small girls! So anyone above thirty is considered old? I have half a mind to bundle you up to my house to show you what an 'old' man like me can do." He exchanged amused looks with Ian.

"Ha-ha, you wish. Don't over-exert yourself trying to prove to anything to me." I said laughing. We had come in Ian's car, a black Jaguar, and I wasn't sure what the plan was. I wondered if Ian would mind dropping me off on campus because there was no way I was going with them to any hotel. I wasn't going to let anyone put me through that again.

"Hey, guys, I think I'll just get a cab back to campus," I said. I decided against asking directly for a ride and prayed that Ian would offer to drive me back since I didn't have enough money for a cab. Tobi shot me a loaded look, but I ignored her.

"Don't be silly; it's too late to get a cab. Why don't you come with us and we'll drop you off in the morning?" Ian said.

"No way, man, not after last time," I said, smiling. "But thanks for offering."

"You know you can always join us," Ian joked, winking at Tobi who stared stonily ahead. I wondered why she was upset. Sometimes she just pissed me off. I was the one facing the prospect of having to go back to campus in a cab at this time of the night with no money for the fare.

Terry pulled Ian to the side where they conversed in low tones.

"What's up with you?" I asked Tobi when the men were out of earshot.

"There's nothing up with me. What's up with you? Why do you always have to be so difficult? You had known the plan before we came out."

"What's the plan? Please tell me; another night of listening while a disgusting married man humps you all night? Look, you're my friend, and I love you, but I can't condone what you do. I understand why you do it even though I think there are other ways to make money without having to sell yourself. Don't go rubbing what you do in my face and believe that I will be okay with it. And just in case you don't know, there's nothing right about having sex with a third person in the room; it is just sick." I tried to keep my voice down, and I held my arms close to my sides and clenched my fists to avoid gesturing, which I did when I was upset. I didn't want the guys to know we were having an argument. How dare she think I was okay with all this bullshit? The fact that I had allowed her to persuade me to come out wasn't enough – she had to stick it in my face every time.

"If that's how you feel, then I guess I won't stop you from taking a cab," she said with considerable restraint. She turned away, and I could tell that, like me, she was fuming inside, but Terry and Ian had finished scheming and were now walking back towards us.

"Here's what we'll do," Ian said, slapping his palms and rubbing them together. "We'll drive down to Terry's place so that he can pick up his car and then he'll drop you off. Is that okay?"

I looked at Tobi, uncertain if it was a good idea to be left alone with Terry, but she didn't meet my eye. Her face was resolute as she stared at a spot in the far distance.

"Don't worry; I'm harmless. I'll just drop you off unless you say otherwise," Terry said, grinning. "Okay, let's get out of here."

We went to Terry's place, and he picked up his Porsche Carrera. I had never been in a Porsche and was a little overwhelmed. I sat on my hands feeling slightly uncomfortable. Here I was, alone in the car with a man I barely knew, who had made it plain that he wanted to sleep with me. Was I doing a stupid thing? Maybe I should have gone with Tobi.

"Hey, you can relax, do I look that scary?" he asked, and I shrugged.

"I got you something," he said, nodding towards the back seat. I looked behind my seat and saw a colourful paper bag. I picked it up and pulled out a box.

"Oh my God, you bought me a phone!" I exclaimed. It was a sleek yellow Nokia 3510i, and it actually had a colour display. Most of the students on campus had plain Motorola and Nokia monochrome phones.

"Tobi told me you'd lost your phone, so I took the liberty of getting you another one. There's an MTN SIM card in it. I've loaded it with N10, 000 credit."

My eyes widened: that was a lot more than my monthly allowance. What was the proper etiquette in this kind of situation? I didn't think it was right to accept it if I had no intention of doing anything with him.

"Look, Terry, this is really generous of you, but I don't think I can accept it," I said, turning around to place the bag back on the seat.

"It's fine. I'm giving it to you, no strings attached. You don't have to do anything you don't want to." He paused. "I really like you; you're gorgeous, smart and principled. I admire that... and you dance like a dream. I like that you speak your mind; your boyfriend sure is one hell of a lucky bastard."

My face grew hot beneath his praise. "Ex-boyfriend," I corrected him.

"Excuse me?"

"My ex-boyfriend; we broke up five days ago." Suddenly I found the pattern on my purse fascinating, and I fidgeted with the strap; I hoped he didn't take the fact that I was now single as a green light.

"Wow, I'm almost tempted to shout for joy, but I know it won't change anything between us. How do you feel?"

"You don't want to get me started... he was my first love," I sighed.

"Hmm... Was he also your first *'ahem'*." He mock-coughed.

"What? None of your business," I replied, not too harshly.

"Tell me about him; what was he like?"

I looked at him, wondering if he was really going to listen. My friends were sick of hearing me moan about Wale, so I welcomed the opportunity to talk about him. My handsome Wale, with his beautiful brown eyes that I could just fall into, his soft sensuous lips and his beautiful long fingers that wrapped around my waist when he held me.

I talked about Wale all the way to campus.

CHAPTER 20

"You're going on a date with Terry!" Monica exclaimed.

It was Tuesday afternoon. We had been slouched on Monica's bed watching a VCR on the small TV in her corner when my phone rang. Not many people had my new number so I had a good hunch who might be calling.

"Halloo," I answered.

"Hi, how are you doing?" a husky voice asked.

"I'm lovely, thanks. See, I knew you had an ulterior motive for giving me a phone."

"Ha, you got me... I won't call you if it bothers you, though." Terry laughed.

"No, it doesn't bother me. What are you up to?"

"I'm just leaving work. Are you busy? I feel like having Chinese food, but I'm not looking forward to eating alone. Would you mind keeping me company?"

"Hmm, that's sounds nice; I could do with some Chinese food," I said, laughing. "All you'll be getting is the company, though." I was already getting excited. Chinese restaurants in Lagos are expensive, and I loved Chinese food, so the thought of having some without having to pay for it was a very welcome prospect.

"Trust me; that's plenty. I'll pick you up at seven."

"See you then," I said, hanging up.

I turned to beam at Monica, who was sitting with her mouth open.

"It's not a date," I insisted.

"Who are you and what have you done with Jade?"

"Come on, Monica, don't go all judgmental on me; he only wants the company to go get Chinese."

"Why didn't he ask his wife?" She narrowed her eyes at me.

"It's not a date," I repeated. "I love Chinese food; andTerry is offering it with no strings attached. He's a really nice guy. You shouldn't put people in boxes. Just because he's married doesn't mean he can't have any female friends." I was trying to sound nonchalant, but I don't think Monica bought it.

"He bought you a nice phone with N10, 000 credit, and is taking you out to an expensive restaurant, and you really believe it's for nothing?" Monica was not letting me get away with this one.

"If it really is so innocent," Monica continued, "call your dad and tell him about Terry."

"We both know I'm not going to do anything that stupid. Not everything has to be black and white, and this is my grey area. Look, Monica, I know myself, and I trust myself. I know nothing is going to happen. I'm not going to get physical with him, and I have informed him several times of the fact. Whatever he gives me or does for me, he is well aware of what I can or can't offer him. And that's good enough for me." I sighed. "I guess I'm feeling a little battered and self-destructive, but you know me; I'm responsible so you'll just have to trust me."

"What about trusting him? You would be putting yourself in a compromising situation. God forbid, if anything should happen, if he were to turn out to be a rapist no one would believe that you hadn't gone along willingly."

I thought about what Monica said. No one would believe a girl who had been receiving gifts from a guy if she claimed that he'd raped her. Everyone would blame the girl for leading him on or would call her a liar.

"I hadn't thought of that." My face lit up as I thought of a way of rectifying the situation. "Why don't you come with us?" I suggested. I saw the excitement in her eyes even though she tried to act indifferent. Monica, like me, received only a small allowance from her parents and any opportunity to eat out was welcome.

"Are you sure he won't mind?"

"Well, he wanted company…" We chuckled.

It was when Terry called to say he was outside that it occurred to me that he might have come in his Porsche. I informed him that I had a friend coming with me. He didn't seem to mind. Unfortunately for Monica she had to curl up tight in the seat behind me.

We went to Golden Gate in Ikoyi. I had only been there a few times with my parents, and it made me feel slightly grown up to be there without them. We had a lovely meal, Monica and I being greedy and gorging till we could stuff no more food into our bellies. Terry charmed Monica so much that I could tell that she was no longer seeing him as an Aristo and more as a likeable personality. When we got back to the hall, Monica went ahead inside and left me alone with Terry in the car.

"Thanks, I had a great time and so did Monica," I said.

"My pleasure. I know Monica was supposed to be your bodyguard, in case I tried anything inappropriate." He smiled knowingly.

"I don't know what you're talking about," I laughed. "Why would I need a bodyguard with you?"

"Ah, don't worry, I understand these things. I think I passed this time; maybe next time she'll let me take you out alone," Terry said, looking into my eyes, and in spite of myself I felt a tiny shiver of excitement run through me.

"Erm…" I didn't know how to respond to that. Was that a blatant come-on? Or did he just want to spend time with me as a friend? My mind decided it had to be the latter because surely I couldn't keep hanging out with him if he kept coming onto me... that would be leading him on, and I so wasn't leading him on because he already knew where I stood in this relationship – or non-relationship. "I guess you'll have to ask her nicely?" I replied shyly, hoping it was the right answer. He threw back his head and laughed.

"Okay, thanks once again for dinner... and everything," I said, making a move to get out of the car. He leant towards me and kissed me on my cheek.

It was only the next day when I grabbed my bag on my way to class that I noticed the fat envelope in my bag. It contained N30, 000.

"Oh my God!" I screamed, alarming my roommates, one of whom upended the entire case of brown powder she was applying, over herself. They shrieked in response, in fear of whatever had made me scream, before asking me what was wrong. I laughed happily, telling them I'd thought I'd seen a rat, and I ran out of the room followed by their angry swearing.

I spent the first period daydreaming about how I would spend the money. As Professor Ade droned on about law, the individual and the state, I tried to keep my mind on what he was saying, but it was pointless. I made plans in my mind to go to Collectibles and Talk2me after school to buy some clothes. These two boutiques were the most popular among students who could afford them. I imagined myself in my new and expensive outfits; for once I wouldn't have to visit Yaba Market, the closest market to school, to buy my clothes. I always had to prepare myself mentally to go shopping in Yaba; the hustlers yanking at your arm from every side, trying to force you to look through their wares draped over their arms and shoulders, or the ones trying to get you to have a peek at questionable jewellery wrapped carefully in white handkerchiefs to give the illusion that the items were stolen goods and hence worth more than they would be sold to you for. Women, shouting in your face in Pidgin English, "Aunty, you want do your hair?" regardless of the fact that you're sporting a new hairdo. The pushing and the shoving, the irascible motorcyclists, inconsiderate of any road user except for their own kind, sometimes pinching your bum and speeding off through the bustling crowd causing people to jump and scream obscenities at their receding backs.

I dreamt of getting another pair of lovely low-rise jeans to give my favourite pair a break once in a while. Not once did I wonder why Terry was so generous when I wasn't giving him anything in return. He'd already said he liked me and wanted to take care of me. Not all men are monsters, I thought, and not everybody wants something in return for their acts of kindness. I'd called Terry on my way to class to thank him for the money, and he said he'd snuck the money into my bag because he knew I would have given him a hard time before taking it from him.

"What makes you think I need the money?" I asked. "I am perfectly content with what I have."

"You're so predictable,' he laughed, 'but one thing I know is that girls always need that lil' bit extra. I don't want you to lack for anything when I'm around to give it to you."

That was just what I needed: an open invitation to ask for anything I wanted and not to have to give up something for it. How many girls would kill to be in my shoes right now? I smiled, feeling smug.

I went shopping alone; I knew Monica would ask too many questions and read too much into what wasn't really a big deal. I had taken money from a married man who liked me – so what? It wasn't like I was doing anything wrong. I spent almost N20, 000 on clothes, shoes and accessories, and came out smiling. I even got a cab back to campus. It felt good not to have to check how much I had before getting into a cab; it felt really good knowing I would have nice clothes to wear to class the next day and would not have to feel miserable every time I looked into my wardrobe. I got back to my room in a good mood which quickly dissipated as soon as I put my new clothes in my wardrobe. Their presence in my wardrobe only highlighted the fact that my former nice clothes now looked old and shabby and my relatively newish clothes looked tacky and cheap. It suddenly dawned on me that I would need a lot more than N30, 000 to change my wardrobe and my lifestyle. Having only a few lovely items of clothing meant I would either wear them so often that people would get sick of seeing them or I would wear them only a few times, alternating them with my old clothes, but then people would still recognise the new clothes. Wouldn't it be nice to wear an outfit only once or twice and never have to wear it again that semester? Reluctantly I decided to wear my new clothes only on special occasions, like on dates or to parties, and stick to wearing my old outfits to class. Yeah, that would work.

    I lay on my bed and shut my eyes. I had never been a materialist girl; I had always been happy with what I had and turned a blind eye to the things I couldn't afford. But now, all of a sudden, it seemed possible that I could have it. I resented this feeling of inadequacy where before everything had either been enough or just wasn't important.

    I hadn't spoken with Tobi since the night at the club three nights earlier. I wondered if she was still upset with me. I dialled her number, and it rang off twice, but I knew

Tobi was wary of picking up unknown numbers. I tried one more time, and she picked up on the fourth ring.

"Hello, who is this?"

"Hi, Tee, it's me."

"Me who?" she asked, even though we both knew she wasn't fooling anyone.

"So obviously you're still upset with me?" I said, with a nervous laugh in my attempt to inject humour into the conversation. My first instinct was to apologise, but I caught myself. I was always the one doing the apologising, even when I had done nothing wrong.

"Is this your new number?" she asked in a toneless voice, ignoring my question.

"Yep, apparently, I have you to thank for that. Terry bought me a new phone."

"No problem. So what phone did Terry get you? I hope it was a really expensive phone. I would be so embarrassed if he bought you a cheap phone." Her voice was beginning to get excited. "You should hear the way he goes on about you. That guy has got it bad, are you sure you're not using any jazz on him?"

I laughed nervously. "He got me a Nokia, and yes, it's a nice phone. I like it a lot. He even had it loaded with N10, 000 credit. But I think you're exaggerating: he just wants to be friends. In fact, we spent the journey back from the club talking about Wale."

"Oh no, Jade! You didn't! Why would you do that?" Tobi exclaimed.

"Erm, because he asked? What's wrong with talking about Wale?" I asked, confused.

"Jeez, isn't it enough that you go on and on to me about how you've lost the one and only love of your life? Do you have to start blabbering about it to the whole world?"

"Tobi, don't you think that's a bit harsh?" I asked, hurt. What was more natural than talking about something if it hurt you? About trying to find someone who would understand the pain, someone to empathise with and comfort you, to tell you it wasn't your fault and that there was nothing you could have done to change what happened?

"Jade, you know me," she said in a mellow voice, "I'm just giving you the harsh realities without any trimmings. You're making yourself seem like you were dumped and are broken-hearted. It's not a good look; you should never show a guy, any guy, that you're broken-hearted about another guy. You have to seem untouchable like nothing can hurt you."

"Umm," I said, nodding my head absentmindedly even though I knew she couldn't see me.

"Yeah, trust me; I know what I'm talking about. Already you're giving Wale too much props with the fact that he broke up with you; don't make it worse by making out that you're devastated. You need to get out there, have fun and show no remorse. It's always worked for me. When guys see that you won't be affected by a break-up, it makes it harder for them to leave."

"Hmmm, I'm not sure I agree with you." When Wale broke up with me, I'd acted as if I didn't care and he went through with it.

"Well, I can only give you the best advice, whatever you do with it is up to you. So, what's up with you and Terry?" she asked conspiratorially.

"Erm, nothing." I wondered how much I could tell her. I decided to keep the N30,000 Terry had given me out of our conversation. I told her about the dinner.

"Interesting," she commented, "you sound like you're beginning to warm up to him."

"Er, certainly not in the way I imagine you're talking about. I enjoy his company, but there's no way it can go further than us being friends. I don't feel any physical attraction to him and even if I did, there's no way due to the fact that he's married and with kids."

"Yeah, yeah, whatever," Tobi said, laughing. "When are you guys next hooking up?"

"Nothing's planned yet… for some reason, I don't feel right about that question. Terry and I are not dating!" At least, I didn't think we were. I really did enjoy his company; he was easy to talk to without any complications, and his maturity and the fact that we didn't have any mutual friends made it easier to talk as I felt that whatever I told him would remain between us.

CHAPTER 21

I realised I was making excuses to do what I wouldn't condone: this wasn't me. I was a good girl, I followed the rules, didn't cheat and was satisfied with everything I had – and so I made up my mind; I wasn't going to go out with Terry anymore. I'd always prided myself on being principled, and hanging around with him was a threat to my principles. The part I couldn't make up my mind about was if I should tell him not to call me anymore, or to ignore his calls and hope he would get the message. I knew with a firm conviction that I was never going to have sex with Terry; first of all, I was still a virgin. Yep, at the age of twenty, I was still keeping myself and hoped to hold on until I got married. Secondly, I tried picturing myself with Terry, and I shuddered with revulsion each time. It wasn't anything to with him physically; it was what he represented and what getting involved with him would make me. So I had two strong reasons not to have sex with Terry and enough reason to keep away from him."

It was now eight days since I had spoken to Terry – nine days since our dinner. Although I had planned to let Terry know that I wasn't interested in going out with him anymore, I was so inherently nice that I knew I would probably wouldn't remain adamant if he pushed. I convinced myself that he wouldn't, but my experience with men led me to believe the contrary. They refused to take "NO" for an answer, asking ridiculous questions to wear down your defences, holding out for a "maybe" and then convincing themselves that it meant a "YES".

Terry wasn't the only one I had been avoiding. I'd missed the classes I took with Wale last week and this week but today I couldn't afford to miss my philosophy class because there was going to be a test after the class.

"Don't worry," Deji had said to me that morning as he informed me of the test, "you can sit by me, and I'll hold your hand."

"No thank you," I said, laughing. "Please, can you lend me your notes? I'll make photocopies."

I had a free period before philosophy; I was confident that I had enough time to study for the test. With all the friends I had in class, no one had thought to inform me of the test until this morning. Not that I was surprised: most of them probably hadn't cracked open their notes yet, and a few were already discussing seating arrangements for the lecture theatre in such a manner as to be able to copy off each other. Not that I was a goody two-shoes and felt above copying, but I seemed to have a knack for getting caught every time. One time one of my classmates was copying off me during an exam, and I was the one who got reprimanded. Monica's theory is that I wear emotions vividly on my face; apparently, I had looked so guilty, and the other party had looked so calm that it was only natural to think I was the one cheating.

I walked to the small photocopying room at the end of the row of classrooms. There were two photocopying machines there, but it looked as if one was broken as there was a long queue at the other; I stood at the end, getting worried. I was sure Deji would want his notes back as soon as possible. I was beginning to consider asking him to let us study his notes together when I noticed a familiar figure near the front of the queue; it was Wale. My breath caught in my chest, and my first instinct was to run, but I had two options. Option 1: I could go back to class and try to study with Deji which would be painful as we would have to wait for each other to finish reading each page and I didn't think we had enough time for that. It also meant I wouldn't be able to concentrate on the parts I had trouble with. Option 2: I could walk to the front of the queue and beg Wale to photocopy Deji's notes along with his. The masochistic part of my brain decided on Option 2. I walked to the front, wary of the angry eyes following me. I got to Wale and took a deep breath.

"Hi," I said, smiling. Wale jumped, and I derived a little pleasure from the startled look on his face.

"Hey." He recovered and smiled back at me. "How have you been?"

"Great, great. You?" We were speaking to each other like strangers, trying hard not to say the things we really wanted to say. The people in the queue behind him were beginning to mutter.

"So, what have you got there?" I asked, pointing at the book he held. It occurred to me that he was there for the same reason that I was.

"Philosophy?" I guessed, raising my eyebrows and smiling.

"How do you know?" he asked, taken aback.

I held up Deji's notes, and he grinned.

"I guess we've both been avoiding each other," he said.

Finally, Wale was at the front of the queue. He handed the book over to the boy making the copies and showed him which pages to copy in duplicate.

"In case you're wondering, the other copy is for you," he said to me over his shoulder. That was one of the things I had loved about him; he was so intuitive and knew what I needed without having to ask me. If only he had been intuitive enough to know that how much I loved him... would it have made a difference?

"Whose notes are these?" I asked as he handed me a stapled copy.

"Sade's," he said, without missing a beat. I narrowed my eyes at him: not that it was any of my business if anything was going on between them, but the quick way he had answered definitely sounded guilty.

"Well, it beats trying to make sense of Deji's notes." Now it was his turn to narrow his eyes at me, and I tensed up, hoping he wasn't reading too much into it. All of a sudden he burst out laughing.

"Why would you borrow Deji's notes? He's not exactly the best note-taker." I laughed with him, getting the joke. Deji wasn't what you would call a serious student, and he was proud of the fact that he got by without having to put much effort into his studies.

"His were the only notes available. No one else would part with theirs so close to the test."

Wale paid for the photocopies, and we walked towards the lecture theatre in silence.

"How ironic that I've been avoiding you all this time, and I bump into you now," he said, breaking the silence. His voice was thick with an emotion I couldn't place. I wondered if it would be appropriate for me to say all the things that were running through my mind a mile a minute. For instance, could I tell him that I missed him and that my life seemed like a black-and-white movie without him in it? Could I tell him that I would give up everything to have him kiss me now? I wished time would stop, and we could spend eternity here, in this moment, with him next to me; it was torture when he wasn't there. It was simple, and yet it was complicated. It was harder because I could see in his eyes that he still had feelings for me. But I knew we were both fools and this moment was going to pass without either of us admitting anything.

"I know. It's not as bad as I thought it would be," I lied, my eyes betraying me, Wale nodded in agreement.

"I know!" he exclaimed. He was lying, too. His voice cracked when he spoke.

Sade was waiting for Wale front of the lecture theatre, and I could have sworn I saw a look of fear in her eyes when she saw me. I might have imagined it, though, because the next minute she was smiling at me.

"What's up? Long time," she said.

"Nothing much," I replied, making an effort as well. "You?"

"I'm just there, you know." She shrugged. Wale handed her notebook to her.

"I saved you a seat," she said to him. Then she turned to me, that annoying smile still on her lips. "Sorry, I don't think there are any empty seats where we are."

"That's alright; I'm sure Monica saved me one." I felt like punching the surreptitious bitch in the face. It would probably do her some good: straighten out that crooked witch-like nose. "Okay, I'll see you around," I said, half-waving.

"Wait," Wale said, grabbing my arm as I turned to walk away. "Sade, please can you give us a moment?" I saw her face fall as she turned to walk away. A part of me felt victorious and elated, but I didn't want to get into anything to do with us now. Not before a test and not when we both had some quick studying to do.

"No, Wale, not now. I need to get Deji's notes back to him, and we both need to study."

Wale's face closed up, shutting me out completely. "You're right; this test is paramount." He let go of my arm. "Good luck and see you around."

"You too," I replied, wondering if I had done the right thing. I would have given up a million tests to get the chance to talk to him. I watched him walk inside and prayed that he wouldn't give up on me.

* * *

"I'm bored," I moaned.

Monica and I leant against the railings in front of her room on the second floor. The balcony looked out into the middle of the hall with the raised stage-like platform. It was 5.45 p.m., and I was still recovering from the effect bumping into Wale had on me.

"Me too," said Monica, throwing back her head and letting out a cry of frustration. "Where does a young lady get some action in this crappy place?"

"I think we're doing something wrong; everyone else seems to be having fun. Maybe it's the company I'm keeping," I said, pouting.

"Yeah, right," Monica laughed. "You're even worse than I am."

We stood there in silence, watching the comings and goings of the world below us.

"You know, you could call Terry to take us out," Monica suggested.

"Really?" My jaw dropped. "I thought you didn't like the idea of hanging around married men?"

"Hey, I'm not the one he's pressuring to sleep with him. I can have the free lunch without the guilt." We both laughed. I put my arm around her shoulder.

"That's why I love you; you're such an amazing friend," I said, my voice dripping with sarcasm.

"I try; I really don't get enough appreciation for the work I put in. So, are you going to call Terry?"

"No way, darling, you'll just have to find your own Aristo." I hugged her tighter to me; she pulled away and shrugged off my arm.

"You know who else we can call if we're really bored?" she asked warily.

"Who?"

"Yomi."

"Yomi?! No way, I think I would rather call Terry before I called Yomi. Just forget it." Yomi hadn't given up hope that he and I would hook up, and he was always on my case. The last thing I wanted was to make him believe I liked him.

"Maybe not for you but for me," she said, avoiding my eyes.

I did a double take. OMG, did Monica like Yomi? I thought about all the times she'd had to wait for me whenever Yomi chatted me up, and I felt sorry for her.

"Not that I like him or anything" she went on. "But I'm horny. I haven't had sex in like, two weeks."

"Eh, okay, I really didn't need to know that. You can hook up with Yomi on your own; you don't need me to be there. I think going alone will definitely improve your chances. Just as long as you know what you're getting yourself into." I shrugged, acting like I wasn't surprised that she was into Yomi, but I was stunned. I knew that Monica could take care of herself, but I couldn't help but be worried. Yomi was a notorious knicker-chaser, and the worst thing was that he boasted about his exploits.

"Are you going to call him?" I asked Monica.

"Nope, you will." She batted her eyelids at me. "I can't just call him out of the blue. Please, just call him – that way he won't know what's hit him when I unleash the 'Monica effect'."

"You are such a joker," I laughed. I thought about it for a minute: maybe this was what I needed to do to get Yomi off my back. "I'll do it." I whipped out my phone. "Do you have his number?" Monica read out his digits to me from her cell, and I dialled. It only rang once.

"Hey, hunny," I said in a sweet tone, winking at Monica. "What are you wearing?"

"Hi, sweetness," he replied. "It could be you, all you gotta do is say the word."

"Idiot, you don't even know who this is," I laughed down the line. "You're such a pig."

"Ah, it is you!" he exclaimed, recognising my voice. "I've been gagging for you like a dog for choice meat, um uh uh." I heard the sound of him licking his lips: eww. "So, to what do I owe the pleasure of this phone call?" he asked, employing what he probably imagined was a sexy tone.

"I just felt like hearing your voice, what are you up to?"

"Nothing important, why do you ask?"

I looked at Monica; she was making hand gestures and mouthing something, but I couldn't for the life of me understand what she was on about. I figured she was just excited; I'd never seen her that animated. I nodded and held up my palm, signalling for her to calm down.

"How long will it take for you to get here?"

He hesitated. "Are you messing me about?"

"Why would I want to do that? I'm bored and need company."

"Really? Give me ten minutes."

"Come to room C204," I said before he hung up.

"He's on his way," I said to Monica, tucking my phone into the back pocket of my jeans. "What was all that about?" I mimicked her gesturing.

"Erm," she sighed, "I was signalling for you to hang up."

"And why were you doing that?" I frowned. "You haven't changed your mind, have you?"

"I have. I was just thinking about it; I didn't believe you were going to go ahead with it. Now it's all happening a little too fast."

"You're joking, right? This idiot is going to think that I have a crush on him and that I chickened out at the last minute if we don't go." I raised an eyebrow and folded my arms across my chest. This babe was killing me, I thought. Note to self: never take Monica seriously again.

"Or he could think you played a prank on him; to get him to stop stalking you." She shrugged, a small uncomfortable smile playing around her lips.

"Eh, we're still going; if you chicken out, I'll just have to tell him that you have the hots for him."

"Come on; you wouldn't."

"I so would."

"I know you won't; nothing you say will make me go."

"Okay, fine, we'll just have to find somewhere to hide so he doesn't see us when he comes and then spend the rest of the night in boredom when we could be hanging out at his place watching a movie, sipping Baileys on ice and munching on Mr Biggs chicken and chips or shawarma from Wrap'n'go." I sighed. I wasn't trying to bait her; I had just built up the experience in my mind. Plus I figured none of us had to do anything we didn't want to do. I was the one Yomi was after, but I felt safe in the knowledge that I wasn't going alone. Anyway, Yomi wasn't a fool; once he saw Monica with me, he would realise that nothing was going to happen between him and me. Hmm, actually, knowing Yomi, it was more likely that he would think he was in for a ménage à trois.

"Let me think about it... are we definitely going to get shawarma?"

"I'm sure we can get whatever we want. We'll just have to work on Yomi together." I could see that she was beginning to come around.

"Fine," she agreed reluctantly "I'll just need to change my outfit." She looked down at her outfit in disdain.

"There's nothing wrong with what you're wearing."

"I know, but I'm not going to seduce a man in this. There's no way I'm giving him a chance to wriggle through my fingers. If he arrives before I'm ready, just wait for me."

I nodded. Yay, it had worked. It's funny the way things had turned around so quickly; a few minutes ago I would rather have eaten my own feet than hang out with Yomi, and now I was the one looking forward to it, albeit for my own greedy reasons.

I leant forward on the bannisters, peering more closely at the students going back and forth below. I wasn't really focusing on anything or anybody. I hoped Monica was ready before Yomi showed up. I wasn't prepared to keep up the flirting with him; that was going to be Monica's role tonight. My role was to watch some decent TV instead of watching Yoruba movies on the VCR.

My mobile phone rang. I fished it out from my pocket and checked the caller ID. It was Yomi.

"Hey, I'm standing outside C204, are you here?" I said when I picked up the call.

"Yeah babe, come downstairs; I'm parked outside." I should have known he wouldn't want to come upstairs. Probably avoiding girls he had promised to call and didn't. It worked out even better this way; I didn't have to pretend that I was interested in him while waiting for Monica to get ready.

"Oh, I thought you were coming up to meet me. I'll be out in a sec," I said and hung up. I went into Monica's room to check if she had found something to wear. She was sitting on her bed, bending over to do up her shoe straps.

"Is he here?" she asked.

"Yep, he's parked outside, waiting for us to come and meet him," I said, flopping beside her on the bed.

"Okay, does he know I'm coming?"

"Nope, I didn't mention it."

"Cool, what do you think?" she asked, standing up and stepping in front of me so I could assess her outfit.

"Hmm, not bad," I replied, nodding. Monica was wearing a pair of Harlem pants, a tight-fitting T-shirt and high-heeled shoes: sexy in a casual way. "Ready?"

"Yup," she replied, grabbing her handbag.

When Yomi saw us approaching, he jumped out of the car to open the passenger door for me. He brushed his lips against my cheek as I stepped closer to get in but I could see his eyes were fixed somewhere below Monica's neck. I smiled to myself. I couldn't blame him; Monica was wearing a padded wonder bra that was working miracles. He didn't stand a chance.

"Hey, thanks." I pressed a fist against my lips to keep myself from bursting out into laughter at the way his eyes bulged at the sight before him.

"Yeah, sure," he replied, looking at me for a fraction of a second before turning back to Monica. "Are you coming with us?" He leant towards Monica as he spoke, a cloying smile playing across his lips.

"What do you think?" Monica replied coldly, fixing him with an icy stare before getting into the back seat. Really? Was that how she was going to seduce him? Yomi didn't seem to mind; in fact, his already annoying smile grew even wider.

As we headed toward Yomi's place, he lost no time in abandoning any pretence of being interested in me. I felt the sexual tension building as he tried to draw Monica into a conversation about her love life, to which he had never paid any attention in the past, and Monica continually brushed him off with monosyllabic responses. I was beginning to wonder if this was such a good idea. It was one to thing to be bored on a Friday night and stuck indoors with nowhere to go, and quite another to be trapped in a house with two horny twenty-year-olds. I prayed that I wouldn't have to go through another Tobi-and-Ian hotel-room type scene.

"So what are you up to this Friday night? Doing anything interesting?" he asked, trying to catch Monica's eye in the rear-view mirror.

"Duh," she replied.

"Oh, of course, no, I meant, you know, I was wondering if you were up to anything later, you know, going to a club or something."

"Yeah, maybe. Can we stop at Wrap'n'go to get shawarmas?" she asked without batting an eyelid.

"Yeah, that 'd be great," I spoke for the first time since getting into the car.

"Whatever you ladies want," he said magnanimously. I hoped that meant he was paying.

We had left campus through the front gates that lead into Fowora, a bustling town with roads badly in need of repair. The contrast between the well paved roads and the imposing buildings of the University campus and the tired, worn out façade of Fowora town, was glaring. In Fowora, the houses were coated with a fine layer of dust and the sun's rays bounced off the dirt and seemed to multiply. In the four years I'd spent in the university, I'd come to love it as my home, although I couldn't claim to understand its residents. In the sheltered school campus, it was easy to pull-off a fake lifestyle. Girls clad in designer gear costing more than both parents' monthly salary, or wearing revealing outfits that would cause parents to burst out in a "binding and casting" fit. Boys with appalling manners, acting cool and walking with exaggerated swagger. But outside the campus gates, these students jumped into the rickety buses that passed for public transportation, ducking their heads to avoid being seen by anyone they knew.

It was all going to plan; we got our shawarmas, which Yomi paid for, and then we headed to his place. It was messy and smelly but nothing that I couldn't handle; I had grown up in a house with three boys. I had been looking forward to watching cable TV; unfortunately, the reality was that the main dish was connected in the main house. On the boys-quarter TV, where Yomi stayed, you could only view whatever channel was being watched in the main house. My heart sank. I caught Monica's apologetic look; she hadn't been interested in watching TV and the fish she had sought to bait looked as if it was already hooked and ready to be sautéed.

I sighed, hoping that whoever was watching TV in the main house was tuned to something I would like to watch. It was a small consolation that Yomi had a bottle of Baileys, but I had to have it without any ice and in a questionable mug. I looked around the small living room. There were no sofas, only a couple of dirty-looking bean bags which Monica and I sat on; I was glad I was wearing a pair of jeans and not a skirt. There were a desk and a chair in the corner, and I assumed that was where Yomi did his reading, although the idea of him reading was hard to imagine. There was a pile of books beside the desk, and I noticed a Scrabble box lying among the pile.

"Let's play Scrabble!" I bounced up and down on the bean bag in excitement. I crept off my seat towards the Scrabble box on my hands and knees and reached for it with a big grin on my face. Monica shot me an irritated look. To be honest, I was surprised Yomi had a Scrabble board; he seemed more like a Monopoly guy to me.

"I don't like Scrabble; it belongs to my sister," he said.

"Come on; it'll be fun. I mean what else are we going to do all night?" I caught Monica and Yomi exchanging a glance. Really, these two were like dogs in heat.

"I don't like Scrabble either," Monica said, triumph glowed on her face. Come on! This wasn't a competition.

"Looks like we have something in common, so what would you like to do?" Yomi asked her.

"Well, we're bored, there's nothing on TV, and we don't want to play Scrabble – so how about Truth or Dare?"

Really? That's what she came up with? Yomi's eyes lit up. I knew that nothing I said at this point would matter. Now I knew how it was going to go down I wasn't so sure it was worth coming all this way for.

"Fine," I sighed, giving up. "Monica, truth or dare?"

"Dare," she said, slowly looking into Yomi's eyes.

It all pretty much went downhill from there. I don't know what I had expected, but it was evident I wasn't getting a ride back to campus that night. Monica and Yomi had conveniently forgotten my existence.

It was only 8.30, but I couldn't wait to get out of the tiny, funny-smelling flat. I called Deji, pleading with him to come and get me.

"Sorry babe, I'm on the Island," he informed me, sounding as if he couldn't wait for me to get off the phone. I heard feminine laughter in the background; I didn't need to be a genius to figure out what he was up to.

"What time will you get back?" I asked quickly; if there was even the slightest chance that he could come and get me tonight, I was willing to take it.

"I'll advise you not to wait up," he said, laughing. "Just hang in there, I'll call you tomorrow."

"Bastard," I muttered down the line, hoping he had heard me before he hung up.

Now I was stuck. I had three options: no, scratch that, I had only two, I thought as I watched Monica and Yomi engaged in their very offensive PDA. I might have been their only audience, but I would have expected a bit more decorum. I felt like slapping their heads together. So my options were to get a cab or to call Terry. Getting a cab would mean digging into my already insufficient allowance and calling Terry would mean I thought it was okay to remain friends with him. It shouldn't even be an option. I considered dragging Yomi out of the pile of lips, arms and legs on the floor and threatening him to take me back to my room, but something within me had grown slightly less averse to calling Terry. I was inclined to blame it on the alcohol and the fact that I was watching a form of pornography which affected me a little. Surely, this would be a dangerous time to call Terry.

CHAPTER 22

I called Terry.

I'd had to. I had run out of options and spending my money on a cab without a Terry in my life would mean I would have to live on peanuts for the rest of the month or go back to Daddy with a concocted story about how I needed money for an assignment or a school project.

Terry had been happy to hear from me. He didn't ask why I had been avoiding his calls, or why I hadn't called him until now when I needed him. He said he was glad of an excuse to leave the house. I resisted the urge to ask about his wife and kids. Neither Monica nor Yomi noticed when I left, and I guess neither of them cared. They had been kind enough to relocate to the bedroom as their lay-down dirty dancing got a little more intense. By this time I had polished off half the bottle of Baileys. I was now in what I called my "happy tipsy euphoria".

"Hi," I said, leaning into his car from the passenger-side window.

"Hi yourself," Terry replied, reaching across the passenger seat to open the door for me. I got in, shut the door and tucked my hands beneath me. I never knew what to do with my hands in a car when I wasn't driving. I caught a whiff of his cologne, and before I could stop myself, I inhaled deeply. He must have taken that as an invitation because he leant over and brushed his lips against mine briefly. His lips were soft, and I was taken aback. In my inebriated state, my indignation came in the form of an embarrassed giggle. I tried to be upset, but I found that I didn't have the energy and at the back of my mind I really didn't care.

"You're drunk," he pronounced, proud of himself for coming to such an obvious conclusion.

"No, I'm tipsy. Big difference." I grinned at him, and he grinned back, like a big bad wolf. My, what big teeth you have.

"Where to? Do you want to get something to eat?"

"Nope, I'm good. I had a large shawarma."

"Well, I can't take you back to campus."

"What? Why?"

"I haven't seen you in ages, and here you are, right in my lap and drunk. I'm not throwing this opportunity away," he said, laughing.

"I knew calling you was a mistake," I laughed.

"Then why did you?"

I ignored his question. "What if I insisted on heading straight back?" I asked.

"Ah, I'm a gentleman at heart. Are you sure you want to go back to campus?" Terry posed his question in a way that suggested I would be missing a lot if I said "yes". He picked up my hand and massaged my palms, and then my wrist, slowly working his way up my arm. His hands were strong but gentle, and I felt delicious shivers explode in my head. I laid my head back against the headrest and shut my eyes. The only sound in the car was the sound of our heavy breathing. He lifted my hand and slipped my middle and ring finger into his hot moist mouth. It was as if he had hit a secret button and broken a dam between my legs. Blood rushed with incredible speed to my head, and I felt woozy. He rolled his wet tongue around my fingers, slipping it between and around them, causing me to moan softly. It was such a strange feeling to me. He wasn't touching me anywhere private, but the effect could not have been more profound. What was he doing to me? Was it the alcohol? In that instant, I knew I had a quick decision to make. If I let him continue it would get way out of hand. I felt my inner consciousness struggling to get out from behind the dense cobwebs built up in my mind from alcohol consumption. I didn't want this: not with him, and not in this place. His other hand was beginning to creep up my blouse, and I summoned up the will to brush it away. I pulled my fingers from his lips.

He looked surprised.

"Wow," I said. "That went crazy for a second."

"You looked like you were enjoying it." He winked at me.

"No, I wasn't and even if I was, I can't do this with you, Terry, and you know why."

"Then why did you call me?"

"Because I needed your help; you didn't have to come if you didn't want to. I'm sorry, but I just need a lift." I hoped I wasn't hurting his feelings, but we both knew if I'd had a car I wouldn't be sitting here with him.

"Ouch." He strapped on his seat belt and started the engine.

We drove in silence all the way to campus. I was relieved that I had stopped him when I did. I liked him as a friend, and while I wasn't proud to admit it, I had missed him, financially.

"I'm sorry," I apologised again as we pulled up outside my Hall.

He didn't respond. He switched off the engine and sat back with a sigh. I wondered what the etiquette was in this kind of situation; could I get out of his car now? I decided to wait to see if he would say anything.

"Look, Jadesola, I like you a lot," he said eventually, turning to face me. "That's the only reason I would leave my house to come and pick you up from some guy's house at this time of the night." He held up his hand as I tried to interrupt him. "Please, let me finish. I'm not like the other men out there; I don't want to use you; I just really enjoy your company. You make me feel young and alive, and I like that about you. I also like that you seem to enjoy my company as well and are not just hanging out with me because of what you know I can give you." He paused. "I know you're a good girl, and I respect that; that's why the last thing I want you to feel is that you have to avoid me. If you just plain can't stand me, I can handle it; I'm a big boy, but if you're scared that I'll take advantage of you, you can put your mind to rest because I will never touch you again. Well, not unless you want me to," he added with a mischievous grin.

"Okay, thanks," I said, fiddling with my fingers. I felt shy; I had never been shy around Terry because when I met him, I thought he was a douche bag. But now there was a difference; whenever I looked at Terry, I was beginning to see so much more. I saw a good man... okay, maybe not very good... I mean, he was still making sexual advances to a girl barely out of her teens in his car while his wife and kids were sleeping soundly somewhere safe. Nonetheless, I saw someone I could talk to without any fear of being judged and someone who would actually listen. I saw a friend.

He nodded. "Make sure you go straight to bed."

"Yes, Daddy," I teased.

He reached into his jacket and passed me an envelope. I didn't know how to react. I assumed it was money; it was a fat envelope. I took it from him and looked inside. It was full of cash and MTN phone credit scratch cards.

"Wow, why are you giving me this?" I hoped he didn't think I was ungrateful. I wondered if I should refuse it but a big part of me really wanted the money. Hey, I had nothing to feel guilty about; I hadn't asked him for it. The saying that "there's nothing like a free lunch" kept ringing in my ears. I had heard stories of men who gave out money even when they weren't having any sexual relations with the recipient; I convinced myself that this was one of those cases. I considered myself extremely lucky.

He shrugged. "As I've told you, I know what it's like to be a student, and it's even more challenging when you're a girl. I just thought you'd like a little extra to add to what you get from your parents."

"Thank you, this is really kind of you." I opened the door and slid out.

"I'll call you tomorrow, okay?" he said, bending to look at me through the passenger-side window.

"Okay. Bye." I waved and walked to my room.

Lying on my bed, I reflected on the day. It had been a pretty eventful day, from bumping into Wale, to the experience at Yomi's and then with Terry. I looked through the contents of the envelope. There was N20,000 and N5000 credit. A lot of money from someone I wasn't even having sex with. Maybe he truly meant it, and he wasn't going to push me to do anything I didn't want to do, but judging from what happened this evening he probably didn't have to. I got a sense that I was playing with fire, and wondered if I could avoid getting burnt. I couldn't help getting excited. It was as if I had my very own magic knapsack where anything I wished for would appear in it. Okay, not to get carried away, I knew it didn't work in quite the same way, but I also knew that some girls slept with men and came away only N5000 richer if they were lucky – and here I was, not even one kiss, and I had gotten a phone, phone credits and N50,000. I didn't have anything to fear from Terry. Not that I believed everything he had said but the fact that he had stopped when I asked him to had given me confidence in his character.

Terry called the next day, which was a Saturday, and he took me out to dinner at Saipan in Dream Plaza, on the Island. This time, I went alone, wearing a lovely summer dress I had bought that morning using some of the money he had given me. The dress was bright yellow; it was off-shoulder and had a full skirt that stopped just below my knees. We took the lift to the restaurant, and I tried not to stare at the large and imposing frames and the lovely marble walls. We had cocktails at the bar before we proceeded to our table. I had a Piña Colada for the first time, and it felt so grown up to be having cocktails in a bar. The food was fantastic, and I had to resist stuffing my face. When Terry dropped me off, he asked if I still had some of the money left and said that he could give me more if I wanted. I smiled and told him I was fine. I mean, he had only given it to me the night before. I wondered if it was a test or if he actually believed I could have blown N20,000 in less than a day.

I had a weird dream that night. I dreamt that I was walking down the road with Josh, my old crush. I had an eerie feeling that I was being watched, and I held on tight to Josh's hand. It was the middle of the night, and there were barely any cars on the road. The odd car passed once in a while, their headlights on full glare. I noticed that the headlights were like eyes, with pupils darting back and forth like feelers sending out some sort of ultrasound wave to avoid a collision. There was no one driving these cars; the cars moved serenely, heading towards their pre-programmed destinations. Some of the cars had wild eyes, but there was this sleek silver car with slanted eyes that looked like a sexy horse; I could have sworn that there was steam coming out of its grids on both sides of the car, as if from flared nostrils. The car cut through the other docile cars in a beautiful pattern; just looking at it made me weak at the knees. I watched it from a distance, and as it approached me it winked; I swooned. The car swung around when it reached me, and the passenger door flew open; I was enticed by the power and the apparent wealth the car represented. I let go of Josh's hand quickly and jumped into the car without a backwards glance, shrugging off his hand as it grappled for mine. Once in the car, I looked around in awe; there was no one else in there; I was all alone. It was the poshest car I had ever been in; the upholstery had diamonds in them, and they glittered and sparkled. Despite the diamonds, the seat I was in was incredibly soft and cushy. There was a dim light in the car, but no one could see inside from the outside because the windows were misty. There was a face pressed tightly against the window where I sat; I saw the lips move in screams of panic and fear, but I couldn't hear a word it said. None of it seemed to register. I felt as if I was in a bubble of excitement and everything outside that bubble was hazy. There was a large screen on the dashboard in front of me and my destination flashed before my eyes in a big font. "Paradise- Innocence lost", the screen read; in a much smaller font below this, it read, "Please press the GO button to proceed". I searched the screen, my eyes darting back and forth over it, wondering if there was something I was missing. I squinted and peered more closely at it, trying to locate the button. I was getting exasperated; I felt around the screen for anything that felt like a button. There was the sound of pounding coming from outside; fists were being pummelled into the roof of the car hard and fast. It was very distracting; I needed to concentrate.

"Where the hell is the GO button?" I asked aloud in frustration. The car started in a convulsion; it was as if it had heard me. I pulled my seatbelt on in haste, my hands shaking with anticipation and excitement. In my dreamy half-conscious state, I knew we were heading somewhere fabulous. As if we were in a sci-fi movie, the car began to move – not horizontally, like the other vehicles, but vertically, rising above the other cars and like lightning we were off. I shut my eyes and clutched the armrests tightly. The vibration got worse, and I felt as if my whole being was being shaken to the core. Blood rushed into my head, making it feel like a floating balloon. I couldn't feel anything above my neck. The car's convulsion stopped as suddenly as it had started, leaving me dazed. I supported my head in my hands. My eyes had stayed shut throughout the duration of the journey which had taken less than a minute. With my hands still supporting my head, I opened my eyes slowly. I could tell from the amount of light streaming in the car that it was daylight: either that or this place had some serious street lighting. I took my hands off my face and lifted my eyes. We had travelled to a fantastic place indeed. It was such a beautiful place, and the people walking the streets were perfect. Maybe too perfect: not one hair was out of place. I could even see an amazingly white beach, with a picture-perfect azure sea just beyond it. Had we journeyed out of Nigeria? My sleep-fuddled brain could not imagine where I was. Surely there were no beaches in this country as perfect as this. The people here were definitely Nigerian, but the place... the place was too good to be true. As soon as the thought left my head, the car began to fade from beneath and around me like a veil being slowly pulled away, and I found myself on the streets, standing with what had looked like perfect people from the comfort and safety of the car. There was a metal brace clasped around my neck and shackles on my feet; a chain running down from the neck brace was looped around my wrists, and it continued downwards to join the shackles on my feet. My knees buckled from the impact of the shock, and I fell forward. I reached out to prevent myself hitting the ground. I held onto the first thing my hand touched. It was someone's arm; I steadied myself and looked up. The face that stared back at me was blank and unfeeling. It belonged to a young girl; she was probably my age, but she looked haggard and drained. I gasped and apologised. Only the women were in shackles; the men held chains and whips. The beautiful clothes on the people were gone and had been replaced by dirty and torn loin cloths, exposing bare, heaving chests. I was the only woman without a slave master, and the men sneered at me as they led the women along the path to what, a minute ago, had looked like a beach but was, in fact, a dirty swamp. I heard a snarl behind me and turned to see one of the women sink her teeth into the man that held her chains; she grabbed the whip from his hands and, swinging it with considerable force, she brought it down on his back. The man screamed and let go of her chains; as the chains hit the ground, the woman stumbled over them, and as she fell, the man kicked her in the head and walked away. The woman was now crouched in the dirt; she grabbed her head in both hands and let out a series of blood-curdling screams. The throng of people walked by her without a glance and no one stopped to help her. What was this place? I backed away from the woman in quick jerky steps, my heart racing as I spun around, trying to figure out what to do, which way to go. I noticed some buildings on the other side of the throng of people, and I fled towards it, bumping into zombie-like bodies in the process and shoving them out of my way. Hands reached out to grab me as I ran and I pushed them away forcefully. I ran into the wall of one of the buildings too quickly, and I put out my hands to stop myself. I felt the impact as a dull pain shot through my arm. I swung around fast, bumping the back of my head on the wall in the process. I slid down the wall, sinking down onto my haunches and began to rock myself, slowly at first, and gaining momentum. I needed to get out of this nightmare. Was I awake or still sleeping? In my dream, I tried to pinch myself, but nothing happened; I just kept rocking, back and forth, really fast, like a swinging pendulum. I felt myself floating upwards. I was looking down on my other self, still rocking, back and forth, back and forth. I woke up slowly, feeling as if I was being pulled slowly through a tiny tunnel. The first thing I registered was a throbbing headache. I rubbed my temples and sat up. The dream had felt so real, and I pressed my palm to my heart and raised my eyes heavenwards, thanking God that it was only a dream. I sighed and shook my head, rooting for my phone underneath my pillow and checking the time; it was 6 a.m. It was Sunday so I had two more hours of sleep left before I had to start getting dressed for church. I lay on my bed, staring at the ceiling.

I hadn't seen Monica since Friday night at Yomi's place, so I headed to her room as soon as I got back from church. She wasn't in her room so I called her phone. She picked up on the fourth ring.

"Heeey," she greeted me cheerily.

"Hey, Mon, what's up?"

"Nothing much, darl. What's up with you?"

"Same old, same old. I just went to look for you, and you're not in your room. Did you go home for the weekend?"

"Eh, nope," she said vaguely, "but I'm fine; you don't need to worry about me."

I wondered why she was evasive and then it dawned on me.

"Oh!" I exclaimed. "Did you go to Yomi's place?"

"What do you mean, go?" She giggled. "I never left."

"Wow, you prosy. You mean you guys have been at it since Friday night?"

"Yep and you're interrupting." That annoying giggle again. "This has been the most amazing weekend ever! We must have done it in every position imaginable."

I wrinkled my nose and held the phone away from me. Blergh, talk about too much information!

"We've barely eaten all weekend; I bet I've lost a ton of weight."

"Okay, okay, I get the message. You've had lots of fabulous sex. When are you coming back? I'm bored." If things continued like this between Yomi and Monica, it was beginning to look like I would have to find myself another BFF.

"I'm not sure. Tomorrow morning, I guess. There's no way I'm coming to campus today; I'm too knackered."

I went to my room and sank onto my bed. Maybe I should read a book? It'd be good to stay in bed all afternoon, curled up with a good book. I picked a Marian Keyes novel, *Rachel's Holiday*, from my wardrobe and lay with it unopened on my chest. I scrolled through the contacts on my phone. So many random people: no one I wanted to hang out with right now. Hmm, I thought as I scrolled past Deji's name; nah, he was probably at home. He always went home during the weekend. My finger hovered over Wale's name. This was what happened when you were bored, and your good-for-nothing friend had abandoned you to have sex with a guy who'd fancied you for ages. What would I say if I called Wale? I just wanted to hear his voice, maybe check up on him. I tried to picture his face: what would he be doing on a Sunday afternoon? We used to spend our Sundays watching pirated DVDs; was he now watching movies with someone else? Defying the smart part of my brain that was warning me no good would come of it, I pushed the dial button. I held my breath; as soon as I heard the dial tone, I lost my nerve and hung up. I exhaled loudly: that was close. I didn't want Wale to think I was desperate or still fixated on him. I wanted him to believe that I had moved on. I felt better all of a sudden. I had gotten over my foolishness, and my craving for the sound of his voice had vanished, to be replaced with cringing disapproval that I had almost made a fool of myself. My phone vibrated, and I picked it up without checking the caller ID. It was at that instant that I realised my mistake. "Oh shit! Caller ID."

I knew who it was before I heard his voice.

"Hello, who is this?' he said hesitantly. "Sorry, I just saw a missed call from this number."

"Yeah, hi, sorry, this is Jade." I laughed: a shrill and annoying sound. Of course, he wouldn't have known that I'd lost my phone. I wondered if he had ever tried to call me. I felt a small pleasure from imagining that he had. It must have driven him crazy if he couldn't reach me; had he been wondering if I had blocked his number?

"I think my phone dialled you by mistake; it does that sometimes." Shit, shit, I cringed inwardly. What a lame excuse. I closed my eyes and took a deep breath. Calm down, Jade; I chided myself.

"Well, I thought it was someone that didn't have any credit and was flashing me. I was only returning the call." He sounded weird; his voice was a little high, and he was speaking too quickly.

"No, no, I have credit," I said in a funny voice, smiling into the phone as if he could see my face.

"Where are you calling from? Is this your line?"

"I lost my phone so I had to get a new one."

"I'm sorry to hear that. So how have you been?"

"Oh, I'm great – you?" I was so far from great right now. His voice was making my heart do funny things. I closed my eyes briefly, savouring the sound of his voice. It wouldn't last, this conversation. It would be over just as quickly as it had started. I had to soak in all of it. How he sounded, the expressions I imagined him making as we both struggled along with the conversation. I felt a light fluttering in the pit of my belly.

"Couldn't be better," he replied.

Silence. Neither of us said anything for what must have been a few seconds but seemed like an eternity.

"So..." He sighed. "I'll let you get on with whatever you were doing. It was nice talking to you."

Shit, it was ending. I had to do something to keep it going. I racked my brain quickly for a safe topic. My stupid brain betrayed me: nope, nothing. He was waiting for me to say something now. I could hear him breathing; was it my imagination or was he hoping I would say something, too?

"I'm bored," I blurted out. As soon as it came out, I regretted it. Wale would think I only wanted to talk to him because I didn't have anything better to do.

"Me too," he confessed.

"How come?" I asked.

The line was silent for a few more seconds; I imagined him shrugging.

"It's been exactly one month, two weeks and five days," he said in a solemn tone. My heart leapt with hope. In the time we had been apart, we'd both avoided the topic, choosing to talk about anything but that. The fact that he'd brought it up now must mean something.

"In all that time I never thought I'd be so happy to see your number on my phone," he continued. "What made you call?"

Should I repeat the 'phone accident' story? I decided against it. If he was honest, then I owed it to "us" to be honest as well. I exhaled slowly.

"I miss you," I said, my voice breaking. "I've missed you so much. I... I've been trying to understand why you felt we couldn't work through whatever we were going through. I keep asking myself if there was anything I could have done to change your mind."

"Where are you?" he asked urgently.

"I'm in my room, why?"

"I'm coming over."

I hung up grinning like the cat that got the cream. I combed my hair and touched up my makeup; my whole body was tingling with anticipation. I paced around my room waiting for Wale. My hands trembled, and my palms were damp. I ran my palms down the sides of my dress to keep them dry. I found myself peeping out the window to see if I could spot him coming, my heart hammering against my ribcage. Thank goodness I'd called his phone; this was it. We were finally getting back together. I tried to visualise what I would do when he walked in. I imagined jumping on him and wrapping my legs around him. I would kiss him long and hard, lock my arms around his strong neck and never let him go.

CHAPTER 23

I heard a hesitant knock on the door. My hands seemed to have gone numb, and I willed them to open the door and let him in. I looked everywhere but at his face, hoping he couldn't tell how nervous I was.

"Hi," he said, breaking the silence. "You look beautiful." He spoke in a low voice, and I had to strain to hear him.

"Thanks," I replied, self-consciously brushing my fingers through my hair. Wale walked to my corner of the room and sat down on my bed without any invitation. I followed suit, perching gingerly on the far side of the bed; I picked up my pillow, propped it on my lap and leant forward on it.

"What's up?" I asked, pressing my hands hard into the pillow to keep them from trembling. My mind ran through the reasons for him being here. It could be one of two things: either he was bored and wanted company, or he had come to try and make things work between us. I prayed that it was the latter. If so, it must have been very hard for him to come here, not knowing if I would say yes or no. I made up my mind to make it easy for him if it came to that. The last thing I wanted was for him to chicken out and be unable to express his feelings.

"The things you said on the phone – did you mean them?"

I looked up at him and felt his eyes bore into my soul. I had told him that I missed him, but he hadn't said anything back. And yes, the fact that he had rushed over when I'd said it wasn't exactly a bad sign, but I didn't want to be the only one admitting everything. Didn't he have something to say to me? I kept quiet and saw a look of exasperation creep across his face; he knew what I was doing. Even face to face with something I had wanted for so long, I was still too stubborn to stop playing games.

He sighed. "I've missed you too; you can't even imagine how much."

My heart leapt with joy and everything around me seemed awash with light. I needed to watch what I said so that I wouldn't blow this. Who knew? We could be back together before the end of the day.

"Why did you break up with me?" I just had to know. I'd been asking myself this question every day since that evening he'd told me we needed a break. I could see then that he hadn't really meant it, that he still felt deeply for me, so why had he gone ahead with it? I needed to know so that I wouldn't be walking on eggshells around him, hoping that I wouldn't cause him to break up with me again. He stared at me for what seemed like an eternity before he spoke. I knew that he hadn't expected me to question his breaking up with me when it seemed as if we were on the verge of making up. He looked uncertain for a fraction of a second.

"At the time it seemed the right thing to do. I was really upset that evening. The thing is, you have a lot of male friends, and I can't understand the way you interact with them. I'm not saying that it's wrong for you to have male friends; I'm just saying there need to be some boundaries. How would you feel if girls played with me the way you do with Deji, for instance? I bet you wouldn't think it was funny."

"You know it doesn't mean anything, Deji is just my friend," I said, "and we've always played like that."

"But it's not about you and Deji; it's about me...us, this relationship. You have to be considerate of my feelings. How do you think it makes me feel?"

"I'm sorry," I said, my voice breaking. "But why didn't we just talk about it like we're doing now? Breaking up with me was a little extreme."

"Was it? I'd been trying to talk to you, dropping subtle hints so as not to upset you; breaking up with you was the only way I could get your attention."

Now I felt awful. Had I been so horrible? I had convinced myself that it wasn't my fault and that he was just a power-seeking monster.

I looked down at his hands, those long, soft and beautiful hands. I hated apologising and if I was going to do it, I didn't want to see him gloat.

"I'm sorry I was such a horrible girlfriend," I murmured, my gaze fixed on one of his knuckles. He was silent. I risked taking a peek at him. He was smiling at me. He put his hand under my chin and lifted my head to face him.

"Hey, you wouldn't know how to be a horrible girlfriend even if you tried."

I smiled back at him, wondering if he was going to kiss me now. We were staring into each other's eyes and it seemed like the right thing to do. Just then a couple of my roommates, with lovely timing, burst into the room, arguing loudly. They stopped as soon as they spotted us but then continued as suddenly as they had stopped. Obviously, the urgency of whatever they were arguing about was too much to be ignored.

"Let's go for a walk," Wale whispered in my ear.

"Good idea," I said, jumping off the bed. At that moment, I hated my roommates; couldn't they have stayed away for five more minutes? Just one kiss would have been enough to get Wale and me back together; now this talking and making up bit was going to take a lot longer. Aargghh!

We walked out of the hall in silence, and at one point he reached out his hand for mine. He held it as if it was the most precious thing in the world to him and I felt an overwhelming rush of love for him. We walked side by side, past the small rooms crammed with double-decker bunks and all sorts of student life paraphernalia, past the smelly bathrooms, down the shabby stairs, past people walking in a leisurely way; it was Sunday evening after all. We walked through the gates and crossed the main road to the bus and taxi park, which doubled as a mini market, where for dust-tinged and the local women sat on stools displaying their wares of fresh fruits, biscuits and sweets. At the end of the short dusty road, we followed the path around the Engineering Faculty until we got to the Lagos lagoon. We sat down on a large rock facing the calm water. It had been more than ten minutes, and we hadn't spoken a word to each other, but our hands were still clasped tightly together. I stole a glance at him and caught him staring at the lagoon surface with such intensity that I wished I could read his mind. He felt my gaze and turned to me; his expression softened, and his mouth eased into a smile. Even though I knew he still liked me and I sensed that we were about to get back together, I was still a little nervous.

"So, here we are," he said with forced cheeriness.

"Yup," I responded. "Why didn't we ever come here? It's beautiful and private."

"That's because it's Sunday. I bet there's a lot of shady stuff going down during the week."

"We should come down here every Sunday evening then," I said, realising too late the implication of my words.

He didn't respond, and I wondered if he had heard me. He studied my face intently as if looking for information written there.

"There's something I need to ask you," he said finally.

I braced myself for his question.

"Has there been anyone else?"

This threw me, if only because he knew I was a virgin.

"Anyone else... what do you mean?" I asked.

"I'm sorry if I'm forward, but it's important for me to know." His face was an expressionless mask; he kept his eyes fixed on me as if fearing he would miss something vital if he looked away.

I looked down at my hands for a few seconds, and then I lifted my eyes to his.

"You know I've never been with anybody; I would never do that." "And there's no one hoping to come into the picture?"

I could see hope in his eyes. I laughed. "If you're asking whether you have any competition, you'll just have to find out yourself. What about you? I heard you and Sade have become quite the couple." I jutted my chin at him and smiled to make it seem as if I didn't really care about his response.

"Nothing is going on between Sade and me," he answered quickly.

I raised my eyebrows quizzically.

"Really. In fact, Sade has a boyfriend now."

I couldn't help wondering if that was why he was here with me. Sade no longer had time for him? I was tempted to point this out, but I restrained myself. What good would it do?

"I think that we should get back together," he said, taking hold of my hand.

Was that it? I didn't know what I was expecting – but it wasn't this emotionless proposal. I felt as if I was playing a part in a drama and had to say my lines from my head and not my heart.

"What is it?" he asked when I didn't respond.

I shrugged. "I don't know, I just... I feel like there should be more."

He shook his head. "I don't understand. What do you want from me?"

"I said I don't know." I shook my head. "I would very much like us to get back together," I choked on my words, "but we obviously haven't resolved whatever issue made you break up with me in the first place. How do I know you won't do it again? The next time you feel I'm not behaving the way you expect your girlfriend to act, how can I trust you to bring it up with me and have a conversation about it? Even if it turns into an argument or a fight at least, we'll both know where we stand with each other."

He sighed. "Jade, I'm sorry I broke up with you. At the time it seemed like the right thing to do. But I'm making this promise now: if you agree to go out with me again, I will never break up with you."

"What does that mean?" I narrowed my eyes at him.

"I'm saying that if we ever have any issues, I'll do everything in my power to resolve them and that if we do ever decide to part ways, the decision will be yours to make. I'm hoping this will help you understand how serious I am about this. What we have is so special; I haven't been able to get you out of my mind. These last weeks have been the most torturous weeks of my life, and I don't want the misery to go on – not if you're willing to have me back."

I looked into his eyes, glistening in all their sincerity, and I felt my eyes moisten. How did he know exactly what to say? I will never forget that moment; it was perfect. The evening light doing a dance on the lagoon, the light breeze, and even the squawk of the seagulls felt as if they had their special place in that moment. I felt as if I had lost myself and all that remained was a vessel filled with so much love that it threatened to explode any minute. He saw my response in my eyes and smiled: a smile of relief and exhilaration. How had we managed to stay apart all this time, feeling the way we did for each other?

    He wrapped his arms around me, and I laid my head against his muscular chest. I could hear his heart beating, and it sounded like the most beautiful sound in the world. I promised myself there and then to never be too far away from these arms. For in them, I felt complete.

CHAPTER 24

Despite my joy at being back together with Wale, I had a nagging thought at the back of my mind. Would it be wrong to keep seeing Terry? I tried to convince myself that I wouldn't be doing anything wrong. He was only a friend, after all, and nothing was going on between us, physically or emotionally.

Wale and I resumed our relationship, and all was well with the world. I had Wale to love me and hold me. We spent most evenings and weekends together, always touching as if we couldn't believe the other was real. We did almost everything together; we fed each other and took long walks talking about our dreams and our future. We existed in our own little bubble of happiness. On the other hand, I also had Terry. He was easy to talk to and with him, I could be anyone I wanted to be; nothing I said shocked him, and he didn't chastise me for any profanity I used. I could be an angel today and Jezebel tomorrow. I was free to play-act, and I got paid handsomely for it. I was now used to taking money from Terry; it was no longer an issue. It was assumed that he would give me money at the end of our dates, almost as if he was paying me to spend time with me. He never asked me whether I had any money or not, he just kept giving, and he never asked what I spent the money on. He was the "perfect older friend". I teased him with my body even though he never made any more sexual advances towards me. I wore cleavage-revealing blouses and figure-hugging dresses on our dates; I knew I was playing with fire, but it was too much fun, seeing the lust in his eyes, knowing that he couldn't have me. I began to take it for granted that our relationship would always remain that way.

With Wale, I tried my best to be the perfect girlfriend. I stopped flirting with the boys in school, and whenever we were together, I gave him all of my attention. I now took better care of myself, thanks to the money I received from Terry. Wale wondered about the outward change in my appearance, but it was easy to fool him that my clothes and shoes had cost a pittance and that I had a way of making money go a long way, or that I was getting more money from my dad. Sometimes I marvelled at how easy it was to keep Wale in the dark. I always took his calls, even when I was out with Terry. Terry didn't seem to mind. But I never picked up Terry's calls when I was with Wale. I communicated with Terry mainly by text to avoid any awkwardness.

Yes, things were definitely going my way, and I hoped they would for a long time, but it wasn't long before my little bubble burst. One evening I tried calling Terry but he wasn't picking up his calls; I hadn't heard from him in a week, which was strange. We usually went out at least once a week. I left him a message and assumed he would respond. When I hadn't heard from him by the next day, I tried calling again; this time, I only got his voicemail. I left him a couple of cheery messages, masking the anxiety in my voice. Was he trying to avoid me? I pushed the thought away. I didn't know what I would do without Terry in my life; the very idea made my stomach churn. It had been two weeks since I had received money from him and I had spent almost all of it, believing that he would replenish my diminishing stocks when next I saw him.

I didn't hear from Terry the next day or the day after. I was beginning to get desperate; I was now trying his phone up to ten times a day, and still getting no ring tone. It was as if he had just disappeared. I consoled myself with the thought that he was probably out of the country on business or on holiday – but why he wouldn't have let me know?

I couldn't honestly say what I'd been spending money on; it just seemed to fly out of my hands. I always paid whenever I went out for lunch or dinner with my friends. I bought clothes for an exorbitant price at the "car boutiques" held every school-day afternoon in the car park, where girls sold clothes bought on sale from the UK or the US. I went to fancy hair salons outside campus every other week instead of washing and straightening my hair myself or going to the cheaper salons on campus. I splurged on weekly manicure and pedicure treatments. I couldn't imagine living without what I had come to regard as bare necessities.

But now my nails were chipped, and my hair urgently needed attention. It didn't occur to me to paint my nails and fix my hair myself; I was only concerned about which of my friends I could borrow some money from until Terry got back in touch with me. Surely it wouldn't be long until he called me back.

I began to rack up debt with no means of repaying it. I ran my mind back to the last time I saw Terry. We'd had a lovely time, and there'd been no indication that anything was wrong.

One Tuesday evening, six weeks after I'd last heard from Terry, I realised I was completely broke. I couldn't think of anyone that would be willing to lend me money. The week before I had actually borrowed some money from Wale; I'd called him up and asked him to meet me in the faculty car park after his class.

"Wale, I need 5000 naira," I'd said.

His features creased into a frown. "What? Are you okay? What's wrong?" He held my shoulders and bent forward to look into my eyes.

I looked away and cocked my head to the side, scratching my neck. "Yeah, I... erm..." I licked my lips. "I'm fine, I just... I need to pay for something and, well, I need money to pay for it."

"No, something's wrong – what is it? You can talk to me."

"No, you know what, don't worry about it. I'll just ask Monica if she can lend it to me," I said, turning to walk away but he grabbed my arm and pulled me back to him.

"If you need the money that bad, I'll get it for you. I just wish you'd tell me what it's for."

I bit my lip and shook my head.

"Okay, at least promise me that you're all right."

I smiled then; he was going to give me the money. I reached up, standing on the tip of my toes and wrapped my arms around his neck, kissing him full on the mouth.

"I'm okay. Thank you so much. I'll pay you back, I promise."

"Sure," he muttered in a flat voice. He didn't hug me back.

I had tried to be careful with the 5000 naira, but now it was all gone. How had I managed to live on 7000 naira a month just a few months ago? It was ridiculous that I couldn't even make 1000 naira last one day.

I thought Terry again; it seemed as if he was the only one that could help me out of my predicament. So I did what I should have done in the first place; I called Tobi. After all, I had met him through her.

"Hey, Tee," I said when she answered.

"Hey, boo, I was wondering when you were going to call," she responded smugly.

"Why is that?" I asked.

"Well, I saw Terry on Friday night..." She paused for effect. "I'm guessing that's why you're calling."

"What?" I feigned that I was hurt. "I was just calling to speak with my lovely friend."

Tobi grunted in response.

"Okay, yes," I went on, "and to ask about Terry. Did he say anything about me?"

"I don't know if I should say anything. Sweetie, I think you should just forget about him. You had a good run, I'll give you that, and I still can't believe you never slept with him. He must have the patience of a saint!"

"You know I can't sleep with him; I love Wale."

"Ugh, spare me. Like love can put food on the table or shoes on your feet."

"So what did Terry say, *now*?" I asked impatiently, deliberately ignoring her statement about Wale.

"He wants you to stop calling him, says you've left over a hundred voice messages already."

"What? I can't believe he said that... but did he say why he's avoiding me?"

"Oh yeah, he also said he's fed up of 'smelling what he can't eat'."

"Yuck," I said, and then I sighed. "That sounds fair, I guess; I just wish Terry had given me some sort of warning."

"Why? Would you have reconsidered?"

"No, I guess it would have made me feel less... I don't know if 'abandoned' is the right word. He could have at least told me." I stuck out my bottom lip like a little child.

"Apparently, he didn't think it would take this long for you to get the message."

I sighed again. "The weird thing is that I actually miss Terry. He had become more than just a chequebook to me."

"Hey ho! Don't tell me you have feelings for Terry!"

"It's not as bad as it sounds. I just thought I had become more than just the girl he wanted to sleep with. When next you see him, can you just tell him that for what it's worth? That I'm sorry if I ever led him on and that I miss him?"

"You really want me to tell him that you miss him? I don't think that's a good idea. It just makes you sound pathetic."

"Just tell him exactly what I said, okay?"

"Sure, no problem."

"The thing is, I guess I've known all along why Terry's been avoiding me. I just didn't want to admit it to myself. He's only human after all, and when he made the promise never to pester me for sex, a part of him must have held out some hope that I would find the idea of sex with him attractive the more time I spent with him. And he was right. The idea of sex with him was terrifying, but I had thought about it. But now that it could be the only thing that'll get him back, I find myself considering it even more. But, Tobi, I can't do that to Wale. He knows I'm a virgin, so sex with Terry would really complicate things. Wale has been so patient with me, willing to wait until I'm ready; I just couldn't do that to him.'

Tobi listened as I rambled on and she promised to speak with Terry on my behalf.

Terry called me that evening. As soon as I heard his voice, my hands tingled, and I felt heat radiate through my chest; there was hope for me yet.

"I've just spoken with Tobi," he said, as soon as we were done with pleasantries. "She made me realise that it was harsh to cut you off without any warning. But considering our relationship, I thought it was the best thing to do at the time. You have a boyfriend, and I'm sure you'll be happy with him, without me getting in your way."

I took a deep breath.

"Thanks for calling me back, Terry. I do understand why you decided to cut me off. I guess I'd begun to grow too attached to you." I hesitated; was there anything as too much honesty? "And the lifestyle that came with spending time with you."

"Can I ask you a question?"

"Of course."

"What is it that you want from me? You know we can't just be friends; I definitely want more than that. But you need to think about what you want."

I thought about his question, remaining silent for several seconds.

"I want what we had before."

"Babe, I can't give you that anymore. I think calling you back wasn't a bad idea."

Oh no! I was going to lose him again! Now that I had him on the phone, I was going to do whatever I could to make him see me again. Hopefully, he would give me some money.

"Wait, don't go," I pleaded. "Can we meet somewhere?"

He paused. I could tell he was surprised by my request.

"Do you have something for me?" he asked, his voice sounding hopeful.

"Yes," I responded quickly. "I do." I squeezed my eyes shut, my heartbeat racing. I felt as if I were in a car that was spinning out of control; it was going to crash, and there was nothing I could do to stop it. I clenched my free hand into a fist, my nails bit into my palm.

"I can pick you up in an hour," he said. "Say, around seven. I'll call you when I'm outside."

"See you then," I responded. A part of me was relieved that I was going to see him again, but the most sensible part of me was terrified. I covered my face with my hands and let out a small cry. I wasn't sure I could go through with it but felt I had to sacrifice something for everything he'd given me.

I went to see if Monica was in her room. I found her lying on her bed, watching TV.

"What's up?" she said, instantly concerned. "You look like a fish out of water."

"I need your advice." I paused, wondering how to proceed. "You know how Terry has been ignoring my calls for the last six weeks? Well, he just called me, and I asked if we could hook up."

"So, what's the problem?"

"He thinks we're going to do it." I expected shock and admonition, but Monica remained calm.

"Did you give him that impression?"

I nodded. "I just panicked, Terry was going to get off the phone, and I know if he had, I would never be able to get to talk to him again, and I need money! Who else will give me money just like that?"

"True, you have been very lucky with him. He knows you're a 'Vee', right?"

I nodded.

"I think you can get away with a 'BeeJay'. You've done it before, haven't you?"

"Erm, no."

"Jeez, are you kidding me? Don't worry. It's easy, just remember not to bite. It's not like eating a sausage; it's more like, well, licking an ice lolly. And you have to look like you're really enjoying yourself."

I grimaced.

"Well, what other options do you have? Most girls would kill to be in your shoes. Do you know what these Aristo girls get paid for a night? They're lucky if they get up to N10,000 for sex, but you must have gotten close to half a million from this guy."

"He hasn't given me up to that amount," I protested, smiling. Somehow Monica had made it sound like a compliment, and I was flattered. But then it hit me. "Oh no!" I exclaimed. "I can't believe I'm actually going to go through with this. Before I met Terry, I was perfectly happy with my allowance and now... I can't imagine how I could have survived on it. Arrgghh! This feels like a nightmare."

"Would you like me to come with you?"

"Would you? Thanks, Monica," I said, sincerely grateful. At least I wouldn't be alone.

"Sure thing. Call me when he gets here."

At 7.20 p.m., just when I was beginning to wonder if Terry had changed his mind, he called me to say he was outside. The atmosphere in the car was tense. I could tell Terry wasn't happy that I'd brought Monica along. I sat in the front seat with my shoulders slumped and stared ahead at nothing in particular. I was preoccupied with what I had to do; I kept imagining how it would be, and I couldn't wait for it to be over and done with.

We had dinner at a Lebanese restaurant on the Island, and afterwards, we went to a secluded hotel a few minutes from the restaurant. It seemed that Terry had gotten a room earlier as we didn't stop at the reception desk but just went straight to the lifts. My body followed Terry down the long corridor to the room that was to be the place of my defilement, but my mind was far away. For some inexplicable reason, I felt that it was something I needed to do. I was hoping he would give me at least 50,000 naira, so I could pay off my 25,000 naira debt and survive for the next few days without having to change my lifestyle: one which I saw as necessary to be happy and to keep holding onto the façade I had built up. I wondered how this would go down. Would he want to have small talk with me and make it seem as if I was doing it of my own free will, or would he just pull down his pants and wait for me to pleasure him in a way I had never done to anyone before? In a manner which I felt was both disgusting and degrading?

"Please let it be over quickly," I prayed.

In the hotel room, Terry smiled at Monica and me and asked if we wanted something to drink. I shook my head silently, while Monica asked for a Coke. She plunked herself in the armchair, turned on the TV and flicked through the channels. I wished I could be as composed and as confident as Monica was but then again, she wasn't the one going to the slaughterhouse. I was glad she had insisted on coming with me; at least it would minimise the risk of Terry raping me when he realised I wasn't going to go all the way with him. Terry brought Monica her drink and gestured for me to come with him. I looked at Monica, and she gave me a sympathetic look. "Good luck," she mouthed. "Remember, no teeth." I swallowed hard and, bracing myself, followed Terry into the adjoining room. There was a queen-sized bed in the centre of the room, but Terry ignored it, choosing to sit in the armchair in the corner.

"I've missed you so much," he said. I stood where I was, a few feet away from him, my arms and shoulders tense, not sure of what was expected of me.

"Come and sit down," he said, patting his thighs.

I shook my head, covering my mouth with my hand. "Let's just get this over with," I said in a strangled voice. My chest tightened, and I felt a horrible sensation in the pit of my belly.

Terry angled his head at me. "Are you sure you want to do this? You can back out now; it's not too late."

Yeah right, I thought; easy for you to say. I was tempted to ask if he would still give me the money if I backed out but I already knew what his response would be. I nodded, hugging my arms around my chest.

    The room was silent for a while with me just standing there and Terry, sitting and looking at me. What was the thing to do in this situation? It didn't look as if he was going to point me in the right direction; it was up to me to take the initiative. I closed my eyes and took a deep breath. I had made up my mind; this was going to happen, so it was up to me to make it less uncomfortable than it was. I willed myself to want to do it, and I felt a boldness take over me. When I opened my eyes, I looked into his and smiled seductively at him. I walked over to where he sat and, not breaking eye contact, I bent forward, running my hands down his thighs from his knees to his member. His eyes widened, and his lips stretched into a grin. Oh my God! I can't believe I'm about to cheat on my boyfriend. With a married man! I shook my head to get rid of my thoughts. I felt him suck in his breath as I rubbed my hands over his fast expanding groin area. I unzipped his jeans, and his member sprang up at me. I held it in my hands and in spite of myself, I felt a pleasurable thrill run through me. I rubbed my hands on it, going up and down from the tip to the shaft, over and over again. He reached for my blouse, undid my buttons, and reached into the cups of my bra to free my breasts. I heard his sharp intake of breath as my breasts sprang out of their confines, my nipples hard and aroused. I felt him harden even more. This was wrong; I shouldn't be enjoying this. I moistened my lips and took a deep breath as I put his tip between them. He groaned loudly, which encouraged me further. I sank to my knees between his legs and took all of him into my mouth. He grabbed my breasts with both hands and grazed my nipples with his thumbs. A soft moan escaped from my lips; it felt so good, the fullness of him in my mouth and his hands on my breasts. I felt a stirring in the pit of my stomach and a pleasant moistness further south. I twirled my tongue around the tip and sucked on him hard, putting all of him in my mouth and letting him slide out again until I felt that my jaws couldn't take it anymore. Just when I was about to give up, he grabbed my head and pushed it down on him hard; I spluttered, but he didn't ease up. When I looked up, I caught sight of his face; his eyes were glazed over in ecstasy, his mouth was open in a silent swoon. I whimpered, shaking my head to loosen his hold. He let me move my head up a little but then, shifting his weight onto his feet, he thrust himself back into my mouth, going back and forth rapidly. My eyes widened at the discomfort in my throat and my eyes filled with tears. He shuddered and jerked, groaning, and I felt my mouth fill up with his sticky semen. As soon as he let go of my head, I jumped up with a muffled cry, cupping my mouth with my palm, and ran into the bathroom. I rushed to the sink and spat; I kept on spitting till I felt like I had no saliva left. I rinsed my mouth several times to try and get his taste out. I felt like a worthless rag, used and abused. I stared at my reflection in the mirror and turned away in disgust. I looked and felt like a prostitute, with my breasts hanging out and my mouth sore. I straightened my clothes and my hair as tears ran down my face; I tried to stop them but couldn't. Just as I felt ready to exit the bathroom, the door swung open, and Monica rushed in. She saw my tears and rushed to my side, gathering me into her arms. Her concern made me cry even harder until the sleeves of her dress were damp.

"Did he give you the money?" she asked after a few minutes. I sniffed and wiped my face with my palm.

"Erm, no. Not yet," I said in a small voice. I didn't care about the money now. I wished I hadn't done it. I had gone against everything I used to believe in. The innocent child within me grieved. How was I going to face Wale, after what I had just done? I had betrayed him and cheapened what we had. I had insulted it and trampled it in the dust.

"What?" Monica exploded, her nostrils flaring, and I started out of my self-pity. "Come on; we have to go after him, quickly." She let me go and raced for the door. It took me a moment to comprehend what she meant, and I felt cold all over. That would be the worst thing ever if I had just gone through that for nothing. The rage and shame washed over me: rage that he would be cruel enough to humiliate me in such a manner and shame that I had let him. I was worse than a prostitute; at least they got paid for what they did. I hurried after Monica, and we ran towards the lifts, hoping that we hadn't missed him. He wasn't by the lifts, so we raced to the stairs, running down two steps at a time. We must have looked like madwomen as we ran out through reception, our bags swinging and our chests heaving. Terry was driving out of the hotel car park by the time we got outside. He slowed down as he passed us. Believing that he was going to stop, I hurried to the car, trying but failing miserably to look calm and composed. I tried to calm the pounding in my ears; it had all been a misunderstanding. He wouldn't really have left without us, and without giving me some money. I got closer to the car and reached for the door on the passenger's side, which was when I saw the mischievous look in his eyes. His lips curled as if the sight of me left a bad taste in his mouth; then he threw his head back and sniggered. Before I could blink, I was sprayed with dirt and gravel as he revved the car. "No, no, no, no, this isn't happening!" I cried as I brought my fist crashing down hard on the boot of the car before the car shot forward and out of my reach.

"I swear, if I catch you, I will kill you!" I screamed after his car, my heart sinking to the bottom of my shoes as a wave of self-loathing engulfed me.

CHAPTER 25

That was the second time in my life that I'd felt suicidal; the only other time I'd felt like this was when I'd seen Josh with my best friend, Alexia. I contemplated the various ways of ending it. I stared at the door handle of the taxi longingly as we drove across the Third Mainland Bridge from Ikoyi to the university. I felt a dizzying pain in my chest as if my ribs were being constricted and I couldn't breathe. Tears rolled down my face as I sat, head bowed, shoulders slouched. I folded my arms over my chest and gripped my sides as if I was trying to hold myself together. Monica kept glancing at me in concern, but she didn't say anything.

There was only one person who could save me, who could make me feel human, but I couldn't confide in him. I needed to see him, to have him look at me the way he did, to remind myself that I wasn't completely worthless, that I could be loved and that someone did love me.

It was late that night, a few minutes to eleven, when I showed up on his doorstep with red, swollen eyes. As soon as I saw him, I broke into a fresh batch of tears. He took me in his arms and led me inside. I could tell he had been asleep, and I had woken him up. As I sobbed and whimpered in his arms, my nose running and my lips quivering, I waited for the inevitable barrage of questions, but they never came. He just held me and wiped my tears and runny nose till I tired myself out and fell asleep. I woke up the next morning still in his arms.

"Hey," he said, stirring to see my face. "You gave me quite a scare last night. Are you okay?"

I nodded; I did feel a lot better. In the bright light of morning, it was easy to imagine that last night had never happened. I smiled up at him and tried to come up with explanations for my behaviour. I could say it was that time of the month, or I could lie that I lost my grandma – but then he would want to pay his respects to my parents and would want to come for the funeral. I could say I had a big fight with Tobi, and we were no longer friends. But what had we fought about? Hmm, maybe I'd tried to talk her out of going to a married man's house, and she had lost her temper, calling me a goody-two-shoes. Surely he couldn't dislike her more than he did already. I smiled at him, ready for whatever questions he had. He smiled back at me.

"Are you okay to attend lectures? I don't know about you, but I feel like just staying in bed all day."

I smiled gratefully at him because even though I felt better, my body ached all over, and I felt like I had just been through a meat grinder.

"Let's stay in bed," I agreed.

"Okay," he said, disentangling himself from me and getting out of bed. "I'm going to get breakfast; you just stay there and rest." Sliding his feet into his slippers, he strode out of the room, still in his pyjamas.

With Wale gone, my mind was free to wander, and I pondered the events of the night before. A part of me was convinced that I'd deserved the way Terry has treated me and I felt cheap and worthless. I wondered what must be going through Wale's head. At no point did it occur to me that maybe he was waiting for me to tell him what had got me so riled up. The worst part was that I was itching to call Terry. I needed to offload some of my anger, to tell him what I thought of him and what he'd done to me.

I peeped out of the door to check that Wale was nowhere in sight; then I took out my mobile phone and toyed with it for a few minutes, trying to pluck up the courage to dial Terry's number. Eventually, I shut my eyes tight and pressed the call button; at worst he wouldn't pick up his phone.

"Hello," he answered, and I almost dropped the phone in shock. I hadn't thought about what to say as I hadn't expected him to pick up.

"Erm, hi, it's me," I said shyly, half expecting him to hang up on me. This wasn't the tone I should be taking; I should be screaming down the phone at this son of a bitch who had taken advantage of me and had made me feel worse than I'd ever felt in my life.

"Yes, what do you want?" he asked coldly.

"Why, Terry? What did I ever do to you?" I asked, tears beginning to pool around my eyelids.

Terry laughed a dry mirthless laugh. "Are you serious? Why are you trying to play a game you'll never win? Look, you're not like Tobi, and you'll never be like her. I would advise you to give up now and face your boyfriend and your studies. Do you think I'm a fool? You say you have something for me, and then you throw me a bone like I'm a dog."

"But Terry..."

"You said I didn't tell you the last time, so I'm telling you now. Don't call me again." He hung up on me.

I stared at the phone, dry-mouthed. If I'd felt horrible before, there wasn't a word in my vocabulary to describe how I was feeling. So that was it? I had made a fool of myself and risked my relationship with Wale for nothing? I resolved there and then that I would never again put myself in such a compromising situation. I was going to start over, cut back on my expenses – okay, maybe exaggerate some expenses to my parents to get more money – but I was never going to let any man make me feel this way again.

By the time Wale came back in with breakfast, two loaves of bread and some Akara (fried ground beans), I was composed and smiling. This was the boy I loved with all my heart, and I was going to protect our love with everything in my power.

CHAPTER 26

When I made my resolutions, I had meant every word and had no intentions of wavering. It was evident that the kind of life Tobi lived was not for me. I couldn't handle it. But as strong as my resolve was, my relapse still happened; when it did, however, it came in stages. I had been exposed to a world of easy cash and had got to the point of beginning to condone it. So while I remained faithful to Wale and to our relationship, unconsciously I perked up whenever a particularly nice-looking car drove past me, hoping the driver would notice me and stop to chat me up. When I went out clubbing with my girlfriends, I would choose to stay with them in VIP whereas before I would have been itching to get to the regular club where I could dance without feeling self-conscious.

A month after the incident with Terry, I was already living my artificial life; I didn't even feel like me anymore. It was one lie or the other to get my parents to keep giving me money. I was also getting adept at stealth. Whenever I saw a girl to whom I owed money, I would duck into the nearest hiding place – behind a car, under a bed or beneath the desks in class – until the coast was clear. I stopped picking up their calls and stayed away from my room as much as possible. I was always in Wale's room; it was the one place no one thought to look for me.

One Friday afternoon Tobi called me.

"Hey, chick, what are you doing tonight?" she asked.

"Just hanging out with Wale; what's up?"

"Well, that's boring – so, change of plans; we're going out tonight. I have a surprise for you."

"Fine, see you later," I responded dryly. Another night of watching her pick up guys or the other way round: whoop de doo!

"Aren't you going to ask what the surprise is?"

"You said it's a surprise, so I want to be surprised when you get here."

"Fine, be like that, bitch," she said and hung up. I knew she wasn't really mad; she was just playing up with her drama queen antics. I shrugged and went about my day.

In the evening, Tobi called me to come outside.

"Why don't you come inside?" I asked. "I'm not ready yet."

"Fine," she grumbled. When she came up to my room, she was bubbling with excitement.

"Hurry up, come on, come on," she kept saying, as I applied my mascara and put on my shoes.

When we got outside, I turned to her.

"Wait, who's picking us up?"

A huge grin broke out across her face. "That's the surprise!" she exclaimed, fishing out her keys and running towards a shiny metallic red Honda CR-V.

"Wow."

"What do you think?" she asked, leaning back against the car and throwing her hands up as if to showcase it.

"It's beautiful." I ran my hands over the car and felt just how smooth and shiny it was. I couldn't help but feel a tiny bit of envy. Here I was, almost penniless, and my friend had so much money that she could buy a car.

"How can you afford it?" I asked, forcing a smile.

"I have a friend who owns a dealership. He gave me a good deal." She waved her hand dismissively.

"Congratulations, I'm really happy for you," I said.

"Thank you." The smile she gave was patronising. "Let's go," she said, tossing her hair back over her shoulders.

I was a bit wary; I'd never seen Tobi drive and wasn't sure if she even could. Would it be rude of me to ask? I mean, she'd driven the car all the way here from Ibadan or wherever she'd come from, hadn't didn't she?

It turned out that she drove like a maniac, with no concern for her safety or the safety of the other drivers on the road.

"So who taught you to drive?" I asked, half mocking, half serious.

"Ha-ha, I can drive nau; just because you've never seen me drive doesn't mean I can't."

"I know you can drive; I was just wondering if anyone taught you or if you taught yourself."

"Don't worry about that; you're in safe hands." She turned in her seat to get something from her bag on the back seat and the car swerved dangerously close to the car in the next lane.

I pulled my seatbelt across my chest hurriedly and did the clasps. I held on tight to my seat and prayed that we would get to our destination in one piece. Tobi looked at me and burst out laughing.

"Come on; my driving is not that bad."

"Just keep your eyes on the road, yeah?" I said, staring straight ahead.

By the time we got to the club, I was fighting the urge to pee my pants. We'd had up to five near-misses. My armpits were clammy, and my heart was in my mouth; I was just glad the drive was over. We entered the club, and as soon as we walked into VIP, I noticed a man in a polo shirt and jeans staring at Tobi. She glanced at him and looked away, feigning disinterest. I noticed, and I was slightly relieved. Hopefully, it wouldn't be one of those nights when she would be occupied throughout, and I would be stuck sitting by myself, trying to repel the attentions of randy men with the well-used statement that I had a boyfriend. I doubt if any of them believed me; they just grunted and proceeded to convince me of the reasons I needed to leave my "broke-ass" boyfriend and go home with them. While I felt uncomfortable with the thought of being close to anyone but Wale, I toyed with the idea that I could find another "Terry". A guy I could lead on with only the promise of sex, while he showered me with money and gifts.

As soon as Tobi noticed the guy staring, though, she started acting weird. He kept watching us, but he didn't approach. I didn't understand what game Tobi and this guy were playing, and I was uncomfortable. I expected Tobi to go and talk to him, or to tell him off, but she just ignored him. She acted as if it was normal.

"Tobi, why is that guy staring at you like that? Do you know him?" I nudged her and nodded in his direction.

She smiled a weird smile. "Yeah, don't you know who that is?" she whispered.

"Erm... I don't think so. Who is he?" I inched closer to her so I could hear her response.

"He's the owner of Bramblings Shopping Centre."

"Hmmm." So what if he owned one of the largest shopping centres in the country? I took a closer look at him. He wasn't particularly ugly, but there was something about his face that sent shivers down my spine. He seemed like a man who would do anything to satisfy his hunger, physical or sexual. He wasn't particularly fat, but he had that protruding belly that Nigerian men carry so valiantly, large and perfectly round.

"How come you even know what the owner of Bramblings looks like?"

"Why is that important?" she chided, still whispering.

So we sat through the night, resisting all advances and pretending we were having a good time. At this point, I had an idea of what was going on. The fish had been hooked as soon as we came in; now we were just waiting. Tobi bought us drinks – expensive ones – and she actually paid! Usually, she let guys pay for her but today she didn't welcome any attention from other men. It was as if Tobi was putting on a private show for this Bramblings guy. When she decided she wanted to dance, she pulled me up and proceeded to deliver her sexiest moves. I was a bit uncomfortable; when I dance I like to have the ability to move my limbs as I see fit, but as Tobi was now in my personal space, I was reduced to bopping my head and making small movements. It definitely wasn't for my benefit. To my relief, she was done with her dancing after a couple of songs.

"We're leaving," she said, grabbing her purse off the chair and leaving me to follow.

"Okay," I said, rolling my eyes at her retreating back.

I took my time, downing my drink and gathering up my stuff in no particular hurry. Since Tobi hadn't given me much notice, she could damn well wait for me. I couldn't help but notice that her admirer was no longer on his seat; knowing that it wasn't a coincidence he was leaving just as we were, I took even slower strides. I just hoped Tobi wasn't going to change her mind about dropping me back on campus; she had promised to take me home tomorrow, so she was going to spend the night in my room and then give me a ride home in the morning.

When I got to the car, Tobi was seated behind the wheel, drumming her nails impatiently on the steering wheel, and the big belly guy was nowhere to be seen.

"What took you so long?"

"Hey, calm down. You should be the one apologising for leaving me behind." I was halfway in the car, my bum on the seat but one leg outside the car. The door was ajar, and I held onto the handle.

"Whatever." She waved her hand dismissively. "So anyway, I'm going to Babatunde – you know, the Brambling guy's house. Would you like to come or do you want to take a cab back to school?"

"What? Just like that?" My mouth dropped open in disbelief that she would treat me in such a manner.

"Look, I'm sorry, I know I promised to take you back to campus, but I can't pass this opportunity up. Babatunde has asked me to follow him. He's waiting in that Range Rover." I looked in the direction she was pointing, and sure enough, there was a Range Rover parked on the opposite side of the road, with its lights on.

"Tobi, you know I don't have any money, and I'm trying to manage with the little that I have. I can't afford to pay for a cab, but I really cannot go through another night of listening to you having disgusting sex with some guy."

"Eh, okay, that 'disgusting sex' paid for the car you're in."

I rolled my eyes at her.

She let out a long breath and rubbed the back of her neck. "Just come with me, okay?"

"I can't see that I have any other options, as long as he doesn't mind."

"Okay, let's go. Shut the door."

"Erm, aren't you going to ask him if it's okay?"

"No need; he'll find out when we get there."

"Fine by me," I responded, shutting the door and settling into my seat.

We drove behind the Range Rover to Victoria Garden City. The front of the house didn't look as impressive as I had expected and I was a little disappointed. For the house of the owner of a massive shopping complex, I had expected it to be big and imposing. We drove in as the gates opened, and saw a magnificent mansion. The reason why we couldn't really see much of the house from outside the gates was because of the gigantic compound. We parked the car where we were instructed to by the uniformed security guard. We wouldn't want to mix up Tobi's CR-V with the Mercedes and Bugatti.

We followed Babatunde into the house, our faces betraying none of the awe we felt. It was a typical day after all, and we went into stinking rich mansions all the time. I thought the décor of the house of the house was garish; it reeked of money, almost as if the walls had been plastered with the real thing. There was even an eight-foot golden statue of a lion at the entrance.

As we walked behind the man, I thought it a bit weird that he hadn't said one word to us. Who invites people to their house and doesn't speak with them? He didn't even seem surprised that I had come along nor did he ask our names. In fact, he barely glanced at us. We walked into a beautiful living room, and he spoke for the first time, asking us to make ourselves comfortable before striding off.

Tobi and I sat down, with me perched gingerly on the edge of my seat. Wow, I thought, looking around. This was like, the most expensive house I had ever been in. The over-the-top chandeliers, the soft plush cream sofas and the carpets looked as if they had been installed that morning. They were spotless. A steward appeared and asked if we wanted something to drink. We shook our heads, and he nodded expressionlessly and walked away.

We sat there waiting, barely speaking to one another, slightly paranoid that there were cameras everywhere and that we were being watched. We were just beginning to relax when a man wearing a suit came to summon Tobi. I remember thinking that she must have nerves of steel to do this all the time. Babatunde gave me the heebie-jeebies; he could easily be a serial killer. He obviously had zero social skills. No hello, no introductions, and I found out from Tobi later that he hadn't even approached her at the club; he had sent one of his guys to talk to her. But when had this happened? I hadn't seen her talking to anybody; I needed to start paying more attention to things happening around me.

Tobi smiled at me and stood up.

"I'll be okay," she said as if she knew what had been going through my mind.

"Be careful," I whispered in response.

I wondered what I was going to do to while away the time she was gone. No sooner had the thought crossed my mind than a maid came to inform me that my room was ready. I looked around me to check if perhaps she was speaking to someone else. She smiled and gestured for me to follow her. She led me into a lovely comfortable room and showed me around as if we were in a hotel – the minibar, the en suite bathroom, how to use the TV on the wall – and then she left me to my devices. Nice! At least I wouldn't be bored waiting for Tobi. I dropped my bag on the floor and flopped onto the soft queen-sized bed. I grabbed the TV remote from the bedside table and flipped through the channels. I fell asleep watching *Fresh Prince of Bel Air* and was woken up by Tobi shaking my shoulders.

I groaned. "What time is it?" I sat up and rubbed my eyes.

"Babe, you will never believe how much Babatunde gave me." Her eyes sparkled, and she was grinning from ear to ear like an idiot.

I frowned. "How much?"

"Two... thousand... dollars!" she said, pausing after each word for maximum effect.

"Whoa!" I shrieked, sitting up quickly. "You're kidding."

"Nope," she responded smugly. "And he asked me to give you this." She handed me a few notes. My eyes widened in surprise and glee. I took the money from her and counted it. Three hundred dollars! That was almost fifty thousand naira.

"Aaaaaah!" I squealed. I jumped up from the bed and did a dance.

"Shh, not so loud," Tobi said.

"Wow," I said, trying to catch my breath.

"I don't know; I wondered the same thing."

"Wow," I said again. I fanned myself with the money and burst into laughter. Three hundred dollars! And I didn't even have to do anything!

"Is it okay if I go and say 'thank you' to him?" I straightened my rumpled clothes in a bid to make them look presentable. I'd thought of taking them off last night and sleeping in my underwear, but I'd been paranoid about doing that in such a strange place. Plus there were no locks on the door.

"I don't think that's a good idea; we should just go. Don't worry; I already thanked Babatunde enough for both of us."

"Right." I gave her a knowing smile.

"Let's go, come on." She got off the bed and dragged me out of the room.

"What's the hurry? Let's see if we can order some breakfast now."

"Trust me; we need to leave."

"Why, what is it?" I looked at her carefully. She did seem a bit odd.

"Tobi, are you okay? Did he hurt you?" I moved closer to her, whispering. He did look like a psycho.

Tobi shook her head. "It's not important, but can we just leave now?"

"Okay, sure." Grabbing my bag, I hurried out behind her.

Tobi drove me back to my hall to pick up my things and then she dropped me off at home. Throughout our journey, I kept thinking of how I was going to save and manage my money. I was really excited. I had to admit that I was lucky. Keeping the grin off my face was hard. I could afford to pay off all my debt and still have money left over.

"Thanks, Tobi," I said, reaching over to give her a hug. She winced in pain when I squeezed her shoulder. I looked at her with concern written all over my face.

"Tobi, seriously, you need to tell me if this man hurt you." It felt slightly awkward for me to be asking Tobi these questions. We never discussed what happened with the men she slept with.

"Don't be silly. Of course, I'm all right." She looked as if she wanted to tell me something but was fighting an internal struggle.

"You can tell me anything." I dropped my voice so that she could hear the sincerity and concern that I felt. "I promise, I won't tell anybody."

Tobi smiled, and I felt her shutters coming down; the vulnerability in her eyes disappeared. She was now calm and in control.

"I'm great. Hey, I've got two thousand dollars, baby! I couldn't be better."

"Okay, if you're sure." I sighed, disappointed that she was shutting me out.

"I just need a favour," she said as I turned to open the car door.

I turned back to her.

"Babatunde wants me to come back next Friday. Will you go with me?"

"Tobi, I don't think we should go back there. That guy is scary, and he's clearly hurt you even though you're pretending it's nothing."

"Look, he didn't do anything to me that I can't handle," she said defensively. "This is the first time I've ever been paid this much. I told you yesterday; I'm not passing up this opportunity. I'm going to milk it for as long as I can. You can come with me, or I can just ask someone else."

I thought about it. Since Tobi said she was fine, who was I to say she wasn't? I could do with getting some more money without having actually to do anything.

"Fine, I'll go with you," I agreed, feigning reluctance. I was already counting the dollars in my head.

CHAPTER 27

The following week went by in a blur; I had money in my purse, so life was definitely better than the week before when I'd had to count every penny before making even the smallest purchase. I spent most of my evenings with Wale, and I felt that our relationship was great. It had lost a bit of the initial intensity and passion, but I still loved him, and we couldn't keep our hands off each other. It was weird, but I felt as if our relationship had been more intense with Terry in the picture. On some level, the flirting and game-playing with Terry had stirred up something in me, and I was able to express with Wale what I couldn't do with Terry. I felt ashamed to think that that could be the reason. I had felt as if I was invincible, that nothing I did with Terry would ever affect my relationship with Wale as long as I never let Terry touch me. But I was beginning to realise that I hadn't been immune to the charms of a good-looking, older and mature man, no matter how hard I tried to deny it. Would I have cheated on Wale if Terry wasn't married? In fact, I had cheated on Wale with Terry. What was wrong with me? Did I have no conscience? I had conveniently stored that particular memory somewhere so deep that I was beginning to imagine that it hadn't actually happened, or that it hadn't meant anything. We'd had sex; the fact that it was oral didn't make it less wrong. Somehow I managed to face Wale every day without the guilt killing me, and this made me think that maybe I was not as 'good' as I believed I was.

Lately, I sensed that Wale was beginning to want more. I found myself constantly removing his hands from between my legs and pressing my knees tightly together whenever his hands wandered. I had no problem with him touching my thighs, but when he started trying to probe deeper, it made me uncomfortable.

"I just want to touch you," he said one evening. We were making out on his bed, and I had just pushed his hands off. I made a face.

"I told you, I'm not ready for that yet."

"I'm not asking you for sex. Surely you've been touched there before."

"Never!" I lied, my mind flashing back to Alex, the randy guy in Tobi's so-called uncle's house.

"I'm just worried that things will go too far and get out of control," I added.

"I can control myself, don't worry about that." He leant away from me and narrowed his eyes. "Why don't you want me to touch you?"

"I told you, I'm not ready," I said, countering his suspicion with a steadfast gaze.

"Are you worried I'll discover something I won't like?"

"Like what?" I had a feeling I knew what he was implying.

"Like the fact that you're probably not a virgin."

"What?" I blinked rapidly, my mouth hanging open, and shook my head. "You didn't just say that."

"Jade, we've been dating for over two years, and we've never seen each other naked. No one, apart from me, actually believes that you are a virgin, and all my friends think I'm an idiot for falling for that crap." He was beginning to raise his voice, and he made sweeping arm gestures as he spoke. I reached for him with the intention of placing a hand on his shoulder to calm him down, but he flinched away from me, getting off the bed and pacing the length of the room. I bit my bottom lip, fighting back the feeling of rejection. My hand hung in mid-air for a fraction of a second before I withdrew it. I was hurt that he wouldn't let me touch him. I lifted my chin and faced him.

"What friends? Are you listening to your friends that have never gotten laid, or is it, Sade?" Damn Sade, constantly trying to sabotage our relationship even though he insisted they were just friends and nothing more.

He stood up and glared at me; I knew something bad was coming.

"Where were you coming from that night?" he asked, his tone so low that I had to strain to hear him.

"What night?" I asked, trying to keep my cool. I had frozen over on the inside. I wrapped my arms around myself to stop myself from shaking. I wasn't ready for this question: not now. And I knew that I was the worst liar. No matter what I said, he was going to know I was lying.

"Don't play dumb. You know the night I'm referring to. Who is the man that made you cry so much? Christ! You must think I'm a fool. Tell me, who was it?" He stood in front of me and pulled me up from the bed so I was standing in front of him. His eyes were hard, his beautiful face was flushed, and his nostrils flared. I couldn't look into his eyes so I chose to stare at my feet.

"I wasn't crying because of a man; I'd had a fight with Monica," I mumbled without conviction. Where had this argument come from? If only I had allowed him to touch me like he'd wanted.

"What? Don't lie to me. Someone saw you in a hotel with some guy."

"Who saw me?" I asked, sounding bolder than I felt. The words of Shaggy "It wasn't me" flashed through my mind and if I hadn't been in such a serious situation, I would have laughed. I wasn't going to admit to anything, I mean, I was still a virgin so it didn't really count.

"I can't tell you, all I can say is that it was a very reliable source. What have you been getting up to, Jade? I've noticed so many changes in you since we got back together. Something isn't quite right. You're beginning to act like a 'big girl'. And the way you spend money. I'm worried about you. You need to be careful about what you're getting into. I knew that Tobi girl was a bad influence on you."

"Wale, you don't have to worry about me, I'm not getting myself into anything. How did we even get into this conversation?" I smiled at him, willing the tension out of his body. "Please, can we sit down?"

He nodded and sat down. I sat facing him and continued.

"Your source was right; I was in a hotel that night." I saw fear in his eyes and something else: anger?

"I went with Monica," I explained. "She was on a date. I was only keeping her company, making sure she was safe and then we got into a fight and she completely lost it."

I made a mental note to tell Monica what I had said to Wale. Not that he was going to ask her, but you never know. It wouldn't hurt to make sure my alibi was tight. She would be upset, but I could handle her. I wasn't going to lose Wale over something as ridiculous as that night. Plus I didn't even get paid for it!

"So, that's the reason you were so upset?" he asked. I saw the struggle in his eyes, and I felt ashamed that I was doing this to him. I could see that he really wanted to believe me. A part of him must have felt on some level that it was all a load of bollocks, but I was confident that he would choose to believe me.

"You know how I get. I rarely cry, but it only takes the tiniest situation to get me upset. It was just a misunderstanding I'm sure we'll get over it." I looked at him and smiled. He didn't smile back, but I could see that the storm was over. He sighed.

"Please trust me; I've never done anything with anybody. And the only person I want to do it with is you." I took one of his beautiful hands in both of mine.

"When? Jade, I love you, but I'm only a man. You can't expect me to wait forever."

I nodded as he spoke.

When I'd told Wale I was a virgin, I had also said that I intended to remain that way until my wedding night. However, the decision to remain a virgin until my wedding was a decision I had made easily; I had never been in a relationship, and so I had no idea how difficult it was to do. Now I couldn't even remember why I'd made that decision. The idea of waiting until marriage seemed really ambitious. That decision had changed over time to waiting until I felt I was ready.

"I understand where you're coming from and can I just reassure you that I don't intend to keep you waiting forever. I just want to get to a point where I'll be satisfied that it was my decision and that I can handle whatever happens afterwards." I played with his fingers. He slipped his free hand under my chin and raised my head so I could look up at him.

"Hey, whatever happens, we'll handle it together. Look, I love you. You know I do, and if you love me too, you shouldn't be afraid."

"I know, please be patient with me. It'll be soon, I promise."

That Friday I went with Tobi to Babatunde's house. The next morning he sent Tobi away with the same amount of money for both of us as he had the week before. I really could turn this into a business: offering chaperoning services for wayward girls who didn't want to be left alone with strangers. I smiled to myself as Tobi, and I changed our dollars for naira at the black market.

This time, I would be more careful with my money. Since I didn't have Terry or any steady stream of ready cash, I was going to make my money go a long way. Also, I had to be careful with Wale; I didn't want him getting any more suspicious than he was now. Knowing now that he had spies around, I had to be extra careful and cover my tracks. He would flip if he knew I was going with Tobi to do what she did.

The next time Tobi and I went to see Babatunde, he sent her away with 500 dollars for me. That was 200 dollars more than I had been expecting and I was overjoyed. But I sensed that something was wrong. Tobi wasn't herself as she drove me home. She was short with me and seemed irritated by my presence.

"What's wrong, Tobi?" I asked as she parked in front of the gates to my parents' house. "Did I do anything to upset you?"

She glared at me without saying anything, and I braced myself for accusations, real or imagined. It wouldn't be out of character for Tobi to find fault and get upset when there was nothing to be upset about. All of a sudden, she sighed, and her whole stance relaxed.

She looked at me, her features grim.

"I don't want you to come with me to see Babatunde anymore. I'm sorry, I know that you're enjoying getting all that money without having to work for it, but there's always a catch. You need to remember that."

I gasped and covered my gaping mouth with my palm. I didn't realise how much I had come to rely on the money I got from Babatunde. The disappointment I felt was thick and overwhelming. I felt desperate. It had become my source; I couldn't go back to depending on my allowance.

"No, don't say that. But... are you going to continue seeing him?" I asked.

"Yes, but that's really none of your business," she snapped, frowning at me.

"Was it something I did?" I persisted. Surely, there had to be a reason for this decision. I knew that she needed me there, more than she needed the money he gave her... okay, maybe not more than the money, but I knew she wouldn't go there alone; she would have to find someone else. She was too scared of him. I had seen the fear in her eyes when she spoke of going to see him, and she was fearless when it came to a lot of things. What was his pull on her? And if she was so afraid of him, why did she keep going back? It wasn't like they had a relationship; as far as I knew he'd never called her, but she kept to her Friday night appointments religiously. That was the only time they saw each other. So what kind of hold did this man have on my friend?

"I didn't want to have to tell you, but he wants you."

"Oh," I said, realisation dawning. Tobi was only trying to protect me.

"Listen," she said, "I know there's no point warning you because you're a 'good' girl but stay away from that man – he's evil."

There it was again: the fear I'd seen in her eyes. I heard the tremor in her voice, and it gave me goose pimples and caused the hairs on my arms to rise.

"Why? What did he do to you?" I asked in a whisper as if he could hear us. I didn't really expect her to answer, knowing how private she was, but my curiosity got the better of me.

Tobi looked lost. When she spoke, her voice sounded lifeless, as if she had withdrawn from her body and only an empty shell remained.

"He is a sick, depraved man. He's made me do some things that no one should ever be asked to do. At first, it wasn't too bad; I felt I could handle it. It was kinky, but it was okay, you know. I had my limits, and I thought, surely, it couldn't get any worse. But it did, Jade; it got really, really bad." Her hands shook as she spoke.

"How bad, Tobi? And why do you go back there? Is it the money?"

She looked at me with those lifeless eyes as if I had just said the most stupid thing she had ever heard.

"Money? I would give it all back to disentangle myself from him. He says I can only leave when he's done with me. Until then I have to do as he says."

I was shocked to hear her speak in such a manner. What would Babatunde do to her if she left him? Would he kill her?

"Can't you just tell him you've had enough and leave? I'm sorry; I didn't know it was this bad. I feel terrible about this – like I've been profiting from your pain."

She looked down at her hands. When she raised her head, the life was back in her eyes.

"Nah, it's fine," she said. "I'm... I'm fine. Thanks for the concern but it's not a good idea for me to take you with me next time." She waggled a finger in my face. "Can you imagine, I told him you were a Vee and were saving yourself for marriage and do you know what he said?" Without waiting for me to respond, she continued. "He said, 'No problem, I'll just go in through the back door'." She laughed. "Do you see how sick he is?"

"What? Like anal sex?" I asked, screwing up my nose, and we both laughed.

"Oh my lord, you are so naïve, I swear," she said, slapping her hand on her thigh.

So that was it? Maybe he made her have anal sex with him, and that was why she thought he was such a terrible man. Even though I imagined it was sick and yucky, surely people did it all the time. It couldn't be all that bad.

"Thanks, Tobi. I guess I had a good run, but what am I going to do now?" I was worried; it really was the end of my lucky streak. I couldn't imagine that I would be able to get some other guy to keep giving me money without having to give up anything.

"I know, but you really have to make up your mind about losing your virginity. What are you keeping that thing for anyway?" Tobi asked.

I turned away from her and looked out of the window. Tobi had lost her virginity at the age of thirteen to the French teacher in secondary school. Then she had acted as if she'd won some sort of race. Tobi had boasted about it, about how she'd made him beg for it and how grateful he always was when she "took care" of him. I'd always smiled, indulging her when she talked about it, but I knew for a fact that the man had been sleeping with a couple other girls in our class, not to mention the girls in the classes above us or even the classes below.

How was I supposed to explain to Tobi that I wanted my first time to mean something more than just two people satisfying their urges? I wanted the whole fairy tale, with a happily-ever-after thrown in.

"I'm just not ready yet," I responded, without turning back to face her.

"Well, it's up to you. I can hook you up when you're ready. The people I'll hook you up with pay very well."

I turned to look back at her.

"Okay, thanks," I said with a smirk. "For nothing," I finished under my breath.

I was desperate, but not that desperate. I would just have to stick with my good old allowance.

I hugged her goodbye and watched her drive away. As soon as she drove out of the driveway, I turned around and walked in through the gates deep in thought. The security guard greeted me with smiles and exaggerated servitude. I had formed the habit of passing him a few hundred naira for no reason, just because I could, but this time, I ignored him. Even in my distracted state, I didn't miss his disappointment. On entering the house, I said hello to my mum and dad who were having breakfast and responded to their questions about school and my health and if I was eating properly; then I went up to my room and threw myself face down on my bed. I lay there for a few hours, ignoring my siblings calling out to me, anything from "Did you eat the Suya I put in the fridge?" to "Come and get your stuff out of the hallway!" They gave up when I didn't respond. For the life of me, I couldn't understand why everyone had to be so loud. Couldn't they just come and find me?

So I stayed where I was on my bed, daydreaming. If I were getting this much money when I hadn't even slept with anybody, surely I would be rolling in it once I actually did it. No one would know what I was doing. I could have all the money I wanted to buy all the things I needed to be comfortable. I could afford to keep up my five thousand naira body lotion and other such things I needed on a regular basis. I searched for ways to justify what I was contemplating. I couldn't take the decision lightly; as much as I wanted all those things, letting go of my virginity would be like losing a unique part of me. I had come to depend on it as a part of my image. Something I was proud of: that at the ripe old age of twenty, with all the promiscuity that was rampant on campus, I had been able to hold on to it. Losing it would change everything; it would change my relationship with Wale and my relationship with the opposite sex in general. At the moment, I had lots of male friends, and that's all they were. Was I naïve in thinking that the fact that I was a virgin closed the door on any "will we or won't we?" speculations.

I made my decision. I was ready. But if I was going to do this, it had to be special and memorable for both of us. Wale was slightly more experienced than I was but I believed he had only ever been with one girl before me. And that had been ages ago. I had to prepare, I wanted everything to be perfect, and so I went shopping.

CHAPTER 28

On Tuesday afternoon, after my three-hour-long Law 402 lecture, I went to find Wale. I found him in one of the lecture halls having a conversation with a lecturer. I sat in a chair a few yards away and proceeded to wait for him. He spotted me after a few minutes and excused himself. I stared at him unashamedly as he strode towards me, a smile on his face. I marvelled that this beautiful creature belonged to me. I thought about what I had planned for that night, and I felt the blood rush to my face.

"Hey," he said, bending over to kiss me full on the lips. How amazing it was that I responded so easily every time he touched me. Every fibre in my body sprang alert with the slightest provocation.

"Hey you," I said, taking his hand and letting him pull me to my feet.

"You look beautiful," he said, a hungry look in his eyes.

I smiled and rolled my eyes at him. "Hold that thought... I need your room keys. I have a surprise for you!"

Wale's eyes widened, but he didn't say a word as he fished in his pockets for his keys and handed them to me.

"Be sure to be back for 6 p.m. No African time, or you'll miss the surprise," I warned, and I kissed him goodbye.

It was almost 4 p.m., so I had just over two hours to prepare. I hurried to my room to pick up the things I had bought, and then I headed over to Wale's place.

I checked my phone; I had received a message from Wale telling me he was slightly nervous about the surprise. Good, that made two of us.

"Don't be," I texted back.

I got to work setting up the candles and getting everything ready. The room slowly darkened; it looked as if it was going to rain. It was now 5.15, and I was almost done. I needed to get Wale here now or else he would be stuck wherever he was until the rain stopped. By then all my efforts would be wasted and who knew when I would be able to pluck up the courage to try to do it all over again. No, it had to be today.

I texted Wale to ask where he was and to tell him to start making his way to me before the rain started. Not long after I sent the message, I heard the sound of rain pouring down on the house, drumming out a rhythm on the roof like a child hitting a saucepan. I heard it hit the ground in large sloshes as puddles formed in no time.

So that was it, I thought, resigning myself to spending the evening alone in Wale's room. I brought the CD I'd burnt for the occasion out of my bag. I slotted it into the CD player, and the room was filled with the gentle crooning of Sade Adu. I had turned out the main lights and the light from the scented candles I had laid out flickered and gave the room a lovely calming glow. I changed his sheets to the new green and blue flowery ones I'd just bought, and I sprayed my perfume all around the room. I stood back and admired my work; it was perfect. Wale's presence would make it complete; I missed him already. I had on a black lacy teddy under a silk dressing gown. I had considered getting some wine but who was I kidding? Neither of us were big wine drinkers. So instead I got a bottle of Baileys for myself, and a bottle of Malibu and a can of Coke for him. I figured the alcohol would come in handy as I was very nervous. With everything ready, I lay on his bed and waited for him.

I love the rain, the way everything feels mellow, and the cleanness of the air afterwards. It affects people too; they tend to be happier afterwards as if the rain has washed away their troubles.

I was nervous, afraid of what I was about to do. I knew it would change my life and the way I viewed the world around me. I was opening one door and shutting another behind me forever. No matter how Tobi put down being a virgin, this was a huge deal. I had taken some painkillers in anticipation of the pain I was bound to feel. I wanted everything to be perfect; I had even purchased some condoms from the tuckshop in my hall, which had been a cringe-worthy experience; it was like I had the word "SLUT" written in red across my forehead.

Even as my mind was telling me I was wasting my time hoping Wale would show up in this torrential rains, in my heart, I knew he would find a way. I hadn't told him what I was planning, but he must have sensed it. The joy in his eyes had been unmistakable when I'd asked for his room keys and had given him a time frame to get back.

I tried ringing his mobile, but I couldn't get through; the signal was always bad when it rained heavily. I was beginning to drift off when I heard a gentle knock. I roused myself from my slumber, my heart catching in my throat. I opened the door; Wale leant against the doorframe. He was dripping wet.

"Howdy, ma'am," he said with a beautiful grin, tipping an imaginary hat. I smiled back. I was so happy he made it. He'd found his way to me through the rain. I held the edges of my dressing gown closer together in a play of chastity and batted my lashes at him coyly. Then, as if I'd suddenly changed my mind, I eased the robe off my shoulders and let it fall to the ground. I heard his sharp intake of breath as he pushed himself off the doorframe and walked in, kicking the door shut behind him. I laughed as he covered the distance between us. The electricity between us crackled, and I didn't care that he was getting me wet as we grabbed at each other passionately. My heart was so full and overjoyed. I felt as if I had made the right decision; he was my soul mate, and I loved him with all of my heart.

Everything was fantastic – no, beyond amazing, much more than anything I had ever felt in my life. He knew where to touch me and for how long. I ran my hands all over him, and his skin was soft and smooth. He was cool from the rain, and my warm palms hungrily tried to steal some of his coolness. It was the first time we'd been completely naked with each other. We stood looking at each other; we were finally going to do this. I handed him a condom, and he rolled it on. I was tense.

"Relax," he murmured in my ear. "I'm going to be gentle, I promise." I nodded. I trusted him completely and tried to relax. He laid me down gently on the bed and climbed in next to me. There was a moment of fumbling, and then a sharp, searing pain. I clenched the sheets and let out a scream. The painkillers didn't help. He covered my mouth with his.

"Is it in?" I asked, blinking back tears. It was a silly question. I knew it was. It hurt like crazy down there. He smiled at me.

"Are you okay?" he asked, and I nodded. Satisfied that I was okay, he thrust and I lay still, flinching with every thrust and waiting for the discomfort to shift. It didn't. After six thrusts, I couldn't take it anymore, and I pushed him off me.

"I'm sorry," I said. "It's just too painful."

He bit his lower lip and cocked his head to the side. "I think I know why. Do you trust me?"

"Yes," I responded without any hesitation. Wale smiled at me, and I smiled back.

"I'm going to try without this," he said, pulling off the condom. "Tell me if it feels better."

"But isn't that risky?"

"I'll be very careful, don't worry."

And this time, it was so much better. Thrills of pleasure ran through me with each thrust. At first, I was unsure of what to do. It felt a bit clumsy as I struggled to keep rhythm with Wale's thrusts. I bit back a soft moan self-consciously; the last thing I wanted was for him to think I was trying to emulate the girls in pornographic movies but after a few minutes I let go as I felt my body consumed, waves of fire and ice crashing through my veins in a heady combination. I allowed myself to be carried away – much to my chagrin, as that meant that I lost control over the sounds that I made. I whooped and hollered, swooned and moaned, and as I felt myself dangling over the edge I screamed out his name, whipping my head back and forth. He held me tighter as he shuddered and he groaned into my hair.

"You're so beautiful," he whispered in my ear when it was over. "I love you." I felt my spirits soar, and a huge grin spread across my face. I pulled a pillow over my head, embarrassed about the way I had behaved, like a wild animal.

"What?" he asked, trying to yank the pillow off my face. "Are you shy?" I took a peek at his face over the pillow; he was laughing at me.

"How was it?" I asked, looking anywhere but at him, cringing even as the words left my lips. He stopped laughing, and a soft smile spread across his face; he yanked the pillow from me. His eyes locked with mine as he brought his head down, his lips finding mine in a soft and sensuous kiss.

"It was the best thing that has ever happened to me," he cooed. "How was it for you?"

I felt my eyes moisten. "It was beautiful, perfect, everything I ever wanted my first time, and even more so because it was with you," I responded, my voice breaking.

He held me in his arms till I fell asleep and I was still in his arms when I opened my eyes the next morning. I snuggled closer into him and sighed happily. Everything was going to be alright.

I called Tobi the next day to talk about it.

"Finally! Congratulations, we have to celebrate."

I laughed along with her.

"So, how was it?" she asked. "Give me all the gory details."

"Nope, sorry, not going to happen."

"Come on," she prodded.

"All I can tell you is that it was incredible! I will never forget it."

"I can hear the satisfaction in your voice. Go, Wale, who knew he had it in him, eh?"

"Eh eh, don't start." I hated it when she took the mick out of him.

"So... now that you're 'unplugged', you can come and join me in the business."

"Erm, I don't know, it just feels wrong. I've thought about it, but I don't know if I could do that to Wale."

"Eh, yeah, it's a little late for your conscience to be making an appearance. Why did you decide to lose your cherry? Why now? If you were still getting money from Terry or Babatunde, I think you would still be clinging to that thing like a monkey to a banana."

"That is such a horrible thing to say, Tobi. Are you implying that I lost my virginity just so I could become an Aristo chick?"

"That's exactly what I'm saying, babes."

Ooh, the nerve of her! I was boiling inside, even though deep down I knew she was right – but there was no way I could admit that to myself. If I did, then what would that make me?

"Screw you," I said and hung up.

I was surprised to find that I wasn't as upset as I felt I should have been; after all, Tobi had planted the idea in my head in the first place. So now I was no longer a virgin, I hadn't thought I would feel this liberated. I had expected a tinge of regret, and I had thought that I would miss it, but so far none of my previously anticipated feelings had surfaced. All that was there was a tremendous feeling that I'd been set free to do whatever I wanted to now. I had held out as long as I could; I was almost in my final year of university, and I intended to enjoy it. I was in my fourth year of a five-year degree. With all my disgust about Aristo girls forgotten, I set about doing what I previously despised. How to start? Tobi had mentioned that she could set me up, but I wanted to do this with as few people knowing about it as possible. I wasn't like Tobi; I couldn't just meet up with some guy who expected sex that same night and would pay me for it. That was just plain prostitution, no matter how much you sugar-coated it. I wanted another Terry, someone to take me out on dates and give me money. The sex could be an added benefit, not assumed or expected at the end of every date. My very own sugar daddy, to be more precise. In my bid to justify myself, the irony was completely lost on me. Who better to be my Terry than my very own Terry? Yes, I know, he had taken advantage of me and humiliated me, but I totally got what he did and where he was coming from. In fact, it meant he had balls and was not a pushover. Could I really blame him? I had been taking and taking for months and giving nothing in return.

So one day, I plucked up the courage to call him. I withheld my number and dialled his number. My heart was pounding loudly in my chest, and I wondered if I was making a horrible mistake. I could be setting myself up for the second round of humiliation. I had to take the risk since I didn't know anyone else. His phone rang off, and I let out my breath and relaxed when he didn't pick up. I would try to call him back later, I thought, about to tuck my phone into my back pocket of my jeans, but then it rang. Private number.

"Hello?" I answered tentatively.

"What do you want?" a gruff voice asked. It was Terry. What the...?

"Erm, what do you mean? You called me," I responded nervously.

"You just called me with a withheld number; what is it? I thought I told you not to call me again."

I was surprised; I looked around, wondering how he'd known I'd been the one calling.

"How...?"

"Don't worry about that; look, I have to go. You have to stop this. If you need money, I can't help you. You're not like your friend, so stop trying to emulate her lifestyle and stop calling me."

"Can I see you?" I asked. I was hoping that he would give me some money one way or another.

I heard him sigh.

"What are you up to?" he asked.

I closed my eyes and rubbed my forehead with my free hand. I was trying to block out the fact that I was talking to a married man and that I would be cheating on Wale. Surely I was going to hell.

"The thing that was holding me back before, well, it's not there anymore," I said in a muffled voice. Gosh, I sounded so cheap and tarty, I chided myself with disgust.

"I'll pick you up at 8 p.m.," he said and hung up.

What the hell was I doing? I couldn't stop to think this through because I knew it was definitely a bad idea. But somehow I felt compelled to make this mistake. Who knew? At the end of the year, I could be driving my own car around campus. After my classes, I went back to my room. I went to a salon on campus, and I had blonde highlights done. I was going to wear my new corset top with a pair of jeans and my new pair of high heels.

I was ready by 8 p.m. I had told Wale I was going to one of the lecture halls to read. Hopefully, he wouldn't try to find me as I hadn't given him an exact location. I had just told him my phone would be on silent. I checked myself out in the mirror, and I had to admit that I looked irresistible. I was showing the right amount of cleavage to drive any man crazy, but not too much. I was wearing a corset that made my small waist look even smaller and a pair of jeans that hugged my hips in all the right places.

Terry called my mobile to let me know he was outside and when he saw me his face lit up like the American sky on the Fourth of July. A shiver of excitement ran through me. It was different this time; it was just him and me, and it was almost like the old days, the conversation and the flirting. No games, no pretence, no charades. We both knew what was going to happen.

We went straight to the hotel; I had expected dinner first, but I wasn't put off. The sooner it was over, the faster I got paid. As soon as we got into the room, Terry asked me to strip. It was over in less than ten minutes, but it felt like ages. It had definitely been a huge mistake. He didn't even take one item of his clothing off. He asked me to bend over, spat on his finger and rubbed it in me– so no need for me to get wet first, then.

And that was it: ten minutes of grunting, thrusting, discomfort, waiting and praying for it to be over. I wondered if I was required to pretend like I was enjoying myself, to moan and writhe like I had seen in my limited exposure to pornographic movies. I settled for staring at the patterns on the bed sheet and keeping quiet. No point encouraging him. He rubbed his hands all over me, hitting my bum and obviously having the time of his life. I guess I had to get used to this. It wasn't too bad; I thought, just before his hand came down hard across my bum.

"Ow," I whimpered as my eyes prickled. Terry stiffened and left out a groan as he came. I stiffened in response, relieved that it was over. He disengaged his body from mine, and I felt his eyes on me, but I refused to turn around until he turned away and walked into the en-suite bathroom to get cleaned up and I put my clothes back on.

"That was great; you have a stunning body," he said when he emerged from the bathroom. He was obviously happy with himself. I just nodded.

He drove me back to campus and when he parked he reached into his pocket and gave me some money. My face fell.

"10,000 naira?" I spat out. "Are you kidding me?"

"You're very lucky; I pay prostitutes a lot less than that."

I resisted the urge to slap him across his smug face.

"I'm not a prostitute." Of all the insults.

"Hence the amount. Now get out, I need to get home to my wife."

I looked at him with as much hatred as I could muster. Without saying another word, I got out of his car and slammed the door hard. It was my fault; I deserved to be used and treated like dirt. I willed myself not to cry; this was only a minor setback. There was only one thing to do – go crawling back to Tobi.

"Okay, fine. You were right," I admitted to Tobi on the phone that night. "And I need your help."

"Of course, you do. You need to be very smart with these guys or else they'll take advantage of you. And yes, I'll help you." I wondered if she knew about Terry; if she did, she didn't let on about it.

CHAPTER 29

The first guy Tobi set me up with was very nice. Not nice-looking, mind, but he was nice to me. He must have been in his mid-forties. He had a bit of a paunch but to be fair, you'd be hard-pressed to find a middle-aged man who didn't. On our first date, he took me to a nice restaurant in Ikeja, which is on the mainland. Needless to say, I was nervous, but Tobi had assured me that he was safe. She knew where he lived and where he worked so she could find him easily if anything happened to me. It was a beautiful evening; the food was fantastic, and I ordered some of the most expensive things on the menu, just to check his reaction. He didn't flinch. Good, I thought. The only downside to the "date" was that I wanted to run for cover every time he opened his mouth. His English was appalling, and he had quite a strong Yoruba accent. Speaking English with a strong Nigerian accent is understandable, but dreadful English with a strong Yoruba accent is just plain punishable. I listened to him boasting about how much money he had, and name-dropping about this or that celebrity that was at his house the other day. Like, who cared? I ought to have been paid just to listen to him, but Tobi had advised me that it was best to stroke his ego.

So I said things like, "Wow, you really are an amazing guy."

And, "I'm so glad I met you, you've had the most amazing experiences."

And, "Really!" Cue eyes widening and mouth formed in an "O". "No way! Awesome."

By the end of the night, I could tell he thought I was in love with him.

As we walked to his car, I turned to him and put on my best shy schoolgirl impression.

"Thanks for dinner, sir," I said, folding my arms across my chest. His eyes immediately flew to my cleavage. I rolled my eyes. This was too easy. "But I'll be going back to campus now; I have a test tomorrow, and I need to go and prepare." I crossed my legs with my right foot on tiptoe behind the left. With my chest pushed out, I rubbed my arms and rocked from side to side like a little girl. He literally licked his lips like a hungry wolf.

"Haba, no o. You cannot go back nau. Don't worry ke; I'll take you back *sho* that you can read. Or you can come to read in my hotel."

"But sir, I won't be able to concentrate. Your company is distracting; I know I won't be able to read if you're there." I pushed my hip out to the side, and his eyes almost came out of his skull.

"Ha-ha, young girl. I know you're just *tee-sing* me. Come on, let us go. No worry; I'll take care of you."

"I'm not sure. I'm afraid you'll just forget about me after you've gotten what you want."

"Rule number one, don't mention anything about money," Tobi had said. "You're not a prostitute, so never, ever discuss money. Let him feel he has to show you what he's worth; he has to prove it to you. Most of all let him think you want it more than he does."

"Me?" he said, beating his chest. "Never! I will take care of you, no worry."

"Promise?"

"Of course, yes. Anything you want, just ask me. Ha, if you give me what I want, walai I will make you happy." He licked his forefinger and then raised it in the air.

I smiled a massive smile. That was what I wanted to hear. I stood on tiptoe and gave him a peck before getting into his car. And that was how Aristo number one swam happily into my net. Sex with him was uneventful; I think on some level Tobi must have chosen him as my first for that reason. He was undemanding and only took what I was willing to give. He seemed very grateful for it as well.

Outside the bedroom, he treated me like an over-indulgent father, letting me have my way without putting up much of a fight. We went out for dates wherever I wanted to go. He called me one afternoon a couple of weeks after we met. I was on my way to class, and I was running late.

"My little yum yum," he said as soon as I picked up the phone. It made me cringe every time he called me that. I was nobody's little yum yum.

"Look, Alhaji, I can't talk right now, I'm on my way to class. What do you want?"

"Haba, can I not talk to my schweet'art again?"

"Alhaji, I've told you, I'm late for my class."

"Ah, okay o," he said, resigned. "I just calling to te you that I haf send the drifer, 'e will pick you up in the efening. I want to see my yum yum tonight."

"No, Alhaji," I said, "we didn't agree to that. You can't send your driver to pick me up unless I agree to see you, do you understand?"

"Okay, shorry my dia," he apologised. "So when I will see you again?"

"I'll call you after my class and then we can arrange something, okay?" I hung up.

That conversation pretty much summed up our relationship. But while I felt I had some control over when or how he saw me, I didn't have much control over his wallet. He kept that thing on a tight leash, relinquishing his hold only after he was satisfied.

Tobi set me up with Aristo number two three weeks after setting me up with the first one. Aristo number two was older than the first, but I wasn't picky. He was Nigerian and had been resident in the United States until a couple of years back when he'd come to work for one of the international oil companies on a contract. He'd left his family in Florida and went back to visit them as often as he could. My dates with him gave me a glimpse into another world. He took me to places like the American Embassy and the Boat Club. We went to private beaches where we rode Segways on the sand and jet skis in the ocean. He didn't pay me as well as Aristo number one, but I enjoyed the time we spent together. He wasn't demanding in the bedroom, was happy to take whatever he could get, and I did my best to make him feel comfortable. He'd told me he didn't have sex with his wife anymore, so I think he was satisfied with me: I liked to believe so.

People were beginning to notice something different about me. As one of my colleagues put it, "Damn girl, look at that ass!" Okay, so jokes aside. Apparently, I looked and acted like a different person now. Another friend said that I had the look of someone who was having sex regularly. The things people come up with!

"How you can tell if someone has sex regularly?" I'd asked her, a small smile playing around my lips, and she'd looked at me out of the corner of her eyes.

"You can just tell," she had said. Food for thought, I guess. What I was itching to say back was that only someone who isn't having sex often enough has the time to think up such rubbish.

The way boys treated me changed; they were more alert whenever I passed them or walked into a classroom. Even the lecturers were nicer to me. They smiled at me and gave me extensions on my assignments.

One day I went to see Dr Williams to hand in an assignment that was a week overdue. Dr Williams shared an office with a female lecturer, and when I walked in, she gave me a nasty look; I was taken aback, wondering if I had done anything to offend her. I didn't take any of her classes so I drew a blank.

"Good afternoon, ma," I said, as I curtsied. She didn't respond so I went on to speak with Dr Williams.

"Hello, my dear," Dr Williams said with a huge grin on his face.

"Good afternoon, sir," I smiled back at him. "I came to hand in my LW405 assignment."

"You know that assignment was due last week. What are you doing bringing this to me now?" His tone was serious, but he still had a smile on his face. Was this a test?

"I know, sir, I'm sorry."

"So what are you going to do for me?" he asked. A loud hiss rent the air as the female lecturer scraped her chair back and sprang to her feet. She eyed us and stormed out of the room, muttering something about evil daughters of Jezebel and hellfire.

"Don't mind her, too much religion; she doesn't know how to enjoy life." He excused his colleague, stroking his chin. "So, back to your assignment; I'm afraid I've already marked the papers for your class. You know it makes up 20% of your grades this semester. If you want me to help you, you have to make it worth my while." He was still stroking his chin. He licked his lips and had a hungry look in his eyes.

I had anticipated this kind of behaviour; one of my classmates had tipped me off about what to do to get him to take my late assignment.

I pushed an envelope full of money to him across the table. Thrown off; he leant forward to pick up the envelope, looked inside and, apparently satisfied with its contents, held out his hands for my assignment.

"Not what I had in mind, you know, but it will have to do," he said, the lust in his eyes not diminished by the sight of an envelope full of money.

"Thank you, sir," I said, giving him a knowing smile and doing a mock curtsey.

"Er, Jadesola," he called out when I was at the door. "Next time, make sure you hand in your assignment in time. I'm not going to take money from you the next time."

"Okay, sir," I said, and I left his office.

Even my parents noticed the change in me. One day my dad made a seemingly innocent comment like, '"What have they been feeding you in school? Your bum is getting bigger." My mum had looked up sharply and our eyes locked, but she didn't say anything. When my dad left the room, she called me to sit by her side, then she proceeded to tell me about the dangers of sex, about how she'd been a virgin when she married my father and how she would like the same experience for me. I listened to her talk without saying a word. I nodded in all the right places and shook my head in some. It felt weird for me to be having this conversation with my mum now; I was twenty, for crying out loud! I deserved a medal for holding onto my virginity for as long as I did.

Really, Mum? I'd thought. That ship has like, so sailed! It was glorious, Mum.

I just need everybody to get off my case. The way everyone was going you'd think I was the first person in the world ever to have sex.

CHAPTER 30

A month went by, and I was now an expert at lying. Every word that passed through my lips was a lie. My brain was on a lie-default, and I had to do a manual reset to tell even one truth. I was lying to my parents, to Wale and Monica. I even lied about what I'd had for breakfast, not because I wanted to but because I couldn't help myself. The only person I was telling any truths to was Tobi and even those were half-truths. I was still very much in love with Wale and to my knowledge, he thought I was the best thing since sliced bread. I still spent a lot of time with him; sometimes I showed up at his after my dates, just to erase the memory of old men slobbering over my body. It wasn't like I saw the men often – once or at the maximum twice a week – but I could call them up whenever I needed anything, and they would get it to me. I had managed to change my wardrobe completely, getting rid of my former cheap clothes. Most of my clothes were worth more than the allowance I still received from my parents. Whenever Wale asked about something I wore, I just lied about the value or said that it belonged to Tayo, my older sister. If he spotted any holes in my lies, he never alluded to them.

One evening Tobi showed up in my room; usually, she called me before coming over. She said she needed me to accompany her somewhere, but she wouldn't tell me where.

On the way, she told me how Babatunde had finally gotten tired of her and that she was now free. And very rich, I thought to myself. She drove to Surulere and parked in front of a small clinic.

"We're here," she announced, getting out of the car. She walked towards the clinic without waiting for me. Classic Tobi, I thought, hurrying after her. I didn't need to be a genius to figure out what we were doing in a shady-looking clinic at this time of the evening. By the time I got into the clinic, Tobi was already speaking to the lady at the reception desk. She asked to see Dr Femi; she had an appointment. The receptionist looked at her with cold eyes and a downturned mouth; I looked at Tobi to gauge her reaction. I expected her to be rude to the woman or at least to react in a similar fashion, but she didn't seem to have noticed the woman's attitude. The lady ignored us for a few minutes, staring intently at an outdated-looking computer, looking up only once to give Tobi a once-over. When she finally spoke to us, it was to direct us to take a seat in the waiting room, which was half full. There was a middle-aged woman in traditional attire with a couple of empty seats next to her, and we headed in her direction until we got a whiff of her pungent body odour. Tobi and I shared a look and kept walking. There were no more paired empty seats so it meant we would have to sit apart but Tobi got a nice man next to an empty chair to give up his seat. We had been waiting for over an hour when a nurse came and gave Tobi a pill to swallow. While we waited, Tobi and I talked and joked about everything and nothing, but not once did we talk about what she was about to do. Or about whoever it was that had gotten her pregnant. We were there for another couple of hours before the same nurse came to get us. She took us to through the back door of the clinic to an outhouse. The room was bare except for a table and a chair; the nurse asked Tobi to strip, put on a hospital gown and lie down on the table. Surely it wouldn't have killed them to put a bed in there instead of a rubbish table? Perhaps the intention was to make the patient feel as uncomfortable as possible.

Tobi did as the nurse asked without any arguments. It looked as if she was just going through the motions, not asking any questions; then it occurred to me that this wasn't the first time she was doing this. The doctor came in, a young man in his early thirties, and he asked me to go back to the waiting room to wait for Tobi. I gave her a quick hug, and prayed that she would be okay, and then I left her alone with the doctor and the nurse. I went back to the waiting room to wait for her, glad I had brought a book along to kill time. The book was called *Watermelon*, by Marian Keyes, and I became so absorbed in it that by the time I was called to come and get Tobi, it felt as if I'd only been waiting a few minutes. Tobi was sitting up on the table, weak and pale. She asked me to get her bag, and when I handed it to her, she pulled out a large brown envelope and handed it to the doctor. He looked inside, nodded and left us alone with the nurse who was busy tidying up. I helped Tobi get dressed, and the nurse saw us out, something akin to pity in her eyes. Tobi was in no state to drive so I drove us back to campus. I asked her to stay over, and she agreed. I let her sleep on my bed, and I slept on a spare mattress on the floor.

I was taken aback by the incident. And frankly a little disappointed in Tobi. For someone who slept with men for money, you would think she'd have had the sense to protect herself. I promised myself there and then that I would never let that happen to me. I was going to be extra careful, and any man that refused to wear a condom would just have to deal with the rejection. You would think that in this day and age, with all the education about the risks of sexually transmitted diseases, that people would never have unprotected sex. The problem was that a lot of people felt they were invincible, especially the rich ones. I hoped pregnancy was the only thing Tobi had "caught".

Weeks passed uneventfully. My cycle of wake up, go to class, see one of my Aristos, go to see Wale continued. I began to notice the changes to my body now. My boobs were bigger, and my nipples tingled sometimes, but I'd thought it was normal due to all the sex I was having. I'd been eating a lot of rich food, and my belly was beginning to get slightly rounded. I needed to cut down on the dinners or be more disciplined whenever I was out and just have a salad or something light.

One Friday night, a few weeks after I'd accompanied Tobi to the clinic, I felt like going out. I asked Wale if he could take me clubbing but he already had plans with some of his friends to play video games. I couldn't believe he was blowing me off for that. Tobi was out of town, so that left Monica. I asked if she'd go clubbing with me but she'd already made plans with Yomi. I couldn't call Deji because frankly, Wale would see that as a stab in the back and it could be grounds for another break-up.

Although I was tempted to give up, I felt restless. I didn't want to be alone today; I felt as if I needed to surround myself with people or I'd go crazy. I considered surprising Wale and showing up at his games night. It would be fun for a few minutes, but I knew I'd get bored quickly and regret it.

I was walking along the corridor to my room when I saw Aisha; the girl Tobi said was a dominatrix. She was leaning against the balcony facing two other girls. From what I'd gleaned from Tobi, Aisha was in the big leagues; she only dated politicians and celebrities. Everyone respected her even though she wasn't very nice. I'd tried to say "Hello" to her a few times, but she always ignored me.

"Hey! Cute blouse," Aisha called out. I stopped and looked around me before I realised she was talking to me. I was wearing a close-fitting black satin halter-neck top.

"Is it Chanel?"

"Yes, thank you," I smiled, pleased that she was talking to me.

"We're going to the launch party of a new club in Lekki, do you want to come?"

It was like manna dropped in my lap; suddenly I was glad that no one else had had any time for me. These were the girls I needed to hang out with. I was getting sick of the small fry Tobi threw my way; I was so ready for the big time. And if there was one way to get into the big league, Aisha was it.

"Yes, I'd love to." Just try and stop me!

We got to the club around 11 p.m., and it was already in full swing. We made our way to VIP, and the owner of the club came to get us at the door. Sitting in the VIP section of a club had become a force of habit. I couldn't imagine going to a club now and not being in VIP. Maybe except when I was with Wale, but then we rarely went clubbing together. He took me to the cinema and house parties, but he was nervous about taking me clubbing. His excuse was that he'd been threatened a few times on campus by cult boys who thought they had a chance with me if they got rid of him. He figured it would be the same in a club, and he could end up seriously hurt. I welcomed his reluctance. The last thing I wanted was to be approached by one of my Aristos when I was out with him.

CHAPTER 31

Aisha had disappeared with the owner of the club, and I couldn't see the other girls we had come with. So it looked like I was on my own. I sat at the bar and ordered two shots of Baileys on ice. I looked around and saw some girls that I knew. I waved at some and nodded at others. I used to think the VIP section was so pretentious and that surely these people couldn't be having any fun but by now, I couldn't imagine anything different. The thought of being in the main club, struggling to bust a move on the crowded floors, pushing against sweaty, who-knows-where-they'd-been bodies was extremely unappealing. It was interesting how much I'd changed since meeting Terry. Some guy came over to ask me to dance; I danced with him and let him buy me drinks. At one point during the night, I needed to use the bathroom. I excused myself and made my way to the ladies – that was when I saw Babatunde, with his scary piercing eyes and his borderline psychotic stare. I felt a rush of excitement mixed with a strong perception of danger. He'd told Tobi that he wanted me, and it was there in his eyes; I felt naked and vulnerable beneath his glare. If I'd had a lighter skin tone, I would have been red all over. My face grew hot, and my heart beat faster. I had to walk past him to get to the bathroom. Not once did he take his eyes off me as I looked away and pretended not to have seen him. In the privacy of the bathroom, I smiled to myself. This was my chance to get in the big league. I touched up my makeup and looked myself over in the full-length mirror. I wriggled my hips and pushed up my bra to ensure that my breasts were being shown off to their maximum potential. When I emerged from the bathroom, I scanned the club for Babatunde, but I couldn't see him anywhere. As I made my way towards my previous companion at the bar, my path was blocked by a slim guy in a dark suit and dark glasses. He told me his boss had asked him to bring me outside to the car. I didn't need to ask who his boss was; I had been half-expecting it. I was slightly nervous, remembering all the things Tobi had said about him; she had warned me to stay away from him but how bad could he be? On the other hand, I was excited; if I went home with Babatunde, by this time tomorrow I could be $2000 richer. I smiled to myself as I followed the dark-suit guy. On the way out, my former dance companion grabbed my arm from behind, trying to catch my attention; I figured he couldn't remember my name but that he'd seen me walking towards the door.

"Where are you going? Come back with me; I bought you a fresh drink!"

"Erm..." How could I let this man down easy? He was tugging me away from Dark Suit now, and I was trying to yank my arm from his grasp. What happened next was like a scene from a movie. Dark Suit turned around to see what the commotion was about and seeing, let's call him Desperate Man, yanking on my arm, he flicked back his jacket to expose the butt of a gun. Desperate Man immediately let go of my arm and threw up his hands. He let me go so suddenly that I stumbled toward Dark Suit who caught me in his arms and steadied me. I walked out of the club with my head up trying to pretend that nothing unusual had just happened, that I had men with holstered guns at their waist escorting me from buildings all the time, but inside I wondered if I knew what I was getting myself into. Dark Suit led me to an Escalade and opened the door for me to get in. Sure enough, Babatunde was in there with his big, bulging eyes.

"Hello," I said, wondering if I was meant to curtsey as I did to anyone who was a lot older than me.

"Good evening, my dear, come, sit down, I won't bite." He sounded normal, like somebody's father. Not how I'd imagined he would sound.

"Thank you," I said, climbing in next to him.

"I like you, okay? And I'm going to take you to my house," he said.

I studied his features; he had a large nose with hairy nostrils, his ear was large, fat and fleshy, the lobe full and rounded. His lips were small and thin, and he had a rounded double chin. His eyes bulged as he spoke and I found myself both fascinated and repulsed by him.

"Okay," I responded, my hands folded in my lap to keep them from trembling. I watched the skyline of Lagos, the only city I had known since my birth, as we rode in silence. The familiar sights looked different tonight, but I knew that everything was the same, the only thing that had changed was me. I had finally made it to the big times; there was no going back for me after this. I could have it all; the car, the designer clothes and the love of my life.

When we arrived at his house, there were no preambles like the first time Tobi and I had come; he led me straight to his bedroom. I didn't know what Tobi was so afraid about, apart from the fact that he wanted his dog to watch, and he asked me to pretend that I was his sister, and we were going to play "hide the sausage" in the cupboard when the adults were not looking. That must have been one twisted childhood. I could bear it; the thought of $2000 kept me going through the night. The poor sick twisted man. I wondered if he was married;

there wasn't a wedding ring on his finger and no family pictures that I could see.

I had prayed that he wouldn't want to "go through the back door" as Tobi had indicated, and not once did he even make reference to it. He was very nice. The next morning he paid me and sent me on my way with $3000! That was $1000 more than Tobi had been getting. He said he'd had a good time, and he wanted to see me next Friday and was I available. Was I ever! Then he said something that made me slightly troubled; he said he hoped Tobi had told me what he liked and that we were going to do that next week. He told his driver to take me wherever I needed to go.

I wondered why he was so pleasant; I hadn't been expecting that. I had imagined some kinky things would go down, and yes, I know, what went down is up there with the kinkiest, but Tobi had made it sound terrible.

Tobi called me later that day, sounding frantic.

"What do you think you're playing at?" she asked, shouting at me from the other end of the line.

"Calm down! What are you on about?"

"One of my friends just called me and said she saw you leaving the club with Babatunde. Please tell me she was lying."

What was it with all these people and their spies? Was there nothing that could remain secret in this town? I rolled my eyes.

"And so what if I did," I retorted, smiling to myself as I thought of the money burning a hole in my handbag.

"You know what? You sound like an idiot right now. I'm coming down there now." She hung up.

I was tempted to leave my room and switch off my phone so that she couldn't find me. I felt slightly guilty that I had gone with Babatunde behind Tobi's back but in my defence, there hadn't been an opportunity to call her and let her know where I was going. I decided to stay put since I had nothing to feel guilty for. It wasn't as if he had been her boyfriend and she had been in love with him. It was only business, after all.

In just over two hours, Tobi rushed in like a whirlwind and opened her mouth to speak, but I put up my palm to stop her.

"Before you start, there's something I'd like to say." I moved past her to shut the door; my roommates had gone home for the weekend so we had the room to ourselves. I saw Tobi making an effort to calm down.

"I'm sorry, okay? I'm sorry I went home with Babatunde. In my defence, I didn't go after him, he came after me, and he didn't give me the option to refuse. I know you're worried about me, but you don't need to be. I'm a big girl, and I can handle him. Last night wasn't that bad – seriously, it's nothing I can't take."

Tobi shook her head.

"First of all, that's a lame excuse; you can always say no, I'm sure he didn't hold a gun to your head. Secondly, how could you be so naïve? You've only been there once, and you think you can handle it? Did he ask you to come back next week?"

I nodded.

"Please don't go," she pleaded, and I could see she meant it. "I've driven two hours to beg you never to go to that man's house. I would never do that for anybody else."

"Tobi, he gave me $3000!. How can I just let that go?"

"I know the money is very tempting, but you'd be selling your soul." She looked down for a moment as if pondering something, and when she looked up, I could see the determination in her eyes.

"If you go to see Babatunde on Friday, I'm going to tell Wale everything!" she said.

I was shocked that she would threaten me. This wasn't Tobi; she would never do that to me. She knew how much I loved Wale – how much he meant to me. I searched her face, but I couldn't find any trace of malice or hate in her eyes. I sighed.

"What is this really about? What did that man do to you?"

She looked away. "I can't tell you that. It's too horrible."

I took her hands in mine.

"Please, you have to tell me, what did he do that was so bad? And why did you keep going back?"

She looked at me as if trying to decide whether she could trust me.

"You can never repeat this to anyone. No one, not even Wale. Promise me."

"I promise."

"I'm serious, no one, ever."

I nodded. We both sat down on my bed.

"I'm so ashamed, Jade; the things I did..." Tobi covered her face with her hands.

"Why did you do them?"

"I don't know what he did to me. I couldn't control myself. The second time we went over to his place, he said something in my ear and I found myself obeying everything he asked me to do. It was almost as if I was trapped in my body and someone else was doing all those things." Tears poured down her face.

"What things? What did he make you do?"

She looked me in the eye.

"I can't bring myself to tell you; all I can say is that it involved his dog and a haggard old woman." Her face contorted in disgust at the memory. Then, all of a sudden, she grabbed my blouse and shook me, tears and snot flowing freely down her face. "That baby! That monster I aborted, I don't know if it was fully human or half dog!"

I gasped and shouted "Jesus!" involuntarily as a terrible shiver ran through me. She let go of me as suddenly as she had grabbed me and dashed out of the room, flinging the door open with such force that I half-expected it to fly off its hinges. I was in too much of a shock to chase after her immediately. After a few seconds, it occurred to me to check that she was okay; I ran after her with my heart in my mouth, hoping she hadn't done anything rash.

I searched for her for almost half an hour before I found her in the bathroom sitting under the shower. She was soaking wet, her clothes torn, and she had scratches all over her body as if she had tried to take off her skin. She was eerily calm, and it was scaring the crap out of me. I went to my room to get a towel and a change of clothes. I dried her off in the bathroom and persuaded her to change her clothes. I didn't want anybody asking questions.

When we got back to my room, I held her for a long time. There was a nagging question at the back of my mind: why had she kept going back? Why hadn't she run after the first time? I couldn't ask her in her state so I decided to let it go.

"I know what you're thinking," she said as if she could read my mind. "You're wondering why I kept going back. It's simple: Babatunde said I had to. He said he owned me, and he could do whatever he wanted with me until he was sick of me. Those were his exact words. He said he would ruin my life if I disobeyed him. I laughed in his face and told him to do his worst; nothing would make me come back. That was the second night we went to his place. He said my mother would die if I didn't come back and still I laughed in his face, but then the next day, my sister called me to tell me that my mother had fallen ill all of a sudden. They took her to the hospital, but the doctors didn't have a clue what was wrong. Jade, I have never been so scared in my life. I rushed down to the village to see her, and she looked terrible. There was nothing ordinary about her illness. I called him immediately and begged him to make my mother better. I told him I would come back to see him the following Friday, and as soon as I got off the phone, my mum was better." Tobi sniffed at the end of her story. That was when the penny dropped for me. My pulse raced and my eyes widened.

"What is it?" Tobi moved away from me so that she could look at me, and I could read the alarm in her eyes.

"What will he do to me if I don't go?" my voice trembled.

"I can tell you what to do, but you're not going to like it."

"I'll do anything," I said. I had to protect myself and my family.

"I went to see a man who is powerful in the spiritual realm and he told me that if I wanted to be free, I had to burn every penny Babatunde had given me."

I gasped and covered my mouth with my palm. That was the last thing I had wanted to hear.

"But wait a minute – how do you know that it needs to be that extreme? Surely there had to be another way."

"There is no other way," she said. "I've had to burn all the money and everything I ever bought with it."

"Oh, wow, but maybe I can avoid it. Babatunde didn't do anything fetish to me." Tiny beads of perspiration formed on my forehead and I wiped them off with the back of my hand. My hands felt clammy and swollen.

She looked at me as if I'd just said the stupidest thing she'd ever heard.

"Did you have sex with him?" she asked.

"Yes."

"Then, trust me; he's taken something from you. That's what he does. The first night breaks down your defences and gives him an opportunity to use something from you, for him to be able to control you."

"Then how come you were jumpy after the first night?"

"I guess I must have sensed something off about him, but I chose to ignore it because of the money. It's not worth it, though; I wish I'd known that then."

I put my face in my hands and groaned loudly. When I lifted my head, I took a deep breath. "I'll do it," I decided. "I'll burn the money. Sorry, I doubted you."

"It's okay; I'm just glad you're not going to see that monster anymore. Come on; I need to take you to see my guy. He'll be able to help break whatever bond Babatunde may have put on you."

I wasn't sure I wanted to go with her to a spiritualist. I had been brought up in a Christian home, and I still went to church. My mother would freak out if she knew. But in the light of everything Tobi had told me, I figured it wouldn't hurt to try. So we set off to see the man, who lived only fifteen minutes away in Surulere.

I was expecting an old, weird-looking man, with charms hanging all over his body, residing in a ramshackle hut. But in fact, he was clean-shaven and dressed in a pair of jeans and a t-shirt, and the house was quite nice and modern.

He led us into a semi-dark room; the fragrance from the incense burning on every visible surface filled the air. We sat down on two of the big cushions arranged around an altar decorated with shells, cowries, little kernels and pine, oak and fig leaves.

Tobi brought the man up to speed on my plight. When she finished, the man stood with his head bowed for a few minutes; then he looked up and stretched out his hand to me.

"Give me the money he gave to you."

I scrambled off the cushion and walked slowly towards him, my eyes drawn to the bundle in my hands. Trembling, I placed the money in his outstretched hands and walked back to my cushion with my head bowed, and my shoulders slumped. I watched the man as he danced around the altar; I needed to be certain that it wasn't a trick. Tears glistened in my eyes as I mourned for the life I could have lived with that money and the life I had dreamed I would live by sticking with Babatunde. I grieved the things I had done to get that money; it was all in vain now.

The man uttered incantations into the flames on the altar, which flared up as he spoke. I held my breath as he placed the bundle of dollars into the fire. He gestured to us to come closer, and we both hurried to the altar, our eyes fixed on the orange flames lapping at the edges of the notes. The bundle charred quickly, the greyness spreading slowly towards the middle, converging in on itself. I held on tightly to Tobi's hand, restraining myself from snatching the money out of the flames, and she squeezed my hand back. I didn't realise I had been holding my breath until the notes were charred. I let it out in an audible rush of air. I felt numb, and my head felt light. I held onto Tobi for support.

"Congratulations, you are now free. Whatever Babatunde has on you is now useless," the man said to me.

"Thank you, sir," Tobi, and I chorused. I was going to curtsey, but Tobi had dropped to her knees in front of the man, bowing to him with her hands clasped in front of her chest. I felt ridiculous standing there so I followed suit.

"Be very careful what you do from now on," the man warned, looking me in the eyes when we got off our knees. "Especially with that baby; your life is tied to it." A flicker of confusion crossed my face and then realisation dawned on me. He must be referring to the baby Tobi aborted.

"Oh no, you mean Tobi." I hiked my thumb in her direction. "I can't be pregnant." I laughed shakily, relief flooding through me. The man's mouth fell open and his brow furrowed. Tobi looked away quickly. He looked back at me and narrowed his eyes.

"Are you sure?"

"Yes, very sure." There was no way I could be pregnant. It just wasn't possible. The air in the room was beginning to stifle me, and I couldn't wait to get out of there.

Tobi handed the man an envelope. We thanked him once again and hurried out of the house.

CHAPTER 32

In the car Tobi pondered over the man's revelation.

"But why would he ask me to look after the baby? There is no baby!" she shouted, getting agitated. "It doesn't make any sense. He's usually spot on. It's not like him to make a mistake." She was silent for a minute. "I can't still be pregnant, can I?" she asked, her voice trembling. "I know because I felt that thing slide out of me. And I haven't slept with anyone since." She looked at me. I threw up my hands and shook my head.

"Don't look at me. I'm still reeling from the fact that we've just burnt $3000. Sorry, I can't help you."

Her eyes widened, and her mouth fell open.

"Why didn't I see it?" she said, slapping her palm on her forehead. "Look at your boobs; they're huge!"

"What? Yeah, isn't it normal when you start having sex?"

She gave me that look again, the one that said I was stupid.

"Anyway, I can't be pregnant. I've never had unprotected sex," I stated with an air of finality, hoping Tobi would drop the topic.

"Right," she said.

"Where are you going?" I exclaimed as she drove past the turning that would have led us to campus.

"We're going to get a pregnancy test kit."

"What? All because some crazy man said something about a baby? What if he's wrong?"

"He's never wrong."

She repeated that statement an hour later when I emerged from the bathroom with the pregnancy kit that seemed to believe that I was indeed pregnant.

"Impossible," I said in shock.

"Do you know who the father is?" Tobi asked, and I kept shaking my head.

"I don't understand; I've never…" My words hung in the air when I remembered that rainy night, four months ago. "No, it can't be, it can't."

What was going to happen to me? I couldn't keep this baby. I was only in my fourth year of university; I still had one year to go to get my law degree. This baby was going to ruin my life. Oh, Wale! He'd asked me to trust him that night, but he hadn't kept his word. I felt betrayed.

"What am I going to do?" A million and one thoughts were flying through my head. My head felt hot, and my skin tingled as tiny beads of sweat formed on my skin.

"What do you want to do?" Tobi threw the question back at me. She was sitting with her legs crossed on my bed, and she seemed unperturbed by my predicament.

"I don't know; I just know that I can't keep this baby." I sat down beside her and with my elbows in my lap, I put my head in the crook of my arms and folded my hands over my head.

"Do you want me to take you to the clinic?" she asked, and I groaned and lifted my head. I nodded in resignation.

"But I have to tell Wale."

"No, you can't tell anybody," Tobi warned, her eyes flashing.

"But it's his baby; he has a right to know."

"You cannot tell anybody," Tobi reiterated firmly.

I sighed. "Tobi, this is such a huge mess. I need to think about this."

"Yes, fine, whatever you need to do, but the sooner we sort this out, the better."

"Okay," I said, nodding. I sank further into the bed. I was exhausted. I hadn't fully recovered from the activities of last night and then all the excitement this morning – and now this. I felt as if my body was about to shut down.

"In the meantime, I'll book an appointment with Dr Femi. I'll let him know it's urgent."

"Okay," I said again.

Tobi stayed with me till I fell asleep, all the while rubbing my back.

When I woke up six hours later, my head heavy and groggy, I looked around for Tobi, but she wasn't there. I fished for my phone, checking under my pillow, but it wasn't there. I found it in the back pocket of my jeans. I had five missed calls. One from my mum and four from Wale. I didn't feel like speaking with anyone but wanting to avoid any confrontations I dialled Wale's number.

"Hey," I said, my voice husky from just waking up.

"Hey you, where are you?"

"In my room. What's up?"

"Are you just getting up? It's 7 p.m.! What did you get up to last night?"

"Nothing, I'm just exhausted." I briefly considered telling him about the baby. I still believed he had a right to know. Also, a part of me hoped he would want us to keep the baby. Even though a baby was the last thing I wanted, I had always sworn that I would never have an abortion. The thought of murdering my child was unimaginable; I'd always thought you had to be irresponsible to get pregnant, with all the information available on safe sex, but here I was in the same boat. I didn't know what to do. On the one hand, a baby would ruin my life but on the other, an abortion could ruin my chances of ever getting pregnant again. I'd heard stories of women not being able to have children after numerous abortions. Scenes from Nollywood movies flashed before my eyes: of husbands throwing wives out of their houses when the doctor confirmed that it was indeed the wife's fault that the couple couldn't bear children, that she'd destroyed her womb with too many abortions. The husband, resplendent in his innocence and on his high horse, not remembering the numerous girls he'd persuaded to have the same procedure his wife was being persecuted for having. I decided to take Tobi's advice; I wasn't going to say anything to Wale until I'd made up my mind about the baby.

"Do you want to go and get some dinner?" he asked. "And maybe come back to my place? I've missed you." I knew what he meant by this, and it triggered images of sex. For some reason, those images made me feel nauseous.

"Please give me two seconds," I said hurriedly, "I'll call you back."

"What is it? Are you okay?" I heard him ask as I flung the phone on the bed without cutting the line and flew off the bed. I knew I couldn't make it to the bathroom; I found the nearest empty bucket and emptied the contents of my stomach into it. When I was sure that nothing else was coming back out, I carried the bucket to the bathroom to clean it. As I walked into the bathroom, I stopped in front of one of the mirrors and stared at my reflection. My face looked funny; it was my nose. How come I'd never noticed it? It looked slightly wider and bulbous. I looked at my boobs and my belly. How could I have missed the signs? I still had my periods, which was weird. Weren't periods supposed to stop when you were pregnant? I tried to remember when I'd had my last period, but all I could remember was feeling as if I was about to have my period; I couldn't remember having one. Shit! I was even more stupid than the girls I used to think were dumber than doorposts for getting pregnant. At least they knew when they were pregnant. I hadn't had a clue. I wasn't used to watching my periods; they came when they came, and if I'd missed a month in the past it hadn't been a big deal because I hadn't been having any sex.

It was so weird that I was feeling pregnant now: nausea and the fatigue. Twenty-four hours ago I'd been fine and not pregnant. And now I was pregnant, and it seemed as if my brain had just received the message as well.

I went back to my room and called Wale, but he wasn't picking up his phone. I lay back on the bed, fully intending to go back to sleep, but a few minutes later I heard a knock on the door. I knew who it was even before I opened the door.

"What's up?" I asked as he entered.

"I should be asking you the same question. I heard you throwing up; are you okay?"

"Oh, that... yeah, I think I ate something that didn't agree with my tummy. I'll be fine."

"Aw, you poor baby," he said, giving me a hug. "How are you feeling now? Do you want to go get some dinner?"

I groaned; the thought of food made me feel nauseous again.

"I don't feel like eating anything."

"Did you eat lunch?" Wale asked, cocking his head and narrowing his eyes at me.

I shook my head.

"Come on; we have to get you something to eat."

He took me to get some spicy vegetable stew with large meat chunks and to my surprise I was ravenous. I wolfed it down. I could tell the fact that I had eaten pleased him, though it might also have had to do with the fact that he liked being right. He'd known what would make me feel better. He took care of me that night, and it got me thinking that he would be an amazing father to our unborn child. I couldn't imagine him changing a nappy or bathing a baby, but I could see him being there, a strong tower that our child could always run to. He would nurse him when he fell ill just as he'd taken care of me. I thought all these things and I fell even more in love with him.

"Why are you looking at me like that?" he asked. He was tucking me into bed, and I was staring at him with glazed eyes, lost in my dream of the future: our future.

"Nothing," I said, smiling. "I was just thinking how much I love you and how lucky I am because you're so amazing."

"Wow," he said, taken aback. He placed the back of his palm on my forehead. "Nope, you're not running a fever. Where's that coming from?"

"I don't say it often enough, do I?"

"You rarely do, ever."

"But you know I do feel like that, right?" I tried to sit up, but he pushed me back down gently.

"I know you do, in your own way." He kissed my forehead. "Sleep tight, babe, I'll see you tomorrow. Make sure you call me if you feel worse."

I wondered what he meant by saying I loved him "in my own way"; it somehow seemed like a loaded response.

"I'm fine, don't worry." I watched him walk to the door. "I love you," I called out to him for good measure.

"Go to sleep, Jade," he called back to me.

There was something niggling at the back of my mind, but I was too tired to dwell on it. It was the next morning that I realised what it was. He hadn't said he loved me back.

CHAPTER 33

I was self-conscious now. I wondered if anyone could tell that I was pregnant. It was Monday morning, a mere couple of days after I'd found out. It had taken a lot of willpower to peel myself off the bed this morning. All I wanted to do was sleep.

In class, I found it hard to focus on what the lecturer was saying; my head kept spinning, and it was an effort to keep it off the table. It didn't help that the lecturer was droning; his voice was giving me a headache. When I couldn't take it anymore, I dug out my sunglasses from my bag and got up to leave the class.

"And where do you think you're going, young lady?" he said, raising his voice, and I winced at the sound. I held my hands to my ears and hurried out of class. He must have said something derogatory because a few seconds later, I heard the class erupt in laughter. Let them laugh; I was going back to bed, and I planned on staying there for a long time.

I woke up that evening feeling as if I'd been through the grinder. How long was this going to continue? I couldn't take it anymore. I made up my mind. I couldn't keep this child; it was already ruining my life and it wasn't even born yet.

My phone rang, I checked the caller ID. It was Deji. I groaned; what did he want?

"What is it?" I said as soon as I picked his call.

There was silence on the other end for a few seconds.

"I was just calling to see if you were okay. I came to see you earlier, but your roommates said you were sleeping."

"I'm fine; you don't have to worry about me."

"Okay, if you say so." He hesitated. "What happened to you in class today? It's just so unlike you, Jade. Something's wrong, and I'm worried about you. You're different, like a whole other person, and you don't even talk to me anymore."

"Oh, yeah, sorry about that. It's just, you know how it is with Wale," I said, wondering how I could get him off the phone. I needed to call someone else. Someone who could help me out of my situation.

"Yeah, I understand. Just, if you ever need to talk…"

"I'll remember that thanks, Deji," I said, realising too late that I was short with him. I felt bad. He was only trying to help.

"Deji," I called before he could hang up. "Thanks, I appreciate it."

"Anytime, babe." He hung up.

I wondered if he liked me, but I shook the thought out of my head. Deji was a player; there was no way he was capable of having real feelings.

Now that my phone was free, I went to find a private place to talk. I walked to the back of my building, looking around to make sure no one was around before I dialled Tobi's number.

"Hey, did you get me that appointment?" I asked as soon as she picked up.

"Hello to you, too."

"Babe, I can't take it anymore, I'm going crazy. This has got to be the worst feeling in the world. Why anyone would want to get pregnant on purpose is beyond me," I moaned.

"You're hilarious," Tobi said, laughing. "Didn't you feel this way last week?"

I shook my head. "No, I didn't, that's what's so weird. As soon as we found out, I've been feeling like crap. I'm constantly nauseous. I thought that was supposed only to happen in the mornings – I mean, it's called morning sickness."

"It's a deceptive name, isn't it?" she said, still laughing.

"The appointment?" I asked, ignoring her.

"So you've made up your mind. Are you sure?"

"I couldn't be surer. If I feel like this now, I can't imagine how I'll feel when I get bigger."

"Okay, I called Dr Femi, and he said he could see you on Thursday. He can't do any earlier. I'll come down in the afternoon, and we'll go together."

"Thank you so much, Tobi. I'll guess I'll have to find a way to survive till Thursday."

"No problem, but remember, you can't tell anyone, do you understand? You can't afford to have something like this following you around."

"Yeah, I know, you don't have to tell me. I'm not stupid," I said defensively.

"Okay o, don't bite my head off. I'm just trying to help."

"Sorry."

"See you Thursday – take care of yourself. You can call me anytime you need to talk, okay?"

"Sure, see you then," I said and hung up.

I went to get something to eat and then just lay in bed reading a book. At 11 p.m., my phone rang. It was Alhaji. Shit! I'd forgotten I had an appointment with him. I should have called him earlier to let him know I was ill. I let it ring off. As soon as it went off, it started ringing again; it seemed that Alhaji wasn't going to give up easily, but I was in no mood to deal with his wounded ego so I switched off my phone and went to sleep.

I had a weird dream on Wednesday night. I dreamt that I was in hell, and evil-looking babies tortured me with pitchforks. I woke up more tired than I'd been the night before. I put the dream down to an over-active imagination and a guilty conscience. Everything was going to be fine as soon as I got rid of this baby. I could go back to being my old flirty self instead of a mere shadow.

I avoided Wale all week because I was paranoid that he would suspect something was wrong. He called me every day, trying to get me to come over to his room. I knew he was horny, and that was why he kept pestering me, but I wasn't in the mood. I didn't think I would ever be in the mood for sex again. I mean, what were the odds that the first time I ever had sex, I got pregnant? Was I being punished?

On Thursday evening Tobi arrived to take me to the hospital as promised and on the way she filled me in on what to expect from the procedure. I winced a few times. Jeez, it sounded horrible; but I didn't want to consider the alternative. It occurred to me that I was missing something important.

"How much will it cost?"

"Only 50,000 naira," Tobi said.

"Why is it so expensive?" I gasped.

"Femi is a qualified doctor, not a quack. Don't worry; I have the money; you can pay me back later."

"Thank you," I murmured. "I don't know what I would have done without you, Tobi."

When we entered the clinic, I got the feeling that something was not quite right. The receptionist was not at her post so we sat down and waited. There was a big lady sitting a couple of seats away from us; her voice was the loudest of anyone's, and she seemed to know what was going on. Her blouse was slightly too tight for her and her flesh strained uncomfortably against the fabric.

She was slightly out of breath from talking a mile to the minute. Everyone else was speaking in low voices, but this woman seemed to want the whole room to hear her story. From what she was saying to her companion, I gathered that a young girl had come in earlier for an abortion and was now bleeding profusely; they were afraid she was going to die. (She'd heard this when the nurse had come to get the receptionist). My blood ran cold at the thought of what lay ahead of me. I looked at Tobi, and she held my hand.

"I've done it a few times; you'll be fine. Dr Femi is very good at what he does," she whispered to me.

"Yes, but... what if it's true? What if the girl dies?"

Despite her reassurances, Tobi's confident look faltered.

The receptionist came out wringing her hands in distress. If we had been in doubt about the seriousness of the situation, her expression and mannerisms confirmed our suspicions.

"Please, everybody, you have to leave, the clinic will be closing now," she announced.

Voices rose in protest; people had been waiting for hours to be seen by the doctor.

"You can stay, or you can go, but the clinic is closing. If you leave quietly, I will call each of you to reschedule your appointments, but if you refuse to leave, we will have the police come and throw you out," the receptionist threatened.

"Well, that settles it. Come on, let's get out of here," Tobi said, getting up. I was surprised to find that I was relieved that I wouldn't be having the procedure today. As much as I didn't want to be pregnant and as much as I wanted to get rid of the baby, I'd become paralysed with fear at the thought of the procedure. We walked outside in silence, the darkness of the night enveloping us totally as there'd been a power cut; NEPA had struck again. The clinic was the only building on the street with any lights on.

We walked past a black RAV-4 on our way to Tobi's car, and we heard someone sobbing loudly. Tobi walked past the car without glancing at it; I tried to do the same, but a strong sense of curiosity overwhelmed me. I couldn't help myself. The person crying must have some form of connection to what had happened in the clinic, and I wanted to know the details.

CHAPTER 34

I peered into the car; I couldn't resist. A young girl, about my age, was slumped over the steering wheel, her face buried in her arms. I tapped on the window to get her attention.

"Hey! Are you okay?" I asked.

"What are you doing?" Tobi turned back, frowning. "Are you crazy?"

The girl lifted her head; it was Aisha. She stared past me as if she couldn't see me. She was breathing heavily and sniffing; she wiped her face with her palms and seemed to be calm for a few seconds. All of a sudden, she began wailing and crying again. She hit her head repeatedly on the steering wheel.

"Come on, let's go. Leave her alone," Tobi said, taking my shoulders and trying to move me away from the car. But I resisted. For some reason, I didn't want to leave Aisha alone. Surely there must be something I could do to help.

"Hey." I tapped harder on the window. Aisha, sobbing, wound down her window. Tobi sighed, obviously frustrated, and I scowled at her. If she didn't want to help, she could leave. Tobi rolled her eyes, hissed and walked to her car.

"Just hurry up," she called out to me. "Some of us still have to drive to Oyo tonight."

I nodded, holding up my palm to get her to calm down.

"Hi, Aisha. Are you okay? Was she your friend? " I asked, pointing in the direction of the clinic. "Is she going to be okay?"

Aisha shook her head. "Not my friend, my cousin." And then she sobbed louder as if she had just realised that the fact it was her cousin made the situation much worse.

"Is she going to be okay?" I repeated.

"Okay?" She looked at me as if I was mad. "She's dead."

I gasped.

"I'm so sorry," I said hurriedly. "Is there anything I can do?"

Aisha looked at me, tears streaming down her face, her eyes filled with sorrow and fear.

"I don't know what to do. I'm in so much shit. I'm so dead." She banged her head on the steering wheel again. "I need to find a way to transfer her body. The clinic won't have anything to do with it. They need to protect themselves so they're going to claim they never treated her; what am I going to do? What will I tell her parents? I picked her up from home this evening; how am I supposed to tell them their daughter is never coming back? That they need to come and get her body? What will they tell people happened to their daughter? Everybody is going to blame me, but I didn't do anything! She asked for my help, and now I'm the one in trouble! My life is over." She wrung her hands, and then she covered her mouth with her palm to stifle the whimper that escaped her lips. Her shoulders shook as she sobbed and she sniffed with every breath she took, wiping her wet face and runny nose with the back of her hand.

I looked at Aisha, and I felt sorry for her. There was nothing I could do to help her; I was beginning to regret speaking with her. I should have listened to Tobi and minded my own business.

"What exactly happened? Do you know what went wrong?" I asked out of fear for my situation. An icy chill swept through me; it could have been me in there.

"I have no idea, I wasn't in the operating room, and the doctor had run away by the time they called me in. She was just lying there, bleeding profusely. I watched her die, and those bastards stood just stood there – useless people. I begged her to keep the baby, but she wouldn't hear of it. Her boyfriend wanted the baby too, but apparently, it wasn't his. The baby belonged to a married man, and she didn't think she could live that kind of life, letting her boyfriend raise another man's baby. Plus he's not rich; he works for a GSM company, but he's just managing. And now she's dead. That's it; her life is over. She was in her final year, you know. She was going to London for her Masters next year. So stupid." She clenched her fist and slammed it into the steering wheel.

"Listen, I have to go," I said, seeing Tobi walking towards me with her nostrils flaring. "I'm sorry about your cousin; please accept my condolences."

She looked up, and she had a desperate look in her eyes. For the second time, I wished I hadn't gotten involved.

Tobi grabbed my hand and pulled me away from Aisha's car.

"I'm sorry," I said, looking back at her. Aisha just sat there with her shoulders drooping. She stared into space, her face puffy, her eyes red and her chin trembling.

"Listen," said Tobi. "This means Dr Femi isn't an option anymore. I don't anticipate that the clinic is going to be open for a couple of weeks. We can't wait that long. I have someone else..."

"Are you joking?" I asked, incredulous.

"What?"

"You can't honestly tell me that you still expect me to go through with it after what just happened. Aren't you afraid?"

"Oh, that," she said, brushing it off with a wave of her hand. "Look, that was just an isolated event. You can't let it stop you from doing what you have to do. I promise that that's not going to happen to you."

"But how do you know? How can you guarantee that it won't happen?"

"Jade, do you know how many times I've done this? Four times! Four! One, two, three, four!" She counted on her fingers. "And am I not still here? Am I not fine? You don't know the full story; maybe there was something wrong with her before she had the procedure. Maybe she already tried to get rid of it by herself beforehand. You can't base your decision on that." She was making a lot of sense, but I had made up my mind.

"I agree with you, Tobi; I don't know the full story, but neither do you. When I agreed to have the abortion, I didn't realise I would be risking my life." I sighed as the full realisation of what I was saying hit me. If I kept this baby, my whole life was going to change, and I couldn't imagine it would be for the better. The first thing I needed to do was to tell Wale; I prayed he would take it well. It would be great if we could tell my parents together. To assure them that we knew what we were doing and were prepared to take full responsibility for the child. I had a bit of money saved up: not much, but it would have to do till I found a job. I had no idea what sort of job I could find, but I was determined to remain optimistic. I was worried about how my parents would take the news. As much as I knew they loved me, I could see them chucking me out and disowning me. They were lovely people, they were, it's just, I knew how much they cared about their image. My mother had made a statement once that if any of her daughters got pregnant, or any of her sons impregnated a woman, before marriage, that they'd have to leave the house that day.

"That's about the dumbest thing I've heard you say," exclaimed Tobi. "You can't keep this baby! Look at you, you have a good life, parents that care for you, guys falling over themselves when you talk to them, and a boyfriend that loves you. Do you think any guy is going to want you if you keep this baby? The stretch marks, wobbly belly and droopy boobs, not to mention your reputation – no self-respecting man is going to want to marry you after you've had a child. What will your parents say? You think they'll help you? Give you a place to stay and money to look after that baby? How are you going to survive? Jade, you cannot have this baby."

Her words sunk in and it felt as if the air was being sucked from my lungs. I took rapid breaths. What was I going to do? The reality Tobi painted was a lot worse than what I'd had in my head when I made my decision. But I couldn't go through with the termination. The dream I had last night flashed vividly in my mind. What if I died? That was it; I would go straight to hell where I would be tortured by evil babies with red horns, holding pitchforks. I would rather live my life on earth in hell than spend eternity being tortured in real hell. The irony of my situation hit me; if only I'd had this much clarity before – before I did what I had no business doing in the first place. I should have remained firm in my beliefs and my faith. Fine, I know I hadn't been a saint when I was a virgin, but then only God knew my secret sins. I'd prayed to him and believed that he would forgive me, but now the sins I had committed in private were going to be exposed for the entire world to see. It didn't matter that girls my age were doing the same thing I had done: having sex. They all managed not to get pregnant. I was going to be judged and ridiculed. I was going to be called names like slut and prostitute, the girl who couldn't keep her legs together or her panties on. I could take the easy road and wipe out the evidence – but what if I ended up like the dead girl, then what? A voice inside said that I wouldn't be around to care what people thought about me then. But what about my parents? My family? They would never live down the shame. They would be the family whose daughter died from an abortion. My panic attack worsened. My head felt as if it was overheating; I could almost see steam seeping out of my skull, and my vision was getting blurry. I needed to talk to Wale, and I need to do it tonight. I just knew he would make me feel better. I needed his strong arms around me; I needed him to reassure me that it was going to be okay.

"Maybe you need some more time to think about it. About how much this will destroy your life," Tobi said in a soft voice.

"Tobi, I'm afraid. I feel like all these things happened for a reason. I know it sounds insane, but I feel like this girl dying tonight, of all nights… I feel like it was a sign, telling me not to make a costly mistake. I have a strong feeling that the same thing will happen to me if I go through with it." I told Tobi about my dream.

"So that's it? The reason you don't want to get rid of the baby is that you had a stupid dream?" she sneered.

"No, don't trivialise it. Do you remember the man's warning? Something about protecting the baby?" I saw the look in her eyes. "You see, you know it too, you said it yourself – the man is never wrong. He knew about the baby before I even knew I was pregnant. I've made up my mind; I'm telling Wale tonight."

Tobi sighed. "Fine."

"Thank you." I checked the time; it was a few minutes past 9 p.m. He would still be awake. I dug my phone out of my bag and dialled Wale's number.

"Hey, babe," I said. "We need to talk, can I come over now?"

"What's it about?" he asked, with tension in his voice.

"I'll tell you when I see you," I said, hanging up.

"Very bad idea," Tobi said.

"I trust Wale, he loves me, and he always says, whatever happens, we're in it together. Will you come with me?"

"Only if you want me to."

"I want you to."

"Okay, but I'll stay in the car; this is something you need to do alone."

We made our way back to Breamston University in silence.

"Good luck," Tobi said as I got out of the car in front of Wale's room. I walked to his door, contemplating how I was going to break the news.

"What is it? Are you okay?" Wale asked as soon as he opened the door to let me in.

I shook my head. "Please, let's sit down." I walked towards his bed, and he followed. I took a deep breath, deciding to go straight to the point.

"Remember the night we had sex for the first time?" I asked as soon as we were seated. He nodded.

"Well, I'm pregnant," I announced, cringing as I spoke. I watched the expression on Wale's face go from one of concern and worry to shock. His mouth fell open.

"How do you know? How long?" he asked, blinking rapidly and swallowing hard.

"I took a test." I took another deep breath; this was harder than I had thought it would be. I had a quivering sensation in the pit of my stomach. "I think it happened that first night, so I would say four months gone. Although I can't be certain until I see a doctor."

"Shit!" he exclaimed, slamming his fist into his hand. "What are you playing at, Jadesola? How could you get pregnant?" I suddenly realised that I was afraid; the possibility of him rejecting me had not crossed my mind before now, and I felt my chest constrict.

"You're speaking like it's my fault." I frowned and looked at his face, full of righteous anger; his chest was heaving, and his lips were a thin line. My eyes were drawn to his; they were cold, like a stranger's. I couldn't believe it. I stared into them, pleading. This wasn't the Wale I knew; he would never speak to me this way.

I watched him become as cold as a stone. He got up and walked away from me. When he turned back to face me, his face was expressionless.

"It's not mine, it cannot possibly be mine," he said.

I was thrown and confused. Had he not heard me right? Could he not remember? He had taken off the condom! Anger shot through me. How dare he?

"B... bu... but..." I tried to speak, but my throat was so tight from anger that I couldn't push out the words.

"Look," said Wale, "I remember putting on a condom that night and every time after that. Do you think I'm blind or stupid? I know what you've been doing. I tried to lie to myself. I managed to convince myself that you were different, but I was wrong. I know that now. You're no better than a prostitute. And now you're trying to pawn another man's child off on me. You must be crazy!" Spittle flew from his lips as he screamed at me, the veins in his neck straining against his skin. His eyes were wide, and he jabbed his finger in my face as he spoke. I shrank back from his rage and his hurtful words – words that cut me deeper than I had ever been cut. I felt as if this was a really bad dream; I would wake up soon, and the nightmare would be over. There was no way Wale would say all those hurtful things to me.

"Wale, think about what you're saying," I pleaded with him.

"Get out!" he shouted at me. "I don't ever want to see you again."

I shut my eyes tight, and tears squeezed through my lashes and down my face. I opened my eyes to see the face I loved more than life itself looking down at me with so much hatred. And the irony was that I didn't blame him. It was my fault: all of it. I felt my world crumble around me as I got up and left him without saying another word, my shoulders slumped and my head down. I felt uncontrollable tremors rocking my body as if I were in the throes of a terrible fever.

Tobi jumped out of her car and ran towards me as soon as she saw my tear-stained face. I held out my arms for a hug but she ran past me, and the next thing I heard was her shouting.

"You bastard! You don't deserve her." And then I heard what sounded like a punch, followed by Wale screaming in pain. Tobi strolled out wringing her wrist. She smiled at me and shrugged. "You know I got your back. Damn, that sucker has a hard face. Come on." She placed an arm around my shoulders and led me to the car.

CHAPTER 35

I was now about five months pregnant, I couldn't tell for sure how far gone I was since I hadn't been to see a doctor or a midwife, nor had I had a dating scan. I was basing my pregnancy on assuming I had conceived that first night with Wale. My previously flat belly was now slightly rounder; I could have gotten away as being slightly bang-bellied, but for my boobs and my nose. What was the deal with my nose? It just wasn't right; it looked as if someone had thrown a rotten tomato right in the middle of my face. And my boobs were spilling over my bra. I needed to get much larger bras, but I wasn't in the frame of mind to go shopping, especially bra shopping. I hated bra shopping.

People in school were already beginning to suspect that I was pregnant. The fact that no one knew for certain meant that Wale had kept his mouth shut, and I was grateful to him for that. Very few people would have been able to miss an opportunity to put their ex's business out in the open, especially in a delicate situation such as the one I found myself. They would spread the word quickly about my infidelity and how another man had impregnated me to avoid anyone thinking the child was theirs. We were officially broken up, but I couldn't bring myself to hate him. Everybody asked me why we had broken up; we had seemed so perfect together, so happy. There were rumours going around that he had broken up with me because I was an Aristo chick, which wasn't entirely untrue. I just wondered if he would have broken up with me despite the rumours he had heard about me if I hadn't gotten pregnant.

Now that people were acting funny towards me, I needed all the friends I could get, but for some reason, I was getting the cold treatment from Monica. She'd stopped picking up my calls, and when I'd confronted her in class, she'd looked up briefly from the novel she was reading and simply told me she was busy. She'd probably heard the rumours and had chosen to keep as much distance between us as possible – probably to avoid catching what I'd caught. Our relationship was already strained as I'd kept her at arm's length after losing my virginity. I knew she would suspect what I was up to if she knew I was now having sex, and I wanted to avoid the questions about where I was or what I was doing. Before the rumours about me had spread around campus, we'd had normal conversations in class and sometimes we got lunch or dinner together; I'd always paid, and she'd never complained, but now she ignored me whenever our paths crossed and I'd given up trying to get her to speak with me. I assumed she avoided me to prevent people from thinking she was an Aristo chick as well. Or perhaps Yomi had instructed her to. Whatever reason she had, it hurt, but I didn't hold it against her.

I was beginning to get used to this kind of treatment. It helped me realise how shallow the people I had surrounded myself with were. People I was familiar with on campus turned their heads when I walked by, pretending not to see me. No one called me or invited me to parties. The only friend I had was Deji.

He'd confronted me about the rumours one day after class.

"Hey," he said, walking towards me as I tried to get out of the classroom as quickly as possible. I could feel several pairs of eyes on me now, judging me. He caught up with me and put his arm around my waist.

"Hi," I responded, looking up at him and smiling. "Are you sure you want to be seen with me? Everybody seems to think I've caught the plague."

"Yeah, about that – is it true?"

I sighed. "I wish it wasn't." He nodded. We walked out into the courtyard overlooking the faculty and, with his arm still around me, he led me to one of the platforms in a quiet corner where we both sat down.

"How are you holding up?" he asked. "Are you okay?"

"Yeah, I guess I am, considering. I just didn't think I would be so alone, you know. Some days I'm so miserable, wishing I could just put an end to my misery." I laughed dryly. "Look at me being all dramatic. I bet you're considering getting me committed to a psychiatric hospital."

He drew his eyebrows together, and I saw the worry in his eyes.

"I was only joking; I wouldn't actually do it," I said hastily.

"So what is he doing about it?" Deji asked with noticeable anger in his voice.

"Who? Wale?" I asked.

"Yes, Wale, who else? He is the father, isn't he? Where is he? He should be here, protecting you, carrying your books and making sure that you and the baby are safe," he said, a vein throbbing on the side of his head.

"You know we're not together anymore, right?"

"Yes, I heard, but does he know about the baby?"

I nodded. I saw realisation dawn in his eyes.

"The spineless bastard. I always knew he was no good, the next time I see him, I swear, I will bust his face open." He was worked up now, and I smiled softly at him. It was nice to have somebody on my side.

"It's okay. I don't blame Wale. Just don't get into trouble because of him; he's not worth it," I said, stroking his arm to calm him down. He grabbed the hand on his arm and held on to it as we sat quietly

Deji's expression was intense, and he looked like he had an internal struggle.

Then he asked me a question. I didn't quite hear him, as he'd mumbled it.

Had he asked me to marry him? No, that was so unlikely and so random. But he took both of my hands in his. He looked very serious and earnest. I knew then that I had heard him right.

"Look, Jade, I know this is not the ideal situation but... I'm in love with you. I've known that I loved you for a couple of years now. We've been friends for as long as I can remember, and I know that this might seem weird – that's why I never said anything or made a move. I've tried to stop feeling this way, but I can't help it. I'm sorry that I've put this on you now but I care about you, and I want to take care of you."

I heard everything he said, but I had no logical response. I couldn't imagine two of us together; I had known him for so long that I'd come to think of him as my brother. He was friends with my siblings, and he got on well with my parents.

"You would marry me even though I'm carrying another man's baby?" I asked.

"To be honest, it's not the best scenario, but I would rather have you with everything than not have you at all. I can take care of you and the baby. I know I'm not the most intelligent guy in the room; I don't even know what I'm doing studying law, I'm probably never going to practise it, but I've got some things going on the side that's making me a bit of money. I'm only here because I promised my dad I would get a degree. Once all this is done with, I'll be able to focus on my business full-time." He spoke with so much passion that for one moment I allowed the picture he painted to envelop me. To imagine that I could love him and we could get married and raise a family together. I would have the baby and then come back to finish my degree. We would get a nanny to look after the child while we were either away at work or in school. I would be safe and secure, free from ridicule. I would be somebody's wife and somebody's mother. It felt so good to dream that things could be right after they had gone so wrong and I allowed myself bask in this, if only for a moment. But deep down I knew I couldn't do it. I loved Deji, but I wasn't in love with him, and it would be a grave injustice to pledge my life to him even as I pined for another man. I was still very much in love with Wale. I couldn't do that to my very good friend; what kind of marriage would we have? It might start off great, but it couldn't possibly end well. Gosh, I could only imagine how many girls on campus would give their left foot for Deji to propose to them. I felt tears pooling slowly in my eyes, threatening to fall. I tried hard not to blink, to keep the tears in. I ached to wipe my eyes discreetly, but Deji was still holding my hands. Why couldn't this be Wale sitting here next to me, asking me to marry him? To be his partner in this life. I knew the answer; it was my fault. I had blown it – and for what? I didn't even have anything to show for it. I was in a difficult situation; I had to let my dear friend down gently without hurting his feelings.

"I love you, Deji…" My voice caught in my throat, and I blinked rapidly. The tears that had been threatening now fell with wild abandon. Deji saw them and looked down at our hands, biting his lip.

"But you're not in love with me." He finished the sentence for me, his voice sad. "I know that. I know you don't love me now. I just wondered if any part of you feels like this could change in future, that you could grow to love me. I'll be patient, and I won't put any pressure on you." There was hope in his voice.

"I don't know; at the moment I don't think I am capable of feeling anything for anyone else. I appreciate what you're proposing and how much you're willing to give up, but I'm sorry, I can't do that to you. I'll just have to go through this alone, but I don't want to lose you as a friend."

He let go of my hands and wiped my tears with his fingers. "I understand. I'm such an idiot for making things awkward. Will you forgive me?" He smiled at me.

"Only if you forgive me for rejecting the most amazing offer anyone's ever made to me," I responded.

His face brightened, and he pulled me into a hug and kissed my forehead. I shut my eyes tight, enjoying the sensation of being held so tenderly. I pulled out of the hug and opened my eyes to find myself staring into Wale's eyes. I read something in them that I could only interpret as pain and longing because they were mirrored in mine. I wanted to look away quickly, to pretend that I hadn't seen him, but I couldn't tear my eyes away from his. It was as if he held me captive and I was too weak to break free. We stared, caught up in our world, and I felt Deji tense next to me. He'd let go of me and had become distant.

Sade was with Wale. She reached out and took his hand, and as they walked past us, she hissed.

"Slut," she said, loudly enough for me to hear. Wale flinched and looked away, breaking the spell.

"Don't ever call her that," he said in a stern tone.

"Whatever. I've always told you about them, haven't I?" Sade retorted, not bothering to whisper.

"Great, my humiliation is complete," I said, stinging from the insult.

"What are you doing?" Deji asked in annoyance. "He could totally see that you still have feelings for him. It was written all over your face."

"Huh, we only broke up a month ago; of course, I still have feelings for him."

"I know, I know, but you don't have to show it so much. Next time you see him, you have to pretend like he's not even there. People may treat you like crap now but if you keep on acting as if you deserve it and as if you have no pride or dignity left, they'll keep treating you like that."

"What if I do deserve it, and have no pride left."

"Then you fake it. From now on, you have to hold your head up and never take an insult lying down," he said, holding his head up and putting on a haughty look. He made a face, and I laughed in spite of myself, and his face broke into a huge grin. I looked into his happy face, and I wondered why I couldn't fall in love with this kind and handsome man.

I called my parents beforehand to let them know I was on my way home and that I had something important to tell them. They were waiting for me in the living room.

"Jadesola, are you pregnant? Shey o ti lo'yun?" my mum asked as soon as I walked in. She was distant, not looking me in the eye; that's how I could tell she was mad. My dad sat next to her, staring at the floor, and I hated myself a little bit more for doing this to my parents.

"Yes, Mummy, I am. I'm sorry." Tears spilled down my face. "I know I'm such a disappointment to you, and I even thought of getting rid of the baby to avoid embarrassing you, but I just couldn't do it."

My mother gasped and sprang up from her chair. "Never," she said, enveloping me in her arms. "You are my child, and you are only human. You will never be an embarrassment to me, do you understand?"

I nodded, sniffing back my tears, my shoulders heaving.

"God forgives, so who am I to hold this against you?" She held me at arm's length and looked me over. "How far gone are you?"

"Five months."

She nodded. "You should have told me sooner. I hope you haven't tried anything stupid to try and get rid of it."

I shook my head.

"Good, that's good. Jadesola, your father and I are very disappointed in you. We thought you, of all our children, would know better than to conduct yourself in this way."

I was aching to protest. "But Mummy..."

She held up her hand to stop me. How could I let her know that I had held onto my virginity for as long as I could? It hadn't been my fault. It was Wale's fault. I swallowed my words.

"We are a family and families stick together. We will help you in whichever way we can, but you will be responsible for your child. You will bathe, feed and take care of it. I took care of my children; I will not take care of another person's child, do you understand me?"

"Yes, Mummy," I said, as relief flooded through me. So I wasn't going to be homeless after all. I hugged her again. "Thank you, Mummy." I stole a glance at my dad. He was still sitting with his head bowed. I went to him and knelt down in front of him. "Thank you, Daddy," I said, clasping my hands in front of me as a show of gratitude. Without a word, my father stood up and walked out of the room. He hadn't looked at me once, the whole time. My mother touched my shoulder.

"Get up; it's okay. Give your father time; he'll come round." She patted the sofa next to her. "So where is Wale in all this? I'm not expecting him to marry you, but I hope he's taking full responsibility."

I should have expected this question, but I wasn't ready to answer it. How could I tell my mum that I would have to raise the child on my own? I had introduced Wale as my boyfriend to my parents and my siblings a few months after we'd started dating. He'd come by a few times during the holidays to spend the day with me or to take me out for dates. He'd played video games with my brothers and exchanged gossip with my sister. I hadn't told my family that we weren't together anymore so it was only natural for my mother to expect that he would take full responsibility. I said the first thing that came to my head.

"He's fine, Mum. He was pretty nervous at first, but he's gotten over it, and now he couldn't be happier that we're having this baby together." I knew she would find out eventually, but for now what she didn't know wasn't going to hurt her.

"Good, I'm glad to hear that. Like I said, your father and I will help in any way we can, but I need you to call Wale so that we can speak with his parents. The next step is for us to arrange a meeting with them to discuss how to handle the situation, don't you think?" She put her hands around my shoulders and held me close to her. I could smell her flowery perfume, the same one she'd worn for as long as I could remember. I felt her soft breath as she pulled my head to her chest, cradling me like a baby. I took a long breath, savouring the moment, trying not to panic. This could be the last time my mum ever held me to her bosom. Once she learnt that my boyfriend had rejected me, would she find it harder to support me?

"Yes, Mummy, they're in the US on holiday. I'll call them to arrange something as soon as they get back," I lied again. How long could keep the lie up? My mum let go of my head and pulled her arm away from around my shoulders.

"What kind of parents travel to the US when their son impregnates his girlfriend?" She snorted derisively. "Obviously, he hasn't told his parents yet. Okay, let me know as soon as they get back. It's always best to sort these things out when it's still fresh on the ground."

I nodded. For now, I was relieved. The biggest hurdle was over; I had told my parents, and they hadn't freaked out. I felt the gloomy cloud that had followed me ever since I found out I was pregnant lift a little. About Wale and my break-up, we would cross that bridge when we got there.

Now I needed to break the news to my siblings before they heard it from someone else.

My sister was the first one I told. I sat with Tayo to watch a Nollywood movie in her room, all the while pondering how to tell her. I can't remember what movie it was and was only half paid attention to it. All I remember is that it was starring Genevieve Nnaji and Omotola Jalade, my two favourite Nollywood actresses. In the middle of the film, Tayo sighed loudly and grabbed the remote control; she paused the movie.

"Okay, what is it? What's wrong? Do you need money?" she asked, impatient.

"What?" I asked, puzzled. "What are you on about?"

"You've been sighing from the moment you walked in. Do you want something?"

I figured it was a good time as any to tell her.

"I'm pregnant." I went straight to the point.

"Shit Jade, are you fucking kidding me?"

"Hey..."

"I thought you were a virgin?"

"Yeah," I shrugged. "It kinda happened the first time." I scrunched up my nose.

"Shit, that is messed up."

"I know."

"Okay, let me think. Do you want me to take you to get it removed?"

I shook my head hastily.

"Just wanted to let you know," I said. "by the way, I already told Mum and Dad."

"Fuck, Jade, are you seriously out of your mind? You can't have this baby; you're throwing your life away."

"Look, please, I already made up my mind. And, seriously, can you like tone down the swearing?" I said, raising my palms.

Tayo stood up, and her face was full of concern. I admired and respected her, and I thought she'd be more understanding than my other siblings, but I was wrong. She asked about Wale and she couldn't understand why I hadn't just got an abortion like any normal girl would, especially after Wale denied any responsibility. I didn't tell her about my dream; I knew she would make light of it. It was important to me, and that was all that mattered.

I spent hours crying in my room afterwards.

The next day she came into my room.

"Hey, lil' sis," she said. I ignored her. I had just come out of the bathroom and was getting dressed. She stood in front of my lingerie drawer, so I walked around her to get my things out. She moved out of my way to give me access.

"I understand why you're mad. I would be mad too. It's just, I was thrown, you know. You've always seemed to have your head on straight. I just didn't want to accept that this was happening to you. I guess I should have been more supportive instead of fighting you. It's your life, and it's your decision. I'm here to help if you need me." She gave me an awkward hug from behind, let go quickly and walked to her room. The people in my family were not big on showing affection.

"Thanks," I said in a low voice, just before I heard the door shut. I knew she'd heard me.

I couldn't handle telling my brothers so I asked if my mum could tell them. She later told me that they had taken it well and had all promised not to give me any trouble over it. I was already going through enough without them making things any more difficult.

CHAPTER 36

It was three months since I'd discovered I was pregnant. Three long months that I'd been apart from Wale, but the wound was so fresh, it could have been yesterday. Apart from the pain of being away from him and not seeing him whenever I wanted to, things were beginning to get better. I was seven months pregnant, and there was no doubt in anyone's mind that I was pregnant. It was no longer an interesting topic so people had stopped talking about me and moved on. They were nicer to me now. Random people offered to help me do things. They gave me their places in queues and gave me lifts around campus. Even Monica was talking to me now.

I still attended lectures; I was determined to keep going to classes until the day my baby was born and would get back to my studies as soon as I left the hospital after the birth. The lecturers were respectful enough not to ask me any questions; in fact, most of them pretended not to notice, except for some of the female lecturers who felt it was their responsibility to impart snippets of wisdom under the guise of giving advice.

It had been a typical day, nothing special about it. I dragged my heavy self out of bed and went to my classes. The springs of my bunk bed were beginning to dig into my hip as I could only manage to sleep on my left side. I wondered if I would need to commute from home; I thought longingly of my soft and comfortable mattress there. But it would be too much for me to commute every day unless I had a car, and since I had fallen short of my goal of getting a car, I was confined to foot patrol. I went to my classes and then Monica, and I walked back to my hall together. I was wary of her friendship now that I knew what she was like but she had stuck to me as soon as our classes were over. She said she had something to tell me.

"What is it? Tell me now." I was beginning to worry; I hated it when people left me in suspense.

"Don't worry, I'll tell you when we get to your room," she insisted.

"I can't stand this – how can you tell me you need to tell me something and then say you'll tell me later."

"I just think it's better if I tell you in your room." She wasn't budging, so I hid my impatience and listened to her talk about nothing, all the way back to my room. It had better be something important or else I was going to tear her a new one.

"Okay, tell me now," I demanded as soon as we stepped into my room. A couple of my roommates were in, but they were watching home videos and were so engrossed that I doubted they would listen to our conversation.

"Okay, just sit down, please."

"That bad?" I asked, settling myself at the edge of my bed.

"Depends." She took a deep breath. "I'm telling you this because you're my friend, and I wouldn't want you to hear about it from just anyone." I snorted at her casual use of the title "friend" and nodded.

"Wale and Sade are dating," she said, looking at me intently, trying to gauge what my reaction would be. "Sade has been running around campus, broadcasting it to everyone who cares to listen."

"And...?" I asked, pretending that I didn't care.

"Erm..." She looked confused. "That's it; that's what I wanted to tell you. Are you sure you're okay?"

She'd probably expected some drama; I was, after all, carrying Wale's child and barely three months after we had broken up he was already shacked up with his friend. The one who had always hated me, from the day I'd begun dating Wale. The one I had always told him had a crush on him. The one he'd told me was only a good friend and nothing more. I felt my blood run cold, and my chest felt as if it was going to explode from the weight of it all. I couldn't allow Monica to see how much her "news" had hurt me. I had been holding out so much hope and faith that he would come back to me. I'd dreamt up scenarios where the baby was born, and he realised that he'd made a mistake abandoning his child and the love of his life. That he'd make a grand gesture, and I would run into his arms, giddy with glee, and we would live happily ever after.

"Yes, I'm okay. You don't have to worry about me, we broke up months ago, and he's allowed to see other people. But thanks for taking the trouble to tell me, and for your concern." I smiled at her to convince her I was fine. I hoped she would leave.

"Okay. If you need me, I'm just round the corner." Taking the hint, she patted me on the shoulder and left me alone.

All my hopes, dashed, with my dreams of us eventually getting back together, and there was nothing left. Only darkness: heavy, uncomfortable darkness. I tried to claw my way out of it; there had to be a silver lining somewhere. Every negative thing that I had heard or felt about myself came crashing through my mind. From Josh – how he could never acknowledge that I had feelings for him and that I was never good enough for him – to Terry, to all the men I had known; I was never good enough for any of them. I was just a useless waste of space, and no one would ever want me; no one could ever love me. A tiny voice in my head tried to argue that it wasn't true: my parents loved me, Deji had said he loved me, even Wale had loved me once. But I shut the voice down. They'd loved what they thought I was; if they knew the things I had done, how low I had sunk, not even my parents would love me then. That was when I decided to take my life; it wasn't worth living, and all I was bringing to the people who loved me was pain and shame.

I thought it over calmly in my head while the TV made dramatic noises in the background. My roommates were exclaiming about the movie now and were adding their commentaries to the action being played out on the screen. They were just over a couple of metres away from me, but it could have been a few hundred kilometres.

I felt weird, and deep inside I couldn't believe I was contemplating suicide. I was calm and at peace. It felt like the right thing to do: nothing dramatic, nothing over the top. I looked through my things for pills, any pills – painkillers, sleeping pills – but I couldn't find anything. I decided to run down to the shops to try and get some medicine. It was better this way; I would have a wider variety.

"Where are you going?" one of my roommates, Rita, called to me. "Come and watch this movie, it's really interesting, you don't want to miss it."

"I need to get painkillers, I have a nasty headache," I lied automatically.

"It's okay; I have some aspirin." She got up to get them for me.

"No, no, it's fine. I'll get some myself," I protested.

"Don't be silly, take these. Unless you think my aspirin is not good enough for you."

"Fine, thank you," I said, taking the aspirin packet from her.

"Come and sit down, let's watch together."

"Sorry, my headache is really bad; I just want to lie down."

I took the pills back to my corner and sat down on my bed. I didn't want to have to think about what I was about to do. I needed to work fast before I changed my mind. I wished now that I had gone ahead with the abortion since dying was a common factor between that and what I was about to do. At least with the abortion, I could have had a chance to keep my reputation, Wale and a lifestyle I had worked so hard to cultivate. I had told my Aristos that I was pregnant, and they had melted away, crawling back to wherever they had crawled out from like snakes. I don't know what I had expected; I hadn't expected them to care anyway.

I was worried that my roommates would hear me as I popped each pill from the blister pack but they didn't even look up from the screen. There were ten pills in total. I wondered if that would be enough; I figured it would just have to do.

I got a bottle of water from the fridge by my bed and swallowed the pills a couple at a time. When all the pills were gone, I downed the rest of the water in the bottle and lay on my bed waiting for death. I expected it would be painless; I figured I would fall into a deep sleep and never wake up. I wondered if I should leave a note but I didn't have anything to say. I decided I would send a text to my parents and my siblings, just telling them how much I loved them. It seemed to me like the best idea in the world, so I sent the texts and switched off my phone. I didn't want anyone calling me and waking me up while I was asleep.

The pain came in slowly; it started from the pit of my belly and built up like the pressure within a volcano before it erupts. This is what it feels like to be dying, I thought to myself. I tried to be quiet, to hold the pain in, but it became too much for me. I moaned and then my moans turned into screams. I heard my roommates rush over, shouting in alarm. They would have spotted the empty blister pack in the bin by now; they would know what I had tried to do. The last thing I remember before I blacked out was a hand being forced down my throat and a forceful attack of nausea. I remember throwing up the contents of my stomach into an empty bowl and then there was the soothing, rocking motion of nothingness.

EPILOGUE

Tobi sat on the edge of my bed, swinging her feet to and fro as she watched me stroke the little head on my lap. She wore a grey pinstripe suit over an ivory blouse, with a bow at her neck and a tight skirt that stopped just below her knees. Her hair was held up in a tight bun, but a few tendrils had escaped, falling in curls on each side of her face. She looked as beautiful as ever. I looked at her, and I wondered what my life would be like if I had never gotten pregnant. I shook the thoughts out of my head; I was happy now; it wouldn't do me any good to go down that road. Tobi worked for one of the major investment banks in Lagos as a hedge fund manager. She had her money now, and she didn't need to sleep with any man for money. I turned the envelope over in my hands, admiring the expensive-looking invitation. Tobi was getting married; from what she'd told me her fiancé was loaded; he owned two houses on the Island and was very good-looking. But she was in love, and wouldn't have cared whether he was rich or not.

I forced a smile in her direction, and she returned an equally forced one. I swallowed the lump in my throat. I only had myself to blame for what happened to me, but I couldn't help thinking that my life would have been so much better if I'd never met Tobi – though I couldn't blame her for the choices that I had made.

I'd tried to kill myself, but I hadn't succeeded. I had been seven months pregnant. It seemed that the 'will to live' of the child within me, had been stronger than my desire to die. Only my family and close friends knew what I'd tried to do, and they'd taken it in turns to act as some security to me, against myself. Eyes everywhere, watching my every move. Watching my phantom of a life wilt away. It had taken years for me to get over my self-hatred: in the pursuit of money, I had turned what had been a promising life with prospects for a bright future into one of depression and despair. It felt as if I didn't deserve a way out, an escape from what I had done. It hadn't take Wale long to get over me. I wonder if he'd heard about my weak suicide attempt; if he had, I would never know. He hadn't come to see me in the hospital nor had he called.

That was ten years ago. I stopped taking anti-depressants last year because now I have so much to be thankful for. I still live with my parents; I'm fine now, but they wouldn't hear of me moving out. I had gone back to Uni to try and finish my degree, but my heart wasn't in Law anymore. People had looked at me as if I was crazy when I'd decided to change my major in my final year, meaning I'd have to spend three extra years in Uni, but I didn't care about that. I knew deep within me what I wanted to do: something I could do in solitude with little interaction with the outside world. I wanted to write. So I had dropped out of Law and finished Uni three years later with a degree in English Literature.

I wrote a number of children's books, and I was lucky enough to have had some of them published. I don't get paid much for them, but at least I'm doing something.

Moni – that's my daughter's name, though her full name is Monifa, which means 'I am fortunate' – loves reading my books, so I keep writing them for her.

Moni saw her father, Wale, for the first time two years ago; she was eight. I had discovered where he lived a day before. A mutual friend had mentioned it casually, throwing it in the air as if it was nothing. She probably felt that it was too long ago; surely I wouldn't care what he did or what he was up to. But I did care; I scrambled for her words like a dog amongst scraps thrown from the dinner table onto the floor. I etched the description of his house in my mind. I knew the place; it wasn't far from where my parents lived.

So that day I had taken a different route to Moni's school.

"Mummy, why are we going this way?" she'd asked.

"I found a short cut," I had replied.

"Don't be silly, Mummy; if anything, this is a much longer route. See, we're going past Bingles Hotel, and we could have cut across this road on Shomolu Road which would have taken us to school a lot faster," she said precociously, looking at me as if aliens had stolen my brain.

"Yes, well, there's nothing wrong with taking the scenic route, is there."

"Fine," she'd sighed. "I guess this road is a lot nicer looking, plus there aren't as many potholes."

That was when I saw him. He was so much more handsome, but there was something different about him. I couldn't put my finger on it. I hadn't seen him in eight years, so I didn't expect him to look the same. It was something about the way he carried himself as if he was constantly wary: the look of someone that lived his life walking on eggshells.

I had stopped by the corner of his house, looking in through the gaps in the gate. It didn't occur to me to stay out of sight, to spy from a hidden spot, so that they couldn't see me. That was when she came out, and I understood why he looked the way he did.

Sade had put on weight, and I took great pleasure in seeing that, but what she had lost in looks she had made up for in attitude. I heard the way she spoke to him, and I felt sorry for him. She'd looked up then, and our eyes met. She'd sneered at me and looked away as if I wasn't important, but then her eye had slid to the angel by my side, tugging at my hands impatiently.

"Let's go, Mummy, come on. I don't want to be late for assembly," Moni pleaded. Wale must have heard her, for he looked at us then. The wary look on his face disappeared as he stiffened visibly and his eyes went cold. I looked away; I held my daughter's hand more tightly and walked away briskly. Moni had to run to keep up. I felt the tears stinging my eyes and then sliding down my face.

"Mummy, slow down, you're hurting my hand," Moni cried.

"I'm sorry," I said, slowing down and easing my hold on her hand. I brushed my tears away quickly with my free hand.

"Who was that man, Mummy?" she asked, looking up at me with her innocent eyes.

"Nobody, baby, just an old friend." It was beginning to dawn on me that I'd made a mistake; I should have gone this way on my way back from dropping her off instead of bringing her with me.

"Is... is that my dad?" Her voice sounded so fragile that I stopped in my tracks.

"Why did you say that?"

"I just figured that must be him. He's the one in the picture you always carry in your bag. I asked Aunty Tayo, and she said he was my dad." When I saw my sister, Tayo, I was going to give her a piece of my mind. She'd had no business talking to my daughter about her father.

"When was this, honey?" I asked.

"Oh Mummy, it was ages ago. Grandma and Grandpa told me about him too. They asked me not to ask you about my dad. They said I was never to mention him to you. That it made you do crazy things when you thought about him. It doesn't make any sense to me; you love my dad, don't you? Why else would you still have his picture?"

How was I supposed to respond to such a question? I felt as if my whole family had been ganging up on me behind my back. How dare they say these things to my daughter? While I understood their motives, I felt they had crossed the line. They had no right. I looked at my daughter's face, and my heart melted. That explained why she'd never asked me about her father. She was very intelligent for her age, and she made things a lot easier for me. She looked so much like her father, but I liked to think she was more like me in personality. One day, I was called into the headmistress' office; Moni had refused to participate in a class experiment unless the teacher called it something else. She had argued that calling it an experiment was patronising to her class. In her words, an experiment was something that had never been attempted. That's why it was called an experiment: an experience of something that exists only in the mind. What they were doing had been done so many times, and it had a known outcome, so why was it being called an experiment? That reminded me so much of the arguments I used to have with my lecturers. I missed that.

Tobi's wedding invitation made me think of Wale. I had fantasised over the years that he would wake up one day and realise that he had made a mistake and that he still loved me, and we would get married and live happily ever after. I couldn't get him out of my mind, and I woke up the next day still thinking about him. So that morning, naturally I'd convinced Moni that we should take the "scenic route" to her school.

'Mummy, look, there's my dad,' she said in a conspiratorial tone as we approached Wale's house. He was walking towards the gate of his compound, carrying a black bin bag in his hand. My heart stuck in my throat as it occurred to me that if Moni and I continued walking, we were going to cross paths with Wale. I turned around sharply; it wasn't too late to take the other route, we could still make it to Moni's school in time for assembly.

"Mummy! What are you doing?" Moni whispered. "Come on; he's right there. You should talk to him."

"No, Moni, let's go the other way." I looked over my shoulder now; he'd spotted us, and he stopped. He looked sideways towards his house and then looked at us; we were standing right next to his bins. He looked as if he was weighing up his options: to keep walking towards us, or to turn around and head inside his house with his garbage.

"Come on." I grabbed Moni's hand and pulled it. That was that. I hurried away, expecting her to follow, but we'd only taken a couple of steps before she yanked her hand from my grip.

"Moni, what are you doing!" I shrieked. My mouth fell open as my daughter strode purposefully towards her father, her chin stuck out defiantly. She stopped a few feet away from him, and I watched as they studied each other. Moni's face was serious as if daring him to deny that she was his. I saw Wale do a double take. Moni looked so much like him, and I think for the first time he saw it too. His forehead wrinkled as he stared at her, and the shake of his head was so slight that I almost missed it; his gaze flickered to mine. I didn't know what to do so I smiled stupidly and gave a small wave. He looked back at Moni and flinched. The bin bag fell to the ground with a loud rustle and clink of metal, glass and other discarded objects hitting the ground, and without a word Wale turned around and strode back into his house. I walked to where Moni stood frozen, staring at the spot where her father had stood a few seconds ago. I wrapped my arms around her, and as I held her something broke in me. I had heard people use the expression "I saw red" to describe a feeling of intense anger – and I had never been able to relate as much as I did at that very moment. I could take him rejecting me when I had needed him the most but how dare him treat my daughter in such a manner. I grabbed Moni's hand and dragged her behind me as I stormed through his gates. I pounded at his front door with my fist, ignoring the pain that shot through my knuckles.

"Mummy, let's just go," Moni said in a low, dejected voice but I ignored her. The door was opening, and I planted my feet firmly on the ground, preparing myself for the verbal assault I was about to launch, but what I saw stopped me in my tracks.

Wale stood there, and his eyes were bloodshot; he looked as if he'd been crying. I didn't know what to do. I was prepared for war, not this. The anger built up inside me slowly melted away, and all that was left was hope.

"Would you like to come inside?" His eyes pleaded with me.

"I... I... I don't think that's a good idea," I said, my eyes wide. Moni stuck her head out from behind me, and I felt her hand tugging on my dress.

"Mummy, please." I looked down at Moni's upturned face, her little brown eyes and pert nose so similar to that of the man standing in front of me.

"Is she...?" Wale had a soft expression on his face as his eyes fell on her. Instinctively I wrapped my arm around Moni's shoulders. As I looked from him to Moni, I felt a sharp pain in my stomach, like a knife twisting in my innards, and I winced. Moni looked up at her father, her face beaming, and it hurt. I took a deep breath and held her in front of me.

"This is your daughter, Moni." They stared at each another, and I coughed softly to break the silence.

"We have to go," I said, gripping Moni's shoulders and steering her away.

"No, please don't go, stay a few minutes." Wale raised his palm.

I shook my head sadly.

"I just... I feel like I've just found a piece of me and I... she's my child!" He cocked his head in amazement.

My mind flashed back to the way he'd treated me all these years, and I felt some of my previous anger slowly seeping back into my veins; I took a deep breath to calm myself.

"What do you want from me now?" I said. "Surely you must have known she was your daughter – how could you not know? But you never even bothered to be certain she wasn't yours before you turned your back on me. On us." I felt the tears before they came, hot and angry. I didn't want to cry, not in front of him. I turned around and walked away from him.

"I'm sorry," he called out. I could hear him coming up behind us and when I whipped around my face was only a few inches from his face.

"That is not good enough," I said, baring my teeth and pointing a finger in his face. "All it took you was three months, three months! Ha!" I threw my face and my hands heavenwards. "Did you know that I..." I whipped my head around to check if Moni was within hearing distance. She was standing by his gate, a few yards away from us, and she was kicking her shoe against the concrete driveway. At any other time I would have told her off for ruining her shoes but today it didn't matter. I looked back at Wale, his shoulders hunched and his arms hanging limply by his side, and my chest felt hurt and exposed. I felt as if I had managed to rip open a wound that had been healing and now it hurt just as much as when it had been fresh. I narrowed my eyes and lowered my voice. "Did you know that I tried to take my life?" I asked, the tears dancing around my eyes. I would not let them fall if I could help it. "You never bothered to check on me; you didn't care if I was dead or alive. That was all I meant to you. I would have..." I paused to sniff noisily. "I would have died for you, you promised me. Do you remember? You promised me; you said that if anything happened, we would handle it together. Well, you are a cruel, evil man. Why should I care what you want now?"

"I just... I feel so stupid. All these years. I thought you lied to me. It wasn't easy for me either, you know." He scratched his head. "I'm sorry, I shouldn't have cut you off completely, but Jade..." He lowered his voice even more, and I had to strain over the blood rushing in my head to hear him. "You hurt me incredibly, all those men. Did you think I wouldn't find out?" His eyes were boring into me, and I felt my cheeks burning. I tore my eyes away from him and looked down, but he wasn't done.

"You cannot even begin to imagine how I felt, how much I wanted to hate you. You used me, and you lied to me. What was I to you? How much could I have meant to you that you would do that to me?"

My mouth fell open, and I started to protest, but he held up his hand to signal that he had more to say.

"I did what I did to protect myself, I felt like everything you'd ever told me was a lie and that there was no way you were pregnant with my child, not when we were always so careful. I just... I never allowed myself to believe that any part of it could be true. But now that I know..." He rubbed his palm over his face, looking haggard. "I want to be part of my child's life." His eyes flicked to Moni; she was leaning on the gate posts, and her eyes were fixed on her father as if she was drinking in as much of him as she could just in case she never saw him again. I saw the look on her face, and my heart melted. I wondered how hard it must have been for her to have grown up without her father, knowing he lived a few streets away and wasn't interested in her. I smiled weakly at her, and a wide grin spread across her face. I couldn't remember seeing her so happy. I frowned as the thought crossed my mind that Moni might be holding out some hope that her father and I would get back together.

"Are you sure this is what you want? Once you commit, you can't change your mind." I held my breath, my heart beating fast; I was giving him a way out. If he decided to walk out on her after this I would hunt him down and tear him apart, I swore solemnly to myself.

"I would never walk away from my child." There was certain awe in his eyes as he looked at Moni and I believed him.

"What about Sade, how will she react to this new development?"

His face fell as he realised that there was another factor to be considered. He inhaled deeply through his nose and then exhaled slowly through his mouth.

"I don't care," he said calmly. "If you let me, I promise that no one is going to keep me away from my child."

I nodded; I felt a shiver run down my spine at the steely determination in his voice. Our eyes met, and I felt my skin growing hot as the years melted away; I saw us, the way we had been then, and I had to restrain myself from reaching for him. I wanted to pull his head to my chest and stroke it gently while he held me tightly in his arms. It was too much to dream that there was still hope for us. It was enough for me that he was going to be in his daughter's life from now on.

There was no way we would make assembly now. Moni hated being late and usually she was grumpy when she knew she was going to be late, but today was different. I held her hand, and she swung our hands as she walked, a spring in her step. She skipped a few times along the way; her face glowed, and her eyes sparkled as she sang out loud. My heart soared as I watched her and I found myself singing along to her song.

THE END

About the Author

Bolaji Eyo lives in Hertfordshire, UK, with her husband and two lovely daughters. She owns and runs Sophianna's Bakery, a bespoke wedding and celebration cake business. Her second book is non-fiction, titled, "Things I wish I knew before I said I do" and is on track to be released before the end of the year. When she doesn't have her face stuck in a book or writing, she can be found in the kitchen, making pastries and cakes. She is also a Certified Business Analyst Professional.

Acknowledgment

I give God all the glory. I was raised to put him first in everything I do and this has never steered me wrong.

I would also like to thank the following individuals who without their contributions and support this book would have stayed half-finished on my computer:

My husband, Emmanuel, for his love and encouragement.

My mom, dad and the rest of my family, for encouraging me to release my hold on this book and to just let it fly.

Sola Njoku and Busola Taiwo- my beta readers. I appreciate all your honest feedback and all your help and advice.

Sarah Quigly, my amazing copyeditor.

Kenny Oshinowo, for creating such beautiful artwork on the initial book cover.

Special thanks to Deefrentng, for their patience with my multiple alterations to the book cover design and for doing such a beautiful job. Thanks so much Debola Olomo, Ugochukwu Okafor and Uju Nwobu.

Thanks to Hammad G. for an amazing job on my final book cover.

Sola Sonaiya, I know we haven't spoken in years but you were my first role model. You played the piano, spoke German, wrote books, you were intelligent and beautiful; everything the young girl in me aspired to be.

Last but not least, thanks to all the beautiful people who helped me make the tough decision on my book cover.

Thanks for reading! Please add a short review on Amazon and let me know what you thought!